The Coreseu Chronicles Book Four

ellen c. maze

Anathema
The Corescu Chronicles Book Four
By Ellen C. Maze
©2020, 2022 by Ellen C. Maze Sallas
All rights reserved.

ISBN: 978-1-7340474-7-9
V03122022
Also in Kindle eBook

Cover photo © Fernando Cortes – Spain, 123rf.com
Cover Design: Elizabeth E. Little, Hyliian Design
Little Roni Publishers, LLC
www.littleronipublishers.com

The following is a work of fiction. Names, characters, places, and incidents are fictitious or used fictitiously. Any resemblance to real persons, living or dead, to factual events or to businesses is coincidental and unintentional.

Let's stay in touch!
Enter your email address to join my newsletter. You'll receive exclusive deals and special offers, and be the first to know about new releases. *You can unsubscribe at any time.*
I included a free book!
https://dl.bookfunnel.com/z0c7dpe1am

PUBLISHED IN THE UNITED STATES OF AMERICA

Anathema
(Anathema)

1. ANATHEMA, Anathema (English pronunciation: An-ath'-em-ah)
(Greek pronunciation: Ow-a-they'-mah)
—Greek for accursed,
Cursed, a religious ban or excommunicated thing or person.

2. ANATHEMA, Anathema (English pronunciation: An-ath'-ay-mah)
(Greek pronunciation: Ow-a-theh'-mah)
--Greek; like the above but in a good sense; a votive offering, a gift.

ALSO BY ELLEN C. MAZE

Novels
Rabbit: Chasing Beth Rider Book One
Rabbit Legacy   Book Two
Rabbit Redemption Book Three
Anomaly: Beyond the Rabbit Book Four
Conundrum: The Lost Rabbit Book Five
Vestige: Fathers and Daughters Book Six

The Judging: The Corescu Chronicles Book One
Damascus Road: The Corescu Chronicles Book Two
Tree of Life: The Corescu Chronicles Book Three
Anathema: The Corescu Chronicles Book Four
Novus: The Corescu Chronicles Book Five

PARANORMAL SHORT STORY COLLECTIONS
22 Sideways: Twenty-Two Bloodthirsty Tales
Tiny Tales, Bizarre Tales Anthology
Loose Rabbits of the Rabbit Trilogy
Feckless Tales of Supernatural, Paranormal, and Downright Presumptuous Ilk

1

The eyes of the Lord are in every place,
Keeping watch on the evil and the good.
Proverbs 15:3

THE AROMA OF ELIZABETH HAWKEN'S TAINTED BLOOD drew Mark to Anthony Agricola's house with its delectable power. Eight weeks had passed since the vampire Mark called The Other and Tony knew as Rakha polluted her blood. She did not know; the creature fed her his blood after sending her into a swoon. And now he was dead, shot by police. Was he gone for good? Who could know?

Mark watched her setting plates with Tony's wife and pondered his responsibility. He and the woman were strangers, having been barely introduced in her father's hospital room two months ago. The only reason he had come this afternoon was because of the delightful pull in his middle. His old master's blood mixed with hers and called him to *taste, enjoy, imbibe, because, oh! How delicious is the blood of a brother!*

The blood of a brother.

Tony Agricola and Sarah Tracey, his wife, both carried vampire blood in their veins that summoned Mark in the same way. The difference being Tony was actually a vampire while his wife, like Elizabeth Hawken, were simply *infected.* This made them "immortal" while remaining human.

And I would sink my teeth in all of them if I were a different kind of monster.

Mark allowed a tiny grin at his thoughts—he had never been a monster. Not like that, anyway. Now, he and Tony sought deliverance. It was a process, for Mark's spirituality was in its infancy. He spent three-hundred-and-eighty-years killing sinners, taking their blood—all in the name of God. In Mark's mind, he had been cleansing the world. But he had misinterpreted his bloodlust and God sent Tony to show him the error of his ways.

"There is only one Judge," Agricola had told him, and although the road to this awareness was bloody and regrettable, as a result Mark no longer drank from humans.

1

Or vampires, he thought with a new grin.

Across the space, Elizabeth peeked over and returned to her task, she and Sarah setting the table, decorating for guests expected later in the day. Mark would not attend. Tony Agricola's friend and ministering partner, John Jenkins, was taking a full-time ministry position at his home church. The party would be a baby shower for John's wife. Who would be in attendance? Mark did not think on it more than a moment, planning to head off before anyone arrived.

And why was Elizabeth Hawken here? From his hospital bed, her father a had instructed Mark and Tony to have no further contact with his daughter. Because of Rakha, Miller knew they were vampires… But here she was. Whatever caused him to relax his edict Mark did not know, but he had nothing to fear—the woman was in no danger.

"Isn't that Tony's friend, Doctor Corescu?" Miss Hawken whispered to Sarah and Mark's superior hearing picked it up.

Miss Hawken? Really? He scolded himself at the label. She wasn't a teenager but was twenty-six and had been married and divorced.

But she doesn't know about vampires.

On this point, Mark agreed with Tony; there would be no need to share their secret with her. The list of those aware of their predicament was short—John Jenkins knew but lied to his wife who saw Paul attack Tony the night the world changed for the preacher. John told Opal that Paul was insane, not a supernatural entity. Sarah Tracey knew, but was convinced they'd all be delivered soon and could put it behind them. And retired police detective Jonah Miller (Elizabeth Hawken's father) knew but decided to keep it to himself, even from his retired detective wife. Mark's years had taught him that for a vampire, secrecy was best.

Elizabeth again glanced at him and shook her head to Sarah.

Why am I here?

Besides the draw of her blood, his ruse had been to check on Tony now that the excitement had died down. But in truth, Mark had come to check on the girl.

That's what she is, really, a random female…

But she was more. His mind turned to Hope Brannen, the woman God sent to involve Tony Agricola in Mark's life. This is the way Mark saw it—he'd judged sinners for centuries until a beautiful young woman turned his head one day, along with coincidental cues drawn from his dreams. Mark's life came to an abrupt halt and her involvement eventually led him to where they were today.

2

And she's off riding horses…

She moved with him to his German estate and this moment—Mark glanced at the wall clock for clarification—this moment, she would be tacking up her newest showjumper for a lesson with an Olympic riding coach.

Ms. Hawken glanced at Mark a third time.

Does she see me as a vampire?

He held her eye for as long as she'd match him. This time, she didn't look off. Instead, she widened her eyes and inclined her chin, her expression reading, *"What?"*

He grinned, she won, his gaze dropping to the floor. For a split second, she reminded him of Hope.

Well, Hope of nine months ago.

Hope, before she gave up on Mark ever biting her neck. Before she afterward, turned her energy into horses, horse training, Olympic coaching sessions, and German showjumping barns.

At that moment, Elizabeth set her items to the table and walked toward him. He put his hands in his pockets and waited, inside asking again, *what am I doing with this woman?*

"Doctor Corescu," she said, her soft California accent pleasant to his ears, "do you want to help? You must feel pretty strange standing against the wall when everyone else is working."

Mark grinned wider and shook his head. "On the contrary. I'm quite comfortable avoiding senseless labor."

"Ah," she said with a glance to Reverend Tracey setting placemats around the long table. "Throwing a party for a friend is senseless?" She crossed her arms and looked into his face, awaiting his answer.

She hadn't come close but kept a polite distance, the proper spacing between virtual strangers. Mark licked his lips and prepared his next pithy remark, his inner voice saying, *you are acting very strangely…*

"My reply would not be polite, so forgive me," he said finally. It seemed important just then for him to know what she was thinking. He looked into her mind and her eyes widened as if she sensed it. Then, she blushed bright pink, her palm to one cheek.

"Oh, gosh," she said with a smile. "My head rushed. How weird!"

She did not understand what had happened and Mark had a notion to send Tony a question. *"What does Ms. Hawken think we are? She seems suspicious, but what does she know?"*

From the backyard preparing the gas grill for their feast, the man responded, *"Jonah, me, and Sarah agreed to tell her that the man she knew as Rakha Tep was a psychopathic killer. None of us want her to know the truth…"*

What Tony didn't say was the part that Mark knew by heart. Tony's famous ending, "why tell her when God will deliver us soon?"

"You are very strange," Elizabeth said then, but her smile remained, and her eyes twinkled with what she wouldn't say. "Okay, then, go on." She swished her hand at chest level. "If you're not going to help, you can't stand there watching us. You're distracting me."

With that last muted flirtation, the young woman turned and rejoined Tony's wife at the decorations. Mark watched her go. She was Hope's height and weight, but a brunette where Hope was blonde. And Hope's sky-blue eyes were even brighter than Paul's had been, where Ms. Hawken's kind hazel eyes spoke of a wisdom beyond her years.

Elizabeth had returned to her duties but swiveled to see his face. He hadn't moved, still leaning against the wall, hands in his slacks pockets, and he gave her the same smile as before.

"Sarah, look at that man over there," she said, her eyes in Mark's but speaking to her friend. The reverend turned her head and chuckled before going back to her work. "No, look at him. He's not helping. What do you think he's doing?"

It was a game for the youngster and Mark played along. He blinked and exhaled as if as comfortable as can be.

"I think he's watching you," the reverend said her face to her work. "You probably have him mesmerized. Go see if he's breathing."

"Oh, he's breathing." Elizabeth set her decorations down with finality. "I'm going to make him help us or leave."

Sarah chuckled and finished her last place setting. "We're done here. Invite him to stay for the party," she said, still not looking his way.

Mark knew why, she was a godly woman and married—she did *not* like the way her blood rushed when their eyes met. Elizabeth Hawken, on the other hand, was again coming toward him.

"Sarah tells me that you're a medical doctor," she said, this time stopping five feet away instead of ten. "Doctors are very hard-working people. Go ahead and tell me your rude reason for not helping." She crossed her arms as before with the same playful scorn in her tone.

Mark was enjoying their interaction very much. The Other's blood in her system caused her aroma to tickle his nose and he allowed it until his grin went to the side and she took one step in.

"Cat got your tongue?" she asked, her head tipped to the side.

4

"Wait… your eyes, they're not as dark as I thought." She scrutinized him a moment, her eyes narrowing as she focused on his, as if studying their hue. "Are you from Europe? Is that what I heard? And you have a girlfriend who rides horses, is that right?"

Mark huffed a soft chuckle. "That was quite a number of queries at one time. The answers are, no, really?, yes, and she's only a friend."

Elizabeth closed one eye and hummed as she ticked off her earlier questions, assigning answers in order. Then she uncrossed her arms and offered a gentle laugh. "Rest assured, speaking as a woman, your horse-riding friend doesn't see you as just a roommate."

"Do you want to know me better?" Mark asked off the cuff. After a careful pause she got wind of his dare and offered a demure smile.

"Nah, you're too good-looking. I was married to a good-looking man. That's trouble with a capital T."

Surprised at her reply, Mark chuckled. She turned away, waved over her shoulder, and left the room.

In the kitchen, Sarah whispered, *Will he stay for the party?*" and Elizabeth said she didn't invite him. With a smile and shake of his head, Mark pictured his living room back home and pushed himself there, leaving Tony to his party. He would see her again. The Other's blood called to him much like Tony's did. And he didn't wonder what God was up to; that was Tony's thing. Mark had no inclination to ponder the minutiae of God's workings.

In his living room, he sank into the couch and because he could, watched the party from afar.

2

...For they all saw Him and were troubled.
But immediately He talked with them and said to them,
"Be of good cheer. It is I; do not be afraid."
Mark 6:50

OPAL'S BABY SHOWER HAD ENDED AND THEIR GUESTS
had departed, leaving a peaceful quiet echoing through the gigantic house.
For Tony, the day's highlights included a personal phone call from Jonah
Miller amending his requirement that Tony stay away from his daughter.

"*Look,*" the guy had said when the initial pleasantries were done,
"*Elizabeth told me that she's going to keep seeing you and the reverend and she begged
for my blessing.*"

When he paused, Tony heard the angst in his voice. He'd been
viciously attacked by Rakha, given the full vampire treatment, so Miller had
no confusion of what creature Tony and Mark Corescu represented. But
he also loved his daughter and had only just reunited with her after fifteen
years apart.

"*I'm begging you, man to man, God-man to God-man,*" he added since
Jonah knew Tony loved the Lord. "*Just promise me you'll keep that vampire crap
to yourself. There's no such thing as vampires and my daughter doesn't need to know
there might be. Can you promise me you won't tell her?*"

Tony assured Jonah that he and Sarah would never tell. And he
wouldn't. With an internal nod, Tony's mind traveled to the other bit of
news. John was leaving their team. His excuse was being offered the
position of head pastor at his home church, but Mark and Tony had long
discerned he was ready to leave the vampires behind.

And what about Mark...

Tony strode through the main hall toward the kitchen seeking Sarah
and pondering the doctor and his current fascination with Miller's
daughter. Yes, she smelled of Rakha, but something else was going on.
When he mentioned it to Sarah, she said to *watch and see.* Translation: stay
out of it. Tony grinned; his new wife had truly brightened his existence in

every way. He reached the kitchen and rushed inside. Sarah was sobbing.

"What is it?" Tony asked Sarah leaning over the counter. "What's the matter?" She was not ready to answer, so he gathered her into his arms. "It's okay, shhh…"

They had been married almost three months and this scene played out only when a spiritual trial loomed close. He either read that in her mind or his own intuition, but Sarah had seen something coming, and it had to do with the battle they thought was done.

"What'd'ya see, honey?" Tony whispered nuzzling her neck. She stood three inches taller and, in his eyes, she was the most beautiful woman he had ever seen. "You'll feel better once you share it." She held onto him with one arm around his shoulders and wiped her face with her opposite hand.

"I know it," she said, her voice choking and her face returning to tuck into Tony's hair.

"Whatever it is, we'll face it together. It's no hill for a climber, you know," he said, using a phrase she loved from times that weren't so stressful. Sarah was a gifted prophet of the Lord; she heard, felt and saw into the spirit realm when God allowed it, and He used her to overcome demons. Specifically, in the previous battle with the vampire that turned Mark Corescu. With Sarah's anointing, the demon Rakha finally met his end, riddled with bullets from the muzzle of several Montgomery police officers.

"I love you, honey, so much," she said and with one last swipe of her cheeks she stepped back to separate. "God showed me something awful. I thought…" Sarah gasped, her lips rolling in as she gathered her calm. "I thought we were done, but there's more coming."

Tony gathered vague flashes of what she meant, the vision involved violence against her person, a dark shape, a very tall, angular man, striking her, and when he stepped back, her wounds healed but only after dropping her entire blood supply onto the floor.

"I saw it," Tony whispered saving her the pain of sharing. "What does it mean? Is it figurative or literal?" He waited as she prayed for guidance. Because of the vampire Paul Black, Sarah's flesh would heal as soon as she was injured. She was human, but his ingested blood caused her cells to regenerate like a vampire's. Knowing she would heal gave neither of them comfort from such a violent vision.

As he waited, he was reminded how miraculously God had been aiding his bloodlust since Rakha died. Before that night, Tony struggled

7

with his gut as it pined, sometimes painfully, for the vampire's ancient blood. But now, Tony recited Scripture to feed his stomach. He hadn't experienced the discomfort of hunger since the last battle.

Praise the Lord, thank You for that! he said inside watching for Sarah to begin. He still didn't preach publicly because he felt unclean, but he traveled with Sarah and Big John the past two months as they shared the Gospel to churches around the area.

Sarah chuckled very low and finally looked up. "It's a doozy. God showed me a little more." She forced a grin. "We have to submerge ourselves in His word to succeed. If we slip up, the repercussions are steep."

"They always are," Tony replied but hadn't meant to say it aloud.

Sarah gave him a kind grin. "You're going to be tested. I'm going to be tested. It's going to be terrible." Sarah paused. "I'll tell you more as I figure it out…" She kissed his cheek. "Thank you for loving an odd bird like me."

"You are my world," he said and returned to their warm hug. When released, she said she would head upstairs to her prayer closet. She had designed a spare bedroom specifically for communing with the Lord and it was a beautiful, quiet, and holy place in their vast inherited home.

Paul made a mess of my life, but his money at least keeps us comfortable.

When Paul died, Mark signed his assets over to Tony. The amount was in the millions and Tony thanked God; he'd never been rich and at least he could fight the vampire's curse without worrying about bills.

"Our agent said the bookstore has been sold and reopened." Tony waited for her to meet his eye. Paul bought the store in Old Cloverdale thinking he and Tony would run it together. Even that thought caused Tony's mouth to form a sad grin; Paul abused him in the store the few times they went there and they did not get it open before the vampire's budding insanity ruined his life forever.

Now, Tony, don't be so dramatic, he said inside.

"That was fast," she replied and blinked, composing herself. "Let's go later in the month and see what they did to it."

Tony said they should and she turned for the stairs. He followed with his eyes thinking he should pray, too. What was God doing? What could possibly happen to them now that the most evil of all vampires, the one that turned Mark four hundred years ago, was gone?

Tony remembered lying on the floor beside the demon he called Rakha. He had been addicted to the monster's blood and during their long

8

chats, the ancient vampire had bragged there were more vampires out there. Was Sarah seeing something pertaining to them?

Tony frowned, his mind wandering free down memory lane. He saw the night he asked Sarah to be his wife. And even before he met his bride, he recalled the night his inhuman partner Paul Black thrust his demonic curse upon him. And even further back, he saw his friend Hope Brannen innocently drawing him into a life of vampires and supernatural ministry.

And dammit, it's not over.

Tony closed his eyes to ask for help.

3

The Lord said, "Do not remember the former things,
Or consider the things of old. I am about to do a new thing;
Now it springs forth, do you not perceive it?"
Isaiah 43:18-19

THE SUN DIDN'T CAUSE HIM TO BLISTER AND THIS AMAZED all he met. Yet, the pediatrician affirmed at birth that Joseph Robert Ellerslie was an albino. But today? One month from eighteen years old, Joey no longer met the clinical definition. His hair was decidedly blond, not colorless, his eyes were translucent blue, and his skin—while it refused to tan—it held a smidge of melatonin, enough to keep him flesh-colored in decent light.

And it helps that I'm handsome.

Joey grinned at his inner voice. He heard it first in Kindergarten. Jenny Jakes called him a frog-face and when he stood up to shout an insult in return, a voice in his head said, *"You are beautiful and perfect. Ignore anyone who says otherwise."*

Later in life, Joey recognized that sentiment first came from his mother. Rocking him before bedtime, singing hymns and old Gospels to young Joseph, loving him with her eyes as well as her words. All this was before Luke came into the world. Luke was a wonderful baby brother— Joey loved him—but it wasn't long before everything Joey did paled (haha) in comparison to anything Luke Robert Ellerslie accomplished. Yes, his parents gave their father's name to the second son, too, also bringing to light how they felt about the boys.

And Luke has normal skin...

Indeed, Luke was classically handsome, two years younger, but maybe smarter, more athletic, friendlier to others—but Joey was all those things, too. He lettered in Track, won medals at the Y in the high dive. He earned a 50% Academic scholarship to Huntingdon-Peavey Methodist College. Joey was no slacker.

So why did they gravitate to loving him more?

10

Joey only pondered the question a second and moved on. Luke wasn't to blame. If church life taught Joey one thing, it was that people make their decisions and there's not much to be done about it. If his parents loved Luke more, he would take what they had left over. No big. When he graduated college, had a good job, maybe a wife, he would move away and be done with them. For now, he played nice. This was something Joey knew how to do very well.

He mumbled a few additional observations to the air, his eyes flicking to the rearview mirror. He smoothed his hair and checked his teeth. He didn't need to give Scotty something to tease him about. If he had a blemish, Scotty would be sure to mention it. Especially if he could make Joey appear foolish to the female member of their group, Abigail Abingdon.

Joseph (Joey to most everyone), Scott Montgomery, and Abigail Abingdon had grown up together, attending the same schools from K-5 through twelfth grade. They also belonged to the same church, Ryan Road Christian Fellowship, where Joey's parents were founding and lead pastors. Initially a one-room building, today it had grown to a multi-building facility with over a thousand members. Scotty's dad was the church's legal counsel and Abby's legal guardian, her grandmother, sat in the choir since the beginning.

Joey watched the parking lot entrance and reflected on their friendship. Each had chosen a different college, Scotty attended in Auburn, 45 minutes away, Abigail in town at the Community College, and Joey also in town at the Normandale Campus. Friday, Saturday, and Sunday all three were free and they usually spent part or all of those days together.

Joey switched off his dad's aging Buick. He didn't have a car of his own, although he used to. At sixteen, his dad gave him a ten-year-old Subaru. Within the first year, Joey forgot to check the oil three times, causing breakdowns that grew progressively worse. His senior year of high school, he forgot for the last time; the engine threw a rod and the insurance company totaled the car. Since then, he bummed rides with his friends or begged to borrow his dad's car or his mother's SUV. Joey prayed they were secretly working on getting him one for his birthday, but around the house, all he ever heard was what sort Luke needed now that he was sixteen.

"Hear that, Abba? Their *other* son needs a car, too. Please work that out!" Joey prayed and got out to lean on the hood. Looking toward the entrance, he added a few hints about what kind of car he'd prefer. "Abba," he said under his breath, gaze soft and pointed to the main road, "I'd like a new Mustang. Black with tan leather seats, that cool woodgrain dash, and make it a 5-speed, manual transmission..."

Interrupting his dialogue with the Lord, he thought he saw Abby's truck and shrugged.

"Okay, anyway," he continued to the blue sky, "we better make that a white Mustang. Cooler in the summer. Hey, how about that chameleon bronze I saw in the online showroom?" He winked to the clouds. "Praise You, Lord; it will be done!"

Over the past year, Joey had grown to believe God wanted him to be happy and to dream big. This teaching came down from Pastor Aaron Hawken, a famous televangelist he favored over his parents. His parents' sermons were classically boring, but Pastor Hawken on PLTsings.org gave him hope for the future. Pastor Hawken said he was a "child of the Most High God" and should "walk the walk!"

And drive the drive!

The shiny new automobile faded from Joey's mind as he pondered the day's coming adventure. Abby would pick up Scotty and the three of them head out for a prayer walk. Since sixth grade, they met up Saturday mornings and found a place to pray over. The first time, they did it because Abigail dreamed they should walk around the church and sing praise songs. The following Saturday, Scotty said God told him they should pray around the middle school. On the third Saturday, Joey felt like the Lord wanted them to pray at the mall. Nowadays, one or more of them would spout a prayer destination and off they'd go. Each of them would jot down their impressions on a slip of paper, gather to compare their notes, and set off to pray wherever they decide the Lord sent them.

This weekend, God had sent Joey a single word: *Troy.*

Joey's skin crawled. Why?

Troy.

It was a simple four-letter word that could mean anything; today, it seemed to spell doom.

Joey huffed a laugh and looked for Abby's car. What would her paper read? She had more vivid and lengthy visions than he or Scotty. Maybe she could explain the unease in his gut.

Why is this prayer walk any different from any other?

It didn't make any sense. Joey rolled the paper slip into a scroll and daydreamed until he saw Abby's hot pink Amigo turning into the church.

"ABBY!" Scotty's squeal sounded even from across the parking lot as the tiny Isuzu SUV zipped around the bend, visibly slinging her passenger against his side of the car. Joey grinned at Abigail hunched over the wheel, white-knuckled, with a gleam of mischief in her eye. She was a decent driver, but she enjoyed pretending to be clueless. It was Scotty's fault she teased him so much because he reacted with such drama. Scotty's lips were moving as Abby pulled up, parking beside Joey's borrowed car, the sounds carrying as he got out.

"Geez-Louise, Abby! I'm gonna die in your car one day! Mark my words!"

Abigail gave Joey a wink, the game was always fun, watching his freckled face turn red. Still on the away side of the car, she performed a shimmy to drop her capris into place. All the boys liked her shape, although she bought the culture-line about being a "Perfect 10" by the time you're twelve. Since Joey knew her, she'd been plump. By ninth grade, she had the largest breasts of all their friends. This probably did her no favors in her interpersonal relations away from Joey, but he always appreciated her assets. Before entering high school, she often said aloud that she was fat. These days thankfully, she had embraced her curves and grown into the most confident young woman Joey had ever met.

"It's a wonder we got here in one piece," Scott said to Joey running both hands over his face. "Abby drives like a maniac!"

"At least she's willing to pick you up," Joey replied with a nod to Abby. "We all know whose fault it is you find yourself without a car."

Scott said nothing and positioned himself against the Buick beside Joey. Abby also left it alone, which was gracious considering of the three of them, she was the only one that hadn't murdered a car with carelessness.

"You've been at the beach," Joey said as she joined them at his car.

Abby held up one forearm, displaying her bronzed skin. Hawaiian by birth, any time spent in the sun darkened her skin even more. She swished her long brown hair with an extravagant movement causing Joey to grin. They'd always been platonic which made fake-flirting fun. With his eyes falling to half-mast and his lips vibrating in a characterization of a soap opera slow-motion kiss, Abby leaned in and performed the same trick. Scott noticed and groaned.

"Let's get moving, dang. What'cha got, Joe?" Scott held open his palm. Joey dropped a tube of paper into his hand and Scott unrolled it. "Troy?" He looked at Abby. "Joey Ellerslie brings us troy."

With a *hmmm,* she reached for the note.

Always the comedian, Scott turned in an abrupt movement and repeatedly slapped the hood. "Abigail Abingdon! Let's hear yours! Drum roll, please!"

"Hush, dummy." Joey shoved Scotty's shoulder, his eyes on Abby. "What do you think it means?" he asked.

"Don't be a hater," Scott said and resumed leaning beside Joey. "Dummies need love, too."

"You're not dumb," Abby said fishing in her pocket. "You're just special." With a grin she handed her paper to Joey.

He opened the small square and read it aloud. "Bookstore."

"Troy, bookstore," Abby said. It had happened more than once that they all received similar prophecies. She and Joey both looked at Scott who had started a nod when she said the two together. He continued to bob his chin as they waited and then fell into a head-banging posture, strumming his air guitar and the works.

"Scotty!" Joey barked and punched his shoulder. Their friend laughed and grew still, one hand covering his eyes.

"Ommmmmm," he chanted with drama. Then he dropped his hand and shrugged. "I got nothin'." He wiggled his eyebrows to Joey. "So we drive to Troy. Ahem, YOU drive us to Troy until we see a bookstore."

Before Joey could respond, Abby made a noise of disagreement. "No, I think it's something else. Scotty, think hard. God wants you to participate. Stop making everything a joke."

Scotty sighed and closed his eyes. After a moment he offered in a soft tone, "all I can think of is Dad's complaining last night. He and Mom were talking about a pothole in front of…" He opened his eyes and grinned. "On College Street in front of a bookstore! Hah!" Scotty whipped out his cell and flipped a few pages. He held the screen to Abby and then Joey. "There it is. Dad sent me a picture of the hole to avoid. Look at that sign!"

Joey took possession of the phone and zoomed it. His jaw dropped. "It reads, Now Open, New Owner, Haman Troye."

"Whoa!" Abby said and took the phone from Joey.

"Geesh, Haman's a horrible name. He was a murderer in the Bible!" Scotty said grabbing for his phone. Abby dodged his movement.

"Wait… It used to be the Collegiate Bookstore, remember? Now it's…" Abby squint and reverse-pinched the screen again. "The Ancient Book Man. Huh…"

A cold chill blew past and Joey narrowed his eyes. The sensation had come from his spirit, and he shook his head. "I have a bad feeling."

"What is it?" she asked watching his face. "Because of his name?"

"I don't know. Just… I don't know. Let's go." Joey stood off the fender, keys in hand. "I'll drive. Dad gave me the car for the day."

"That was very generous of him," Scotty said with a snooty air and headed for the back door, leaving the front passenger for Abby. Then when she and Joey were both watching, he pointed at her Isuzu. "I mean, really. Thank Pastor Ellerslie for me. Think how horrendous I look in that pink monstrosity!"

"Watch it, Bub," Abby returned and settled into her seat. "That pink baby got you where you needed to go. She might take offense at your words when you next need a ride."

"She knows I'm only teasing." Scotty rolled down the window and poked his face out. "I love you, Amigo! You are my favorite pink monstrosity, the only pink-monstrosity I love, and I will never love-hate another little car as much as I love-hate you!"

Abby shot a grin to Joey who had dropped in behind the wheel. When Scotty had rolled up his window and fallen still, he shot her a glance. They were ready to start. Abigail nodded and closed her eyes, facing front, her chin tipped upward an inch.

"Father-God," she said in her softest voice, "we want to do Your will this morning. Forgive us of our sins, make us white as snow by the blood of Jesus so we can come before Your throne…"

"Amen," Joey whispered, a half-grin at her *white as snow* phrase, him being so pale already. She prayed for wisdom and protection, and in ten minutes they pulled up to the curb on College, directly in front of the new store. The pothole hadn't been filled but an orange traffic cone demarcated it for pedestrians and cars alike. He turned off the engine and read the cheese-board welcome sign.

The chill returned, and this time, it was laced with dread. *"Don't go in there,"* he heard inside. But he was no chicken and his two friends were already striding to the entrance.

Abby turned, her eyes questioning, worrying about his sudden gloom. Joey forced a grin and followed them in, asking God to be on guard for them all.

4

"Who then is willing to consecrate himself
this day to the Lord?"
1 Chronicles 29:5b

MARK DIDN'T WATCH THE GIRL AT TONY'S HOUSE FOR LONG. Barely had he begun when his cell buzzed, informing that Hope requested he come watch her ride. It was nearing 4 PM and he figured the show barn would be loaded with students and hands.

She wants to show me off, he thought and headed for the garage. She had openly bragged on his appearance the one time he visited the place, saying to a fellow rider, "This is my boyfriend, *DOCTOR* Mark Corescu. Isn't he the most gorgeous man you've ever seen!?"

Mark huffed with a wry grin. She was a pistol, especially now that she had been with him a while.

The equestrian facility was close, only five miles away, and he arrived, park and scanned the sunny afternoon landscape. As he expected, the lot was full and the three Olympic sized arenas were peopled with riders going through their movements. He approached the jumping ring and leaned against a shade tree. He trained his eyes in her general direction and pondered another young woman, Elizabeth Hawken. He did not react when Hope rode close and she called his name.

"Mark!" she yipped.

Pause.

"Hello? Anyone home? My new baby's jumping his heart out and you're not even looking!"

Mark offered a small smile. She had only been "home" three days, returning mainly to meet the lorry that delivered her new equine acquisition. When he didn't respond, she literally *growled.*

"Geez! One lousy minute! You'd think a four-hundred-year-old man could spare one lousy minute for his closest companion!" Hope had spoken her piece at normal volume, blasting part of his secret to anyone within earshot.

16

Mark held his tongue; the other riders paid no attention, likely accustomed to her histrionics. This show barn housed every horse she had tried, so they were familiar with the blonde American and her sassy ways. The shiny palomino gelding came to rest a few feet away and Hope slid to the ground with the grace of a champion rider. With the horse's reins in her fist she met Mark from the arena side.

"What are you thinking so hard about? I wanted to see you but your mind is somewhere else."

She stared into his face, chin tilted up, petite, attractive, and feminine. Before she entered his timeline, Mark had never had a female companion. He enjoyed the challenge, but over time, the young woman grew weary of not getting what she wanted.

She blew a puff of air. "Come on, Mark. What are you doing? And will you please remove your sunglasses while we're talking?" She waited, her eyes wide.

Mark was not in the mood to discuss his distaste for the bright sun. *Monsters prefer the dark,* Mark heard inside. And unlike those days in Whitford City when The Other spoke evil in his spirit, this was Mark's own conscience telling him what he knew, that he needed to square things with God. If the truth be known, since Paul died, he hadn't even tried. Mark *existed,* and that was about it.

But I will investigate Elizabeth Hawken...

"Dammit!" Hope hissed interrupting his thoughts. "Leave them on! Why do I even try? I mean, geesh!" Hope spun away with drama. With the limber joints of a gymnast, she lifted her knee to chest height and maneuvered the toe of her boot into the stirrup. With ease, she grabbed the pommel and swooped upward, landing softly into the leather.

Mark considered the copious shade tree he had chosen to stand beneath and swished off his glasses, saying her name at the same time. Hope froze in place, their eyes locked. Then he held her there. No words, no complaints, no apologies—just holding her eye for several long moments. Flies buzzed around the horse's head, one of the other riders screamed with happiness at something she and her horse accomplished on the opposite side of the paddock, a truck horn sounded at the country road passing the facility. Then, Mark saw Hope's surface thoughts. She was looking at a *vampire,* The Prince of the Night, Count Dracula, and more than that, to her, he was sexy and alluring, she wanted to touch him, see him undressed, feel his hands on her body and his teeth in her throat. Mark looked away and Hope's hand went to her mouth.

17

"You hate me," she whispered. "I love you and you hate me."

Mark repositioned his eyewear. There was no response to such a childish accusation.

"It doesn't matter," she said in the same low voice. "I signed up for a riding school. I leave Monday. I hope while I'm gone you decide if you want me around. I'm not happy being ignored and taken for granted." She did not wait for a reply but turned the horse and trotted off.

Mark watched her go. He didn't hate her. He…

Have I grown indifferent?

"You'll have to quantify your relationship. Or consummate. One of the two."

Mark sucked his teeth. That advice had come from Tony the last time they discussed the young woman living (occasionally) in his care. But consummation for vampires meant drinking blood. Tony knew this, but had said it anyway. Why?

Because he's battling the same demons I am, only now that The Other is dead, they are our own inner-selves craving to drink the life of others.

In the distance, Hope hopped a cross-rail set up by a short man wearing breeches. He called out instructions in German and Hope circled and jumped the obstacle again. Her third circle brought her closer to Mark's position and his heart softened.

"Hope," he said low, but also in her mind. The young woman startled and turned toward him. He removed his glasses again and she trotted over, her eyes asking for an apology and something more. "What is his name, this new horse?"

Hope's countenance lightened and she exhaled, bringing the gelding against the rail, thus inviting Mark to touch her leg if he chose. He did; stretching out one arm, he rest his hand on her midthigh.

"Rusty Binkins," she said with a giggle. "I renamed him. They were calling him 'Big Elephant' in German, but as soon as Herr Gregor gave me the translation, I changed it on the registry. He's a Trakehner. Very rare to see one this color." Her smile was genuine, she truly glowed when horses were involved.

"He is stunning," Mark said and his smile caused her pulse to increase. No matter how angry she was with him for withholding his affection, she was addicted to him as well. Mark added, "He likes you a lot."

"He does?" She lowered her voice and leaned closer to add, "Did he tell you that?"

Mark offered a nod. When he first met Hope Brannen, he had wowed her with his ability to read the thoughts of animals, specifically horses.

"Does he know how much I love him?" she asked still whispering. "Tell him I think he's wonderful…"

"He knows. He reads your positivity. He wouldn't understand the words, but he understands the affection you transmit and the tenderness in your training."

Hope smiled wider, her eyes watering with emotion. "Thank you," she whispered. "I'm sorry about before. I don't mean to be such a witch. I love you so much and we don't ever seem to connect."

This was not the place or time for such a discussion, but Mark offered what he could. "It was never fair to you," he said holding her eye. "To keep you with me because you give me peace. I have nothing to offer you along that vein."

Vein.

Hope appeared to have made the same connection to blood-letting and she blushed. Then her mind sent, *"But why can't we do that? I won't die…"*

Mark reached for her gloved hand. He pushed the leather aside enough to touch his lips to her skin. She sighed but was still smiling when he stepped back.

"Can he jump the green one?" Mark asked referring to the three-foot oxer in the center of the ring. It was the only one she hadn't jumped since they came out. Hope's grin faltered and she shrugged one shoulder.

"Nah, I'm not allowed. Herr Gregor said I need to work on my seat a little longer."

A shadow passed her expression and Mark received glimpses of the German riding coach stalking the women in the tack room, standing too close, touching them on the arm, the leg, the lower back. Then Hope shivered and made an excuse.

"He's right. My leg slips back. He said another few lessons…"

"I will deal with this Gregor," Mark said training his eyes to the little man across the arena. "We'll find you another show barn…"

"No, no. Please. It's nothing. Some men are like that, I'm used to it. I can handle it. Plus, he's a Gold Medalist. And there are four of us in the lesson. I'm never alone.."

Hope gathered the reins, waiting for Mark's agreement. He didn't like it and he wouldn't let it lie.

Hope gave him a new smile. "He's a wolf. Maybe you should stay closer to your chicken so he doesn't pluck her feathers when you're thinking about all the other things you find more interesting." She was teasing, but serious about the accusation.

19

"I hear you," he said with a tight nod and slipped his Raybans into place. "Go have fun. I'm watching."

"Yes!" she replied and jogged her horse to the riding lesson in the middle. He watched the troll-like coach instruct as the women hopped their mounts over cross-rails and then higher poles. Mark gave her a thumbs-up when she looked over. Hope had two things on her mind—horses and how to get her vampire friend to bite her.

Mark sighed. He'd killed a different mortal nightly for four centuries. Now he drank from animals. Did he miss human blood? Maybe. Would he take it from Hope? Never.

Mark watched her finish the lesson and cleared his mind of thinking about blood. He didn't suffer bloodthirst, hadn't since the night Paul died. But he remembered how glorious it felt going down and how powerfully it ramped up his system.

But I'm not a vampire.

I'm supposed to be begging to be delivered.

But he didn't. Not yet.

5

"God resists the proud,
But gives grace to the humble."
James 4:6

HOPE CUT HER EYES TO MARK'S TREE. HE WAS THERE, facing in her direction.

Good! It's too hard to keep his attention!

She didn't look at him again, wondering how much, if any, he overheard from her mental complaints.

I don't care. Let him hear. He owes me…

"Güt! Fraulein Hope. Güt!" Gregor clapped his hands and Hope snapped back to her lesson. The expensive riding coach waved her close and she approached at a lazy jog, the lesson coming to an end.

Hope whoa-ed before her trainer, Rusty towering over the little man. Short and stocky, Gregor's riding muscles—legs and forearms—were the most developed, the rest of him had dwindled to mush. He wore his thinning hair slicked back and covered by a barn logo cap. Maybe he was handsome in his youth, but not now. The toad stepped into her space, her still mounted, and he placed his hand to the top of her boot. It occurred to Hope he had positioned himself to be invisible to Mark across the arena.

Craning his face to hers, he cooed, "*Ja…güt…*very good. You are ready for the *clinic-k-k.*"

His English was fair, but his over-pronunciations were comical. His palm scooted past the thick Italian leather of her riding boots to her knee and came to rest on her thigh, his fingers molding to her muscle.

"But you must perfeck-k-k-t your two-point…" Gregor gave her thigh a squeeze. "Now. Show me."

Hope sunk her weight into her heels, her seat rising from the saddle just the right amount. She took riding very seriously and knew she was good. Gregor popped her rear end.

"You must build dees! You must build dees glutes!" He popped her again and she stood up in the stirrups.

21

He was hidden by her horse from Mark's gaze and Hope resisted looking at the shade tree. Was he even paying attention?

Gregor's left hand cupped the top of her thigh and then ran the length toward her hip. "Yes, your thigh eez gut, but your butt… make it strong." He popped her once more and she sat in the saddle.

"Okay. I'll practice," she said, hiding her irritation at being manhandled. The little man was aware of Dr. Corescu, aware he was Hope's man—she'd told everyone. Bragged on him to each member. So now, his hands were testing Mark and Hope at the same time. Was she open to his advances and would the doctor do anything about it?

In her peripheral vision, movement. Mark was heading toward them, having maneuvered over the three-rail fence. Gregor couldn't yet see him, and Hope shook her head to Mark's gaze, but her mind said, *He's murdered a hundred thousand people; what's one more?*

But that wasn't fair.

He hadn't killed anyone since Tony awakened the "priest" Mark had hidden in his heart for centuries.

Hope's mind shot to the day she met him, at his office, sitting at his desk; Hope saw on sight that he wasn't normal. He was too slick, too handsome, and too *everything*. Hope wasn't a spiritual person, then or now, but her friend Anthony Agricola was certain God put them together. Hope believed it, why not. But now? She wanted *more* than what she signed on for. Mark wouldn't sleep with her, wouldn't touch her, wouldn't even look at her very long. Why was he so distant? So stingy? Gregor's touch disgusted her, but some man should touch her some time, some where. *I'm still desirable. Why did I hang up my stirrups for a man who won't even come near me?*

And he would never take her blood. He swore an oath. And this also made no sense.

Mark had reached them, and she sent to his mind, *"I got this. It's okay."* He heard but disregarded her opinion.

Still at her knee, Gregor noticed Mark finally and backed away. He stated innocently, "Güt, fraulein, one more time and you may rest."

Hope didn't move, her eyes begging Mark to be cool, to keep his head.

For the moment, his stern gaze caused Hope to step Rusty away from both men. Mark stopped her before she dismounted.

"Ride Rusty to the barn," he told her looking her in the eye. He had stopped fifteen feet away from the coach, who looked ready to bolt. Hope didn't move and Mark removed his sunglasses. The sun was setting and his handsome face and beautiful eyes stole her heart as it always did. She

22

licked her lips, slow-blinked, and nudged Rusty to walk to the arena exit.

At the iron gate, she hopped from the saddle, reached for the latch and stole a glance backward. Mark and Gregor in conversation. Mark's head tipped to the side, speaking too low for her to hear. Gregor's shoulders rounded, his hands clasped in front of him. She watched another long moment and the man's head looked away. Mark turned toward her.

He is so dang sexy! she thought, watching him stroll through the sand, appearing as if he floated on air. *What if he's lost interest in me? What if I'm boring? Why's he so selfish with his affection?*

None of these questions had answers, so she'd never ask. Mark reached her and then walked beside her to the barn. When they were in the tackroom alone, he took her face in his hands and looked into her eyes.

"Herr Gregor will not touch you again," he whispered and kissed her forehead.

Hope wanted to say thank you but didn't.

Mark overreacted.

He might have hurt her chances to be chosen for the show team.

Why can't Mark love me and stop interfering with my horse training?

Hope thought these things and didn't hide them from her vampire companion. Maybe he read them, maybe not, but one thing was for sure; he needed to change or she would leave.

Will I eat the flesh of bulls,
Or drink the blood of goats?
Offer to God thanksgiving,
And pay your vows to the Most High.
Psalm 50: 13-14

ANYA'S CHEST WAS A SIGHT TO BEHOLD BUT ANDRONI trained his eyes to her lips. In the local language, she explained how all the girls in the company bragged nonstop on his skills as a lover. Androni did not respond quickly enough and she reaffixed her satiny top and sat upright. Watching his eyes, she pulled the snug material upward so that it bumped against her soft rises, swallowing them into her blouse, and in another moment, so disappeared the smooth white skin. Her fingers found, tugged, and then tied the neckline strings into a bow, all the while, she continued to talk, asking him why he didn't like her, why he refused her offer, why didn't she measure up to Steph, who worked the ticket booth weekdays and had slept in Androni's caravan many times.

Why don't I like her?

He did not ponder the question longer than a heartbeat. It was her aroma. Three hours ago, his nose assured, she'd been in bed with Jarred. The disgusting brute from the elephant pod left his scent on her skin, in her hair, on her clothing, and if Androni had gotten any closer, the man's essence may have even been tasted in her blood.

Her blood...

He was hungry.

Androni had lived two-hundred and fifty years, drinking human blood to remain young and vibrant. He understood he was a vampire but had no teacher. His transformation had taken place over time after an attack he didn't recall. He had been twenty-eight and newly married when one evening, a band of marauders tore through the village, murdering, raping and pillaging. Androni's wife had been snatched from their sleeping

24

quarters never to be seen again while Androni himself had been bound and gagged, blindfolded, and carted away. For a ride that took them all night, he rode balled inside a wooden box. When the horse stopped, rough hands jerked him out and dragged him bodily across what felt like loose sand to his booted feet.

"That'll last a while," a man said in Hungarian and Androni's body fell through space to land hard moments later on a stone floor. Then the world grew quiet. He could not see past his blindfold and could not speak past his gag, so he listened and waited. Hours passed before a sound roused him from a fitful sleep. A dragging shuffling walk, ragged breathing, and a liquidy slurp drew near and in another minute, cold hands gripped his biceps, yanked him upwards, and bit into his throat. Androni lost consciousness, only later realizing what the creature must have been.

And I didn't die.

Anya was crying, watching his face. Androni couldn't worry about her sensitivity. He had a performance in a few minutes and had spent too much time *not* drinking the woman's blood. Now he would be forced to wait to fill the void in his middle.

Why didn't I die?

The night the pillagers fed him to their pet monster, they had expected him to perish. No one returned to check on him and the following night, Androni awoke unbound and leaning against the cavern wall, his blindfold on the floor. He rose to his feet and stepped into the sunshine. It took three weeks to find a village and then as long to work his way back home. By the time he reached his burned-out cabin, his flesh had died, and his tongue yearned for blood.

And I found the circus…

An eruption of faraway cheers widened Anya's reddened eyes and she turned her face to the caravan door. That noise meant Androni the Magnificent went on in seventeen minutes.

At least my marquee reads "Magier" and not "Vampyr."

When he first joined the Company, his exhibit was a clown show where a drooling ghoul haunted a cemetery for virgin blood. He hated the role and after a few months, convinced the ringmaster that he was a much better magician than a devil.

"I hate you! You're a monster! And you're mean and…" Anya's voice choked and she scrambled out the door.

Androni didn't like her tears; his life was about fun and laughter. But he did not stop her. Plus, it was time to go, the grumble in his stomach would have to wait. In a smooth movement, Androni donned his navy-blue velvet cape. The sun had set, which he preferred, and he strolled from the unit, his eyes on the side-tent fifty meters south. Androni had always been able to bear the sun, but the brightness delivered a debilitating migraine. Because of this he stayed inside on the brightest days, which only aided his mysterious circus magician persona.

"Androni!" Billus shouted, his voice spiking on the last syllable. This was the stable boy, taller than the vampire by an inch, but skinny as a bean, with very delicious blood. Androni checked the distance to the tent, the time on his watch, and waved the boy close.

"Give us a taste," he whispered in German. "Fast."

Billus looked left and right, seeking a good place to duck in for privacy. He let blood thinking Androni was a Satanist; no one in the Company knew the truth. Even the ringmaster thought Androni only *pretended* to be the Prince of Darkness.

"Let us do it right here, they will think we're in love," Androni said and the boy grinned, looking even younger than seventeen when he did so. Then he moved into Androni's open arms making himself malleable, so the company "vampire" could reach his throat. With a smile, Androni pulled the boy into his body. Billus enjoyed playing "Lucifer's victim". To keep up the pretense, Androni, who possessed two very sharp fangs, mimed using a knife while pressing one such fang into the boy's neck, in the muscle, and not close to the carotid. Billus flinched. He had given blood dozens of times and was one of Androni's favorites. Although, since the youth bedded the Chinese princess in the tiger tent, his blood was no longer the virginal ambrosia it had been at first.

Beggars can't be choosers, Androni said inside and withdrew, snaking a hand to the wound to press until Billus took over with shaky fingers.

"My hero," Androni whispered in his ear. He kissed the boy's cheek and swished away, leaving Billus standing, albeit a tad wobbly, in the center of the dirt road.

The zydeco intro announced the magier and he jogged to the back flap of his stage tent. In German and Hungarian, the barrel-chested master of ceremonies belted out his name and accolades. Androni burst into the tent to the cheers of six dozen circus goers, mostly women addicted to his show. He scanned the crowd; they were locals, Europeans, no tourists among them tonight. Androni had a thing for Nords, blondes, pink skin, pink lips, blue eyes. So rare where he had been born, which was why he enjoyed the Germans.

But I still ended up with fellow Hungarians! he chuckled inside and chose a woman with a darling face and a humongous, soft body.

He inhaled then, the aroma of the crowds' varied blood tickling his nose with the most delicious pain. He bowed, caught the eyes of his closest fans, and began the dance. And the crowd shouted his name.

Z

For we do not wrestle against flesh and blood,
But against principalities, against powers,
Against the rulers of the darkness of this age,
Against spiritual hosts of wickedness in the heavenly places.
Ephesians 6:12

"I GUESS THAT'S HIM OVER THERE," ABBY SAID, LEADING the team as they inspected the store. Joey touched her arm and she stopped her forward motion. "You okay? You're acting sort of weird."

"I don't know what it is, but I have a really bad feeling," he said low. Scotty would tease him, of course, but he expected Abby to have more empathy. He read their eyes; both of his friends thought he was over-reacting. Leave it to Scotty to speak his mind.

"You're gonna win a trophy for all that drama," his friend said loud enough for other patrons to overhear. "I think he's having a nervous breakdown, cooped up with the Ellerslies all these weeks."

Joey shot him a glare for being loud and for his choice of words. Abby took up for him and moved in to snug her arm around Joey's bicep.

"Come on," she said squeezing tight, Joey's arm pressed into her pillowy softness. She knew it and grinned up at him. "I'll protect you."

She pulled a bit and he followed, feeling better seeing her take it so lightly. She had no fear, so as they approached the man behind the counter, Joey's confidence expanded.

"Hi! I'm Abigail Abingdon. This is Joey Ellerslie and Scotty Montgomery. We want to bless your store."

The shopkeeper lowered his chin, Abigail seeming suddenly tiny before him. "Abigail Abingdon, thank you," he said in a Northeastern accent. "My name is Haman Troye. Pleasure." He raised his eyes to Joey and stepped from around the counter. He put out his hand, his eyes flitting rodent-like across Joey's face and upper body. "Aren't you striking! Ellerslie, you say? Where did you come from? Exactly?"

Joey narrowed his eyes at the stranger's tone. He was fishing for

28

personal details and every red flag in Joey's spirit came alive. Joey didn't shake his hand but stepped backward in two quick paces. Abby covered for his behavior by eclipsing him and taking over the conversation.

"Ryan Road Christian Fellowship. His parents are the pastors, Scotty's dad is the lawyer, and my Grandma's in the choir. So, can we do a little prayer walk?"

Her eyes scanned the store as she spoke and Joey noted Troye's eyes appeared to be on the vicinity of her chest. She'd worn a flowery dress that dropped straight down from her bosom and came just to the knee. The creep's eyes remained there even when she turned back to hear his reply.

"No," he answered inside a chuckle. "I don't believe in it."

"Do you go to church, Mr. Troye?" Abby asked, her fists to her hips and her head to the side. The shopkeeper continued to study her body and not her face, but Abby appeared unfazed. She poked at him again. "You don't believe in what? Prayer, or God, or church?"

He finally raised his eyes to the level of her face, but as he replied, he took a step around her to reach for Joey. "None of the above."

This time, Joey accepted the handshake, commanding himself to grow up and stop being such a chicken. It was just a man. A tall, angular, creepy man. Troye grasped Joey's fingers, his cool grip feeling more like steel than flesh. One, two, three seconds passed along with the two pumps, and he did not release. Instead. Troye stepped even closer and enclosed Joey's hand with both of his own.

"You look familiar," he said lowering his voice and Joey wondered if his friends heard. *"I dreamed about you."*

Joey pulled on his hand; his eyes fixed in the stranger's. That phrase was definitely too low for Abby to hear because she did not react. She walked to Scotty and asked to borrow his Spikenard praying oil. Joey broke into a sweat and tugged his hand again.

"So how 'bout it, Mr. Troye? Let us do a little prayer walk. The whole place will feel lighter and brighter," Abigail said, looking away and unaware of how spooked Joey had grown.

The stranger released him in a sudden move and walked in Abby's direction. He stood beside her; his eyes trained to the ceiling as hers were for the moment.

"Who are you praying to?" he asked as if puzzled.

"Jesus, of course," Abby said as if the man was joking. But he scoffed and shook his head.

"No, ma'am, no Jesus here. You can pray to Allah, how about that?

29

Or Mohammad? How about Buddha or Vishnu? Do you like those?" He had turned his face to hers and Joey watched her eyes from his position. First, she looked confused but then her mouth fell into a wry grin as if the man was pulling her leg.

"There's only one God," she said, and Joey was impressed. Apologetics was not his forte and besides today, he never saw Abigail whip that tool from her shed. "Do you believe in all those little g's?"

He grinned upon her bringing his hands to clasp beneath his chin. "Little g's?" he asked, his voice gleeful. "I doubt a million Buddhists would agree, missy." He smiled, darkly handsome in his spooky, English professor way.

Abby blushed and flirted back. She brushed her fingers to his forearm. "Oh, come on," she said. "You know those little g's are fake."

"Are you a Buddhist?" Scotty asked from the other side, to Joey sounding as if he saw nothing weird in the man's behavior.

"Abigail, Scott, and Joey," he said tipping his chin to each of them in turn, stopping in Joey's gaze, "you may pray your heart out, but not while we're open. I close at nine. If you would like to return then, I will stay open a little later for you."

"Naw, sorry, I have a thing tonight," Scotty said and looked at Abby. "You guys can come back, though."

Abby shook her head. "I'm busy tonight, too."

"Joey Ellerslie, are you busy tonight?" the man asked, holding Joey's eye. "I will remain open for you. Bring a Bible. I would love that."

"Now-now, Mr. Troye, that sounds sorta weird," Abby said in a teasing tone, again coming to Joey's rescue. "We tried," she said to all and again tucked Joey's bicep into her softness. Her bravery gave him courage and he spoke up.

"You should have let us pray," Joey said. Coming up beside him, Scotty made a 'yep' noise. Joey added, "This place feels wrong. We're going to pray outside. You can't … stop…" Joey trailed off as his stomach flopped. Then it flipped. Then a sudden nausea climbed up his esophagus, and the entire time Haman Troye grinned into his face.

"Your friend looks like he's going to be sick." Haman blinked and Joey fell against Scotty.

Abby's contact followed and she tried to stand him up. "Joey! Oh, God - run to the toilet!" Abby pushed him toward the restroom sign.

Joey did as he was told and stumbled into the single-head bathroom, slamming the door. He fell to his knees and retched, and before three attempts, his breakfast plopped into the toilet bowl. He gagged a few more times and sat upon his heels to catch his breath.

What was that? Is that guy the reason I didn't want to come in? Is he fixated on me or is that my imagination?

Joey wiped his mouth with his sleeve and stood. Using the available paper towels, he ran the water and daubed his entire face.

The boy! The boy! That's him!

Joey squeezed his eyes closed so hard that they throbbed. He heard those words in his head and the sound of them filled him with dread.

"Oh, I have dreamed about him!"

This time it sounded like the man Haman Troye, but the exclamation had again, been between Joey's ears.

"The dreams brought me here, and Oh! He is perfect!"

"Stop! Father! Oww," Joey hissed under his breath, his head aching from the voices.

"...The Unseen said he will lead me into prosperity. That he will feed what I lack. That he will be mine... Joseph Ellerslie, come meet your new master! The blood of a brother is superior to all..."

"You okay?" It was Abby on the other side of the door. Then she giggled and said as if to the others, "We don't usually vomit and pray. This is a special occasion."

Joey heard chuckles from Troye and Scotty and he leaned on the sink ledge.

"I'm certain he will be fine," Troye said loud enough for Joey to hear. "While he washes his face, tell me what you think of my store. This is my first day of business."

Joey scowled, the man sounding so nonchalant when Joey felt his life was in danger. *Why am I so upset? This isn't like me...*

"I agree with Joey," Abby replied, and her voice grew quiet as she walked away from the bathroom door, "it's too dark. You'll need lighting as well as prayer to clean this place up."

Joey rinsed his mouth several times and stared at his eyes in the mirror. *That guy dreamed about me? Dreamed-dreamed, or was he just making words? And why don't Abby and Scotty think he's weird?*

Joey opened the bathroom door and found them a few yards away between him and the entrance. He joined them in time to hear Abby continue with, "Not only that, it's a mess. We'd never be able to find anything.

Haman Troye responded with a "Hmm".

31

Abby wasn't done. "Wait, is this the kind of store where you look around and try to see if you want anything you happen to run across? Like a flea market?"

"You are adorable," Troye said then with a glance to Scotty and then Joey who looked away. "You tell me. Will that work?"

Joey saw the man was teasing, but Abby took him seriously. She spun a circle and shook her head.

"No. You need to organize it. Categorize the carnage."

"That's very helpful."

Joey narrowed his eyes as the man lifted a hand and seemed about to drop it to Abigail's shoulder. Then, before making contact, he withdrew and clasped both hands again at his breastbone.

"Will you do this for me, Miss Abingdon? I will pay the right person handsomely to make my store profitable."

Joey's jaw dropped; Abby had been looking for a job for months. Her grandmother gave her spending money, but his friend had grown-up needs now that cost more than twenty bucks. And she had expensive taste in clothing, shoes, in particular. Now this awful stranger offered her employment and she loved bookstores more than anything. He wanted to tell her to say no and run out, but that wouldn't make sense.

Abby began bargaining her hourly wage and Troye looked to Joey, his lips moving to whatever he discussed. Joey heard nothing. The acidic bile climbed toward his esophagus as it had before and he spun on his heel and leapt back into the bathroom.

"Oh, God! This is horrible! Help me!" Joey prayed in his heart, again on his knees before the toilet. His stomach was empty so he heaved until exhausted and then he slumped to the tile to rest on his rump.

"Okay, little Joey. I know you now. You are mine. You can go."

With wide eyes and frantic movement, Joey looked about. There had been a voice in his head—it sounded like Haman Troye, but that wasn't possible. Was it?

"Joey? You okay?" Abigail asked from outside the door. "What do you need? Can I get you something? What can I do to help?"

Joey flushed the unused toilet. He wanted to run from the building. Instead, he rolled to his knees and then stood to lean against the door. It was only one word, but it carried the power of God in its execution. Joey whispered between gasps, "Pray…"

On the other side of the door, she did, and Joey thanked God for his friends.

8

A friend loves at all times,
And a brother is born for adversity.
Proverbs 17:17

TONY HADN'T CALLED HIM, BUT MARK WENT ANYWAY. In his German estate, Hope had spent two days and nights, talking, laughing, playing normal platonic couple, before time to leave for her month-long horse adventure. Now that the house had grown quiet, Mark longed for company. Tony and Sarah's presence always brightened his spirits, so after calculating the time difference, he appeared in Tony's study at 5PM, Central Standard Time. The man sat at his desk and did not startle, likely sensing milliseconds before Mark appeared that he was on the way.

His eyes to his book, he grinned saying, "Hey, Doc." With a few mumbled words from the text, he closed the cover of a red leather-bound Bible. He looked up and his face brightened. "You look good. How's Hope?"

Mark slow-blinked and worked up his response. The affection in Tony's reaction pleased him. *Maybe this man's friendship is enough…*

"Enough what?" Tony asked and stood. "What's wrong?"

"Nothing, everything is fine," Mark said, and it was. He wasn't accustomed to living such a mundane life. He hadn't worked with his hands since the debacle with Paul. Before then, before meeting Hope and Tony, he'd been a physician, had a private practice and stood in for ER doctors on occasion. Now?

"So whiny," Tony said with a wink.

"Whiny?" Mark grimaced. "I am whining, aren't I? This is pitiful." Mark smiled but didn't feel it.

"You must be depressed," Tony said then with mystery. "Depression is when you focus on yourself so much that you can't see what's right under your nose." Tony's face scrunched as he held back a laugh.

Mark's brow furrowed. What was he getting at? Then he smelled her. Then he heard her. Elizabeth Hawken, in the next room, laughing with

Sarah.

Tony burst out a little chuckle. "She just got here. Listen," he said. "They're talking about you."

Mark parted his lips and did as Tony said.

"Have you heard from the doctor?" Elizabeth asked in her soft West Coast accent.

"Goodness, no, honey, he doesn't call me…" (Sarah laughs)

"You know what I mean. Has he called Tony? He's sort of stuck in my mind. Do you know what he asked me at the party last week?"

"What?"

"He asked me if I wanted to know him better. What did he mean? I took it to be just flirting, but I can't forget his eyes when he asked it. I think he was truly seeking an answer."

"Well? Do you want to know him better?"

(Pause and then a sigh) *"I guess. I haven't thought about much else. Also, I dreamed about him two nights in a row."*

"You did? What was he doing?"

"Watching."

"Watching? Watching what?"

"Everything. The dreams made him out to be watching life, not living. He stood by, leaning on the wall, just like he did at the party. But in my dream, he leaned on the wall everywhere. Nothing interested him enough to get off the wall."

"Wow," Sarah said then true sympathy in her voice. *"I think he does that in real life. I think he's lost his place. He had a friend, a roommate for many years who died recently. I don't think the doctor has been the same."*

"I saw sadness in him," Elizabeth said. *"But I sensed something else, something huge. I think I should have said yes."*

"Yes to what?"

"To his question – do I want to know him better. I should have said yes."

"Sarah," Tony called then and Mark turned for the door to the hall. The reverend appeared and startled at meeting Mark's eye.

"Oh! Dr. Corescu! I didn't hear you come in," she said and called for Elizabeth. "We were just talking about you."

Mark and Tony both held their expressions though if she thought about her words, she'd recall both vampires could hear them across the house if need be.

Elizabeth appeared over her shoulder and she met Mark's eyes first with a wide grin.

"There he is," she said with glee and pushed past Sarah to reach out her small hand.

Mark shook it, his mind blaring a new realization: *she's not like Hope at all.* Hope was as attractive, but her blue eyes reflected self-interest, had from the start. Elizabeth Hawken's eyes shone with empathy and an eagerness to soothe another's pain. Mark's grin tucked into his cheek as his mind went this distance and the young woman smiled wider.

"I think you came to see me," she said, the handshake over, she stood at arm's length under his nose looking up. "I'm right, right?" Her voice teased and in his peripheral vision, Tony grinned at the pair of them and took his wife quietly out of the room.

"Don't leak our secret, Romeo," Tony sent to his mind from another room and Mark invited Elizabeth to sit with him on the long sofa. She did, sitting with a cushion between them, her knees pointing his direction.

"Okay, for real, how have you been?" she asked and tucked her hands together in her lap. She wore faded blue jeans and a blue T-shirt that sported a Bible verse across the upper chest. The first line, "I can do all things" was in a jumbo font with the second line barely legible beneath it. Her eyes dropped to her shirtfront. "I hope you're admiring my Jesus shirt, doctor," she teased and met his eye once more.

"Your shirt is indeed part of what I admire," Mark replied and leaned back to cross his ankle over one knee.

Elizabeth was picking apart his compliment and then answered, "How is your horse-riding friend? Tony says she spends a lot of time away. Is she out of town again?"

Mark grinned with a *"thanks, Tony,"* to his mind. "She left for a month-long horse camp. I suspect when she returns, she'll be ready to compete in the Olympics."

"I'd like to meet her one day. You care about her a lot which makes me think she's pretty amazing."

Elizabeth spoke her mind without reservation and Mark saw this in her eyes. He appreciated that attribute, so he also preferred to speak openly when possible. All he need do is keep his vampire secret, which he had been doing four centuries. To soften his reply, Mark softened his tone.

"If you meet her in person, you'll discern within a few minutes that God put us together as He did for His purposes in His timing. We were never destined to be more than platonic." When Mark finished speaking, he realized that on a human level, his explanation opened a door for another woman to enter. He hadn't meant it that way, but a correction did not readily appear.

"Really? Huh, so that explains why since I met you, I felt you are pretty much unattached from everything and everyone."

Mark huffed a wry grin. "You are remarkably perceptive. Have you always been so, or have you developed this skill more recently?" Now he wondered if her mental acuity was morphed by consuming The Other's blood. Elizabeth shrugged one shoulder.

"I hadn't thought of it." She hummed. "It's sharpest with you. Maybe you bring it out in me."

"Maybe I should ask you my question again," he replied and this time she offered a wry grin, knowing precisely what he meant.

"Yes, I want to know you better. Do you want to know me better?" She asked her question, now leaning forward but still sideways to see him on his end of the couch.

Mark did not need to dig around for an answer; it bubbled up without effort. "Yes, very much."

Elizabeth grinned and got to her feet. "Then let's go for a walk. In a very short time, God will show us an amazing sunset over the back pasture. I saw it last night with Sarah and it took my breath away."

She put out her hand, seeming as innocent as a child, and Mark stood and took her fingers. She positioned to walk with him into the hall but before they moved on, he looked down at her small hand in his. The Other's essence continued to tickle his nose but he had no desire to take the young woman's blood.

"Thank God for that," Tony said in his mind and as politely as possible, Mark put up a mental block to prevent further spying.

Elizabeth also looked at their joined hands. "What is it? Are you thinking about your lady friend?"

"Not at all," he said in a soft voice. "Let us watch your sunset."

Mark led her to the hallway and then the back door. He sensed Tony and Sarah had moved upstairs and shortly, he and Elizabeth were crossing the mowed yard for the rear pasture gate. Mark lifted it on oiled hinges and they passed through, still hand-in-hand.

Elizabeth allowed silence for several yards and then she pulled him to a stop and pointed to the horizon. "See how pink it is at the top of the trees?" Mark nodded with a *Mm-hmm*. "Last night, it exploded into a neon lavender. I'd never seen it like that. Sarah ran back in for her phone to catch a photo, but we missed it. Maybe the conditions will be right tonight and it will happen again. I think it all depends on the particles in the atmosphere."

Mark nodded again, eyes trained to the horizon, but most of his mind concentrating on the sensation of her fingers in his. Her head came to his chin and her gentle femininity reminded him of all things right in the world.

She cleared her throat. "Did you know Rakha Tep?"

Mark's eyes widened and she offered a short giggle in response.

"You showed up at Dad's hospital room and something Sarah said told me you knew him. From the past, I mean. This is something I wonder about." She continued to hold his eye, her manner curious, not anxious. When he did not answer within a few seconds, she added with a squeeze of his fingers, "Or when you asked me if I wanted to know you better, you didn't mean for real. Is that it?"

Mark's chagrin was evident and her eyes twinkled. It was Tony's idea to protect her from the truth; he had no qualms about revealing it to her because she carried The Other's—Rakha's—blood; how long would he and Tony be able to keep that hidden?

"How do you know Rakha Tep?" she asked with a new and sideways smile. "You can't go backwards now without admitting you were just a big flirt back there in the house. I got you, see?"

Mark chuckled, releasing a little stress he hadn't realized he'd stored during her inquisition. "What if everything you would learn about me does not fit in what you knew about the world previously? How would you handle that?"

"What do you mean?"

"If I told you I was born in Hungary in 1605, for instance. This is a hard fact, not an exaggeration. That wouldn't seem possible in the way you understand the natural world." Elizabeth's eyes had widened but she waited for more. "If you want to know me better, repeat my first sentence to yourself, understand that it is true, and reconsider if we should proceed."

"You were born in Hungary in 1605," she said as a soft statement and followed it up with, *Hmmmm,* as her mind sought different explanations. Then she said, "I was born in Georgia in 1995."

Mark's grin faltered, wondering where she was headed. He could not read her thoughts, and he tried, thinking The Other's blood should have made that possible. *But, what sort of monster am I these days? I don't drink from people. Maybe I'm more human than vampire…*

"Like a vampire?" Elizabeth said then and Mark's lips parted with surprise. "Not a *bluh!-bluh!-Drink-your-blood!* vampire, but something else." She had said the nonsense words in a Bela Legosi accent and Mark's grin recovered.

"That would be a nice way to put it," he said.

"Okay, expand my brainpan, Dr. Corescu," she said and turned them to walk toward the now-setting sun.

With a spark of inspiration, Mark did not resume walking but tugged her hand and released. "First, contact the reverend and inform her that you asked me. She and Tony know my story and out of respect, I would want them to know."

Elizabeth offered a thoughtful nod and removed her cell from her jeans pocket. She texted so Mark could read it upside down. *I asked Mark to tell me about himself and he said he would if ya'll said it was okay. So far he told me he is over 400 yrs old.*

Mark was not surprised when her phone rang shortly after and Sarah's voice sounded through the earpiece.

"Honey, of course, let him tell you whatever he can," she said with the sincere altruism he expected. *"We haven't told you because some of it is awful and scary. Dr. Corescu will be honest. You can believe him. Tony and I vouch for him all the way."*

Inwardly, Mark beamed at the woman's sentiment and then Tony joined in.

"I agree with Sarah. I asked him not to tell you, but he'll be honest. Brace yourself. If you grow frightened, remember how God pulled us out unscathed."

Mark waited for Elizabeth to look up at him and after thanking her friends, she disconnected the call and did so.

"I'm *very* excited to hear this *huge* secret. It's really built up now!" Her words were jovial and Mark was impressed. He offered a tiny nod and stepped for the sunset. Elizabeth joined him and again put her soft fingers into his. "I was born in Hungary in 1605," she said in his accent and he laughed once.

"In my twenties, I went into the clergy and pastored my village. In my mid-thirties, I was attacked by a demon I later came to know as The Other. He used his blood to transform me into what mankind considers a vampire. At the time, I didn't understand what had happened, so when The Other was killed by locals, I decided to use my bloodthirst and telepathic abilities to judge sinners for God."

Mark paused, tickled at how he summed up four centuries in so few sentences. Elizabeth was silent so he looked upon her face. She nodded in slow motion, taking steps methodically, robotically, her mind rolling over his story.

"Should I continue?" he asked.

She blinked and glanced up, her eyes calm but open wide. "You drank the blood of these sinners and judged them," she said flat and without bias.

"I had the ability to read their sins. I would tell them to repent, accept God's grace, and yes, I killed them—all of them, more than a hundred-thousand by the time I met Tony."

"A hundred-thousand," she repeated in a whisper. She also got them walking again, slow and easy. The sun had set, the landscape lit only by the moon. "You met Tony, and then what?"

Mark picked out highlights, assuming if they became close, she'd gather up details as their friendship grew. "God used Tony to reveal my error and I ceased."

Still stepping through the damp grass, she looked up to his face. "You stopped killing sinners for God?" He nodded. "And so now you're friends with Tony because he helped you."

Mark grinned; it sounded as if he might leave Tony's trouble out altogether.

"But you didn't explain how you know that horrible Rakha Tep."

"Ah," Mark responded with a nod. She faced front again and they continued forward. "The Other is what I knew him as. When the villagers killed him, I thought he was gone forever. I discovered that he was a spirit and last year, he assumed a new flesh…" Mark squeezed her fingers. "You met him as Rakha Tep."

"Oh, God," she said low and with wonder. "That guy really was a demon. I knew it." She spoke low and without excitement, nodding in steady tips. "He wanted to kill me. Kill Tony." She looked up again. "He tried to kill my dad. Why?"

This time, Mark gave her a small headshake. "I can only guess at his motives. Perhaps meeting you was by chance and once he saw you, he found you worthy of his attention."

"How? What do you mean?"

Mark hemmed thinking of the best way to continue. "It is my opinion that an entity like The Other would have enjoyed soiling your faith. This is what he had hoped to do with me in the beginning and then with Tony last summer."

"I have bad dreams about him," she admitted and they stood in place, both facing the same direction. "I was raped when I was fourteen and he used that against me."

Mark sighed, understanding her sudden pain at the admission and how the demon would have taunted her.

Then she wiggled his hand with a small grin. "But before all that, I had kept that secret inside, making it easy game for every demon of hell. Once Rakha pulled it out of me, I have peace. See how God turned that horrible misadventure into a blessing?"

"It was anathema," Mark said enjoying in his own mind how he had used the same word with Tony. "A curse and a blessing at the same time."

Elizabeth nodded with a new smile. "And everything you told me makes everything so clear. His every word and gesture... That horrid meeting in my studio..." She whipped her face to his. "Did he make me drink his blood?"

This time, Mark's eyebrows lifted.

"He did, didn't he? When we met, I lost time, lost my memory of about five minutes. I recalled a bottle in his hand but couldn't remember the rest." She watched Mark's eyes and he finally gave her a small nod.

"I do not know precisely how it happened, but I smell his blood mixed with yours. I detected it in the hospital room."

Elizabeth dropped Mark's hand and stretched out her arms, examining them in the moonlight. "So what does that mean? I'm not any different."

She really meant, *I'm not a vampire,* and Mark inhaled to tell her the rest.

"Ingesting The Other's blood in this way will cause your cells to mutate to resemble his. What it means for you is that you will stop aging and you will heal from injuries in moments."

"What? Wait," Elizabeth mumbled, suddenly unbelieving. "How do you know? For real?"

"Unless God decides to deliver you, you and the reverend have this same affliction. Before you ask, Sarah was infected by my now-deceased partner, Paul."

"Paul? Your friend who died?" she asked, her empathy returned in full. "He did that to Sarah? Oh, God, how awful. And I never would have known. She seems normal as anything." Her eyes went to Mark's in a jerk. "Tony, too? He's the only one that seems odd. Does he have it, too?"

Mark smiled and his eyes may have twinkled, an unexpected joy hitting his spirit. He was about to reveal Tony's secret and a playful grin remained on his face enough for her to ask.

"Tony has it, too? By who? Rakha?"

"Tony is like me," he said and waited. Her brow furrowed and then lifted, eyes wide. Mark continued. "Outside of my control, my partner Paul transformed him last year. He does not drink blood," Mark clarified at the last knowing his friend would appreciate that.

40

"Oh, wow," Elizabeth said in soft wonder. "Then he…" She looked aside in thought, nodding, one by one, more than likely thinking about all the strange things about the man.

A cool breeze whipped past and Mark turned them both toward the house. "Are you frightened or disgusted?" he asked as if there were only those two choices.

"Amazed," she answered in earnest, holding his hand and walking toward the lights of the back porch far ahead. After several moments of silent thinking, she stopped and lifted his hand to the available light. She studied its structure and when she turned it over, Mark allowed it, revealing his smooth palm. She traced his lifeline with one finger and then looked into his face with a new respect. "Your horse friend knows all this," she said and he nodded. "Who else knows? Pastor John? He's really close friends with Tony…"

Mark nodded. "And your father."

"Dad?" Elizabeth's voice squeaked and her eyes went to the side. "He made a big fuss convincing me that Mr. Tep was a psychopath." She rejoined Mark's gaze. "He said Rakha was insane and only *thought* he was a vampire. I had put it out of my mind. I believed him." Then she said to the side, "I never would have believed the truth coming from him…"

Tony and his wife stepped out of the porch twenty yards away. Elizabeth was still in examination mode of Mark's palm and she wrapped her second hand around his fingers. Looking up, Elizabeth smiled when he did.

"You're a good man. I knew it when I first saw you. All this other stuff? It's amazing and I'm sure there's much more to it, but I feel peaceful. I think God is telling me this is exactly what He wanted tonight."

Mark offered a single tip of his chin.

"When can I see you again?" she asked with a glance to their friends on the porch. They were out of earshot of Sarah, but Tony would hear them, and Mark said so. Elizabeth inhaled with wonder. "Wow. I'll remember that. You both have super bat hearing." She smiled at a new notion. "Can you turn into a bat?"

"I never have," Mark said and resumed their motion toward the house. "I will remain at Tony's house a few days if you would like to see me here. At that time, you will answer questions about yourself, savvy?"

Elizabeth nodded with a small grin. "But understand, I'm not near as interesting as you are."

"You would be surprised," Mark said and they had reached the porch.

41

Sarah rushed into Elizabeth and grabbed her into a hug. Mark watched the women go indoors, the reverend offering additional information in a rush. Tony sighed and crossed his arms. Mark turned a triumphant grin.

"It's done," he said to Tony's blank expression. "I will stay with you a few days."

With a general headshake, Tony smiled, too. "You will stay with me a few days," he said as if under a spell.

Mark chuckled and Tony did, too, after a moment and he draped an arm about the shorter man's shoulders. Mark walked him toward the door.

"What do you little humans do at night? Television? Pea-knuckle?"

"Tiddlywinks, actually, and guests go first."

Mark gave him a questioning look, saw him smile and he laughed. Finally, some joy reached his spirit and Mark realized he looked forward to the next day. This was progress.

9

You shall walk after the Lord your God and fear Him,
and keep His commandments and obey His voice;
you shall serve Him and hold fast to Him.
Deuteronomy 13:4

"ARE YOU SKIPPIN? WHERE RU?"

Joey read Scott's text on the lock-screen as he pushed through the swinging doors to the sanctuary. On the forward stage, the praise team led the congregation in the first worship song and Joey crept along the back wall seeking an open chair. Most Sundays, the room was half-full. This morning because of the visiting evangelist team, he saw no empty spots except in the last row. Despite being the pastors' son, the ushers glowered at him as he shuffled past. Up front, left of the stage, he recognized Abby's head and beside her, Scott, in their usual seat. Joey dropped into the last seat on the far right corner and texted back.

"Misjudged time. Make room. I'll scoot down at offering."

He took a deep breath and looked about the room at the singing heads. More than usual, the air pulsed with energy and Joey considered who they had coming to preach. The lobby poster read, "Welcome Pastor Anthony Agricola and Reverend Sarah Tracey!" although Abby informed them the two were actually married. The graphics showed a man and woman in separate photos; the man on the left side, sitting and leaning over folded arms, his expression one of seriousness, and the woman standing, upper body only, waving at the camera. Agricola seemed scholarly, serious, reminding Joey of his dad's business manager. And the woman was a little older, pretty, very skinny, and really happy. Between the two a little lower was a photo of a muscle-bound Black man with the caption, "With guest pastor, Big John Jenkins, Columbus, GA."

On the stage, the song changed and Joey sang along. At the lyric, "Protect me, Lord, Your hedges are so high," the image of Haman Troye flashed across his mind. A surge of adrenaline and a threat of nausea pricked him before he settled it back down by sheer will.

I'm worshipping God, not thinking about anything else… he said inside, his mantra working right away. A third song started up, this one asking God to open the eyes of his heart, and Joey sang louder. Below him, near the front, Abby turned and found his eye to wave over the crowd. He waved back and sang louder.

Watching from backstage-right, Tony stood hand-in-hand with Sarah facing the pastors who spoke to the crowd. John stood on the opposite side across the expanse of the modern stage and when their eyes met, he nodded, sweat beading on his forehead. This would be his last gig with the two of them and Tony prayed it went well. Next Sunday, John would begin as head pastor for Damascus Bible Church in Columbus, Georgia. He was sorry to leave their team, but ecstatic to get away from vampires.

At that word in his mind, Reverend Ellerslie began his boisterous introductions.

"Thank you, Brother Ridley, for that lovely rendition of *Amazing Grace!* Don't we have the best worship leader in all of Montgomery?" Reverend Ellerslie waited for the clapping to die down and he cleared his throat. "I'm so happy to see a standing-room-only crowd today. If you're visiting, please take a moment to fill out the little blue card at your seat. Now, JoAnn and I welcome to the platform our guests, Brother Tony Agricola, Reverend Sarah Tracey and Lay-Pastor, Big John Jenkins!"

Reverend Ellerslie motioned to Tony and they trotted up to stand beside their host. Tony winked at Sarah who had been praying the whole morning and by the way her lips moved as she stood mute, she was praying still. Big John looked mightier than ever in an emerald green suit that brought out his uncommon blue eyes. His bald head shone with excited perspiration and he grinned at Tony who gave him a subtle thumbs-up.

Like Sarah and John, Tony wore a lapel mike and would not need the hand-held. He introduced Sarah as his wife and she took over to begin the message. He stepped behind and stood in support mode while John moved to stand equal, facing the congregation.

For fifteen minutes, Sarah and John spoke to the people about Jesus, His love, and His forgiveness. Tony nodded and said Amen, still not ready to take the full mantle of preaching as a vampire. He had not had any blood since Rakha was killed, and he didn't lust for it either, the steady food of Scripture feeding him every night. But all that, he still felt unclean. So, he waited on God's deliverance before he'd resume the role of preacher.

Tony's ear perked when Sarah moved into her prayer of protection over the people regarding demons. God had gifted his wife with the ability to see devils like he saw mortals. Clear as day. He tuned in and loved her confidence.

"I'm addressing every unclean spirit in this room right now, every spirit of religion, spirits of legalism, spirits of distraction, I bind you in the name of Jesus Christ. I command you to be still and be quiet!"

She prayed a bit more and when finished, Sarah scanned the room. She had worn a simple white blouse with tailored black slacks, as always, the most beautiful woman he had ever seen.

"Jesus said He wants us to preach, teach, heal, cast out demons and raise the dead!" Sarah said to the group. "Every single believer in this room has a job assignment. Tony and John and I are inviting anyone to come to the stage for us to pray for you. If you have an infirmity, a sickness, or if you're depressed. Or maybe you know you have a calling and wonder if we can give you more direction on it – come down. In Jesus' name, we welcome you to come!"

John and Sarah separated and went to opposite forward staircases while ushers readied to control the flow of congregants. Tony remained in the middle, listening to both and ready to step to whomever might need a second hand.

As the ushers collected the tithing plates and the guest pastors called folks to the front for healing, deliverance, or impartation, Joey made his way toward his friends. Halfway there, his path was blocked by those vying for a spot in Reverend Tracey's prayer line. Joey decided to join them.

Why not? I could use some prayer after these last few days. And maybe they'll help explain why I am so freaked out about that Troye guy...

The top of Reverend Tracey's head flickered into view as she ministered. Pastor Jenkins shook hands on the opposite side, so when Joey reached the stage, he'd be in the woman's care. Would she mind praying for something like his fear? The Ellerslies didn't practice apostolic so Joey was not surprised to glimpse his father in the wings seething, his mouth a grim line. He'd invited the Agricola team based upon their fame, but both of his parents feared those who spoke in tongues or called out demons, which is what the Agricolas had done since they took the stage. Joey couldn't help but snicker and when his father caught his eye in a scan of the crowded queue, Joey sent a playful wink. He couldn't see Abby or Scott so as he shuffled in tiny steps with his line, he slipped his phone from his slacks to text them. In their group message, he sent, *"In line. Gonna get some of that blessing!"*

Scotty replied without delay, *"I'm on Pastor Jenkins' side. He better be gentle—he's a giant!"*

Followed by Abby. *"I got mine from P.Jenk—he's so sweet! See you in the Youth Room. 'Member we have AuctionP at one."*

AuctionP – Practice for the Youth Group's fund raiser, entitled, the SOSC –"Service to Others is Service to Christ"—Member Auction. Scott and Abby were lead organizers and Joey agreed to be auctioned off with a dozen other teens to do yard work and household stuff for the winners. Last year, he enjoyed his assignment, laying sod with Brian Gamble's son, Kit. Kit was retired military and for three days in the summer sun, they sodded and swapped tales. It had been a blast. And when that long weekend was done, Joey had lost ten pounds and leaned up better than ever. Win-win.

Joey lifted his eyes in time to watch the evangelist lay hands on a young woman's head and pray in a strange clicking language. He couldn't help it; he flicked his gaze to his mother also backstage and in the wings. She was frowning, like Dad, but also wringing her hands at her breastbone.

They are so sad, Joey mused and not happy about it. They'd been hard on him this past summer, putting a lot of pressure on him to excel in school and make good enough grades for an internship. They had him in PreLaw, but every day, Joey wished he studied anything else.

If I was in charge of my life, ahem… I'd study teaching.

Joey pictured the Vacation Bible School groups he taught the past few years. Children aged six to twelve adored him and he received good marks from their parents in the report summaries. But teaching didn't make the money his parents thought he'd need, so he did what his father did before answering the call to the pulpit—business Law.

Joey swallowed and licked his lips realizing he had daydreamed himself right up to the stage. Two people were ahead of him now and Sarah Tracey was praying in the furthest man's ear. Then the elderly man before him went forward to meet the reverend. Joey saw her clearly now, standing barely ten feet away and awaiting his turn. Reverend Tracey's short hair shimmered in the stage lights, and even with dainty beads of perspiration on her forehead, she appeared cool, happy, and in full control of her world. Her voice sang, not like music, but in a timbre that turned every spoken word into a pleasant melody. Joey grinned at his imagination and then it was his turn.

"Hi, there!" the woman said and reached out one hand for him to take. Joey did, returning the smile, but before he could speak, a familiar voice rang out from the stage center mic.

"Thank you, Pastor Tony, Pastor John! Thank God for you and thank you for coming!"

Joey's father was ending the service. A glance at the wall clock, set there specifically for the pastor staff, revealed the noon hour had come and gone. In an awkward few moments, Reverend Tracey turned her face to her husband standing back and to the side. As Joey watched, with unspoken instruction, Agricola nodded to his wife and turned for Joey's dad.

"That was wonderful!" his dad was saying still to the people, none of whom were looking his way. The crowd wanted to meet the visitors and they remained in the long lines that bled all the way into the front lobby. Agricola stepped close to Joey's father, spoke in his ear, and stepped back. His dad's expression dropped, his brow furrowed, and he shuffled away from the mic. Joey looked back to the reverend as she wiggled his hand to begin and when he peeked to the stage, his father had gone. Whatever Pastor Tony said gave the team more time. Joey grinned that his dad had been rebuked and he faced the reverend.

"That's okay, little Joseph, I will see you again. I dreamed about you…"

Joey flinched outwardly and his skin broke out in gooseflesh. With a sudden urge, he tensed to bolt away from the minister, but her slender hand shot forth and grasped his wrist.

"Be gone, devil!" she hissed, her eyes off Joey's right. He did not resist her grip and she pulled him closer with tender contact. "Hi, I'm Sarah. What's your name?" she asked.

Joey swallowed, his mind racing over the past three seconds. Haman shouting in his mind and the lady preacher casting demons off his person… *Is that what happened?* He stammered his name and the woman grinned and waved over her husband.

"Tony! Come meet Joseph Ellerslie," she called and returned her loving gaze to his. "What would you like to pray about, Joseph? Here's Tony. He'll pray, too."

Joey watched her look to her husband a long moment. Something passed between them and she turned back, same happy smile as before.

She asked again what he had come up for and he said the first thing that came to mind.

"I need a car," he said.

The preacher and his wife both chuckled. Her husband tilted his head to one side and caught Joey's gaze. This man was his height with soft brown hair he wore in a ponytail at the nape of his neck. No longer two-dimensional as in the poster, he had a pleasant face with brown eyes and a goatee, but the longer he held Joey's eye, the more Joey wanted to run.

Why? What is going on? Before yesterday, I was never afraid of anything or anyone. What's going on?

The reverend released his arm and gave him a nod. "Get ready, Joseph Ellerslie," she said with a grin. "God has a word for you and it's big."

Joey thanked her, grew still, and tried to think positive. It wasn't easy.

Not expressly trying to be telepathic, Sarah "thought" to Tony, *"This boy is draped in death."*

He returned a commiserating nod that said he'd seen it, too, in his own way. Tony glanced over the line that had formed four deep and then back to the boy. The pastor's son was a good-looking kid, paler than the norm with wavy white-blond hair, tidy and recently trimmed, with serious blue eyes. He was athletic, his frame well developed, Tony guessed, for running or swimming. But his current expression was of stark terror. Tony attempted to send him some peace, but when their gaze connected, he grew even more agitated.

As if he sees I'm not normal…

But that couldn't be. No one had paid Tony any special attention since Rakha died, and because of his feasting upon Scripture, he sometimes forgot he was a vampire.

He smiled and the boy looked away. Tony told Sarah silently all that he discerned and turned it over to her.

"Joseph, honey…" Sarah took a deep breath. "You and Jesus have a very special relationship. He tells me that you want to make your earthly parents proud and excel in the path they set your feet upon. Is this true?"

"Yes, Ma'am," Joey agreed in a whisper. The boy looked left and right and returned to her eye.

"God is about to move mightily in your life. You thought you had your life planned and you're busily ticking off each element, but last month, you asked Jesus to set your feet onto His path. Is that right? Did you ask Jesus in prayer?"

The young man's eyes widened and he nodded in slow motion, his lips parted.

"He heard you. Right now, God is knocking down walls, opening doors and making paths straight to lead you onto a path that in the end will affect millions of lives. Yes, I said millions..."

The boy had calmed and relaxed his shoulders, listening with great interest. Sarah closed her eyes, choosing her next words. *Help me, Lord,* she prayed and opened her mouth to speak.

"Young man, before you were born, God sent an angel warrior to stand watch over your life. He did this because your calling is that great, that important." Sarah paused, not liking at all the sentence that formed next in her mind, "On the flip side, as soon as Satan saw that special assignment, he also stationed a full-time demon at your side to kill you. That demon waited and watched for an opportune time to terminate you."

Joey stopped nodding and she continued.

"Satan has a contract out on you. He has sensed that God wants to use you in some special capacity and he has tried to kill you over and over. Remember that time you fell off the carousel when you were ten? That was one of the times the devil tried to take you away from God. And I see a fall from a bridge when you were seven... and I also see a near miss playing baseball at fourteen when you were pegged with the ball in the back of your head..."

"Yes!" the boy said in a harsh whisper. "That's right! Dad used to call me Miracle Mike!"

"But Jesus protects His own," Sarah continued. "And You are His, Joseph, bought and paid for. Do you believe what I am telling you is from the Lord?"

The young man's eyes watered and he rubbed away tears. "Yes, Ma'am..."

"This contract will never be satisfied. I have not seen this before, but I have to tell you like the Lord showed me. I see your contract, it has been signed by the devil, and there are many names on it; names of demons and powers and princes that are assigned to carry it out. There are also human names on this contract that I cannot read, but I know that's what they are."

The boy winced as she revealed the hard truth. She lowered her voice and

49

let the rest of her words trickle privately into his ear. "This contract is not on paper and it has no expiration date. You will be forced to avoid this calamity your whole life, pursued mercilessly by your enemy. But you shouldn't fear…"

"But…" he began and Sarah continued, prompted by the Holy Spirit.

"Like King David who could never rest from the sword, this is your lot. But God will give you amazing blessing, too. Overflowing anointing and peace every time you seek Him and His will. You will know Him better than any man in your generation…" Sarah marveled at her own words, inside telling the Lord how amazing it all was.

"I don't understand," he whispered and Sarah had the impression that their entire exchange had been private, that God had closed the ears of those on all sides.

"You're asking God, am I worthy. Am I able," she told him and he nodded once. "The answer is yes to both. You feel like just a preacher's kid, just another guy, but God has raised you into a force to be reckoned with. You will be assaulted by the enemy again and again, but he will never overcome you. No matter how bleak things look, your duty is to praise the Lord. Continue in the faith with steadfastness. Persevere and always keep God's name on your lips. He will never leave you nor forsake you. When trials come, and they are coming, lean on God and His Word. Do not sin and keep yourself from impurity. Do you understand?"

"Yes…" the kid managed.

"Okay, receive this blessing. Tony, John, lay your hands on him, too." Sarah placed her hands on Joseph's head, while her two partners moved into place and did the same on his shoulders. "Joseph, stick by God and you will see amazing things. Believe, grow in faith and love. Right now in the name of Jesus Christ, we pass on the mantel of deliverance and prophecy to this man. Jesus, we pray You protect him and grow him in your grace, wisdom and power. In Your precious name we pray."

That said, Sarah sensed the Word of God lift and she exhaled with a hand to her brow. Tony checked her with his eyes, she assured him she was okay, and he and John took the young man aside to walk him to the lobby. All the congregants that had been on John's side of the stage migrated over and Sarah calmed her mind to continue. There were at least two hundred people left to go and she never stopped until they were done. The boy was in some sort of trouble, but God didn't tell her what it was. Sarah remembered to pray for him in every lull and knew that had to be enough.

10

For all that is in the world—the lust of the flesh,
the lust of the eyes, and the pride of life—is not of the Father
but is of the world.
1 John 2:16

TWO DAYS OF RIDING, SEVEN HOURS A DAY, THREE before lunch and four after, Hope skipped out on day three.

"I'm paying *them;* they're not paying me, and I want to have fun!" she said under her breath as the train slowed to a stop. She and another student slipped out after breakfast and took a leisurely tour of the area. By early afternoon, they decided to end the free day with a jaunt to the local circus.

"*Lassen Sie uns zum Karneval gehen*! Come! *Es ist Spaß*! Fun, Hoop, fun!"

"Carnivale, that's right," Hope said to Anna who led her away from the station.

Mark's house and the attached villages were peopled with Germans, many of them fair- and red-haired. Here, every eye she met was brown and each head, male and female, sported dark, wavy hair, as if they had stepped across the border to Hungary or Bulgaria. She mentioned it to her friend who, by her response, hadn't understood the observation.

Anna replied only, "*Karneval,* Hoop!"

Hope could only nod and allow her pal to pull her along, toward a collection of garish canvas structures. Hand in hand, they walked and then jogged to join the patrons filing in the main gate, a tattered and well-traveled nylon sign stretched above their heads written in German. Hope read the word Karneval and left it there. Anna exclaimed with excitement and jerked her in the other direction, away from the main tent.

"Magier! I want to see Magier!" she said, facing away, her black hair catching the light of the low sun. When they reached the end of the queue, Anna dropped her fingers and hugged herself. "*Magie.* Hocus-pookus." She waved her hands before her eyes as she tried to express herself. "An' he is boo-tee-full."

"Oh...*" Hope replied, with a nod. So her friend had been here before, thought the guy was magical and handsome.

With a half-smile, Hope examined the other circus-goers. The bustling fairground was full of sound, smells, and people, all of them dark or red-headed. Hope tugged at her hairband and pulled it out without thinking. Long bright blonde tresses fell over both shoulders within her peripheral view and more than a few people turned to look her way. No one had hair of a similar shade. Hope did not make eye contact, suddenly self-conscious and she balled her hair around one finger and tucked all of it in the generous scrunchie. The interested parties looked elsewhere and Hope exhaled. She did not want to be part of the show. This village was rustic and a little bohemian. It wouldn't be wise to become separated from her friend. With that thought, Hope reached out and hooked her arm with Anna's.

"*Androni der Prächtige! Magier!*" Anna pointed to the hand painted sign hanging on the tent flap, a poorly done rendering of a magician waving his hands over a crystal ball gracing both sides.

Hope smiled and was pulled up to a smallish and swarthy man collecting the entrance fee. Hope reached into the slash pocket of her riding breeches, but Anna touched her hand and paid for them both. In another moment, he entered the tent. Half the size of a tennis court, the floorspace inside was wall to wall wooden folding chairs and nary a one was empty. Men, women and children surrounded them, all noisy, all carrying their own distinct body odor. They were seemingly as excited as Anna, expecting great things. Hope allowed Anna to pull her to a seat and sat, training her eyes to the stage.

"*Dieses wird groß sein,*"[1] Anna yelped over the boisterous crowd and turned her attention wholly to the front, a sense of switching off to everything else.

Hope rolled her eyes and studied the raised platform. They sat on the third row able to view every inch of the twelve-by-twelve elevated structure. A tent flap hung partly open at the back of the stage and she imagined the magician would enter there. But first… the dark man with the black eyes who had taken their money strolled onto the stage from that curtain and faced the crowd. He had no need of a microphone as he bellowed an announcement in his language, but Hope recognized the word *magier* used more than once. When the man ceased speaking and motioned to the flap, the crowd went wild. And then fell still as a silhouette filled the

---

[1] "This is going to be good." (German)

opening and remained in place.

Hope held her breath, the sudden silence causing her ears to pop. She and a hundred others watched the shape of a man in the opening. When she was certain he would never fully enter, a handheld spotlight illuminated the opposite side of the stage at the very moment a man violently fluttered a red silk scarf through the air toward the tent flap.

"Geh weg, böser Geist!"[2] the man commanded. At his shout, the shape of the man shivered, howled like a banshee, and dissolved from view. The crowd erupted with cheers and Hope covered her mouth. In the weak yellow spotlight, the entertainer turned to the crowd and bowed, and Hope covered her ears now, adjusting to the noise.

Anna had spoken the truth; Androni the Magnificent was... well, magnificent. Hope watched his face, profiled and then three-quarters as his eyes roamed the crowd, familiar, friendly, making contact with individuals and as a whole. They loved him, praised him, and Hope didn't have to speak their languages to understand this. He spoke in long sentences, nonsensical to her English-only ears, but with a soft, round accent she hadn't heard since she'd been in country. He had stepped clear to the other side and was making his way back to where Hope and Anna sat, and now she saw his face full-on.

Oh, his voice... What is he saying?

No one offered any translation, so Hope listened, allowing the sounds to lull her to an easy grin. Then he was impossibly close, directly in front of her, looking at her seatmates, speaking to the matron two women down. Up close, Hope recognized stage rouge applied to his cheeks and lipstick on his lips, his eyelids had been shaded with deep lavender, and was he wearing mascara? The magier left the matron, skipped over Hope and spoke to Anna, leaning forward, his hands on narrow hips below a strong chest visible because of white smock tie strings that hung open. He was clean-shaven, his hair black with reddish highlights reflecting the spot, and it reached his shoulders, unbound and moving with his gesticulations. Hope sought his eye. He hadn't noticed her. He hadn't even *looked* at her. Why? How could he miss her? Not a soul in the room was as pale or blonde.

My hair!

In a nonchalant manner, Hope sneaked her fingers to her scrunchie and yanked it free, piling her hands in her lap concealing the band. The

---

[2] Basically, "Out! Foul spirit!" (German)

soft curls fell over her shoulders and the magier's gaze grabbed her own. Hope swallowed and didn't breathe.

"*Fraulein! Bitte!* Put that away, your weapon! Your weapon!" he belted in English and Hope froze. What did he mean? Was he serious? Was it a tease? Then he covered his eyes and pointed, turning his upper body away with drama. *"Ruf die liebe Polizei!* The love police are coming, Frau!"

The crowd craned their heads to see her and Hope roped her hair back into the scrunchie. That done, the magician moved away, his eyes back on his worshipers, and he began his act.

First, he performed sight gags with his hands, using floating silk scarves followed by an oversized deck of cards. After that, he moved to coin tricks, proving the dexterity of his long fingers more than anything else. Hope had seen it all before, but the old standbys seemed new, like a childhood story she had grown tired of, awaiting the right storyteller to make it live again. She took new notice of the crowd, each of them as entranced as she was. Maybe more. They loved him.

Maybe he's a real magician…

Hope's mind had gone down that trail when she heard the man say, "American." She snapped back; the magier had returned to the place on stage closest to her third-row seat, was leaning forward, hands at his hips, speaking directly to her.

"Pardon?" she whispered, locked in his gaze.

"*Ich sagte…*what do you think of my performance thus far?"

Hope's throat closed as her mind sought a reply. His English, like his German, was lovely, and it also flowed out of him like smooth water, caressing her ears.

Why am I acting like this? Hope blinked.

"What do you say?" The magician slinked off the stage with catlike ease and walked toward the third row, stopping four feet away, as she sat third from the outside.

"*Lassen Sie diese Frau durch Sie gehen.* Let her join me on the stage. *Frau?* Will you help me perform my next trick?"

Hope's eyes widened and she shook her head. The people on all sides urged her along. Anna all but pushed her to her feet.

"*Herr…* I don't speak German," she stammered, having risen. The magier held out his fingers and winked in her gaze.

"*Bitte,*" he cooed low, private, as if suddenly, only the two of them existed in the world. Hope's insides tingled and she thought of Mark. What would he think of this magician? This devilishly sexy Gypsy fixing his lurid gaze on his woman?

I'm not his woman. He can't have a woman. I've been an idiot.

Her thoughts cleared as she grasped the magician's fingers.

"A German tongue is not necessary to do magic. *Magie,* Fraulein, is in the eyes."

Hope thought about that as he led her to the stage. In her experience, the eye *was* powerful. From her adolescence, she had power over men with her eyes. As she allowed the man to spin her face to the audience, she realized that she was wearing her riding attire. Her riding breeches were of course, formfitting, as if sprayed on, and her snug Polo shirt left little to the imagination regarding her proportions. Hope maintained her grin, her eyes flitting to Anna who had the sense to wear jeans.

"Yes, my beauty, stand here. *Standplatzrecht hier,*" he translated. "And watch." Hope gave one nod and stood beside him, facing the audience. "Now, *passen Sie jetzt dieses auf.*"

The magician's hand went into the air, fingers open wide, and he snapped the fingers of his other hand with drama. Then the strangest thing happened; a man's bowler hat flew toward them and landed squarely in his outstretched fingers. The crowd clapped wildly after a universal moment of awe. The magician raised his hand for silence, and he reached his empty hand toward the crowd.

"*Wer trägt einen schwarzen Mantel?*" he said in German and turned his chin to Hope translating, "Who is wearing a black suit coat?"

Seven rows back, a young man stood and held a dark garment over his head. Before she could train her eyes to the magician, the coat was yanked from the youngster's hand and it, too, was sent flying toward the stage. Hope ducked to the side as it came at them, only to watch the item land squarely into the magician's free hand.

"You came to see a show?" he asked the crowd with a gracious bow. "Watch this. *Ich tanze!*"[3]

Hope grinned as the smooth showman shrugged on the coat and hat and tap-danced a circle about her. He began a song in German, the tune she recognized as *Singing in the Rain.* Hope bit her inner cheek, trying not to smile too big, amused and intrigued. The debonair character worked up to a spectacular finale of rhythm, lovely song, and he stopped directly before her—his face to her, his back to the crowd.

"Now, you," he whispered, holding her gaze as sure as steel bonds.

---

[3] "I will dance!" (German)

Hope remained still, not daring to look away from his hazel-green eyes, and he added his next instruction. *"Sie versuchen es,"*[4] he said too low for anyone else to hear. "Lift your hand high and open your fingers."

Hope did not move, still thinking about his voice. There was a good three seconds of silence before the man stepped away and faced the people, a triumphant grin on his face.

"Fraulien! Raise your hand." He was laughing now and did not look her way as he spoke. "You don't have a hat. Fancy American women should always wear a hat when on holiday. I will get you one."

Hope raised her hand, her eyes trained to the magier's profile. He, in turn, kept his eyes front playing to the audience more than ever.

"Open your fingers. *Konzentrieren*[5]… Do you like the yellow one? The one with the blue feathers? That one will go nicely with this interesting outfit you are wearing."

Hope blushed at his teasing tone. She steeled herself and watched the woman's yellow hat through the hazy light.

"Now you will say the magic words," the magier whispered, finally looking at her to elicit a response.

Hope's eyes widened and she said the first magic word she could think of. "Abracadabra?"

The magier looked to the crowd with a goofy wag of his head, and the people guffawed at the American visitor's expense. He quieted them finally with a raised hand and then said to her sideways, "No, say, *'I want that yellow hat!'*"

After an embarrassed laugh, Hope said with false conviction, "I want that yellow hat!"

Barely had the words left her mouth, but the item flew off the woman's head and crossed the air unaided to land squarely in her fingers. Hope yelped and sought the magier's eye.

"How? How did you do that?" she whispered, amazed.

The magician faced the cheering crowd, raised both arms high in the air and shouted good night in English and German. Then, with Hope holding a stranger's felt hat in her left hand and standing in front of the assembly with her jaw slack, the man stepped to the dark corner of the tent and was gone.

Anna ran up to her and walked her off the stage and to the exit,

---

[4] "You try." (German)
[5] "Concentrate." (German)

bustling on all sides with strangers, many of them remarking to her about her time with their hero. Hope walked numbly. Oh, she wanted to see him again. Anna had short-changed him with her description; he was more than beautiful. He was *magnificent,* and Hope would be back very soon. Until then, she lined up her fantasies.

11

Behold, you are handsome, my beloved! Yes, pleasant!
Song of Solomon 1:16

WITH SARAH AND TONY OFF TO PREACH, ELIZABETH arrived at their house knowing the doctor would be alone. How amazing he was, just so interesting, and so peaceful. Everything about him spoke calm, intelligence, and serenity. Is that what four centuries will do? Was he like that before he understood the error of his ways? Watching him toss bread to the geese, Elizabeth marveled at how her entire life had been upended over the course of twelve months. Her divorce had been a catalyst to send her packing to Alabama from California. And although the location had been surely chosen by God, being here had become the largest jolt to normalcy. Meeting Sarah Tracey and her vampire husband, being stalked by a demon who tried to kill her father, and tonight, arm in arm with a four-centuries' old man as gentle as any she had ever known.

He grinned, facing the birds. One nibbled his pants leg when he took too long to throw the next piece. Elizabeth wondered if he'd ever done such a thing as feed a flock of wild pond geese.

And could he be any more attractive?

There was no way. Elizabeth had studied him closely now that they'd visited several times, and she'd memorized his every line. Six-foot-four, slightly taller than her father and an inch taller than Aaron, with a creamy, mocha complexion that complimented his dark eyes and hair. Her eyes fell to his hands—her weakness, always had been. A man's hands could be a woman's best friend, and it had been Aaron's hands she noticed when she first saw him at the pulpit. But Mark's hands… they were large, strong, and the grace at which they manipulated the bread, picking it apart one-handed to flick to the angry birds, mesmerized her. She blinked when she realized she was causing her own arousal. After all, she had only just met the man.

The man?

The vampire.

He flicked his gaze her way and shot her a wink. At the same instant, an angry goose honked and stabbed his leg until he dropped bread on its beak. Mark swished his hands and headed to her position. The moon was full and the sky clear, so his face brought a myriad of sensations to her middle as he drew close.

He tilted his head to the side. "It's a good thing I cannot see your thoughts," he said with mischief and lifted one hand as if asking to touch her cheek. Elizabeth took the last step in so he could. Mark instead rest his open palm to the side of her neck and sighed. "You've grown attached to a mirage," he said without a hint of humor. "I affect this appearance, but that is as far as it goes."

Elizabeth's skin prickled at his bang-on guess of her thoughts, but she played it off. "You must be used to this, women and their longing looks. Is that what you see? Elizabeth Hawken drooling over your beauty?" She had been serious, but she wasn't cross. Mark laughed two huffs and gave her a new smile that she treasured.

"Men and woman have looked at me with lust since I came to be this way," he said low, his eyes in hers. "But in all my years, no one has ever looked at me the way you do."

Elizabeth wondered what he meant. "Like how?"

"Your gaze is selfless, wanting only for my future, my good, my happiness."

He paused and Elizabeth rushed with emotion at his words. He was right; she hadn't put a finger on it, but he was exactly right. She had tried to look at Aaron that way, but he refused to allow it, constantly keeping her at arm's length, maintaining psychological distance. But Mark? He was right in her space and in her eye, exchanging energy like the oldest of friends.

"I see also that you want to know me as a husband." Mark smiled, small and to the side. "This is normal; you're a beautiful young woman with your entire life ahead of you. You will, one day, marry the right man, a *good* man, have children, and be the happiest woman in the world. And vampires will fall into your past where they belong."

Elizabeth shook her head, her eyes watery. "Don't do that." She lifted her hand to his still at her neck and wrapped her fingers around his. "I don't know where all that came from, but don't say that stuff to me ever again." She swallowed, forcing down sobs with determination.

Mark brought his second hand up to cup her neck on both sides, facing her and looking down with unabashed affection. "I have lived so long that I cannot play games, pretend things aren't as they are," he said, his tone gentle. "I must tell the truth, and although you and I are compatible, the plain truth remains: I am not a man, haven't been since 1640."

Elizabeth absorbed the compliment—but... Tony said they would be delivered soon, that God had them this way for His purposes and when He was ready, He'd let them go back to normal.

Mark shook his head as if he knew she'd gone down that path.

"Elizabeth, my beautiful new friend," he said even softer than before. "None of us believe this body will survive deliverance. Do you understand?" He watched her eyes and she refused to speak, the answer too horrible to even give a thought. He said it anyway. "This flesh will turn to dust when God rids me of the curse."

"You don't know that!" she screeched loud enough to startle the geese roosting nearby. They scattered to the water and splashed a distance away. The quiet of the pond gradually returned to the sound of crickets and owls and Elizabeth lowered her voice. "You don't know that! You're guessing!"

She read in his eyes that he could say nothing else on the subject— that was it, the sum of the information: when God delivers them of vampirism, Mark will die. But it just couldn't be. Elizabeth turned her heart to God, still looking into Mark's face.

"Let me keep him, Father. Just look at how wonderful he is. Please, please, please let me have this man. I will take care of him, I promise. I will be the best wife in the world. He can stay—you made his flesh. If You will it, he can stay..."

Elizabeth begged the Lord a few different ways until she gave up and pushed into Mark's space grabbing him around the chest. She'd seen him every day since learning their secret, and so far, they hadn't had much physical contact. After a moment of surprise, he relaxed his rigid posture and the weight of his arms landed on her upper back, his hands, strong but gentle against her shirt, still and comforting. Her next thought did not come from God and she knew it as it past her lips, saying in a whisper, "You can find a new host like Rakha. You can live again..."

"Shhh," Mark said over her head and one hand lifted to stroke her hair. "His process served his master, the devil. To exchange my flesh for another takes submission to the Dark..."

"I know, I'm sorry, I know," Elizabeth said, her voice shaking as she worked to control her emotions. "Just give me a minute to... to... accept that. It's so cruel. So mean... God made you, He could save you, too. I don't understand why He won't..."

Mark stroked her hair again and his nose rested on the crown of her head. He inhaled and then she felt the pressure of his lips kissing her scalp.

"I'm afraid my past prevents me from answering with any authority on why. Ask the reverend. She will have words of wisdom."

"She will, you're right." Elizabeth remained as she was, her cheek to his firm chest. Maybe he would turn to dust when delivered, maybe he wouldn't. How was that different from everyone else in knowing when one would die? Elizabeth pondered that another long moment and decided to say so to Mark.

"You asked me last week if I wanted to know you better."

"Yes," he said low, speaking into her hair.

"And you knew then that you might die when God finishes what He's doing."

Mark nodded and she felt the movement.

"So, my answer is still yes. No one knows how long they'll be on this earth. I want us to get to know each other until we can't anymore." She pulled away to see his face.

He tilted his chin to the side, his brow raised. "I would enjoy knowing you better."

"And you can forget about me thinking of you as a potential husband, okay?" she said and allowed a smile, small but real. "Sarah told me about it. That you can't... you know... make love." He did not react to the embarrassing comment so in the hopes of lightening the moment, she licked her lips with a comical smack. "Before that night in 1640, had you had sex?"

Mark's grin tucked into his cheek with a nod.

"Do you remember it?"

He nodded again.

Elizabeth worked on her next topic, the heavy mood lifting by the second. "We can do this. We know the parameters. Let's relax and continue growing our friendship. If you want to kiss my mouth one day, you know how." She waggled her eyebrows. "Your lips work, I felt you kiss my head."

"They do," Mark replied.

"And as for the other thing." She bared her teeth with a giggle. "I'll try not to look so delicious."

She surprised him, he laughed, first one burst and then several. When he quieted, Elizabeth zoomed back into his space.

"Mark," she said looking into his eyes, "this will work. Let yourself go as much as is safe, and I'll do the same. That way, if God takes you away at the end, we will have had a wonderful time together nonetheless." Mark's eyes shone with a light she hadn't seen before now and he gave her a nod.

"Listen well, my beauty," he said and she loved his word choice with her whole heart. "I am very old and very wise so trust me when I say, there is no way you can dampen your deliciousness." He paused maybe to see her reaction and she nodded for more, unoffended. "When we're together, my spirit is calm. Your blood calls to mine, and although a devil brought this to being, I am blessed that The Other's powerful draw is in an angel like you."

Elizabeth grinned, her heart too big for her chest as it swelled with a new adoration. Love? That's what it was. *Selfless, like he said. I see his potential and only want him to succeed. That's love.*

Mark's face softened and he leaned in, the vampire coming close, heading for her mouth. And although he seemed to think it an impossible thing—for a vampire to kiss like a man—he was wrong. Elizabeth fell into his embrace and found the man from 1640 remembered everything good about kissing the one he loved.

"Elizabeth's here," Sarah said, shooting Tony a huge grin as he pulled the truck to his parking space. The young lady's car sat in her usual spot and when he and Sarah exited the car, he listened for them.

"They're in the back, near the pond," he told her and looked away. From where he stood, they might be in an embrace and he grinned without meaning to. Sarah looked over but saw nothing in the low light.

Big John had ridden with them and he piled out to head to his own car, saying with disgust, "God bless that Reverend Ellerslie! I have never seen such behavior in a man of God!"

"Maybe he's…" Sarah began, and stopped her excuses. He had pushed them out at three o'clock even though there were still people coming up for prayer.

Tony clapped his giant partner on the back as he passed. "Have a safe trip home and give Opal a kiss for me."

In another minute, the big man was driving away and Tony watched Sarah gather her belongings from the back seat.

She gave him a wry grin. "Ellerslie is lucky I'm not the one with the super-powers. I probably would have zapped him unconscious for behaving like that."

Tony laughed once and got them going. "I wonder if I have zapping power."

"You do." She smiled with him and they were quiet a few long minutes, both thinking about the boy with the colossal prophecy.

What Tony had not yet revealed was that he had hypnotically manipulated the church pastor more than once, blocking him from ending the service before he finally did. Twice, Ellerslie approached the microphone, filled his lungs to speak, and Tony tossed him a stern glare warning him to be still. Tony performed his trick a third time and Ellerslie averted his gaze, made his announcement that service had ended, and run off the opposite direction.

Sarah poked his arm. "Did you hypnotize him? John said you were giving him a really mean eye."

Tony offered an innocent shrug. "He needed some help keeping quiet, that's all. You probably saw all sorts of demons on him. He hated us very much." Tony expected Sarah to agree but she hemmed.

"No, he didn't have an oppression. He's just prideful. It's inside, not outside," she remarked looking at the house.

"Somehow, that's worse." Tony wondered about the boy. "You said you saw death on his son, Joseph."

Sarah inhaled and turned with concerned eyes. "I've never seen anything like it before. I saw a spirit stitched to his with golden thread. It looks like cross-stitch..." She wove her fingers together. "It's a generational curse, but God didn't show me its origin."

"Incredible," Tony said with meaning.

Sarah agreed with a thoughtful nod. "I see you mentoring him. Listen out for the timing, but I see you helping him with this."

Tony pondered the boy's prophecy over his life. The devil wants to kill him, has been trying to kill him since he was born, and he will never lay down the sword. *Sounds familiar, Father. Please help him and help me. All of us miserable people love You...*

"You and I are going to pray for this young man every day, okay? He's about to enter a very difficult trial."

"Been there, done that," Tony replied and Sarah leaned close to kiss his shoulder. Life was unpredictable, but Tony had an angel named Sarah and he was thankful.

12

The Lord said, "You must not eat the blood of any creature,
Because the life of every creature is in its blood..."
Leviticus 17:14

JOSEPH STOOD AT DETACHED ATTENTION AS HIS MOTHER delivered last-minute suggestions before he went up for auction. It had been a week since his life-altering experience, first vomiting at the meeting with the bookstore owner and then receiving an amazing prophecy over his life with Reverend Tracey. The seven days in between, he studied his schoolwork, took out the garbage, "hearted" Mustangs on Cars.com and worked hard to forget either of those things happened. He did not want to see Troye again and he feared the woman's word from God might actually be true.

I mean... she knew those things about my accidents!

He had always wondered why he was so accident prone, his childhood a collection of near-misses that scared his mother to death. He ate rat poison as a toddler thinking it was candy. He tried to shave his face with his dad's razor at age four and received twenty-five stitches in his chin. A vicious dog attacked him when he was eight and he received twelve stitches in his arm. And on, and on.

So, the devil has tried to kill me many times? Why has he not succeeded?

The sound of laughing slipped past the third-grade Sunday school classroom door where the teens prepared. His dad was warming up the crowd with preacher jokes. The Fellowship Hall was packed with members and visitors, all willing to pitch in a few bucks for a good cause.

"Joseph, stand up straight and remember to smile. Your brother went for seventy-five dollars last year!" Mrs. Ellerslie straightened Joey's tie and backed off, wishing him luck. Luke had bowed out this time and watched on with a grin. Joey gave him a lazy eye, which little brothers understand—the mom was talking too much. Then his brother opened the door to the hall, allowing the crowd noise in the sanctuary to filter in at volume.

"Good luck!" she said to Joey and pushed him toward his brother.

"Mom, really, look at his suit? Somebody's gonna buy him and never bring him back!" Luke said as Joey reached his side.

"You'd like that," Joey said and entered the hall.

"Hey—if you get kidnapped and taken off to Constantinople, can I have your PlayStation?"

Luke's silly question faded as Joey left them for the meeting hall. The parents and younger students welcomed him to the backstage area and he stood in line with two kids about his age that he didn't know by name.

"Joseph Ellerslie. You're up next!"

Joey twitched at the sound of his name being called and just as quickly relaxed. This was good. He'd heard Henry Logg needed help landscaping his property and was going to bid big. Joey had sent word to the man's wife that he wanted the gig so maybe... *If I can get immersed in some physical labor, I can forget this crap weighing me down.*

One of the parents in the wings touched his arm to get him moving and Joey walked through the opening in the curtain. With humorous swagger, Joey waltzed to the end of the makeshift gangway, modeling his suit by flowing both hands up and down and putting on a face for the youngest kids against the stage. They laughed and pointed, encouraging him to be even goofier than before.

Abby and Scott hooted in unison and waved happily from the second row. Following their lead, the entire youth group whistled and whooped until Pastor Ellerslie held his palms up to a few who caught his eye.

The first bid went out from Mrs. Waites for fifty dollars. Joey scanned the crowd for Mr. Logg, much preferring a job he knew than one he didn't. Mrs. Waites had Luke drive her to Hunstville and back last year. Boring!

"We'll bid one hundred dollars!" Abby shouted and Joey shot his gaze over. He gave her a miniscule *no* gesture, but she only grinned wider. The three of them discussed a month ago that the youth group would buy Joey and take him out for pizza. But this past week, he assured them he wanted to work. What was she doing?

"We have one hundred, do I hear one twenty-five?" Rich Ledbetter of the City Planners Office played auctioneer and his Southern drawl worked right in.

"One hundred fifty!" Mrs. Waites raised her frail arm. "Ya'll stop bidding against an old woman!"

"Two hundred dollars!" Abby lifted her hand again and caught the auctioneer's eye to be sure he heard her over the din. He did but before he could announce the going bid, Mrs. Waites had another offer.

65

"Three hundred and twenty-two dollars and forty-three cents!" she wailed. "That is all this old lady makes in a month, you people. Come on and help ol' granny out!"

"You heard her folks, anyone going to top that bid? Three Hundred twenty-two dollars and forty-three cents, going once? Going twice?"

Joey maintained his modeling pose, strode the length of the stage again, not finding Mr. Logg anywhere. *I'm about to drive an old lady to Huntsville. Great.*

"Five Thousand Dollars. Cash."

A soft female voice from the back was heard over the laughter of the crowd. Joey searched the faces wondering who would have that kind of money and could they possibly be serious.

"Did I hear five thousand dollars? How about that folks? For the kids' hospital! Joseph Ellerslie, Pastor Robert's boy, five thousand dollars. Going once? Going twice?"

Joey could not see the woman who bid but he continued to peer past the bright lights where many in the crowd craned their heads seeking the woman, too.

"Sold! To the young lady in the rear. Joseph, go meet your winning bidder at the settling table." The auctioneer shooed Joey off the stage and called his next soldier to the battle.

Joey walked to the small music-slash-changing room behind the stage to shrug out of his expensive suit.

"Gee whiz! Who'd spend five thousand dollars on a loser like you?" Luke had found his way into the room and was busy hanging up Joey's coat as he removed it. "I hope they understand that you are only manual labor, not a prize for a king." Still laughing Luke handed over his previously stashed jeans and T-shirt.

"Did you see who it was? I wonder if it is somebody from Hitching Hill Baptist. Last year they paid seven hundred and fifty dollars for Tommy Stephens." Redressed, Joey left his suit hanging on the door and followed Luke out of the room and down the hall.

"I didn't see, sorry. I gotta help mom with the refreshments. Text me when you figure it out." Luke sped off in the opposite direction and Joey paused in the quiet hallway.

Please let this be an outdoors job, he prayed and took a calming breath. Then, Joey resumed his trek to the settling table at the south entrance main lobby. The man at the card table looked up with a toothy grin, a friendly older man he recognized from choir.

"Joseph," Bill Johansen bellowed from his folding chair, "you're the star tonight, aren't you! Here is your winning bidder."

An attractive young Black woman stepped forward and, avoiding Joey's eye, she said demurely to Bill, "I am acting as an agent for the winner. He couldn't be here." She then looked up to Joey and smiled. "There is a car outside waiting to take you to your destination."

"Whooo! Very mysterious! I can't wait to hear about it all at church tomorrow!" Bill stood and walked to the door with his characteristic limp. "It's a stretch limousine. Look at that!"

Joey smiled, unsure of how to feel. He said goodbye to Mr. Johansen and exited the building. The young woman did not escort him, which seemed odd. At the curb, alongside a gleaming Lincoln, a sturdy uniformed man appeared and opened the rear door.

"Hello, Mr. Ellerslie. I am William, your driver."

"Hi, thanks, where are we going?" Joey asked thinking it seemed foolhardy to trust blindly simply because someone paid five grand to have him mow grass. The driver looked at his cell phone and then met Joey's eye. "565 Stephanie Lane."

From the direction of the building, Abby called his name. Joey asked the driver to excuse him and he met her halfway as she jogged to the curb.

"Geez-louise, Joey! A limo? Who bought you?" Her eyes flicked between his and the car and back, her smile ear to ear. "Can I come, too?"

"Sure," he said and meant it, but she laughed and waved at the driver who gave her a professional nod.

"Send me a text when you see who it is. I'll tell you what Scotty heard," she said with a conspiratorial tone. "He said a girl from the college asked her sorority to put their money together to buy a cute guy. So you know anyone at A-O-Pi?"

Joey thought about the girls at school and shook his head.

"Well, go on," she said and shoved his chest. "Text me. Scotty and I will tell the others. Go have fun!"

With a last wave to the faces gathering in the windows of the church lobby, Joey fell into the long car and the driver closed the door. Once underway, his focus softened at the various buttons and comforts the limo provided and he pondered who bought him. He still wasn't anxious, but shouldn't he be? None of this was normal. And could a sorority afford five thousand dollars?

"We will arrive in fifteen minutes. Can I get you anything along the way?" William asked through the speaker, on the other side of a plexiglass privacy wall.

Joey said no and looked at his cell. After a moment's consideration, he texted the address to Abby's phone. She returned a thumb's up and told him to have fun. Then, he thought about his parents. Joey pressed his dad's icon but after a single chime, it reported the voice mailbox was full. Joey narrowed his eyes and sighed.

It's okay. I'm okay.. They sent a limo. I guess it's normal. I mean, it was church…

When the car slowed entering a neighborhood filled with spacious executive homes, he retrieved his cell and called Scotty.

"Joey! Who was that woman? Is she a wealthy widow lonely for albino nerd-o's?"

"Hah-hah." Joey said with an edge. "Listen, I wanted to tell you where I am, you know, just in case."

"In case what? What could happen?" Scotty laughed his questions. Joey faked a chuckle and delivered the street address. "Okay, I got it. Try to relax and remember to have fun." Joey disconnected the call as William opened his door.

"Thanks," he said, his voice sounding strange to his ears. He strengthened to say, "Have a good night. God bless you."

"You're entirely welcome," William replied, escorting him to the large double doored entry. He swung the brass knocker that hung larger than a man's head. "I've been to your church. Your dad is a powerful preacher."

"That he is, thanks again."

As he spoke, the towering left door swung open without a sound and no one stood in view.

William pushed it open wider and pointed to the sitting room just inside. "You're supposed to wait in one of those chairs and your host will be here shortly."

"Okay. That's weird," Joey said and entered. "But I guess it's all for charity, right?" The driver smiled.

"Have a good evening." Then he tipped his cap and left.

Joey looked around the lavish foyer and called out a greeting, his own voice echoing back. Every lamp within view was on, tossing a yellowy filter over everything. The decor was decidedly feminine, and Joey imagined his hostess was an elderly widow. What could she need? There were no obvious answers from where he stood so Joey chose a chair. He pulled out his phone. After shooting a selfie of himself to Abby, his head against the flowery wallpaper, he opened the Solitaire challenge while listening for his hostess. Whatever happened happened, and Joey worked on his patience.

13

Withhold your foot from being unshod, and your throat from thirst.
But you said, 'There is no hope. No! For I have loved aliens,
and after them I will go.'
Jeremiah 2:25

"MY DEAR JOSEPH, HOW WONDERFUL OF YOU TO COME!"

At the sound of Haman Troye's voice, Joey snapped out of his doze and scrambled to his feet. The man he most never wanted to see again stood square, hands on his hips, between Joey and the door.

It's him! It's Troye! Jesus, help me!

Finding his voice, Joey sputtered, "Mr. Troye? You're the bidder? Why would you pay five thousand dollars for me?" Joey rallied his strength and watched for his response. Maybe the man wasn't the devil. Maybe Joey *had* been overreacting that first time they'd met.

"I would pay every dollar in my coffers if required," the man cooed entering fully and stepping too close. Joey sat down to avoid their bodies colliding. Haman pulled the opposite chair and sat down before him. "I am anxious to begin."

Joey's eyes searched the room for a weapon or escape; he hadn't been threatened, but his instincts had grown knives. He called out in his heart for God to help and pressed his lips together.

"Aren't you brave! You aren't going to scream?" Haman leaned his elbows on his knees. "You look most angelic. Has anyone ever told you this?" The man reached out his hand and Joey shrunk back, his head slapping the drywall. "Your hair, your eyes…" His fingers made contact with Joey's cheek and Joey pressed his feet to the floor to stand. In a flash, his host was up and pressing him back to the seat.

"What do you want?" Joey stuttered, barely holding on to his peace.

"All I want is you, my son. I am your new master. The fates have given you to me as a gift." Haman took Joey by the wrist and he yanked backward. The man held him fast and grabbed his gaze, leaning in, both of them sitting in the rosy parlor.

"Joseph," he hissed and brought Joey's wrist to his lips. Speaking against his skin, Haman asked, "I know you believe in gods. Do you believe in vampires?"

Joey jerked his captive hand but nothing changed. His devilish host remained close, his mouth to Joey's wrist.

"Please, I don't understand. What do you want?"

Haman increased his grip on Joey's arm every time he pulled back. One more yank and it might fracture. He did not pull again, tears sprouting from the stress.

"I want you to know who I am." The man stood, tugging Joey also to his feet. He maneuvered the two of them to the next room's threshold and pressed him to the lintel, his palms to Joey's chest.

Seeing no escape, he closed his eyes and called to God for help. *The Lord is my Shepherd, I shall not want...*

Haman moved cruel hands upward to either side of Joey's throat. "Look at me," he hissed, speaking in Joey's face so close his fetid breath fell on his cheek. "There is a protocol! Look at me!"

Joey did not interrupt his prayer. Eyes closed, he did his best to ignore his attacker and allowed the Scriptures to go audible. "For God so loved the world that He gave..."

"JOSEPH! Open your eyes or I will kill all of them! The girl! The redhead! Your brother! Your parents! I will slaughter them all if you do not look into my eyes right now!"

Fresh tears welled but Joey did not cry. He met Haman's eye and narrowed his gaze. "You're a liar," he whispered and again closed his eyes. If the guy was going to kill him, Joey wasn't going to help.

"You underestimate me," Haman whispered, his voice bringing chillbumps to Joey's arms. "I know where you live. I've been there. I watched you sleep. I have tasted your blood as you dreamed..."

Joey's eyes flew open and he looked into Haman's reddened gaze. He had awakened with a puncture wound a few days ago. It had been so slight that he hadn't given it any thought.

Has this monster been in my house?

"Your brother sleeps under a green and gold comforter and your mother sleeps with her hair in foam rollers..."

"No," Joey gasped having lost the calm drenching of the Holy Spirit. Haman held him securely by the throat and Joey braced both palms to the man's hard chest. "Mr. Troye! Please! I don't understand. What do you want?"

70

"There it is! I have seen this in a vision. Beg! You must beg for your life to save your family!"

Joey gagged at the stranger's breath.

Visions? Visions?

Joey's mind ran to something Reverend Sarah said on the bema the night she gave his prophecy; she said demons run the earth to and fro looking for people to deceive. They whisper in the ears of eager listeners and do all they can to make humans sin against the word of God. Were these demons speaking to Haman? Specifically about Joey Ellerslie? It seemed so unlikely; why? *Why?*

"Beg or I will kill them all!" Haman barked with fury in his tone.

Joey flinched; he didn't mind begging if it kept his people safe. "Please, please, I beg you. Please don't hurt them."

"Beg for your life!" he said, still nearly yelling inches away.

"Please don't hurt me," Joey whispered, his voice choking with emotion.

"Yesss," Haman cooed, and he dropped one hand to rip Joey's T-shirt as if made of tissue. The violence of the cloth against his skin rubbed painfully and Joey cried out with surprise. Haman flung the ruined garment to the floor and paused, staring into Joey's face.

"Please let me go," Joey whispered losing his courage.

The man grinned and yanked him to his body, his horrid wet mouth opening against Joey's throat. Joey pushed against him and lifted a knee, but nothing reduced the strength with which he was held.

Then, his flesh ripped, knives stabbing and searing pain at the bite. Joey stared at the room his eyes wide with shock. The man was biting him. Then he was sucking, pulling blood with such violence that their bodies pulsed in a monstrous dance standing in a one-way embrace in the center of the room. The fire raged at the wound and then ebbed. Joey's vision faded, the room disappeared, and the last thing he recalled was the sound of his body own hitting the hardwood floor. Joey was gone.

Then...

The sun was too bright.

Joey covered his face. After another few moments of wishing he didn't have to get up for class, he opened his eyes.

He was not in his room.

Joey looked left and right and considered his palms against cool wood planks. He was lying on someone's floor. In a rush, Joey sat up and regretted it. His vision blurred and his head pounded just behind his eyes.

"Ughhh!" he moaned and sat over crossed legs. When he creaked open one eye, he noted his T-shirt ripped and discarded five feet away and one palm went to his bare chest.

Oh, God! That was real? Please tell me it was just a dream!

Carefully getting to his feet, Joey's eyes darted about the room, praying he would not see Haman Troye standing by, wearing his evil grin. Joey took a step out of the sitting room and saw no one about. Sunlight streamed in from every window and the lamps from the night before were still alight.

Please, Lord. Please, let me be alone in this house!

From years of practice, Joey closed his eyes to concentrate on God. He quieted his mind and imagined the Lord standing next to him. In the past, this gave him a sense of calm and peace. Today, he had a new experience altogether.

This morning, he could *feel* he was alone.

The more still he became, the more minuscule sounds he picked up throughout the house. Some of the sounds were obviously from kitchen appliances, but when he heard the sound of the clock at the top of the stairs click the second, he gasped.

"What's going on?" Joey's voice sounded unbearably loud and he made a dash to the door.

Maybe I bumped my head and my ears are whacked out. How am I going to get home? Do I walk? Call a cab? He again touched his bare skin and he looked around for his leather bomber. He found it draped to a chair and he jumped for it and pulled it on.

Now what? I'm going home!

Joey reached for the golden door handle. Attached to it was a handwritten note. He yanked the paper free and held it to wide eyes.

"Lucky boy! I did wonderful things to your body—"

Joey looked at his jeans and they were in order, belt snugged tight just as he left it. He returned to the note, his terror escalating.

"You have been transformed. Don't you feel wonderful? Come to the store tonight. We will continue our love affair…"

Joey swallowed, realizing now that the maniac was wording his note for outsiders. *As if I'd ever show anyone! No freaking way!* he shouted inside and continued reading.

"I will answer your questions and help you with this new hunger. Tell anyone and

72

they'll think you are crazy. Do nothing, and you'll go crazy. See you tonight. -HT"

Joey ripped the note into tiny pieces. It *was* crazy. The whole idea was preposterous.

I'm not transformed!

Yet, here he was, hearing impossible sounds and crawling with a super-awareness.

What about my neck? If he is a vampire…

Joey's hand went to his throat and found no wound. At first, he thought that meant he was in the clear, but the calm was fleeting. In every Hollywood movie, vampires have incredible regenerative powers. Still…

This can't be! God wouldn't allow this! Father, are You there?

Joey waited for anything from above. Nothing. He looked at the closed front door.

Who could I call that wouldn't ask questions?

He considered his options. His Uber app would send a car. A stranger is what he needed.

Joey shoved the bits of Haman's note into his jacket pocket to dispose of later thinking a CSI type could paste it together and read the impossible truth. Not wanting to leave anything behind, he crumpled his tattered shirt and stuffed it into his other coat pocket. Then, nose to the wood, he closed his eyes, readying to open the door.

The sun doesn't hurt my skin; it's just bright. Maybe I'm just confused. Mr. Troye is insane. I've been, what? Assaulted?

Joey shook his head, assured that if he had been molested in any other way, he would know it.

What can I do? I can't face Mom or Dad or even Abby. I need time to think.

Luke and his parents would be at the church for the time being, so with his thumb, he ordered an Uber. Then he pocketed his cell and stepped out of the stranger's house. The manicured lawn glistened in the morning dew without a soul in sight. He'd go home and hide in his room. Since separating him and Luke to their own sacred teenager spaces, his parents stopped visiting his bedroom, *period*. It had been a welcome sanctuary and he was extra thankful of this now. Joey pulled the door behind him and walked toward the road. Maybe by the time he reached his house, he would have a plan on how to set things right. Maybe by then, God would assure him that he was not what that monster Haman Troye said he was.

Joey rubbed his face, unable to predict which way it would go. But he knew the one thing he could do to make the situation better no matter what. He prayed hoping it would be enough.

73

14

For the Lord God will help me
Therefore I will not be disgraced;
Therefore I have set my face like a flint,
And I know that I will not be ashamed.
Isaiah 50:7

SELF-ISOLATING IN HIS LOCKED BEDROOM, JOEY TWISTED the rod on the miniblinds, sending the room into a haze. Not satisfied with the result, he yanked the heavy curtains and a thick darkness engulfed the space. Joey huffed; he still saw everything as clear as day.

That strange light is going to drive me crazy! he thought as he looked about the room. Every surface gave off a halo of light. Some surfaces sent off greenish-blue hues, others gave off bright red ones, and his own arm and hand glowed bright white. Joey closed his eyes and the images were remained his retinas before mercifully fading away. He crawled onto his bed and sat cross-legged on top of the covers.

What now? What does this mean? What is God doing?

Impossible rhetorical questions continued to pop into his mind as he sat still, holding his eyes shut. He prayed a few moments, hoping he might hear from God, but nothing happened. Finally, Joey sighed and opened his eyes.

I'll just have to deal with it. My eyes are crazy sharp, this is nuts...

As in the stranger's house earlier, his ears picked up the smallest sounds. He heard kitchen appliances, the hum of his mother's computer in her upstairs office, even a faint drip of water in the basement sink. He heard it all. And it made him fearful.

But God did not give me a spirit of fear, Joey reminded himself, hoping to be encouraged. But he still trembled. Until he heard from the Lord, he considered himself alone, in a most desperate situation. With a deep exhale, he lay back onto the thick comforter, and stared at the ceiling fan. Every particle of dust on the quiet wooden blades stood in his strange super-vision. He fancied that if he wanted to, he could count them.

What am I gonna do? What am I gonna do? What in the world am I gonna do?
Joey asked himself impossible questions over and over until he fell
into a fitful doze. In his dreams, he was drinking the blood of the vampire.
He was drinking from Haman Troye.

"Joseph Ellerslie. Wake up. I'm waiting. Come home to Papa."
Joey inhaled and sat up. There was not even a millisecond that he did
not know what he had become, having returned to consciousness fully
aware of his horrible situation. What he was not sure of was whose voice
he had just heard. Had it been part of the dream or were his parents calling
him from the hall?

"Is that you, Dad?" Joey called out and listened to the house. The
digital clock near his bed showed a little past one. His parents would be
just locking up the church, probably arguing about how the ushers handled
their jobs. Joey strained his concentration waiting for the voice to return.
He didn't have to wait long.

*"Come on, Joseph! I'm waiting for you. Aren't you the least bit curious about your
new condition? I have answers. Come on."*

Joey shuddered and bile rose in his stomach. Somehow, Haman was
calling to his mind.

*"Pish! I took you for a much stouter gent. Where's your bravado? I thought you
Christian types were fearless…"*

"Shut up!" Joey hissed in his dark room. "Get out of my head!"

*"Such attitude. I'll have to give you a lesson in respect. When should I expect you?
Or should I come to you…"*

"No! You stay away from me and stay away from my family! If you
don't, I'll…" Joey got to his feet in the gloom and pointed his finger at the
air. "I'll kill you!"

*"Grow up. You're not a child. Stop pretending last night never happened. You
have solid evidence of your splendid change. I should think you'd be happy. You spent
your entire life serving a god you can't see. Now, you are god. Feels good, doesn't it?"*

A hot tear fell from Joey's eye and he wiped it away. His fear had
morphed into anger. Joey lowered his head to pray. When he sensed that
Haman was about to interrupt, he raised his voice to a scream, raising his
hands to the ceiling. "Get out of my head right now in the name of Jesus
Christ!"

One short burst of emotion and quiet filled the room. Joey listened,
but no reply came from the vampire across town. Apparently, he still had

his authority in Christ. Joey thanked God and slumped back to the covers.

I can command demons, but I've become one myself?

It didn't make sense.

Satan can't cast out Satan…

Joey shook his head.

So if I'm not a demon, what am I? Is there a middle ground? Is there a chance I'll wake up normal tomorrow? Can I pray myself back to the regular old Joseph Ellerslie?

As he pondered the imponderable, Joey stared at the ceiling and did not sleep.

15

… He has given us His very great and precious promises,
So that through them you may participate in the divine nature
And escape the corruption of the world
Caused by evil desires.
2 Peter 1:4

TONY PULLED INTO THE CRUMBLING PARKING LOT OF THE bookstore, surprised the new owner had not yet repaved it. The buckling concrete was a hazard and if he and Paul had stayed with it, they would have fixed it first. He jumped down from the truck to let Sarah out on her side. "Watch your step. There are booby traps everywhere."

Sarah stepped down from the truck and made her way to the curb. "I see what you mean." She turned to look at the building and grinned. "Looks like they repainted."

Tony followed her line of sight. The new owners had globbed black and gold paint on the marquee-style sign and it now read in hand-painted scrawl, The Ancient Book Man. Tony gave Sarah a smirk and led her to the entrance.

Once inside, neither saw anyone at the counter or in the store aisles, so they fanned out and began to pray softly as they walked, asking the Spirit to bless all who entered there. Tony followed the rows of books on his right and headed to the back, curious that the new owner had halved the store, walling and closing off the rear fifty-percent. Was he living there? Was that storage? Tony's gaze landed on piles of books, some organized, some not. Part of his mind disdained the new owner's business acumen, but the other part tried to pray a blessing.

Without paying hard attention, he overheard Sarah saying hello. A young woman's voice answered and they made small talk, Tony only listening because his ears wouldn't allow him not to. Then the youngster said the name Haman Troye and Tony's gasped. Rakha had mentioned that name months ago when Tony sat under his wing in that desolate cottage. *Rakha claimed he was a vampire.*

"Mr. Troye, someone here to see you!" the young lady's sweet voice called.

Tony's blood ran cold and he sent Sarah, *"Be careful! I'm coming!"* He bolted for Sarah's position, reaching her with supernatural speed. A door in the new wall opened and a man filled the space. Without pause, he swiveled his face to Tony's.

"Well, lookie here…" the stranger said.

Tony's instinct had been correct. His mind raced; he'd been here before—a dangerous vampire loose around innocents. He considered Sarah who because of Paul's blood would heal from any injury. And then the girl, a Hawaiian beauty of not yet twenty in danger mere feet away.

Following his instincts and trusting it was God leading them, Tony said, "Haman! How wonderful to meet you!" and at the same time, pushed into him, closing them both up alone in his quarters. *"Get the girl out. Empty the store. Haman is a vampire!"* he sent to Sarah's mind and blocked the man from leaving.

Tony considered the stranger. Troye faced him, one eye twitching, a sideways grin on his face. So far, it remained unclear if Haman knew Tony was also a vampire. Troye inhaled to speak and Tony held up his palm.

"Wait," he said in a soft command. Outside the tiny apartment, the sounds of people exiting filled their ears.

Sarah said through the jamb of the closed door, "Everyone's gone."

"Lock the front door, walk to the stockroom, exit into the alley and wait in the truck," he told her, remembering the layout of the store. When she resisted, he sent to her mind, *"Please, honey, for me. Please."* With his eyes in Haman's, his wife did as he asked, and he did not allow the man to speak until she also exited the establishment.

"You certainly are careful," he said and relaxed the rigid posture he had adopted in his surprise.

"I am Tony Agricola," he said and did not offer his hand. "Looks like we have a few things to talk about."

"Yes, it looks like we do," Haman replied, his voice controlled and casual. He gestured to a pair of recycled upholstered chairs flanking a dented three-legged coffee table. "Have a seat."

Tony sat after pulling the offered chair several feet back to increase the distance between them.

"You're the preacher my people bought the store from," he said and Tony nodded once, watching his eyes. Haman continued as if he weren't being studied. "I thought you were in Europe. Do you live in

Montgomery?"

"Who transformed you into a vampire?" Tony asked, hoping to control their interaction. It had worked in the past as dealing with unbalanced blood drinkers had become his specialty.

"Why should I tell you?" Haman's eyes narrowed.

"Because I asked politely." Keeping his questions and answers short, Tony hoped to get what he needed without coming to blows. He had not grappled with another vampire in a long time, and it was a scary adventure, even with God on his side.

"Yes. You are very polite. Tell me. Miss Abingdon said you are a preacher. How is that? Can a devil be a god?"

Growing bolder, the man danced around Tony's question, the initial shock of seeing another creature like himself subsiding. Tony tried again.

"Who transformed you into a vampire?"

"Who transformed *you* into a vampire?" Haman replied, mimicking Tony's southern accent.

Tony paused to gather his thoughts, so far, hearing nothing from God. He leveled his gaze and tried to speak as Mark did when he needed to be taken seriously.

"I will ask you one more time. Who did this to you?"

"Are you going to keep asking until I slap you silly?"

When Haman smiled, Tony noted elongated incisors, not hidden and not withdrawn. He hadn't heard from God. Maybe if he stalled, maybe Mark would pop in and help. Tony lowered his chin.

"Let's start over," he said and scooted closer, but still ten feet away. "I was made this way by a vampire named Paul Black. Do you know him?"

Haman's eyes widened and he grinned. "I know *of* him. Paul Black the blacksmith. So, you know his master, Dr. Crump."

Tony nodded, aware of Mark's aliases. "I do. Is he the one that made you like this?"

Haman's face turned wistful. "Oh, I could tell you the story," he said and relaxed back. He kicked out both feet and crossed his ankles. "If I tell you my story, will you share yours? I have lived a hundred years with this glorious Gift and never seen a brother before now."

Tony wanted to keep him talking. "Yes, I'm very curious. How did this happen?"

Troye's eyes twinkled and he winked. "I saw the doctor in a dream..." he began and Tony sat back to hear the tale.

It was in Maine, 1915, when Haman watched the doctor's buggy pull away. With a sharp kick, Haman instructed his gelding to follow. He had been tracking the man's movements for weeks and tonight, he'd finally make contact and look into the mystery of the town's only physician.

Haman had no legitimate reasons to be suspicious; the entire town loved the doctor and publicly lauded his reputation. But Haman saw that Dr. Marcus Corescu didn't belong. His hair, eyes, and skin were very dark, more like a Gypsy or those bronze-skinned Egyptians he read about in his books. And the man was tall, taller than anyone else in town. Haman was a man of above-average stature and he was surprised that this foreign doctor had at least two inches on him. Also, Haman saw right off that this so-called country doctor carried himself with an elegant and aristocratic air, as if he had been raised with money and power. This is one of many reasons the doctor seemed askew—why would a man of obvious wealth and position, who was able to purchase a grand two-story house on fifteen acres, not hire servants to help him keep the place in order? Why would he take a job as a lowly country doctor? Was he a ne'er-do-well? A charlatan? Could he really go house to house treating consumption in the elderly and skin disorders in infants and children as if simply another mere mortal depending on his fellow man for his daily bread? Haman thought not. The doctor had a secret, and Haman would discover it very soon. As he rode, he contemplated the night ahead.

Tonight is the night. I will finally learn what this man has to teach me. And I will begin to live the dreams…

There, Haman had the main reason he suspected the doctor of being more than he appeared. *The dreams.* Ever since his first contact with the dark stranger, he had been having the strangest dreams regarding the doctor's nocturnal behaviors. The first night, he dreamed that the man was a ghost who flitted about his house without touching the floor. That morning Haman brushed his uneasiness off easily and blamed it on a plate of bad beef. But the second and third nights, he dreamed more vividly, and always a voice spoke to him, whispering great and wonderful secrets into his itching ears. Upon awakening, he never could recall what was said, but he had a deep-seated need to discover the answers to his questions.

Last night's dream was the most amazing of all. Haman fell asleep in his bed, but opened his eyes in a strange room in a strange house and watched the tall doctor sucking the blood out of a helpless woman.

"Monster!" he had shrieked in his dreamland, but neither of the figures noticed him. He fell silent and looked on. The woman was not afraid; in fact she was smiling, eyes at half-mast, arms relaxed at her sides. And the man was not fierce, appearing serene, reverent, maybe even praying during the disgusting deed. Before the monster completed his meal, the scene vanished and Haman found himself sitting up, sweaty and panting in his own bed.

And that is when I heard the voice of something...other... That raspy, unreal voice in my head saying, "Haman, you must find out my secret. You must approach me and learn of my ways. You can rule with me. We can rule the world together."

Haman had listened to that voice, the voice of The *Other*; it wasn't really the doctor, but rather an evil entity trapped within him. Haman had been discerning such spirits his entire life and this one possessed the power to work its will through the physician's flesh. All Haman had to do was steal it. As he plotted, The Other came to him again and again, with hints and strategies to acquire what he needed from the supernatural monster posing as a village doctor.

Haman snapped out of his thoughts as the doctor's buggy approached the town gates. He trailed him through town over rugged dirt roads, and only when the sun had completely left the scene and the moon was high, did he finally pull up at the town's only pub.

Haman halted his horse at the neighboring blacksmith's dark doorway and stuck to the shadows to watch his mystery man enter the noisy business. After waiting a few minutes in the shadows, he entered the establishment himself and surveyed the crowd. It took some searching, but he found Dr. Crump sitting alone in a far corner, hat brim pulled low over his eyes, staring intently at a group of boisterous youths in the center of the room.

So this is where he spends his evenings?

Initially confounded, Haman settled into a chair across the room, pulled his own hat lower, and watched the stranger watch the youths.

Haman downed four beers as he waited for the doctor to make a move, but he did nothing but pretend to drink from his stein, his eyes never leaving the boys' table.

What is he looking at?

Haman considered each young man and determined Dr. Crump was scrutinizing a slender, fair-haired boy of around eighteen. This one seemed jovial and popular and his laugh echoed around the room like the sound of bells. Perplexed at the doctor's fixation, Haman remained in place, more than determined to see the evening to the end.

Is this his next victim? Is he stalking this boy?

More rhetorical questions popped into his head and then, the doctor abruptly stood and exited the pub with a flourish. Haman slammed a few coins on the table and hustled out the door to follow. By the time he untied his horse and mounted, Crump's buggy was out of sight around the town square and turning toward home.

Is this it? Stare at some youths and go home for the night?

Haman's curiosity only grew as his horse shuffled along quietly on the grassy shoulder a hundred feet behind the buggy.

If I am to believe these crazy dreams, I will need to see more oddities than this!

Then, as loudly as a brass drum in his mind, Haman heard the raspy and frightening voice from his dreams, a voice he had begun to call The Other.

"Haman! You must approach me. Learn of my secrets. Approach me now!"

Startled by the command of an unseen force, Haman kicked his horse into a rapid trot and eventually into a hand gallop alongside the worn road. Riding only by the light of the full moon, he gained quickly on the slow-moving buggy ahead.

"Sir, excuse me! Sir!" Haman cantered up alongside the driver and tipped his hat with his free hand. "Can I speak with you, Doctor. It is an emergency."

With a tight smile, the doctor slowed his horse, bringing him to a halt along the side of the road. "Yes, my good man, what is it?"

Haman dismounted, smiling to himself, amazed at how the scene was playing so closely to the one provided in his morning vision from The Other. Down to the doctor's very words.

"Doctor Crump, do you remember me? I am the man who sold you your house and set up many other arrangements for you in town. Haman T. Esquire, at your service." Haman bowed low and dropped his horse's reins as he approached the doctor's side. When given this sequence of events in his mind in his morning vision, the doctor had jumped down from his buggy and shook his hand. Haman waited to see if this would come to pass.

After eyeing him a moment, the doctor did just that. He set the brake and hopped confidently out of his seat, landing directly in front of Haman's boots. "Yes, Haman. What is the emergency?"

The doctor looked down on Haman, scrutinizing him closely. He wondered briefly what would happen if he were wrong. *What if I have lost my mind? What if this is just a man and I am a lunatic?*

"Haman!" The unearthly voice thundered in his mind and he blinked several times in succession and gathered his wits.

"I want to know your secrets." Haman whispered. He looked up and down the desolate road and before the doctor could respond, he continued bravely, "I want to know why you suck the blood of the living."

The doctor's eyes widened with surprise and he stepped back. "Are you mad?"

"And I know about the boy with the blond hair. What will you do if I tell him about you?" Haman rested his left hand casually on his hip, but his right had snaked behind him and grasped the dagger he had stashed there. *So far, so good. This is all how I envisioned it. How exciting!*

"Haman, what has gotten into you? You're not making any sense." The doctor's words were patronizing, but now he, too, scanned the surrounding area for witnesses to their conversation.

"I know you are a very powerful creature and you are not a man. I will expose you if you do not share your secrets!" Haman gripped the butt of the knife tighter, not wanting to miss his chance to carry out his next task. Could it be accomplished? If the monster were truly as powerful as The Other claimed, could he overcome him? Haman gritted his teeth and waited.

The doctor sighed and in the bright light of the full moon, Crump smiled slowly and placed his hands into his pockets. *"Tsk, tsk."* He clucked his tongue as if scolding a small child. "How much have you had to drink tonight? You are drunk."

"And you're a vampire!" Haman searched deep for his last ounce of courage and reached behind his back to slice open the palm of his left hand. That done, he whipped the dagger forward, slicing the forearm of the vampire almost to the bone and grabbed the wound with his own bloody palm.

The doctor reacted slowly, as if shocked at the brazen attack. When he finally did react, it was only to laugh.

"You cannot kill me with a knife! This wound will heal in a matter of seconds. Remove your hand and see."

Doctor Crump was chuckling, not at all afraid. He obviously didn't realize his blood had mixed with another. It was exactly as The Other had shown him!

"Heal up from this, then!" Haman gripped the hilt of the knife and shoved it violently into the doctor's abdomen. He pushed with all of his might and with one final effort, pressed all of his weight into the man and they both toppled to the ground.

The doctor did not speak again. He looked at Haman's hand on the hilt of the blade buried into his flesh and smiled. Haman jerked his hand free and stumbled back to his horse, leaving the dagger in the monster's middle. Crump laughed loudly, sitting on the ground, bleeding an impossibly black fluid onto the muddy road.

Wrapping his pocket cloth tightly around his wounded palm, Haman made a grab for the reins and startled his horse to attention. He quickly clambered back into the saddle and spurred the horse on. When he dared to look back ten strides later, the vampire was coming to his feet. In the eerie moonlight, Haman saw him pull the dagger free with a jerk, bring it to his lips and then toss it into the trees.

And he was still laughing.

Standing in the stirrups and leaning low against his steed's neck for optimum speed, Haman rode as fast as his horse could carry him. He could feel the monster's blood beginning to run through his system, burning like acid along the way and he grimaced, holding tightly to the horse's thick mane tangled around the reins. Through the pain, he rejoiced: the unseen *Other* had been correct. Swapping blood wound to wound from the vampire *was* transferring his power!

By the time Haman reached his cottage outside the county limits, he was fully transformed. He packed up his belongings as suggested by the eerie voice in his head and left that very night for the coast. The voice had commanded him to flee to Europe.

"Stay in the Old World and grow. Grow in power, in knowledge and wisdom and I will call you home when it is time."

Haman did as he was commanded and he found the blood of the British to be as satisfying as any in the world.

13

*"Or how can one enter a strong man's house
And plunder his goods,
Unless he first binds the strong man?"*
Matthew 12:29

"IS THE AMERICAN BEAUTY IN HER PLACE, ELI?" ANDRONI asked the carnival roustabout in his own tongue. The Polish expatriate ran errands for Androni over the years and he enjoyed the man's company.

"Third row. Just like last night and the night before and the night before that." Eli clutched his grimy cap in stained fingers. Every member of the company had taken notice of the American woman's repeated visits to his exhibit.

"Give her this note before I go on stage." Androni handed over a folded slip of paper and the man squirreled it away in the brim of his cap. He plopped it atop his bald head and was gone.

Androni stepped up to the curtain flap and considered the audience. He had a full-house and the American shone brighter than the others due to her fair skin and eyes. Plus, since her first attendance, she'd been ramping up her visual appeal with carefully chosen clothing. After the riding habit, the next evening she'd worn faded blue jeans that hugged her form and a snug pink T-shirt that revealed a tiny sliver of a flat midriff. Night three, she wore darker jeans with boots and a baby blue sweater tapered at the waist. Night four found her in slacks with a flowing silk blouse, its sleeves reached her wrists but was open at the neck, revealing a whisper of delightful cleavage. What did she have on tonight? The woman sought Androni's attention and it was because of her determination and brazenness that he made her wait for satisfaction. The women he brought to his caravan he *chose*. They all chased the magician, but he only brought them home if he was the fox and they were the hen.

Ah.

Within another moment, the crowd shifted and he glimpsed her attire. Tonight—the night he would touch her pink skin—she'd chosen a cotton peasant blouse with criss-cross string ties from navel to collar, and she'd left the strings loose, although her delightful cleavage remained hidden.

Androni shrank back, her eyes were scanning for him, blue pools of hunger that promised a vampire amazing things. She wanted the magier to give her some attention, how much, he'd determine when they were alone. And if he played it right, she would offer him her blood. This goal tickled his mind and gut. Androni did not pull her onto the stage subsequent evenings, barely acknowledging her. He'd toss her a wink when he said something flirtatious to the crowd, but that was the sum of it. She came back because she wanted to, and tonight, Eli's message would bring her (hopefully) to his caravan.

Androni allowed the curtain to fall closed and the announcements began. Tonight, he would again ignore her throughout the performance, but at the last trick, bring her on stage. The crowd thoroughly enjoyed ogling her and they loved to mock "the American." It would be a good show, and afterwards, a good introduction.

Hope clutched the magician's invitation in her closed fist and stood before the caravan door. A gruff mustachioed local pointed the way but with her knuckle prepared to strike, her nerve wobbled. She'd been to his show five times.

It's about time he got the hint!

At that inside shout, the door opened, Androni the Magnificent filling the void and giving her a secret grin that stole her voice.

"Ah! My rabid American fan," he said in English backing and inviting her to pass. "Come in. Come in. Welcome to my humble home."

Breathing a thank you, Hope peeked left and right before stepping inside. Once there, she stood on a mat placed dead-center: the kitchen and presumably a toilet room on the right, a low sofa against the middle wall, and a messy mattress on the left piled high with blankets and pillows.

I'm practically in his bedroom…

Hope rolled in her lips wondering what Mark would think.

The magician pulled the door closed with a *whump* and motioned for the lumpy sofa. "Please, sit. Do you have a name?"

When she sat on one end of the couch, Androni tugged close a low footstool and sat upon it, looking up into her face. Hope pushed Mark from her mind and smiled at her host. "Hope Brannen. And thank you.

This is nice."

"Oh, it is exceptionally 'nice,'" he said playing with her choice of words. "You may call me Androni. Some beautiful women call me honey or baby. I would accept that, too."

He flashed a new grin and she flushed. The entertainer had shed his makeup and now only four feet away, Hope fell apart looking into his face. As she noted before, his olive skin and jet-black hair put him in the Gypsy category, but without makeup, his eyes seemed luminescent, as if she might see through them, as in looking through a stained glass window. He chuckled when she had not spoken, the strands of his wavy hair dangling over his brow.

"Ask me a question," he said then, speaking low as if they held secrets already. She did her best to play along and not allow him to see her flustered.

"Are you German? I'm here riding horses, but I'm from Georgia in the U.S.," she said leaving her benefactor out of the telling.

"I am Hungarian," he said with a head bow. "You did not ride horses today, though, did you? Or the day before? I think you might be enamored with Androni the Magnificent, yes?"

Hope's eyes widened, the man saying whatever crossed his mind. She pondered the coincidence that Mark was also from Hungary and responded, "You got me." Then she tried to cover her embarrassment adding, "At least your English is good. I can't speak any other language and everyone here knows at least two."

"We travel across many borders. I speak twelve languages. Does this impress you?"

Hope smiled at the question, thinking what a silly thing to ask. Everything about Androni impressed her; in fact, she could find nothing about him she *didn't* like, other than his brazen questions and spoken observations caused her to blush.

"Tell me, Hope Brannen," he said in the lull, "are you going to attend all of my shows to the end of time?" Hope didn't answer right away, and he continued, regarding her with a steamy gaze. "I find you distracting. Someone, somewhere is missing you. I fear you have slipped your leash." His eyes twinkled then with humor. "If you were mine, I'd double-knot the rope and never let you out of my sight."

The unabashed compliments stunned her and Hope stumbled to reply. But he had a point. Why had she come to his trailer?

He huffed without lowering his gaze. "I am provoking you. I

apologize. I am a barbarian, after all." Androni smiled flashing very white teeth.

Finally, she found a few words. "I'm sorry for distracting you. I think I'm too curious. I can't figure out how you do the tricks. The things that flew into your hand… Back home, magic is just illusion."

"I will tell you how it is done." He inched closer and she caught a whiff of lavender. Was it soap or parfum; she didn't know, *but he smells so nice…* "You've earned it after paying the entry fee five times. Would you like to see? I will show you."

Hope said she would and watched as Androni presented his hands, fingers up and wiggling. He pointed one index finger toward her and just like that, her hair comb slipped free and her bangs fell across her eyes with a feathery swish.

Hope gasped and lifted both hands to tuck her long bangs behind her ears. "How did you…?"

"Like this." Androni placed one hand to his hip and with the other, pointed a finger-gun to Hope's blouse. "Bang," he whispered, breaking into a wide grin.

For a moment, Hope wondered if anything happened, but then a breeze blew into her shirt and she looked down. The small bow she'd tied to close her blouse strings had popped open, revealing the edge of her brassiere. Hope gasped again and retied it. "Your magic… It's real?"

"Oh, yes, it is very real. What else can I show you? I am certain I might reveal everything to someone with eyes as blue as yours."

"That's amazing," Hope whispered and sat up from her perch on the old couch. She had seen Mark move objects in a similar fashion, but he was different. He was *Mark*. To Androni, she said, "That's telekinesis."

"Yes. May I?" Androni held out his hand, palm up, as if asking for Hope to take it. Without thinking, she did. Closing his fingers around hers, he brought her hand to his face. He paused only moments before bringing it to his lips, briefly kissing the top of her hand.

"Uh… thank you," Hope said awkward and embarrassed.

"No, thank *you*," Androni said licking his lips, giving Hope the impression he had *tasted* her. He lowered her hand but hadn't released. The magician leaned forward and placed his left hand on the couch next to Hope's thigh. "Hope Brannen, where is your husband?"

Hope inhaled and cleared her throat. Where was Mark? He wasn't her husband, but he would be the closest man to fit the bill. Did she even know where he was? He might be at Tony's. He was spending a lot of time there when Hope was away or at the barn. Hope's mind raced as she stared into the magier's bright eyes.

"You don't know where he is?" Androni asked, his voice soft and velvety.

Hope made a small noise. Her head was growing fuzzy and she blushed. The magier was bewitching her with his gaze, another magician's trick as real as the others.

"You caught me," Androni cooed, his winning smile in place. "I am hypnotizing you. You intrigue me. I want to figure you out and I am certain that I could get to the bottom of it if I convinced you to open up…"

"You're reading my mind?"

"Yes," Androni whispered, his eyes searching her face as his mind did its work in her head.

"Are you going to take advantage of me?" she whispered without planning to.

"I don't think so. Am I doing that now? Do you want to leave? You can go. I am not holding you against your will. Do you think that is what I am doing?"

Hope shook her head. She didn't want to leave, but… "My head… I feel like I'm going to pass out."

"No. That sensation accompanies this trick. This *mind trick.* Tell me about yourself. Your mind will clear when you stop resisting."

Hope blinked her eyes and each time they reopened, she dove deeper into the magician's gaze. Finally, after trying to decide why the sensation was so familiar, Hope gave up and sank into the couch cushion, a sleepy smile on her face. He said she could leave; she didn't want to. What could it hurt to play the new trick? "Okay, Mr. Magnificent, what do you want to know?"

Androni slipped off the low stool and sank into the couch, his leg touching hers. "Why are you alone? A smart man would never set you loose alone in a foreign country."

With a drunken smile, Hope replied, "Mark trusts me."

"But how can he trust the rest of mankind? You should be protected, guarded, and escorted. Yet you stumble into my tent night after night, alone, with a sadness in your heart as big as Transylvania."

"Transylvania," Hope repeated in a giggle and covered her lips, eyes half open. Androni lifted his hand to her hair and maneuvered a chunk of it over her shoulder, running his fingers to the end.

"A woman like you should smile inside and out. What makes you so sad?"

"Do you think you could make me smile?" Hope asked, not sorry his hypnosis had loosened her inhibitions.

"Oh, Androni can make any woman smile," he said and flashed a new grin. "I only have to figure out what it is that you want. I assume you have all the comforts of life—possessions, a nice home, jewels galore. Yet, there is sadness in your heart and a stifling longing in your eyes." Androni took the ends of Hope's long hair in his hand, feathering it to his touch.

Hot tears welled and Hope swallowed them back. The magier was right. She should be protected, guarded, and worshipped. Where was Mark? She was being hypnotized in a strange man's trailer.

With a resigned sigh, Hope locked on the obvious: Mark was not there for her. This stranger, this magician, saw the truth. She was under-appreciated and overlooked by the man she loved. Hope regarded the magician's adoring gaze, giving her his undivided attention.

He thinks I'm worth his time...

"I fell in love with a man who has no use for me," Hope admitted through clenched teeth. "I can't change him, and he has barely tried to change me. I *am* sad. And I'm lonely, too." Hope wiped away the tears that moistened her cheeks.

"You can cry on my shoulder." Androni released her hair and used the same hand to caress the top of her head.

"No, I'm tired of crying over him. I'm tired of waiting for him to rescue me. I'm tired of waiting for him to *notice* me." Now more angry than sad, Hope raised her head and caught her host's eye. "I'm going to leave him. I don't need his money. He's not my sugar daddy."

Androni seemed dubious. "*Can* you leave him? I sense hesitation, as if you doubt yourself. Yet, I also see you do not fear him."

"No, he's harmless," Hope mumbled, then remembered Mark's true nature. She corrected with, "At least to me."

Then Androni did a curious thing. He got to his feet, stared at her a long moment, and then walked into the tiny kitchen nook, his back to Hope.

"What's wrong?" she asked still sitting and leaning forward. The dizziness had passed.

"Hope," Androni said softly and did not turn or say more.

Intrigued by his tone, Hope came to her feet and took a step toward him. "What? What's going on?"

"There are some interesting images in your mind." Androni tilted his head to the side, his voice carrying a mysterious tone. "Some very interesting images."

Hope worked to recall what she'd been thinking. She'd been answering his questions. Did he really see images in her mind? Could he pick up such things in detail? Like Mark had proven to her in the past? Hope stood dumbfounded and waited for Androni to finish his thought. What had he seen?

"You are playing coy with me, Fraulein." Androni turned to face her but remained across the space. Hope noted wonder in his eyes that had not been there earlier, and a crooked grin began to find the edges of his mouth. A *knowing* grin.

"What? What?"

"This man, this *Mark...*" Androni drew out his words and watched her eyes. "He is not *human.*"

"Oh, my God!" Hope covered her mouth with her hands. Somehow, he had seen the truth. He knew that Mark was a vampire! "Oh, my God!" was all she could say, and she repeated it again as she waited to see the magician's reaction.

"Yes… you read like a fine novel, Hope Brannen. In full color, too. Oh, how you have treated that man. Oh, how you have tortured him…"

Androni leaned upon the sink ledge and crossed his arms. What was he thinking? From his mysterious smile, Hope couldn't fathom. She tried to clear her thoughts, but the longer she stood there, the more images came to her mind concerning Mark.

"I'd like you to stop that, Androni. Please, get out of my head!" Hope reflexively put both hands to her throat and then lifted a shaky finger towards the door. "I'll leave! I will, I promise!"

Immediately, the man disentangled himself from her mind. Hope fell onto the couch, blinking and rubbing her face. What now? What could she say to defend herself? To protect Mark's secret? What had she done?

"I want to find this Mark," Androni said, still boring Hope with a hard gaze.

Hope swallowed and met his eye. "Aren't you afraid? I mean, if you saw what I think you saw?"

Androni shrugged. "Why should I fear him? I've not threatened him. I've not hurt you. I cannot fear my own brother."

Hope's eyes grew wide and she again, covered her mouth.

Of course! His supernatural abilities, his hypnotizing gaze, everything about him gave him away and I didn't see it!

91

Speechless, Hope watched Androni from her nest on the sofa and hoped he stayed on his side of the trailer.

"I am no longer in your head, my beauty, but I have questions concerning your vampire friend. I have been walking this planet for two hundred and fifty years and have never met another of my kind." Androni remained where he was which gave Hope comfort.

"I don't think…"

Androni waved away her excuses. "To think there's another vampire out there; he'd be watching us…" Androni bent at the waist and peered out the kitchen window into the night. "I have always known they were out there," he said, his tone wistful. "I knew I could not be the only one. Especially since I was abandoned by my master."

"Your master? I don't know very much about Mark's past. I mean, we have some history, but he doesn't confide in me." Hope wondered now, finally, if she was in danger.

"How did you meet," Androni asked, his eyes soft.

Hope did not reply but pressed her lips together. What was she supposed to do now? And where was Mark? He never allowed her to be so near disaster and she realized in the silence that she'd come to rely on his telepathic monitoring.

Androni stood up off the sink counter. "Are you going to tell me?" he asked and took two steps toward the couch.

"Stop. Don't threaten me." Hope barked out the first thing that came to mind. "Mark knows where I am, and he'll come if he senses I'm in danger. You don't want to be on his bad side." Did he know? She had not called to Mark in her heart during her interaction with the magician. She watched Androni's face as he puzzled out his next words. Something about him; he was so appealing, maybe even more so than Mark. Hope took a deep breath. At that moment, in three strides, Androni crossed the short distance between them and held out his hand.

"Let us test him. What if I were to kiss you? Would that raise his ire?"

Hope looked at Androni's outstretched hand and then back to his face. His feathery hair hung over his forehead and framed his cheeks as he leaned in. *Was* Mark watching? Would he instantly appear if another man, er, another *vampire* should kiss her? Never having been in such a position, she had no way of knowing.

"Does he kiss you?" Androni asked, his English more accented as the moment heated the room. "When was the last time you were really kissed? Can you remember?"

Hope bit her lip and considered his questions. No, Mark would not kiss her. He pecked her cheek often, but he would never kiss her. Not like a man kisses a woman. But this *magier* would. This vampire magician did not fear his nature. He was willing to give her a bit of the attention she lacked at home. What harm could come from it? Androni wouldn't hurt her. Hope clung to that last thought and reached for his hand.

Androni folded her into his arms. He smelled of sawdust and soap and Hope hung in his embrace for several long moments, her face tucked into the rough material of his costume. He murmured something she didn't understand and stroked her hair. When he mumbled the same words again, this time closer to her ear, Hope peeked out of the embrace.

"What did you say? I only speak English," she whispered, her face inches from his cheek.

"Maybe I was speaking to your lover. Maybe if he's listening, he heard me..." Androni whispered, his soft breath landing on Hope's upturned face. "I said, 'I am about to kiss your woman and I dare you to stop me.'"

"That's not too bright," Hope whispered back, now certain that Mark was going to appear magically at any moment. But she did not turn away from the magician's gaze. When he leaned forward to touch his lips to hers, she did not move back.

It's been so long...

"So far, so good, young Hope. Do you think it is safe? Are we likely to consummate this kiss?" Androni asked telepathically, causing Hope to startle. *"Your mind is open. Your lover must speak to you this way, no?"*

Hope nodded, wide-eyed.

"Then, here we go. And to hell with anyone who tries to stop us..."

Androni's lips touched Hope's tenderly and soon, she fell wholeheartedly into his kiss. Wrapped in his arms, she could almost pretend it *was* Mark holding her, loving her, worshipping her the way she had always dreamed he would. But it wasn't. Mark wouldn't or couldn't love her this way. He had made that clear at the beginning. And why? Even as this vampire magician kissed her more gently than she had ever known, she remembered why Mark would never love her this way. It was because of the blood. Because of *her* blood and his desire for it.

So why can this vampire kiss me? He is not taking my blood...

Before she could dream up an answer, Androni pulled away and put his hands on either side of her face. Hope was light-headed and dizzy, but this time it was strictly sexual.

"He did not come. Did I not kiss you passionately enough?" Androni spoke softly and held Hope's gaze.

"Perhaps he doesn't get jealous," she rasped, fully aroused by the magier's touch. Maybe Mark only showed up when she was in danger, and a kiss was not likely to hurt her.

"I would be insanely covetous of a woman like you." Androni's hands cupped her cheeks and his thumb traced her bottom lip. "Not much of a lover is he, this Mark?"

"He protects me," Hope whispered, wondering what it was she wanted from this man, this friendly and adoring vampire.

"He withholds everything from you, doesn't he? Withholds love, affection, intimacy?" Androni knew it all from her eyes and Hope did not attempt to answer his rhetorical questions. "You wonder why, don't you? And you wonder why he won't take that which he desires the most. From thousands of other people he has taken this one thing. But not from you. He flatly refuses. You wonder why he won't take your *blood.*"

Hope blinked back a tear and swallowed. The man was right; Mark was stingy with everything that mattered. All things pertaining to love, he held back. Hope nodded, and her fists gathered the cloth on the front of Androni's costume. The ache in her spirit grew and her resolve to resist the magier and leave his caravan had all but dissolved. Androni placed a lingering kiss on her forehead and Hope thought she might die.

"I could take your blood," Androni said in her ear. "And I would be very gentle." He smiled, the thought of sinking his aching teeth into the flawless skin of this other vampire's beauty tickled his spirit. Her blood would go down his throat like the food of the gods. But he wouldn't steal it; he would wait for her offer. By the look in her face, she was there. "What do you say? Do you trust me?"

The young woman's eyes watered, likely considering all those times her vampire lover refused her back home. Then she nodded, one tiny tip of the chin.

"He still might come…" she whispered and Androni discerned she was torn on whether she wanted him to do so. He would be as dramatic as possible to draw the vampire to contact him. With tender movement, he repositioned the beauty in his arms. Stealthily he loosed the strings of her soft peasant blouse and ran his thumb beneath the fabric. After catching her gaze to reassure, he used that thumb to tug her blouse downward and

bare her shoulder. Hope's hand went to her bosom, but she was still covered, Androni's attention not at all on her breasts.

"Turn like this." A gentle rotation and her back was against his front and he wrapped his left arm about her waist. His right hand tucked her long hair up and over her opposite shoulder before snugging her in tight finally with both arms. "And be still. This may sting..."

The woman's heart rate and respirations had elevated, but she wasn't afraid. She was exhilarated, certain that when he pressed in, she would be sexually fulfilled. Androni had no opinion on how she perceived the act— he was ready to consummate. Androni decided the circumstance called for a horizontal laceration—if the other vampire turned out to be of a foul nature, at least his woman had not been truly *entered*. With a private grin at his own thoughts, Androni raked one fang to the tender flesh beneath the woman's ear. As predicted, Hope flinched but then relaxed giving Androni no resistance as the small wound leaked her blood onto his waiting tongue.

She moaned then like a woman in the throes of coitus, and Androni shifted one hand to cover her near breast. She had spent so much time in the presence of an untouchable immortal that she had quite worked the experience up in her mind. She had a notion that it was a sign of a vampire's *love* to consume her blood. Androni was happy to oblige. After all, her blood was coursing out of her body and into his own. It *was* an intimate exchange of sorts and he was never one to turn down a free meal.

Androni drank his fill and by the time he was nearly done, the woman began to slip into unconsciousness. She was safe, her heart beating strong. He reached into his back pocket for his handkerchief, easily holding her weight in one arm, and he pressed the cloth against the slight wound. He allowed her to tumble into his arms as he lifted her off the ground, carrying her to his small lumpy bed in the front end of the trailer. As he was tucking her into the rough cotton blankets, she rolled over in his arms, her full lips smiling, her eyes open but glazed. She looked like she might speak and Androni spoke first.

"You are safe, my lovely." One peek at her wound and the blood had clotted; it would heal nicely. "Shhh... Sleep. No harm will come to you. I will watch over you until you awake." Androni tucked the quilt under her side and then carefully lifted her head to free her long hair to the pillow. She puzzled him as her weak smile grew and she parted her lips again as if to speak. No words came so Androni clicked off the lamp above the bed and made as if to stand up. That was when she whispered his name.

"Shhh... You are safe."

He heard his name again, very soft. Androni leaned down until his face was inches from hers and she mustered the strength to speak.

"He's coming," she murmured her eyes closed. *"He saw. He knows. He's coming..."*

Androni pursed his lips in wonder and the other vampire's woman fell into a deep sleep. When he finally stood and crossed to the couch, he pondered her last words.

He saw. He knows. He's coming.

Androni ran his tongue over his lips, the woman's blood providing the most satisfying peace in his middle. When would he arrive? How would he perceive Androni the Magnificent?

For a very long time, Androni thought on these things.

And he was excited.

18

"Who will mourn for you? Who will stop and ask how you are?
You have rejected me," declares the Lord.
"You keep on backsliding. So I will lay my hands on you
And destroy you..."
Jeremiah 14:5-6

THE VAMPIRE'S INTRIGUING TALE HAD TONY AT RAPT attention. Did Mark know any of this? Corescu had been asked about Haman and the other missing vampire, Androni, several times and he always claimed ignorance.

But he is so wise and knowing... it is hard to imagine he was duped. Tony considered the stranger, beady eyes, a hawkish nose, and eyebrows so close together that they touched. *Mark would have noticed him, remembered being manhandled on that country road, wouldn't he?*

Asking questions inside got him nowhere, so Tony worked up some that might help him decide what God wanted to happen now. "Why did you come? Here, specifically? Are you looking for me?"

Haman scoffed. "Besides being a vampire, who are you that I should want to see you? I am here for myself. I am the one important to me, not you." Haman stood from the seat he'd assumed and put his hands to his hips. "Now, it is your turn. How did the blacksmith end up bestowing this gift upon you? A preacher?"

Tony narrowed his eyes. He wouldn't share anything more with the man, not even the truth. Haman emanated evil and in another moment, Tony realized why he sensed it—Haman served the same spirits Rakha served, which had been the worst in hell.

"Did you come here looking for the doctor?" Tony asked, watching for deceit.

"Come close. I will drink your blood." Haman's eyes flashed with malcontent.

"Back up," Tony said maintaining his stern Mark-like tone. "I'm not giving you anything. You need to leave town—"

"Your woman—she carries a vampire's blood. I smell it. Bring her back, we can feast on her together, side-by-side. What is a mere woman between brothers?"

Tony zoomed into the vampire grasping his coat lapels in both hands. "Do not speak of her! Don't you even THINK about her!" he snarled in the man's ear. Up close, Troye smelled of mothballs and mud, and Tony leaned out to glare in his face. He read deep-seated insanity in his host's eyes—the man was unstable before he stole Mark's blood, and now he was full over the hill. Now Tony dreaded what was about to transpire. Whether a divine premonition or his own common sense, Tony was about to have to physically subdue Haman Troye.

"Simmer down," he cooed, his breath putrid to Tony's sensitive nose. "You have quite a thing for me, don't you? You go first." Haman looked aside, bearing his throat. "Go ahead. You'll see. The blood of a brother isn't like any other..."

Tony had heard those words before, Rakha said that to him when he fed Tony his blood. *His delicious blood. The blood that satisfied Tony's hunger for a long, long time...*

"Go on," Haman said again low. "You drink from me, I drink from you, and we go round and round."

Still Tony did nothing. With the vampire grabbed close by his coat and Tony's face inches from his neck, Tony did not respond. In his mind, he recalled Rakha's blood going down his throat. How many times? Oh, the memory caused Tony's tongue to swell with thirst, and he hadn't lusted for blood in months.

"Tony," Haman whispered, his face still to the side, "have you ever enjoyed the blood of a vampire?"

"Yes," Tony whispered, not meaning to answer, but part of him didn't care.

"Was it wonderful?"

"Tony! Subdue him. Stop listening and subdue him." It was Dr. Corescu adding his opinion. Tony did not ask where he was, but he offered the information. *"Hope's in a bind. Get away from Troye. I'll come. Let me get Hope to safety and I'll come. Get away from him."* With that last instruction, Mark was gone, his mental tether evaporated. Tony was again alone.

"Hurry. I don't fear you. I will take your blood by force," Haman said then, low and to the side. "I will drain you and hold you captive. What do you think of that?"

During his monologue, Tony had succeeded in tamping down the old lust and he shook his head. "You're listening to the wrong spirits. Listen to the one warning you that I can destroy you. If you lock horns with me today, you will most assuredly be defeated."

"Release me, I rescind my offer," he said in an evil growl. "You have spent one too many days in church. I control my own destiny, not spirits."

Tony made no move to let him go. If he resisted and tried to break free, would he be able to?

Is God with me?

Tony sought his heart for answers and Haman tensed his muscles. In the past, God gave Tony the strength to defeat his enemy. But since Paul died…

No, since I became a vampire, God isn't rescuing me. He's making me rescue myself. Why?

In a sudden movement, Haman broke free, shoving himself back with the force of his push. He stumbled, found his balance, and squared off. Tony tried one more plea to God in his heart.

"Father, please, I give You all of me. Use me for Your will. This man is dangerous. What can I do to keep these people safe from Haman Troye?"

Then the words of Life came and Tony allowed them to flow, his heart finally joyful at the heavenly contact.

"Beware, you devil…" Tony locked eyes with Haman and spoke carefully. "I am a living saint of the Most High God. His Spirit lives within me and works through me in Power. This Spirit is the very same Force that created the universe. He will not allow you to harm anyone. Me, Sarah, that young woman you employ…"

"Are you threatening me with *God?*" Haman asked in a laugh.

"No, but I wanted you to know who you are up against. More than one of your kind has tried to cross me, and if it is God's will that I be triumphant, you do not stand a chance." Tony opened his arms wide. "When you are beaten and broken on this dirty floor, know well that it was the power of God that crippled you, not the mere shell named Tony Agricola."

Haman tensed his shoulders, clenching and unclenching his fists at his sides. Yet, he didn't move. Tony discerned God had frozen him to the spot and this made him grin.

"What are you waiting for?" Tony taunted, with arms open wide, his head up to bare his unguarded throat. Haman's expression darkened but he did not move. "Didn't you say you'd steal my blood?"

Blood-tinged perspiration popped from Haman's brow as he strained against an invisible captor. Then, a visible weakness rippled across the vampire's frame and he went to his knees with a groan.

After a few shallow breaths, he looked at Tony from the floor. "What is this power you wield? Teach it to me. I beg you…"

"It is the Lord in me. I can do nothing without Him." With Haman's eyes round and full of new respect, Tony posed his most pressing question again. "Why are you here?"

The vampire nodded as if weary to the bone. "You are the master. Okay," he rasped and panted, bending over. "I can't believe it. I can't move a muscle against you. Somehow, I *am* powerless. I can't…"

Tony cleared his throat. "I'm waiting. Who are you here for?"

"A boy," he whispered and said nothing else.

The hair on the back of Tony's neck prickled. "What? Who?" Everything was falling into place, but Tony couldn't see enough to solve the puzzle. He pressed, stepping in, "Who? What boy?"

Eyes cast to the dusty floor, Haman pulled off his shirt. "A boy who will be my servant…"

"What? What did you do to him?" Tony dropped to his knees and grasped Haman's shoulders, shaking him and looking into his face. "Where is he?"

"He is a vampire," Haman said, eyes to the side and a wicked grin on his face. "He will come to me to feed him. We will be together forever…"

With disgust, Tony backhanded Haman's jaw. The vampire's response was to dig into his own pants pocket, shuffle a bit and yank out an ink pen. Tony only took miniscule notice of the random trinket, but Haman jabbed it into his throat. When he yanked it out, dark red blood oozed from the wound, filling Tony's nostrils with the sweetest ambrosia he hadn't enjoyed since Rakha's last donation.

"No!" Tony stood, the room spinning as his old lust ramped. *I will never touch his blood. Never! I have been so good. God help me!*

"Take my blood and I'll introduce you to the boy…" Haman spoke still looking aside, his wound not yet closed. "He's only seventeen…"

Tony told himself that worry for the young man of compelled him, but he zoomed in, grabbing Haman's wound with fangs that had ached to slide out for three months. With amazing pleasure, the new punctures his teeth made caused the blood to flow with volume and Tony clutched Haman's shoulders tighter.

The vampire whispered in his ear, *"They told me you couldn't resist. They said you were pretending. You are a horrible disciple…"*

100

Tony drank on. The man's blood was sweet, thick, and alive. He even tasted a wisp of Corescu. It was horrible and wonderful and Tony loathed and loved it equally. Maybe he was breaking God's law, but for the moment, he needed this. He needed this window into Haman's mind. He needed this to control him better. He needed to find the boy and help him if this monster truly stole his humanity as he claimed.

Tony drank on.

Haman grew silent and his hands thudded to the floor.

Tony drank on.

Haman lost consciousness.

Tony drank on.

"Honey, what are you doing? I have a bad feeling. I'm coming in."

Sarah's mental voice sounded urgent, but Tony did not respond. Minutes later, his beloved tugged at his shoulders to get him to release the vampire, but he didn't. Tony drank on and Haman had been right. Vampire blood *was* surely superior in every way. He had forgotten.

It had been so long.

18

*...Each one is tempted when he is drawn away by his own desires
and enticed. Then, when desire has conceived,
it gives birth to sin; and sin, when it is full-grown,
brings forth death.*
James 1:14-15

"TONY, IT'S AFTER TWO. WE SHOULD BE GOING," SARAH
whispered sitting beside Tony in Haman Troye's makeshift apartment. The
wasted vampire lay on the floor, groggy from blood loss, watching them.

Tony nodded in agreement with his wife's statements. *"What have I
done?"* he asked her silently. *"Why didn't I turn away? Why did the Lord tempt
me like that?"*

Sarah did not reply, but inwardly, she seethed with disappointment,
thinking of the Scripture, "The Lord does not tempt anyone. He has no
evil in Him." She closed her eyes as the image of Tony taking blood from
Haman Troye returned to her mind. The nightmarish sight was difficult to
erase. And the breaking of his vow; Tony had promised to never touch
blood again. He was cleansing himself of the curse. He was daily seeking
the Lord's will. What could have gotten into him if not the devil?

"Sarah..." Tony looked into his wife's face, hurt by her unspoken
private thoughts. *"What are you saying?"*

Sarah offered a tight smile. Her husband wanted to be pampered, told
it was okay, told he could ask for forgiveness and it would be behind them.
This was true as far as God was concerned, but Sarah was hurt. To disguise
her uncommon fleshly reaction, she got to her feet saying, "We need to
get going." She looked at the man on the floor watching her with an
unfathomable gaze. "And you need to clean up before someone sees you
cover in this monster's blood."

In her peripheral vision, her husband considered his soiled shirt.

"Sarah," Tony said in a soft voice and she turned to see his face. *"I'm
sorry,"* he mouthed and at the same time, Troye mumbled something from
the floor.

"Did you say something?" Sarah looked down on the pitiful creature at Tony's feet. He might have been a mighty force in his own mind, but before God, he was merely a lump of clay. "It sounded like you said something."

"You…you…" Haman mumbled again, then he looked at Tony to rasp, *"You can't leave me here starving."*

Sarah almost snapped, "Oh, yes, we can!" but remained silent, reminded she was a woman of God and needed to control her tongue. Inside, she still hurt from Tony's weakness. *"Father, help him. Help him. Help me help him…"*

"I made a mistake," her husband sent then to her mind and Sarah looked at his face. *"But he's right. I can't leave him starving. He'll hurt someone. I don't know what we should do."*

"Get Mark Corescu to come," Sarah returned, hating that they spoke telepathically because of the monster on the floor.

"I tried. He's busy saving Hope from something across the globe. Sarah, this monster turned someone's child into a vampire. We need to find him, but leaving Haman starving is asking for trouble…"

Then Sarah saw the most horrid thing in her beloved's mind: an image of Sarah giving blood to the vampire. "I won't do it!" she hissed cutting her eyes to Haman. "You can't ask me that, Tony! How dare you!"

Tony remained calm, facing her and not looking at Troye. From the floor, the vampire seemed to have caught on.

"Yes, yes," he gasped weakly. "I must feed…"

Sarah's eyes grew small and watered with tears of anger and shock. "What boy? Who is it?"

"He hasn't said," Tony answered low.

Sarah jerked her gaze to Haman and stood over him. "Tell us the name of this boy!"

In a wet gasp, he muttered, "Ellerslie… Joseph."

Sarah's hands went to her mouth. "Tony! The boy's prophecy! This is it!"

Her husband nodded, his eyes awaiting her consent or flat rejection of his plan.

"There's got to be another way," she said her voice cold.

"Sarah, I can't hold him here if he is under the blood lust. He's psychotic. He's dangerous. And if he drinks from me, he'll only grow more powerful." With an apology in his gaze, Tony added silently, *"We sate his hunger and tie him up. You and I will go find Joseph and Mark will come deal with him here."*

103

He begged with his eyes for her to try to understand, but for the moment, all she saw was his mistake causing her an enormous hardship. She shot her eyes back to the demon on the floor. Tony took Sarah's hand.

"You have taken an oath to submit to my authority. Will you honor that oath now?"

"It's not right," Sarah said with force, glancing sideways at Haman paying close attention.

Tony gripped Sarah's hand more firmly and pulled her to the sofa. Speaking low in her ear, he reminded her of their promise to the Lord. "Sarah, you can and you will. We cannot leave him here starving and you know that I cannot feed him. You have to trust me, and you have to submit."

Sarah turned her face away from both men and hid her eyes behind her free hand. She heard Haman shuffling nearer, too weak to stand but strong enough to head for a blood source. She focused her thoughts back onto her husband and cried in his mind. *"I must go to the Father. Let me go!"*

Tony released her and she covered her face with both hands, facing away from both men.

"Father! Don't let this happen to me. Please! I know You do not want this…"

It took a full minute, but a wash of calm entered her mind and Sarah took a deep breath. With courage from her God, she put one arm behind her, not facing the men. Her beloved had set a chain of events in motion by his disobedience that was going to cause all of them to suffer deeply. She trusted her God beyond measure, but for the moment, she burned with resentment for Tony.

To Tony's mind, she said, *"Use a knife. He may not penetrate me. Understand?"* Closing her mind to the anxious fever electricity in the stuffy apartment atmosphere, she concentrated on God. Taking another deep breath, and still not meeting the eyes of the vampires around her, Sarah exhaled for Tony to begin.

Tony explained the rules and Sarah kept her eyes closed, her face to the filthy couch cushion. A small pressure to her inner elbow.

I lie down and sleep, I wake again because the Lord sustains me. I will not fear tens of thousands drawn up against me on every side…

Sarah felt the despicable Haman Troye take hold, and then the slime of his mouth against her flesh. In her heart, as she pleaded with the Father, she struggled with forgiveness of her husband.

Forgive him, Father, and forgive me for hating him so right now.

Sarah's stomach lurched and she pressed her free hand to her mouth, praying for peace and for him to hurry. In very short order, the monster's contact disappeared, she was free, and she clutched her arm to her body. Without another word or gesture, she then leapt to her feet and bolted out the door.

Sarah prayed another fifteen minutes before Tony joined her. He climbed behind the wheel seeking her eye. She didn't turn, afraid he'd read hate in her gaze. She just needed time. Just a little time…

"Thank you. I'm so sorry," Tony whispered, but she did not reply.

Tony informed her that he'd tied the monster up securely and heard from Mark, that he would do whatever was necessary to resolve the situation. Before they reached the house, Sarah had grown a little more peaceful and she touched Tony's shoulder across the truck.

"I forgive you. That was horrible. And I pray right now in Jesus' name that this never, ever, ever happens to me again."

"Honey," he offered and she shook her head.

"You think I'm perfect, an angel, a woman of God," she said and broke into tears. "But tonight, I hate you. I will be okay. I will come back to plumb with God. Just give me some time."

Tony said nothing and she was glad.

19

So then, my beloved brethren, let every man be swift to hear,
slow to speak, slow to wrath; for the wrath of man
does not produce the righteousness of God.
James 1:19

AS AMAZING AS HE WAS, MARK COULD NOT BE TWO PLACES at once. Well hidden in the shadows of the woods that surrounded the magier's dwelling, he trusted Tony's God would help him sort out his emergency for the moment. Hope's error seemed more urgent and Mark watched the small caravan across the clearing. No doubt, the supernatural senses of Hope's new pal had picked him up, but Mark chose to wait. He leaned against a slender birch, arms crossed at his chest, eyes trained to the silver-and-rust structure the traveling *vampyr* called home. Mark's full-length dark gray trench coat blocked the cold wind, but he didn't notice, his mind preoccupied with Hope.

Hope. What had she done? And why had she done it? What were the odds that his lovesick companion would run into another of his kind when he was otherwise occupied? And how long had this wild child been out here on his own? With no master, no direction? The Other admitted to knowing of him but not creating him. So, who? This puzzled Mark the most. He scoffed at the ramblings. None of that mattered now.

Did this fop have any idea what he was doing? What if she decided to stay with this carnival vampire? Would he allow it? He had the power to force his will but had no desire to do so. What would Hope choose? Mark focused on the trailer door. The magier was in there, thinking God knows what. Mark concentrated on his unknown brother and willed him to come out. Standing up off the tree, he uncrossed his arms and put his hands into his coat pockets. His mind clear, he decided he would face the matter as it came without planning or plotting. After all, Mark didn't know how he wanted it to end.

The trailer door came open and a man's form filled the negative space. Mark concentrated on his thoughts. The magier was younger than Mark, or at least, had been when he had been transformed. He was dark and handsome, and his overall expression was one of amusement. Mark also saw in those short seconds the man was a playboy, but he was no monster. The carnival kept him occupied and he had developed quite a system of drawing blood from the mortals in his company while protecting his secret. Taking it all in, Mark stood tall, his expression determined, and waited for the magier to make the first move.

Androni remained at the door of his trailer, fingers on the handle, unsure of what to do. The woman's lover was there, in the dark, under the trees. He knew all of this intuitively, and it felt good to have "switched-on" again after so long. Since the other vampire's arrival, Androni had felt more alive than he had in centuries. His eyesight was sharper, his hearing more acute, and his body... oh, his flesh fairly hummed with excitement.

Androni glanced backward at the woman sleeping across the room. Her breathing was gentle and rhythmic, as it should be. He hadn't harmed her. Surely the man outside would know that. He would not have any reason to be angry. Maybe the vampire would thank him. After all these months beside that beautiful creature and he never laid a hand on her? Maybe he'd done the guy a favor.

Androni chuckled. He'd never know what the man thought if he didn't do something. Taking a deep breath, he took the two metal steps to the ground. The woman's lover was twenty meters away beneath white-barked trees, hidden from the light of the full moon. Yet, Androni hadn't needed any light. He saw the man clearly. He managed a half-smile and nodded, a gesture he hoped conveyed confidence and an invitation to come closer. When the man did not move, Androni took two steps from the trailer and motioned with his right arm toward his door.

Won't you come in? he thought, a laugh in his heart. He wanted to remain jovial, after all, he had not approached this mad woman for affection; hadn't she practically seduced him? Androni remained optimistic and waited for the stranger to approach. After a few more seconds, the man moved toward him. When he left the woods and entered the clearing, Androni moved to the side of his door, and with the flair of a showman, lifted his arm to welcome the visitor inside.

"Please come in. I have been expecting you." Androni hoped he sounded brave because to his own ears he sounded childish and afraid.

When he was close, he stopped and greeted him face-to-face.

In one brief glance, Androni gleaned a plethora of information from the man's mind. The first thing he knew when looking into Mark's dark eyes was that he was powerful, and he knew it. This vampire had seen and done more in his lifetime than Androni could even imagine, and much of it was bloody and abhorrent to the man who had executed the deeds. Mark carried within him an equally great regret. Androni didn't know how to receive all that he'd discerned, so he decided to play it cool with a healthy dose of respect. He waited for the stranger to enter and then followed him in, masking his anxiety beneath an easy smile.

First, the man stepped to where Hope lay sleeping on the mussed bed. Androni locked the door and stayed put, waiting patiently for his turn at the visitor's attention. This vampire was taller and had to stoop to avoid the low ceiling.

Androni pulled out a chair near where he stood and motioned for his guest to sit on the edge of the bed. "Won't you have a seat, Herr? I realize this is a rather small caravan for a man of your stature." Androni suddenly hated the sound of his voice, but his visitor sat next to the sleeping Hope.

The silence lingered as Androni wondered who would begin the conversation. Finally, the man sighed with what sounded like impatience.

Androni said the first words that came to mind. "Welcome to my home."

The vampire's eyes flashed with irritation. "What is your name?"

"My apologies, my name is Androni Miklos. I go by Androni the Magnificent." Androni smiled, but his guest relayed no reaction. "You are Mark, and this woman is yours, no?"

His guest glanced at the woman, his face softening. "Can you own the wind?"

Androni shifted in his chair and watched the other man's face. Was he angry? He tried a new tact. "The woman is headstrong."

His guest laughed aloud, his voice booming in the small space. "I won't keep you, Androni. I can see that everything is under control." The vampire stood.

"Wait. You're not leaving?" With a dash of panic, Androni stood as well, not ready to end his new acquaintanceship. "Aren't you going to take her with you?" Androni hadn't planned on that contingency.

"You seem like a nice fellow, and I'm sorry we are meeting under these circumstances, but I will let you in on a little secret concerning Ms. Hope Brannen."

"Yes?"

"She is incorrigible. I can see that you are a man without guile." Corescu paused as his compliment sunk in, and then continued with a wry smile. "She is aware I monitor her safety and she tests me constantly."

"Ah. And you wanted to see if she'd go through with it," Androni offered in a polite tone.

"I imagine I did," he admitted.

"You're not *angry* with Androni?"

Corescu stepped close and clapped him on the shoulder. "Perhaps she will have learned a lesson. Maybe she'll have it out of her system. At any rate, no, I'm not angry with you. Disappointed in her, but not angry with you. I thought you handled yourself well under the circumstances. A lesser man, mortal or immortal, could have made this her last error in judgment."

"I am a gentleman." Androni flashed his teeth in a wider smile, now wondering what it would take to get the man to stay, his mere presence invigorating Androni to the core. "Are you leaving her in my care?"

"I am not able to take her home this moment. I ask you to allow her to remain here until morning. I will send a car to pick her up around 9 a.m. Then she can decide if she will come home."

"You walk in the day?" Androni asked and when he didn't reply in a breath, qualified with, "I do, as well." Androni waited for more conversation and he had so many questions. How old was he? Where was he born? Did they have the same master? Was that even possible? His guest grunted with impatience and Androni asked. "What do you think she'll decide?"

"She'll return to me. I ask that you keep her safe until the car arrives."

"Of course. But Herr…" Androni glanced at her sleeping form and then back to the doctor, "How can I find you? I have not seen another of my kind since the beginning. My master deserted me and I have never been happier than I am right now in your shadow." Androni watched his guest's face and the empathy he read encouraged him. "I want to know you, and anything I have is yours. Everything I have, I give to you. What do you say?"

Thoughts of traveling alongside such a powerful vampire tickled his mind, but the man's face remained rigid. He was considering Androni's offer, but it was taking too long. Androni fell to his knees, desperate for the man to accept. Taking Mark's right hand in both of his, he begged the man to agree to his wishes.

"Please, Herr. *Kérlek, vigyél magaddal,*" Androni said in his first tongue.

"I will not be in the way. I only want to learn from you."

After several seconds, his guest rolled his eyes. "I'm returning to the States. You may follow me there if you wish."

"*Csodálatos!*"[6] Androni whooped and regained his feet, slamming his palms against the metal ceiling of his trailer, the most agreeable sensation flooding his flesh.

Mark put a finger to his lips. "Tomorrow, when the car comes for Hope, you may come as well. Tell Hope she may go to my house in the country or fly with you to join me in the States."

"Yes, but, wait, please. I have one more week of performances. I do not think I can leave before I have collected my wages." Androni grimaced as he spoke the truth, but he had never been wealthy.

Mark reached for his wallet and turned out every bill. "This will get you wherever you want to go. If you get in my car tomorrow, my driver will bring you to the airport. Do you have a passport?"

"I do." Androni absently counted the first few bills, but when he reached one thousand American dollars, he stopped and pocketed the cash with a whistle. "You won't regret it. I have a lot to offer. A lot more than I can tell you about in this short time…"

"Good enough." Mark clapped him on the back and Androni leaned toward the door.

"No, leave the door closed. Your celebratory racket must have half the camp out of bed. I will depart from here."

"Pardon?"

His guest put a finger to his temple. "If you need to reach me before we meet again, she knows how."

He winked once to Androni and disappeared. Androni gasped. Oh, what wonderful things this vampire could teach a willing student! And what a marvelous magician he would be if he could disappear, too!

Androni's heart swelled with happiness and soon the caravan was filled with the sound of singing. The feckless temptress in his bed slept on, but the promises of the future were now brighter than the moon.

---

6 "Wonderful!" (Hungarian)

20

"All who behave unrighteously
Are an abomination to the Lord your God."
Deuteronomy 26:12

TONY LEANED AGAINST THE PASTURE FENCE LOOKING toward the house. Sarah had not spoken since they returned from Haman's store and he was too confused by the day's events to attempt placations. He had a conviction on him that would not pass no matter how many excuses he invented to explain his behavior.

What do You want from me, Lord? I said I'm sorry. I have no idea what You want!

With his head bowed and his hands clasped, Tony concentrated on the vampire in Europe. The older and wiser Master, who was responsible for Haman Troye's condition. He should know that a mere mortal took advantage of him a hundred years ago. He should know and he should come and take care of it; Tony did not want to ever lay eyes on Haman again.

"Doctor Corescu? Answer me…" Focusing down, Tony pictured the old vampire in his mind and found him crossing a hallway in a cavernous stone-walled space, presumably his home in Germany. *"Are you coming? I need you. Something has happened…"*

With a short sigh, Mark said he was coming and shut him out. Tony wasn't finished.

"Why didn't you admit you knew the vampire, Haman?" Tony sent and glanced toward the house. The only light that burned was the one in the den. He imagined Sarah writing in her journal as she did every night, probably recording the horrible things Tony did to her earlier.

"I do not know that vampire." The Doctor's mental voice was insistent and Tony again closed his eyes to reply.

"Haman Troye stole this curse from you in 1915. He is dangerous and has turned a local pastor's boy into a vampire…" Tony did not hide his frustration. *"Can you take care of him? He is bound and waiting for you but I don't think we have much*

111

time…" Guilty, frustrated and painfully aware of his desperate tone, Tony became quiet and waited for the doctor's response. A few long moments ticked by before he heard a reply. And Tony thanked God it was what he wanted to hear.

"I will come now," is all the doctor said.

Abruptly, Tony was released, the line was down and Corescu was gone.

Tony started the engine and pulled down the long driveway to the electronic gate. It was time to visit the Ellerslies. A brief phone call determined the family did not consider their son missing. That meant Joseph had come home. Tony would go see what Haman accomplished. Was there even a tiny chance the vampire had lied?

Tony wished, but that didn't make it so. No response from the heavens made Tony even more uneasy. Ever since he had his altercation with Haman, he had not heard from God.

He was winging it.

And it felt dangerous.

Haman Troye.

Mark knew the name, but before now, it held no significance. Troye had been a businessman and landowner in the early twentieth century when Mark lived up north. Posing as a country doctor, Mark had bought property from the man. End of contact. To hear the man stole the curse off him a hundred years ago? If he didn't have the proof sitting in a bookstore back room, he'd have thought it inconceivable.

"Haman Troye. Show yourself," Mark sent to the man's mind, telegraphing his will with precision developed over four centuries. Through a hazy mental picture, Troye lounged in a dark space, unbound, his hand rubbing his own belly in an even languid stroke.

"Agricola?" he said aloud in the room, searching the four corners.

"It is Doctor Crump. Turn on the light. This instant."

Haman jumped to his feet and flicked on the overhead light, his eyes growing round. "But I thought…"

"Shut up," Mark said with stern authority. *"Look into the corner. Focus. Do not blink."*

Without understanding, but not willing to disobey, Haman did as he was told. "Yes, doctor. I'm looking…" he said, standing at attention.

Mark concentrated on the water-stained wall Troye stared at so intently and willed himself there. With a whoosh of air across his cheeks, he arrived in Haman's dusty apartment. Mark glared at Haman and waited for the dolt to raise his eyes. For the moment, he appeared terrified out of his wits. With his eyes flitting to Mark, the floor, the ceiling, and the door behind him, Haman finally dropped to his knees and covered his face with both hands.

"I don't understand. How did you find me?" he yelped, muffled as it was through his closed fingers.

"How? I can do whatever I please," Mark said, playing up his role since he had the vampire on the run. He reached down to grasp Haman by his hair. "Come. Let me have a look at you." The cowering Troye rose to his feet pulled upward. He wouldn't meet Mark's eye, so he released the oily strands to grasp both shoulders, forcing the man to stand face to face.

"Really, Haman. Look at me." Mark squeezed until Haman winced. "Why are you afraid? You showed no fear the night you attacked me."

"Doctor Crump, please…" he replied, his voice wavering. "I didn't mean you any harm. I knew you wouldn't die. It was the dream! I dreamed about you and I thought…"

"Ah, yes, the dreams. I see them now." Mark scowled, feeling sullied by merely peeking into the contemptible creature's innerspace. "Your mind is full of such vile notions…"

A young man came to Haman's mind and Mark looked on only a moment before the vampire ran the boy through a few despicable machinations.

"Stop!" Mark spat in disgust and withdrew from Haman's head, the man's private thoughts a dark vacuum, more void than any of the hundred-thousand killers Mark judged in his past life.

Haman did not reply, whimpering from Mark's cruel grip and looking aside.

"Is there any saving you?" Mark said knowing the answer.

The vampire finally swiveled his gaze forward and looked into Mark's eyes. "You speak like Agricola. Have you fallen for the lie? God? The Cross?" Haman spat, the phlegm landing harmless to Mark's lapel. "There is no salvation for vampires. *You* are the weak one." Haman's voice grew hard. "You are despicable to our kind…"

Mark moved the contact from the man's shoulders to his throat and he held him fast, his fingers touching behind his neck. The man's eyes reddened and he grasped Mark's forearms. Mark *tsked*, sensing the words

113

welling up from deep within, the words he spoke to his judging victims for four hundred years. But now he recognized whose will he sought.

"Haman Troye, you are being judged. Repent of your sins and ask Jesus to save you." Mark did not allow him to break loose and Troye strength was as a baby to Mark's greater power. "Father-God, look at this creature. What will you do with him? Do you want me to kill him?" Mark sent Haman a single wink. "I'll do it, I'd be happy to choke his life out right now…"

Seconds ticked by and Mark waited, watching Haman's eyes darted rodent-like, never still. After a full minute with Mark intently watching Haman's face, a flash of light caught his attention. Diverting to the source, Mark beheld another man in the room with them. The man was so tall that his head brushed the ceiling. He wore a gray jumpsuit and a faded blue ball cap, but despite such banal trappings, Mark knew, this was most assuredly an angel of the Lord.

After dropping his eyes from the angel's out of respect, he released Haman's throat, shoving him bodily into the bright being.

"No! Wait! Stop!" Haman bellowed, now struggling with a huge hand clamping down hard on his inner shoulder.

Mark backed further away until his coat brushed the dirty wall and watched as the tall man in gray closed his eyes. With no further ceremony, Haman fell to the ground, crumpled into a lifeless heap. It was that easy. It was that anticlimactic. Mark continued his humble posture and waited for the being to speak.

Am I next? Is this it?

Instead of judging him, the angel spoke.

"This one has made his choice." The man in gray stepped away from Haman's corpse and faced Mark. "He is mortal and has suffered a mortal's heart attack."

Relieved at the nature of the message, Mark nodded once.

The angel lifted an object that materialized from the ether. "Take this dagger to the Little Shepherd. He has sinned and fallen off the path. Tell him he is unclean…"

Mark listened as the man in gray spelled out the Lord's will regarding Tony's rebuke and chastisement. Mark took possession of the familiar dagger, saddened at the memory of when he last saw it. This knife had been plunged into Paul's heart during his struggle with a nosy reporter named Connie Nixon. Also, it was the same knife Paul used to threaten John Jenkins and the knife he used several months ago to force Tony into the vampire's curse. As Mark tucked the evil blade away, he marveled that the item was inexplicably woven into the story of their lives even now. When the angel completed his message regarding Tony and how he would need to proceed to cleanse himself from his latest transgression, he disappeared without goodbye.

Mark gazed upon Haman's corpse. He smelled him; Troye was mortal.

If it is so easy to make that monster mortal, why doesn't the Lord do the same for Anthony and myself?

Mark did not dare ask that question but instead, headed home his way. Like a vampire. At least for now.

21

Are they [angels] not all ministering spirits sent forth to minister
for those who will inherit salvation?
Hebrews 1:14

THE ELLERSLIES DIDN'T LIKE TONY. WOULD THEY EVEN LET him in to see their son? Tony pulled into the Ellerslie's drive and switched off the truck. He had no idea how the boy's parents would receive him. Tony had few choices, so he lifted the heavy brass knocker and let it drop. It swung open without a wait.

"Brother Tony, what a surprise!" After a miniscule pause, Reverend Robert Ellerslie stood aside. "Won't you come in?"

Tony thanked him and stepped into the foyer. Ellerslie led him down a short hall and four more strides to a receiving room furnished with velour couches and medieval tapestries on three of the four walls. He gestured for the sofa.

"Can I get you something to drink? Honey," he called to the side. "Tony Agricola is here."

Tony shook his head and offered another thank you, a bit of hope building inside: perhaps Joseph's behavior hadn't changed. Maybe he was fine. It was obvious that the Ellerslies did not realize their son had turned into a vampire.

JoAnn Ellerslie strode in, chest out, her fingers poised to shake hands. "Well, howdy, Pastor Tony," she said, her accent as exaggerated as her enthusiasm. "Robert! Tuck in your shirt, for heaven's sakes!" She shooed her husband and he excused himself presumably to freshen up. "Pastor, let me fix you a glass of iced tea."

"No, thank you. I need to speak with Joseph. Is he in?"

His hostess's smile faltered at the mention of her eldest son, but she turned her face away and belted, "Joseph! Someone here to see you!" After giving Tony a new, tight smile, she crossed her arms, both of them standing between the couches. "He might not come out. Teenage angst."

"He won't come out of his room?" Tony asked in a gentle voice.

116

Robert Ellerslie joined them and clapped Tony on the back. "You know teenagers. He must have had a doozie of a night after the auction. He skipped church and has been locked up in his room all day."

Ellerslie appeared to be taking his son's odd behavior in stride, but Tony denoted worry hidden in his eyes.

"You haven't spoken to him about it?" Tony asked hoping to learn more from their replies. "He didn't tell you what happened?"

Mrs. Ellerslie dropped into the couch and turned her gaze to her husband. "Bob, did he talk to you? Is something wrong?"

"He's fine, Jo, he's fine." Reverend Ellerslie looked to Tony. "He's fine, right?"

"Yes, he's fine," Tony reassured them both with a tight-lipped nod. "I had a question for him about his assignment. Nothing big. Can I go to his room and speak with him there?"

Ellerslie stepped aside and motioned toward the hall. "Third door. See if you can lure him out."

Tony assured them again everything was fine and left them to find the door. He rapped twice on the wood and paused. Nothing, the room as quiet as a tomb.

"Joseph? It's Tony Agricola." Tony had whispered his words, which a vampire would have no problem hearing. The boy remained silent so Tony pressed his face to the doorjamb and said even softer, *"Open the door. I know what happened with Haman. I can help you."*

Joseph pulled the knob and Tony stepped into the dark bedroom. When the door closed, the kid pressed the thumb lock and faced Tony, his arms wrapped about his own chest.

"What's going on? How do you know?" he whispered in a gasp.

Tony's senses alerted him that the boy had fully transformed. With so much ground to cover, he better cut to the chase. "Come with me for a drive. We should take the explanation away from your parents. You haven't told them, right?"

"God, no! But how do *you* know? What do you think happened?" he asked, frantic.

"Shh, it's okay. You're going to be okay. I just came from the bookstore—"

"Oh, God! You saw him? Oh, God!" Joseph's hands flew to his mouth and he turned to peek out the blinds into the night. "He threatened me. I prayed for Jesus to keep him away…"

"Your prayer worked," Tony said keeping the same low voice.

117

"Haman is being dealt with by another, stronger vampire. One on our side."

Joseph's face whipped around. "What?" he asked incredulous. "You know he's a vampire?"

Tony gave a sad nod. "Come with me. Let me explain in the truck. Your parents…" he said trailing off as if the boy should figure out the rest.

Joseph held his eye a few long moments and then exhaled, turned for the window and lifted the sash. "I'll meet you outside. I'm not facing my parents. What if they see?" His raspy whisper broke and he re-covered his mouth, his eyes huge. *"I'm a monster!"*

"No, walk right beside me. They're worried enough." With his voice soft but meaning it, Tony approached the boy to face him square. "You don't look any different. Just walk with me, right out the door, past them, and I'll make excuses for you. They want to see you're in one piece."

A single tear welled in the boy's eye, his white-blond eyelashes flicking it away. "Why do you care?" he asked and then added, "Did God send you to help me?"

Tony gave him a nod. "You need help and I'm here." He clapped his outer arm. "Let's go. Just act normal."

Tony opened the door and the boy shielded his face from the light. In six long strides, they passed the boy's parents, him on the away side.

"Go on out to my truck, I'll be right there," Tony said stopping in the foyer to face the Ellerslies. "We're going for a drive," Tony said, slowing his movements, his words, and then his own breathing as he held first the Missus's and then the husband's eye. "We'll be back soon, everything is fine."

"Everything is fine, JoAnn," Robert Ellerslie said and nodded.

The wife took longer to fall for Tony's suggestion.

"What's going on? Why is he being so weird?" she said, her tone hard.

Tony licked his lips in slow motion, inside, willing the woman to believe him. No one had taught him the trick but figuring it out had been accidental. Now, he had gotten pretty good at it.

"He's just a kid, he's fine. You know teenagers," he told her, re-using her husband's phrase from earlier. After craning her head to see the front window, she'd see only the dark yard, she gave Tony a slow nod. "We'll return soon."

With a final farewell wave, Tony exited and jogged for the truck.

He wished them well in his heart. If they were this upset about their son leaving without saying goodbye, how would they handle it if he never came home because he had been transformed into a vampire?

Lord, I pray that You will give them peace and comfort in You tonight. They're gonna need it.

Joey sat in Pastor Tony's truck with his face in his hands. He had successfully exited the house and his parents saw nothing peculiar in their oldest son.

Thank God. Now what? What can I say to this Pastor guy? No matter what he thinks, he can't help me. And what does he know about vampires?

Joey was jolted from his worry by Pastor Tony's car door opening.

"How are you holding up?" the guy asked as he switched on the engine.

What could he say? Joey shrugged. Pastor Tony offered a comforting grin which he appreciated. Whatever the guy thought, he was sincere.

"I'm taking you to my house. Ms. Sarah's there. You remember her, right?"

Joey straightened up in his seat. *If that anointed woman knows about this…* "What's going on?" he asked exasperated. "Reverend Tracey knows about it, too?" He watched Pastor Tony's profile and the guy gave one nod.

"We'll be at my house in five minutes. Can you keep it together that long?" he asked shooting Joey a glance halfway through. "She and I both know Haman attacked you. We know he turned you into a vampire—"

"No!" Joey shouted and grasped the dashboard with both hands as new dread flooded his system. He'd had enough and none of this could be real. "LET ME OUT! RIGHT NOW!" he shouted, the cab of the truck too small for such decibels. His driver winced and pulled the truck to the shoulder. Instead of releasing Joey into the night, he turned in his seat and grabbed his bicep.

"Joseph Ellerslie," Pastor Tony said, his voice even but with an edge that surprised him. "Calm. The hell. Down," he said spacing the words and holding his eye.

"But," Joey countered and didn't say more. Agricola's grip wasn't cruel, but it was as if an iron cuff had been clamped there. "Who are you? Why do you care?" he whispered, and Pastor Tony released his arm.

"I am Anthony Agricola," he said and faced front to get the truck back on the road. "And I'm a vampire, too."

Joey's jaw dropped. He watched the man's profile and Pastor Tony said nothing else. The truck had turned onto Wares Ferry and the homes and estates were getting larger and larger. Soon he assumed they'd pull into the Agricola residence where Reverend Sarah Tracey—a woman of God who married a vampire—would try to help. Joey's mind raced in wonder and he held his tongue.

In another minute, Pastor Tony stopped at an electronic gate that inched open on powerful rods. He remained quiet as the truck wound down the long drive and found a parking spot at the front walkway. Agricola switched off the engine and swiveled to see Joey's face.

"Sarah and I know Haman attacked you. Come inside and let us tell you what's going on." Pastor Tony paused and Joey guessed he was supposed to respond. Instead, he only nodded. The man climbed down from the truck and met him at the walkway. The reverend met them in the front door and she hugged Joey around the neck.

"You poor baby," she said in his ear and then led him to another room by wrapping her arm in his. "I'm so sorry your trial went this way, but God is with us. You know that, right?" she asked and expected Joey to agree. He allowed her to pull him to a couch and they sat together.

"I … I…" he stammered. "I don't see how God would allow this to happen. I don't think He did this."

The reverend laughed soft and was still holding his arm so she squeezed it once. "Oh, He did. Remember your prophecy? The devil tries to kill you and God saves you for His purposes. He's doing something here. You'll see."

Tony Agricola was entering now and he leaned on a massive desk across from where they sat.

"Listen to Tony. He has a tale you'll recognize." She gave him another squeeze and faced front with a smile.

Amazed at her composure, Joey matched her posture and Tony Agricola exhaled.

"None of this is simple, but listen," he said, his tone gentle. "I was just a guy working in my dad's church when God dumped me right into this world of real-life vampires. I resisted listening to Him for a long time, angry He let this happen, but Sarah's right. I see now that He made me this way for a purpose. I want you to see that, too. I want you to skip the fear and distrust of God's plan and just let Him lead us."

Joey didn't mean to, but his head had been shaking "no" for Pastor Tony's entire speech. And then, in a blink, a fourth person was with them in the room. In the opposite corner and in his peripheral vision, a tall, aristocratic figure stepped into the light thrown by the small lamp.

"Haman Troye is dead," he said his voice slightly accented. He turned his gaze to Joey and Joey's skin tingled at the eye-meet.

"Mark, this is Joseph Ellerslie," Pastor Tony said then. "Joseph, meet Dr. Mark Corescu. Also a vampire."

Joey figured his mouth was open but he didn't close it. This guy looked the part, handsome, a commanding presence, his every movement catlike and measured—he was what Hollywood had in mind for their sort and this made Joey frown. He himself was naturally pale as a ghost and Agricola? He looked like an accountant. With a sudden surprising thought, he whipped his gaze to the reverend.

"Ma'am, are you—" He didn't get to finish. Sarah Tracey shook her head with a sweet laugh.

"No, it's not my lot, I suppose," she said and sent her husband a look Joey couldn't read. Then her smile dropped and she asked the doctor, "Haman is dead?"

The tall vampire sighed once and crossed to be closer to Pastor Tony. Joey watched them communicate with glances and whispers and he strained to overhear.

"Troye was killed by the hand of an angel ..."

Pastor Tony's eyes widened with surprise. "An angel? You're sure?"

Mark answered aloud, "As sure as the Lord lives. Come. The boy is listening."

Joey parted his lips and shook his head, but the intriguing character took Pastor Tony's bicep and led him from the room. Reverend Tracey made small talk on his left, but he tried very hard to hear what they discussed. After all, it pertained to him, right? When the back door closed and he realized they left the house he exhaled.

"Go ahead, Joseph. Ask. I will tell you whatever I can." Sarah Tracey's eyes were full of the love and grace of God. Joey wanted to sit under her gaze forever and he said so. She laughed once. "Well, it's all Him, believe me. What do you want to know?"

Joey flicked his thumb the way Pastor Tony left. "Who was that? Is he like, the vampire king?" The electricity and power that exuded from the man jump-started Joey's already anxious heart. Only now, instead of being frightened and depressed, he was suddenly hopeful, power being a very attractive quality.

"That man used to be a clergyman in Europe in the 17th Century. He was made this way in 1640."

The reverend stopped speaking and Joey looked back to her face, unaware that he'd been daydreaming. "He's been a vampire all this time?" he asked incredulous.

The reverend nodded. "But he doesn't drink human blood and that's the first thing you need to know. Tony and Dr. Corescu seek to be delivered of the vampire curse. Soon, God will lift it off them so they're both trying to behave."

A shadow passed her expression and Joey noticed. "What? Are you okay?" She waved her hand.

"Oh, yes, but when the men return, you can ask more vampire questions. I want to tell you what God is doing. Will you listen?"

"How did he appear out of nowhere? Is this one of our powers?" Joey asked, not intending to disregard her question.

"No, honey, and you forget yourself. This is not a party."

Sarah spoke with authority and Joey was speared with shame for his behavior. He apologized and she continued.

"The Lord has spared you for a reason. *His* purposes. Never forget who you belong to. You have been bought by a price. A very dear price."

"You're right. I'm sorry." Joey lowered his gaze and tried to concentrate on a prayer. *Lord? What now? How in the world can I be a good disciple and a vampire at the same time? Won't I be thinking of sucking blood all the time? Won't I be dreaming of death and preaching about life? Aren't I going to be a miserable failure in the end?*

"Joseph," the reverend said, her voice in a gasp. Joey looked up and she had flushed forehead to neck and he asked if she was okay. "Yes, but I'm getting a Word…"

Joey remained at attention and waited. Then the woman closed her eyes with a single nod and began to speak, her voice flowing like water to his ears.

"This is what the Lord says. 'You are the apple of My eye. I sing over you day and night. I pray for you to the Father even as you dream in your bed at night. I will never leave you nor forsake you. Hold fast to My commandments. Hold fast to My Truth and My Spirit and you will never go wrong. Hold fast until the End. You are My chosen. My anointed. My love."

Joey opened his mouth in shock. *God is speaking directly to me!*

"Yes! Thank You, Lord! I will hold fast!" Joey hugged himself and closed his eyes. *"But you gotta help me. You gotta help me…"* Joey prayed and Jesus hugged him tight. Best of all, His arms were strong.

122

22

For I know the thoughts that I think toward you,
says the LORD, thoughts of peace and not of evil,
to give you a future and a hope.
Jeremiah 29:11

"DRIVE EAST AND I'LL TELL YOU WHEN TO TURN. THE DRIVE will take an hour."

Tony put the truck in gear wondering at the doctor's morose behavior. When they left Joseph with Sarah, he had thought they were stepping to the yard to speak privately, but Mark instead took him to the vehicles and said they would go for a ride. He had instructed Tony to text Sarah a cryptic message and get them on the road. Between them the doctor had brought along a hidden object, long, slender, and wrapped in black. Tony could only imagine it was a sword by the shape but he wouldn't ask before it was time. Now it seemed they had a destination and Tony chose his words with care.

"What's going on?" Tony attempted to read ahead, but the doctor's thoughts were closed off. He took a guess. "Is Hope okay?"

Mark huffed once. "Ask me another time. We have a pressing matter and it is not my place to interrupt God's timeline."

Tony inhaled. He was in trouble and he didn't know where the sentiment originated, his own guilty conscience or from God Himself. "It has to do with Haman."

Mark did not reply; instead, he turned his gaze to the lights zipping past in the darkness.

"Is this a knife?" he asked with a knuckle to the item between them.

"I will show you when we get to the cabin."

"The cabin?" Tony repeated and Mark nodded once.

The cabin...

Tony recalled the doctor's hideaway from discussions with Paul. The two vampires had used it last year when Reuben was killed. It was remote and private. With increasing dread, Tony attempted to calm his mind. After a while, he asked what Mark thought about Joseph.

Mark did not turn his head. "What's to think? Haman brought an innocent boy into this existence, and he's very hungry." Mark flicked his gaze to the right and Tony peeked over. "Turn in there. We're here."

Tony worked the truck down a gravel road that gave way to red clay, closed in by pines and wild bushes the further they traveled. He had no trouble seeing in the dark, but imagined with his original vision, he'd have been blind since the moon was obscured by clouds tonight. Then a rustic cabin emerged sitting on a tiny clearing, mostly of log with a slatted tin roof.

"This is where Paul hid out when you first left for Europe," he said low, knowing from discussions in their time together. Mark had no reply and Tony discerned his heart still ached with loss. "I'm sorry," Tony offered in a near whisper. "I guess I forgot … how close you were." Then he parked and Mark still hadn't spoken. Whether he pondered Paul or the big thing they were at the remote cabin for, Tony needed to say it. "I miss him, too. I'm sorry he's dead. And that's the truth."

Mark swiveled his gaze in the dark interior and for a split second, and maybe only in his vampire mind, he saw Mark four centuries ago, new to the world of vampires, full of questions and not anywhere near the colossus of wisdom the man was now.

"I appreciate that," he said in the same low tone. Then with a closing exhale, he opened his door, filling the cab with artificial light. He took hold of the wrapped item. "Come, we will begin."

Tony trailed him and once inside, Mark secured the door. He did not light a lamp and the room was dark, only lit by the strange light his new eyes provided. Without words, the doctor unwrapped the item and set it in view on the tattered sofa. Tony gulped. That knife had been plunged into his chest and he remember the sensation as if it only just happened. Mark then positioned him in the center of the single-room cabin, and they stood toe to toe. He placed both hands to Tony's outer arms.

"Relax your focus," Mark said and closed his eyes. Tony did too and waited. "You will see the angel I saw. Let it come."

Mark's voice, smooth and calming, served to help Tony open his mind to the coming exchange. Then, the room filled with light. First a little, but then incrementally brighter and brighter until Tony discerned a man-shaped being in the center of the wondrous brilliance. The angel turned its face to Tony although he could see no indentions of eyes, nose, or mouth. It lifted one arm pointing to the couch.

124

"Take this dagger and plunge it directly into your heart…"

The angel's voice entered Tony's ears but also seemed to bubble up from inside his head. He listened and prayed for God to help him keep his cool, terrified suddenly that his punishment was greater than he could bear.

"You have strayed, Little Shepherd, and your flock is in danger. The blood you have consumed is tainted. It will kill you and you will not fulfill your purpose. You should not have taken that which belongs to the enemy. That which the Lord deems detestable should be totally destroyed. A man of God never takes the enemy's spoils for his own gain."

Tony shivered, the dread creeping close.

"As the defilement leaves your body, do not watch it go. No one must see it go. No one…" The angel swiveled to Mark a brief moment and returned to pointing its face to Tony. *"When it is done, remove your shoes. Seclude yourself. Deny yourself food and drink forty days. Repent, pray, intercede, and thus the defilement will depart."*

The message ended and the angel vanished so abruptly, it was as if it had never been there. Tony's eyes fluttered open. "Sarah. You'll have to tell her."

Mark brought his hands to himself and offered a grave nod. "It is my lot to shepherd your group for this period."

"And the boy," Tony said as a statement. "Explain it to him. Help him…"

Mark nodded and reached for the knife. Tony's skin prickled.

"Where?" he asked, his voice breaking. Mark scanned left and right as if he hadn't considered the mess and then gestured for the wall sink. Tony trudged over with the enthusiasm of a death row inmate and Mark stood beside him as he looked into the porcelain. "Will you…?" He couldn't finish, but Mark nodded.

"When the blade enters, it will push your breath out." The doctor's voice had softened and Tony met his eye. Mark gave him a gentle smile. "Nonetheless, you must lean over the sink and remember to close your eyes."

"No one must see it go, okay." Tony took a deep inhale and braced himself on the edges of the cold sink wall. There would be no way to prepare for what was about to happen so he rolled in his lips, gave Mark one last glance and closed his eyes. "Do it."

Then a sledgehammer pounded his chest.

With a tremendous shout, Tony folded forward, the sensation of Mark's hand firm against the back of his neck nothing to that of his life slipping away. The stab wound did not ache or even hurt, but a dull throb began in Tony's head as his body emptied of blood.

Don't look. Don't look, he mumbled inside and his knees buckled. Before he went down, Mark's steadying support held him over the sink now with two strong hands. He did not have to see the blood leaving his body to know it was going fast. In a haze of dreamy grogginess, the sound of liquid hitting the porcelain reached his ears. The vile substance carried the odor of Haman Troye. Tony convulsed once, twice, and then again, his flesh struggling to cleanse itself.

Then quiet.

With an unimaginable release, Tony's muscles fell lax and he collapsed to the counter, his upper body threatening to land in the sludge he dare not look in to. Then the water was running and gentle hands moved him to the floor, arranging his arms and legs to be lying flat on his back, hands by his sides.

"Be still," Mark said above him and could be heard tending to rinsing the tainted vomit down the drain.

"Almighty God," Tony whispered aloud and in his heart, *"I have sinned against You. You are so good to me and I really messed up. If You will forgive me, I will make sure it never happens again. I repent, O Lord, I delight in Your Word and Your will. I am strong in You."*

Corescu was tugging at his shirt now, unbuttoning, moving it off his person. A cool rag was drawing across his skin, washing the wound that had already begun to close. The doctor's touch was so tender, an immortal being, a vampire, who tended a sinner's wounds with immense care.

"Thank you," Tony whispered to Mark and added to the air, "Thank you, Father, for Mark. Thank you for leaving Sarah and the boy out of it. Thank you…"

"Anthony, your shoes," Mark said and Tony kicked them off in a quick movement and fell still.

"It is done."

Tony creaked open his eyes as Mark stood from the floor and crossed his arms at his chest. The doctor was thinking about Tony's friends. About his wife. About Elizabeth Hawken…

Mark looked down to Tony on the floor and a tiny smirk hit his mouth. "If you wanted me to move in with you, you could have simply asked."

Tony considered his words a few seconds, not accustomed to the vampire making jokes. Then Mark raised his eyebrows and chuckled. He put out his hand.

"Get up. You're done."

"I *wish* I was done. Forty days…" Tony took his help and stood up, feeling weak, but otherwise clear-headed. "Another forty-day fast," he mumbled and looked about the single room.

"This is it. Twelve miles from the nearest human abode. You have a bed," the doctor pointed to one corner. "And not that you'll need it, but the great outdoors was Paulie's toilet before…."

Tony nodded aware that again, the memory of Paul Black worked a sad frown on the doctor's face. "Have you visited his grave?"

Mark huffed. "No," he said and turned away. He crossed to the door and turned to face Tony. "I will leave you with the truck. I will take care of your people."

With one last long eye-meet, Mark disappeared.

Forty days? Forty Days? The Lord will sustain me. I know He will somehow. Somehow. Tony slumped into the lumpy couch and sighed. The last time he went forty days without blood, Rakha came and took advantage of his weakness. What a nightmare than monster had been.

"May this fast end up better than the last," Tony said to the air and chuckled at his rhyme. But seriously, he meant it.

"Can I call you Joey?" Sarah asked and he nodded. She pointed to the stairs. "The first room on the right was John's. I'm sure he'd be happy to know you adopted it."

The boy turned to her with his eyes wide. "Pastor Jenkins lives here?"

Sarah sighed, weary to the bone and worried about her husband. The doctor had taken him away and so far, the only news she had was that they were "okay." She rallied her energy to hide her exhaustion from their guest. "John stayed here sometimes but not anymore."

"Reverend Tracey, where did the doctor go? Will he be back?"

"So many questions," she said with a gentle laugh. "Can I answer them in the morning? Try to get some rest."

"But Reverend Tracey, I can't sleep. Not now. Not anytime soon. What am I going to do all night?"

Sarah recalled Tony's problem with the issue and she sighed. Did she need to sit up with him? Was that what God wanted? She thought about walking the boy to the study when a familiar voice called from the foyer.

"Reverend Tracey? I have returned."

Sarah walked to the front of the house, the boy right behind her. She met Mark Corescu's eyes and he bid her come closer. With a quick glance to the boy, she did and he spoke to her close.

"God sent an angel to chastise your husband for taking Haman's blood. In forty days, he will return."

Sarah's heart swelled with more worry than before. "And what? What else? Where is he?"

Mark gave her a friendly nod. "He is safe. I have some property an hour away and he will wait on the Lord. I am permitted to check on him and I will keep you informed. He is safe."

Sarah read in the vampire's eyes that whatever her husband faced, it had already been horrible. Perhaps the worst was done. With a calming exhale, she gave him a nod. "Thank you. For everything. For caring."

"I have assumed guardianship of your home, of the boy," he said and flicked his gaze over her shoulder. "I will take charge of him. You have done well."

"Well, hah," she said with a weak laugh and sighed. "Thank God," she whispered and turned the new vampire over to the old. Then with a final farewell, she went up to bed. And just for good measure, no matter how fruitless, she bolted the door.

23

Then you will call upon Me and go and pray to Me,
and I will listen to you.
Jeremiah 29:12

HOW DO YOU SPEAK TO A FOUR-HUNDRED-YEAR-OLD impossible creature? Joey watched the doctor wish Sarah Tracey a good evening and awaited a prompt. Should he shake hands? That was stupid... Maybe a nod? Or just say, Hi? Hello? *Greetings?* The doctor finally looked his way.

"Good evening, Joseph. Or do you prefer Joey?"

Joey managed a nod.

The doctor considered him a long moment, tilted his head to one side and then sighed. "Follow me," he said and turned away, passing Joey with a swish of air. He smelled of cologne, musky, pleasant, and Joey followed him, trying to think up an amazing reply. The doctor led him to a large study and pointed to one of two leather recliners. When Joey settled in one, the doctor did, too.

"I am a man of few words. Why don't you let me talk and I might answer a few questions at the end." The man smiled and rested his chin in his hand.

"Yes, thank you, Doctor Corescu." Joey did not relax but he calmed himself in increments. How had he come to be here? A few short days ago, he was a boring kid struggling through Statistics 101. But now? A real-life vampire sat ready to tell him how to be one of the Undead.

"Listen," the doctor said his tone like one of his college profs. "I have murdered one hundred thousand men and women in my lifetime. Only when I met Tony Agricola did I cease that behavior. I no longer drink human blood and as long as we are together, neither of us will permit you to do so."

The edict surprised him, but Joey did not interrupt. *Vampires drink blood, right?* He was missing something, and he waited and listened.

"Haman Troye is dead and the Lord sent Pastor Tony away for forty days. I will stay behind and watch over you, mentor and teach you. I will guard this household until Tony returns."

Joey still didn't know what to say and the doctor leaned forward.

"And I will teach you what you need to know about being a vampire."

Now Joey nodded with emphasis. "Yes, thank you," he whispered.

"There is one glitch."

Joey's hand went to his stomach and it magically grumbled. "Blood?"

The doctor nodded. "Feeding off vampires is also forbidden. Do you understand?" Joey nodded but the man added emphasis. "Forbidden means if you disobey this edict, you will be excommunicated."

Joey shook his head. "No, I understand. Really." He watched the man's dark eyes. No matter what happened in the days to come, he needed them. He needed this amazing creature's wisdom and the reverend's prayers. He didn't need human blood or vampire blood. But that left…

"I drink from animals," Corescu said then and stood.

Joey got to his feet. "I don't want to drink blood. I can't imagine it. I've tried. It's too awful."

The doctor sighed and narrowed his eyes. "Come close."

Joey walked up to him without hesitation, his commanding presence undeniable. The doctor scrutinized him a long time and then took his wrist, putting a finger to his pulse. He shook his head once.

"Your bloodlust has arrived. Ignoring it does not lessen its power." Then he turned for the hallway, tugging Joey behind by the arm. He walked for the back door and led him into the cool night air. Joey marveled at the bright starlight and the halo emanating from every object, but the doctor marched on, pulling him to the pasture gate and through and thru across the wet grass. His sneakers grew damp and they walked on, crossing the expanse until the house was the size of his thumbnail.

"Now," the doctor said and turned to face him. He dropped his wrist and took a deep breath. "Be very still and I will call up some dinner." He found his own words humorous because he grinned then and closed his eyes, tilted his regal head to the dark sky.

Joey waited, his eyes first examining the horizon, the clouds, and the lights of the city off in the distance, but then his gaze landed on the doctor. Taller by a head and built strong, a wide chest and tapered waist, brown hair to his collar and clean-shaven. Joey was thinking about classical movie actors when the sound of hoofbeats reached his ears. He looked toward the noise and a black horse trotted toward them, its nostrils puffing.

Joey shook his head. *Is he going to make me drink this horse's blood? I can't do that! It's disgusting!*

The horse reached them and stopped a few feet from the doctor. He touched its long face and asked Joey, "Are you familiar with horses?"

Joey shook his head. "I can't..."

Corescu shushed him. "You can and you will," he said with authority.

Joey watched him place one hand on the hairy mane and his free hand withdrew a small knife.

"You have fangs, but a horse's skin is thicker than a man's."

Joey's spine prickled with a mixture of disgust and intrigue. He still didn't want to think about drinking blood, but he took a step closer as the doctor touched the small blade to the animal's hide.

"This area," the doctor said moving the knife-tip in a four-inch circle, "is your strike zone and will provide blood without causing the animals undue discomfort."

With the skill and dexterity of a medical professional, the doctor forced the steel into the hide a centimeter and pulled back, making a gesture for Joey to move close.

Joey watched the thick fluid bubble to the surface and inch down incredibly slow and thick. Was he supposed to put his mouth on an animal? The doctor waited. Joey moved forward, eyes on the vampire and not on the horse. Then he smelled it.

Oh, God...

A pulse hit his middle, deep inside, deeper than his stomach. It was something else, not an actual organ, something *inside* Joey wanted that blood and wanted it *now*. With a tiny noise and resisting bile that threatened to surface, Joey surged in with speed, his mouth open to conform to the dusty hide.

Oh, god, oh god, oh god! he screamed inside as the animal's blood rushed over his palate and down his throat. *This is wrong! This is wrong! But OH-GOD!*

Then a strong as steel hand pulled him up and off. Joey resisted and fought to remain attached to the horse's wound, but the doctor shoved him then and he tumbled to the grass on his rump.

Oh, he was in heaven.

It was fifteen minutes before his head stopped spinning and the doctor led him back to the house. Joey was amazed, appalled, but most of all, in love with that horse and the blood it offered.

Oh, God help me.

It was good.

24

And you will seek Me and find Me,
when you search for Me with all your heart.
I will be found by you, says the LORD,
and I will bring you back from your captivity
Jeremiah 29:13-14

CORESCU'S CAR ARRIVED AS HE PROMISED, A SHINY BLACK
BMW Sedan driven by a stern white-haired chauffeur. The vampire's
woman flew into a rage when he suggested they go together to her lover
in the States.

"He doesn't want me!" she had shouted in his tiny caravan. "He only
wants to control me! And now he controls you, too!"

Androni worked very hard to convince her otherwise, but in the end,
she chose a different scenario altogether. Hope Brannen would stay in
Germany, but not in Corescu's castle. Instead, she instructed the driver to
take her to the Equestrian Center where she scoffed that she would stay
with friends until she found a new path.

What would the doctor do? Having no way of knowing, Androni
watched her depart the car and he continued to the airport.

An hour later, Androni boarded a 747 to America alone and he
wondered what would become of the brash, romance-addicted beauty. She
was quite a tasty lamb to be canvassing Europe without a chaperone, but
what could he do? Nothing. So Androni put her out of his mind and hoped
Herr Corescu would not blame him for her choices.

We make our own choices, he said inside, watching the passengers settle
into their various locations. He'd purchased a first-class seat and looked
forward to crawling above the clouds he'd only ever seen from below. The
ringmaster wished him luck, promising his job was always open should he
return. Androni left the bridge standing, but hoped to never come back. A
bright and exciting new life lay ahead in a new country he'd never visited.
With his hopes soaring high, Androni leaned back in the plush seat and
closed his eyes. The sounds of hearts beating, people whispering and

laughing, all living individual lives that each felt was more important than any other… all of this, the humanity, was food for his soul and Androni dozed. In his dreams, he and Herr Corescu joined forces and lived.

Oh, how they LIVED!

Hope watched the hired car pull away; the vampire inside hadn't even looked back. *Are all vampires rude jerks?* Sure, he had begged her to accompany him, but not because he liked her. No, it was to maintain his position with Mark. Androni the Magnificent had no affection for her, no commitment, no *interest.* Hope wiped a tear, refusing to allow more than a single drop.

I don't need *Mark. I only wanted him…*

Hope trained her gaze on the hostel located in the center of the equestrian facility. The truth of the matter was that Hope's husband, the one and only man she'd ever been to bed with, died in a car accident, leaving her with a sizable insurance payout. She wouldn't have to work for decades living off the interest. If she wanted to remain in Germany and ride, heck, she would.

Rusty's the best jumper Gregor's ever ridden—he was serious about that. If I put up with his hands, I'll be on the team. Once I'm on the team, the world will be at my feet.

Hope grinned. Being a top-level showjumper meant celebrity parties every weekend, training rides with the world's best coaches during the week and all the horses and horse-men she could ever want.

But no vampires…

Hope dropped her smile and began her trudge for the house. She'd go to her rented room, shower, and collapse on the bed. Maybe she'd cry a little. It was crazy to think a mythical creature such as Mark Corescu could find her company so compelling that he couldn't leave her side. Crazy? Well… That was a sore spot. Hope's twin, Glorie, had been certifiable, successfully hiding her psychopathy from three husbands, in-laws, and her own sister. But just because Hope's sister went mad didn't mean Hope would, too.

Hope paused her walk and looked at the cloudy sky. *Right, God?*

But she didn't know God the way Anthony and Mark did. Hope wanted to think He was taking care of everything, but she didn't have the inclination to change her ways on His account. Instead of truly focusing a thought toward the heavens, Hope jogged the rest of the way to the room.

When Mark asks me why I didn't come, I'll tell him. He ignored me too long and I don't deserve that. Frowning, Hope set her jaw.

Mark mulled his situation passing the time in Tony's basement. He could seclude himself there and besides the Ellerslie boy asking a question now and then, it was a peaceful place. Hope chose to remain in Europe and Mark didn't know yet how he felt about it. Androni carried no phone, but the driver had been instructed to inform Mark of the job's details. The man had taken Hope to her riding school and the "circus gentleman" to the airport. Mark had been amused at the chauffeur's word choice. Shortly, Mark would need to drive to Atlanta to pick the magician up. Androni the Magnificent meant no harm but adding him to the mix increased Mark's responsibility.

Upstairs, Tony's grandfather clock chimed the eleven o'clock hour. Twelve bells had passed since the youngest vampire took blood for the first time. Mark swiveled his gaze to Joseph, lounging on the far couch scrolling through his cell phone. At midnight, he made the youth text his parents a dictated note: *"I'm going on a ministry trip with the Agricolas. I'll be back in a week."*

The boy's parents responded with outrage, threats, and then rang his phone repeatedly, but Mark instructed him to answer in love but only through texting. In the end, it was three AM when they stopped jabbering back and accepted he'd gone out of town.

Upstairs, the familiar rumble of Elizabeth's car reached his ears and Mark looked toward the cellar door. The boy looked up from his phone.

"Who is it?"

"A friend," he answered keeping it short. "You will remain here. I will bring her to meet you if I feel it is appropriate." Mark leveled his gaze when the youth registered no reaction. "You stay here. Understand?"

Joseph nodded in rapid succession. "Yes, okay. I will."

Mark regarded him another long moment and headed up. When he reached the top, the reverend was showing the young woman to the kitchen. Mark considered the past ten days since he'd seen her and a lot had transpired since their kiss. Then, he did something he thought nothing of until it happened; he checked his shirtfront and smoothed his hair.

Did I just primp? Mark took a step backward, paused, and then turned away from the kitchen and ducked into the nearest restroom. He studied his reflection, deep in thought. Before meeting Hope and Tony, he always looked immaculate without even trying. His daily grooming came in rote behavior and Paul was there to straighten and clean anything that required that sort of attention. These days? Mark found himself on the move so often and unscheduled, that he sometimes did not shower for days on end. Of course, his body odor was nothing like a man's because he did not shed sweat. Instead, when he didn't bathe, his skin and clothing became musty and smelled of dirt. Mark sniffed his arm. It wasn't too bad, but he was not freshly showered and perfumed as when he visited with Miss Hawken in the past.

Marked huffed at his thoughts. He wanted to smell nice; something that hadn't entered his consciousness for hundreds of years. Now with a chuckle, he turned on the faucet and doused his arms to the elbow, doctor style, and used the decorative guest bathroom soap to wash. Then he leaned over the sink to wash his face as well. When he stood to towel away the moisture, he caught his eye in the reflection and shook his head.

Am I becoming mortal...?

Mark froze at that thought, rolling the words about, considering the implications. If God delivered him, would he leave the flesh? Working through the notion added nothing to his evening, so Mark cleared his mind and exited the small room. He headed for the kitchen and Sarah was offering Elizabeth a sandwich. When he reached the threshold, both women turned, but the expression in the young woman's face had become what he lived for—and Mark acknowledged it now. He had grown attached to her, something he hadn't allowed since meeting Paul. Yes, he enjoyed Hope's presence before Paul passed, but she had never been able to break past Mark's heart wall. But Elizabeth Hawken?

"Hey!" she said and rushed toward him without reservation or care.

He hadn't seen her for ten days, but no awkwardness was evident. Mark felt a reciprocating grin spread across his face as she hugged him about the middle. His eye lifted to the reverend who gave him a thumbs up. His arms rested across her back and she laughed when she pulled back.

"You're sort of out of practice," she said without a care and remained close, looking into his face, her arms to his sides. "Where have you been?"

Mark's brow raised by reflex, still not accustomed to being questioned by anyone about his doings, but he covered by pecking her forehead. When her light perspiration touched his tongue afterward, he realized he enjoyed that, too.

135

"Okay, I get it. Don't ask." Elizabeth dropped her arms and walked to the island bar stool. "We're about to have a sandwich. Sarah said there's been some excitement and Tony will be gone a little while."

Mark nodded and remained in the doorway. "This is true."

"She also said I should ask you about the boy." Elizabeth stopped there and Mark looked to Sarah who shrugged.

"Yes, downstairs is a local pastor's boy who has been made into a vampire." He smiled as her eyes grew round. She got off the stool and began asking him questions. Mark held up one hand. "What are you doing right now? Have plans?"

Elizabeth stepped closer shaking her head. Mark gave her a nod. "And you said we can get to know each other no matter what happens down the road." The young woman nodded again. "Then, ride with me to Atlanta. I can fill you in on the way and introduce you to a very interesting European magician once we reach the airport."

Elizabeth smiled wide, apologized to Sarah for leaving her alone, and grabbed her small handbag. "Let's do it."

Mark gave her a nod and ignored his heart, suddenly feeling too big for his chest. It was an odd sensation, but he enjoyed it. He made a decision to introduce her to the Ellerslie boy after she had the tale, so he asked her to wait in the foyer as he returned to the cellar.

"What's going on?" the boy asked coming to his feet as if expecting Mark to invite him up.

Over the past few hours, Joey had been informed of the bare basics regarding the vampire in Europe and Mark shook his head at the kid's anticipatory expression. "Wait for me to return. I will pick up Androni and bring him here."

"Can I come?" he asked his eyes begging.

"No, wait for my return," Mark repeated and turned away. Joey remained in the basement and Mark passed the kitchen to greet Sarah Tracey. "Joey will stay at the house and we will be back with Androni."

The woman gave a serious nod, also informed about Hope and her European vampire acquaintance. He would introduce Elizabeth to Joey later; for now, looking at the boy's confused and anxious expression soured his mood.

If turning mortal means worrying more than ever, then this is what I shall endure, Mark mused with no small chagrin and led Elizabeth to the car. At least the sight of Ms. Hawken always brought him joy and he was very thankful.

25

My brethren, count it all joy when you fall into various trials,
knowing that the testing of your faith produces patience.
James 1:2

BECAUSE SHE UNDERSTOOD HIM SO WELL, ELIZABETH GAVE Mark no grief when he asked her to wait at the concourse exit. The comfortable seating suited her fine and she sent him off with an infectious smile. He hadn't needed to explain; he desired to gauge the vampire's behavior anew before he allowed him access to their people.

As the transatlantic passengers disembarked Mark caught sight of his new ward. Androni made his way across the concourse dressed in the same clothes he'd been wearing the night they met and somehow, Mark wasn't surprised. In their brief time together, the magician made quite an impression—carefree, jovial, and extremely verbose. Three attributes Mark realized were not in his repertoire, might never have been, even before 1640. Still, his grin tucked in the side watching the wild one saunter toward his position, his long gray woolen coat with lapels to the hem flapped with each stride. He stepped with swagger, as if everyone should be wearing red and green patterned britches, thigh-high pirate boots and a white linen shirt buttoned only halfway; it billowed, opening to reveal a strong and mostly hairless chest. The people who noticed him looked twice. Some of the females looked three times. He was indeed striking, and Mark shook his head as their eyes met and Androni beamed him a toothy grin.

"Master Corescu!" he said in an undertone performing a half-bow, one forearm at his middle and one flat against his lower back. He straightened and stood at attention, heels clicking together. "I am your servant."

Mark chuckled. "At least you kept your voice down."

Androni huffed a small laugh. "Yes, I will tamp my over-expression. I am aware that you are a much quieter sort. In the circus, loud is proud."

Mark laughed low. He liked the guy; this could be interesting.

"And thank you. How marvelous." Androni scanned the bustling concourse. Then he looked back to show Mark his wide eyes. "And the plane ride? How wonderful it is! I should enjoy flying all the time if possible. I wonder why people complain about it!"

Mark again grinned, his behavior innocent and childlike. It was nice. So much of the past year had been serious and it occurred to him that moment that God may have sent the youngster to lighten up their morose party.

Androni clasped his hands. "Shall we depart?"

"Let us get your luggage and we'll head out."

"No luggage, Herr. Just me." Androni opened his hands palm up.

All the way from Europe with no belongings. Could he be any more eccentric? With a nod, he got them started in the general direction of where he'd stashed Ms. Hawken.

"And here is the leftover money…" Androni reached into his coat pocket and removed a wad of paper bills. "Fraulien Hope would not take any."

Mark noticed Androni stopped speaking as if concerned the topic angered him. Mark pretended he hadn't brought her up and refused the money. "Keep it. Tomorrow, buy some American clothing. Joseph will help you."

"Joseph?" Androni said as they walked. "He is like us?"

Mark hemmed and then allowed a tip of the chin. "I will introduce you tonight. Our drive home will take three hours, so you will hear the story on the way."

"A three-hour car ride," he said with new wonder. "I have traveled by train many times for longer, but never in a car."

Mark gave him a glance and continued forward through the busy crowd. "You've been sheltered to that extent?"

Androni chuckled with the fingers of one hand over his mouth. His movement drew attention, Mark noticed, as if the mortals felt he was flamboyant—not supernatural. Plus, his costume would serve to convince onlookers of his eccentricity. Mark decided that was fine; no one would peg him as a vampire.

"Herr Corescu, you are not unhappy with Androni for…" he said and drew out his sentence until Mark peeked at his face. "For not bringing your woman, eh?"

Mark shook his head while holding the man's gaze. "She has made her choice." Mark resumed their forward movement and added, "I am keeping an eye on her. If she runs into trouble, I will know."

"You are amazing," the magician said with true awe.

They had reached the final section before Elizabeth would come into view so Mark maneuvered Androni to an adjacent pillar. With the magician's back against the plaster, Mark spoke to him eye to eye, his tone soft but stern. "I brought a friend, her name is Elizabeth Hawken. I would like you to call her Ms. Hawken unless she says otherwise. Also, please call me Mark."

Androni smiled, a twinkle in his hazel-green eyes. He flicked his chin to send a lock of hair from his brow. "Mark," he said sounding out the single syllable with utmost respect. "Your friend Ms. Hawken smells wonderful."

Mark grinned now, knowing Androni referred to her scent transferred to his clothing. Having another vampire around, one who wasn't constantly pretending to *not* be a vampire, would be a nice change of pace. He may be seeking deliverance along with Tony, but Mark decided he would enjoy what pleasures he could before then.

When he started away, the magician followed. Elizabeth met his eye and got to her feet. Mark was again surprised at the emotion her image brought his old heart.

"Oh, she is lovely," Androni said and they reached Elizabeth in another few steps. Mark stood beside her and introduced the magician. Androni bowed ridiculously low and when Elizabeth gave him her hand to shake, he instead kissed the outside of it and tucked his hands into his pants pockets. "My pleasure, Ms. Hawken."

"Call me Elizabeth," she said and Mark ignored Androni's peek his way.

"Wonderful, thank you. And you may call me Androni." His tone teased and Mark enjoyed the sparkle in Elizabeth's eyes as she chuckled at the magician's over-acting.

With no additional small-talk until they reached the outdoor garage, Mark led them to the car. They had borrowed Sarah's SUV and Elizabeth volunteered to sit in the back so Androni and Mark could speak up front. He thanked her and once all were in, he started them away from the airport.

"I am a-shiver with anticipation, *Ma-r-r-r-k,*" Androni said facing the road ahead and enjoying Mark's first name once more. "You have a friend named Hope. A friend named Elizabeth, and a vampire friend named Joey. This is all I have so far." Androni flicked his gaze to Elizabeth a millisecond to add, "I prefer this woman over the other one."

Mark nodded, aware he meant no disrespect. After a small sigh, he decided to begin. "We will be driving to a city in Alabama, a neighboring state, called Montgomery. There, we will reside for a short time in a friend's house. Here, you will meet the homeowner's wife, Sarah Tracey, and our new friend, Joseph Ellerslie." In the rearview mirror, Elizabeth caught his eye and smiled. He returned the gesture, feeling extreme calm because of her presence. "Finally, in a few weeks, you will meet the homeowner and my friend, Tony Agricola. He is also a vampire."

"I am looking forward to learning all about you and your people here."

"Thank you, Androni," Mark said low. "I like you. I wouldn't have brought you near my people if I didn't."

"Maybe you were going to explain this to me along the way, but if I may ask, why wouldn't you take Ms. Brannen's blood?"

Mark's eyes shot to Elizabeth who looked back, her face saying, "answer the man…" She had an expression of humor so Mark tried to be less uptight about it. Androni had no guile and hadn't learned to pick and choose topics around ladies. Mark decided to educate him.

"Androni, learn this," he began and the magician grew still, listening with intensity. "Although Elizabeth and Sarah know my nature, I do not wish to discuss it in front of them. For our association, let's keep the vampire chat between vampires. Savvy?"

"Yes," Androni replied suddenly serious. "My apologies." Silence filled the car a full minute and Androni whispered too low for Elizabeth to hear, "But why? This is puzzling me. Her blood was exquisite—"

Mark held up one finger and narrowed his eyes, not because of Elizabeth, but because thinking about drinking blood was something he did not do. "Do you not know?" he asked the man using the same low voice. "Why did she come see you?"

Androni thought a moment and pursed his lips in concentration. "She was lonely?"

Mark waited.

"She confided in me that although you were together some time, you had never taken her blood."

"Have you not wondered why that is?"

"Well, hmm." Androni hummed looking at the countryside zipping past. "You don't drink blood?" he asked finally and Mark gave a single nod. "Not at all?"

"Sometimes," he replied happy Elizabeth had turned to reading her phone when she realized they needed privacy. "From animals."

"Oh." Androni was still trying to make sense of it. "Why?"

"You have no knowledge of the Creator," Mark said as a statement and the man had no reply. "I was like you once, Androni," Mark offered, allowing his voice to return to a soft timbre. "Thousands of humans fell victim to my bloodlust for centuries. But eventually, the Creator, the God of the universe showed me that bloodlust is a curse and that I should be working for a cure, not feeding the animal within. Tony, Joey, and I expect Him to deliver us from vampirism."

Elizabeth glanced up, a little sadness in her eye based upon their private discussion of the topic. Mark looked back to the highway and waited for Androni to remark. When he did, he sought words that wouldn't make his host angry.

"Mark, you have officially blown my mind."

Mark grinned then and patted his near shoulder. "Good. And we've only just begun."

"Amen," Elizabeth said from the back under her breath. Both vampires heard, but neither remarked.

𝔒𝔟

Blessed is the man who endures temptation;
for when he has been approved, he will receive the crown of life
which the Lord has promised to those who love Him.
James 1:12

"HEY, ABBY. YOU DOING OKAY?" WONDERING IF HE SOUNDED different, more "vampir-y," he thought with a half-frown, Joey said good morning to his favorite girl. He hadn't spoken to her since the night of the auction and had no idea if they were angry he'd disappeared.

"Joey! What happened? Are you ghosting me?"

Her question brought a grin; good old Abigail, reminding him that the world could be humorous. The concept of ghosting was one they had discussed over pizza one night, just the two of them, when each felt they'd been dodged by a date they thought had gone well. Hers had been a boy from a neighboring church and his, a girl he met at the library. For some reason, as they spoke, she got the giggles and had laughed so hard, cola came out of her nose. The memory was a good one and Joey was thankful she brought it up.

"Yeah, sorry about that," he said so she'd hear his chuckle. "My assignment was really weird. I'll tell you about it when I see you."

His mind sought how much he'd actually say when she belted out, "Call your mom, buddy. Your parents are freaking out!"

"To be fair, they're always freaking out about something," Joey said attempting a joke.

"No, they're steamed. Your mom told the Sunday School class she might call the police."

"Geez!" Joey looked at the wall thinking of the doctor, just getting back from the airport. He would *not* want police at his door.

"Yeah," Abby continued. "Can you meet me and Scotty tonight?"

"Maybe," Joey hemmed wondering how to gauge their possible exposure. "Let me check on Mom and Dad. I'll call you back." His friend said okay and Joey walked to the door. He thought to see what Dr. Corescu thought they should do when he heard the man say from several rooms away, "Come to the basement."

Joey turned and jogged to the cellar door.

The clock in the foyer chimed 6 PM as Mark opened the front door. After a private goodnight which included a tender kiss, Elizabeth returned to her car and drove away. Mark did not concern himself with Androni's opinion of his behavior but noticed a wry grin on his face nonetheless. As was his habit, as he reached the threshold, he listened for the location of the house occupants. Joey was on the phone with a female and Tony's wife was running a bath upstairs. From what he overheard of the boy's conversation, the Ellerslies presented a pressing new chore.

"Follow me," he said to the magician and headed for the basement. "We will put out fires beginning right now." The magician nodded and at the cellar door, Mark said at a normal tone, "Joseph, join us in the basement."

Androni raised his brows. "Yes. Let us see this boy."

Mark had filled the magier in on everything he needed to know regarding their situation. More than ever, Mark discerned the man had no agenda. Androni the Vampire was beside himself to simply be with another of his kind.

At the top of the stairs, Joseph stepped into view, his pale blue eyes enormous. "Geez," he whispered and descended, his eyes in the magician's. "So, you're Androni."

"*Androni the Magnificent!*" Androni removed his coat with a flourish, flipped it back and forth like a matador's cape, and then reached inside. When he withdrew his hand, he held a sizable bouquet of paper flowers. "Voilá!"

"Hah! And you're really dressed the part," Joseph said with a wide smile. "You came all the way from Europe in this outfit?"

Mark thought to interrupt them for the business at hand, but Androni flipped a ball from his pocket and held it before the boy's face.

"Dressed what part?" the magician said, moving the ball back and forth, much like a snake mesmerizing its prey. Joseph's grin grew lopsided as he watched. Mark inhaled to again, bring them to business, when Androni lifted his free hand to Mark in a stop gesture. With a sigh, he conceded and watched the trick.

"Oh, you are in love with this magic ball, are you not? You cannot look away. Try, try, try, and you love it too much to look away," he said in a lilting voice, the ridiculous words having the desired effect on the boy's strict attention. "Beautiful boy, if you love it so much, why don't you have it?"

The magier opened his fingers, but the ball did not fall. It appeared to be made of foam and it rose in the air, slow, and inch by inch. Androni watched the boy's face and the boy watched the ball make its way to the low basement ceiling.

"How are you doing that?" Joseph asked in amazement. Without averting his gaze, he asked Mark, "Can you do that? Is he doing that with his mind?"

"What nonsense!" Androni announced with mock offense. "I am doing no such thing! This ball is magic! Can you not see how wonderful it is?"

Joseph's grin remained, looking all of five years old, waiting to see what the ball or the magician might do next.

Mark cleared his throat and Androni shook his head, eyes to the boy. "Take the ball, you delightful boy. Take it and let the doctor speak. He has such important things to say…"

Mark parted his lips to begin, but as Joseph reached one hand for the ball, it flicked out of reach. He jumped after it and it again moved away. The boy passed Mark and the magician and followed the ball across the room.

"Doctor Corescu!" Joseph called in a laugh, leaping and grabbing for the evasive item. "He's a real magician!"

"I do not think you can catch that magic ball. I do not believe you love it enough." Androni sighed and his eyes found Mark's. He apologized with his gaze and nodded, indicating he'd finish up. He turned his face to Joey. "Do you love the ball, boy?"

"I do, I love the ball," he replied laughing with the silliness of the game.

"If you tell the ball that you love it, it will let you catch it."

"Ball! I love you!" Joseph said in a giggle. Without delay, the toy zoomed into his waiting fingers and Joseph whooped with joy.

"That's so cool! Will you show me how to do that?" he asked returning to their position.

"That's enough." Mark gestured and Joseph fell still, his child-like grin in place. "Androni, this is Joseph Ellerslie."

Androni made no movement but when Joseph put out his hand, the magier shook it in the normal fashion.

"Joseph, Androni is aware of what transpired to bring you to this state. That said, I can see you have many questions for him—"

"I do, I—" he began in an excited tone and Mark shushed him.

"In time. Control your impulses. Were you impulsive before?" Mark asked and the boy fell silent, the fun leaving his face, as if he just recalled the violence of his transformation. "You had a phone call. I overheard. Your parents will need to be dealt with."

"Yes, sir," he said looking down. "I don't know what to say to them. I'm… I'm…"

"Listen," Mark said and both men looked to his face. "Invite them here, now, tonight. Your story is this: Tony and Ms. Sarah asked you to join their ministry team full-time and you accepted. You have decided to continue your classes online from here, you have a room and an office. You have decided to move here." As he spoke, the boy nodded and Androni's mouth turned up in a half-grin. "Call them now."

"They won't allow it," he said, his eyes begging Mark to fix it so they would. Mark gave a wry nod.

"This is why I suggest you invite them here. I will vouch for Tony and I will persuade them."

Androni's smile completed and he placed his hands into his pockets and scooted his pelvis once, the grace of his movement drawing Joseph's attention.

"All you need do is keep your calm about you and remember they can't stop you."

"I'm only eighteen," he whispered and Androni made a *shew!* noise.

"Eighteen is old enough," Mark said squaring off with him to meet his eye more directly. "You can do this," he said, pushing his will which took with it, confidence in the task.

Joseph nodded. "Okay." The youngster fished free his cell and with a glance to the magician, he pressed the call button.

Mark listened as his parents barked and then shouted for him to come home, but in a very calm voice, Joseph asked his parents to come to Pastor Tony's house. After refusing twice, they conceded and were gone.

Mark gave Joseph a nod. On impulse, he plucked Androni's foam ball from Joseph's hand and turned for the stairs. He needed to speak with Sarah and get her up to speed and there should be less magic and more concentrating on their situation.

"Remain here and allow me time to greet your parents," he said his back to his guests. "I will call you when it is time to come upstairs." Mark wasn't asking and he didn't wait for a reply.

Wholly enamored, Joseph simply turned to Androni and began asking about his magic. Mark trotted up the stairs marveling at how his life had changed.

And become very human.

I guess this is progress… he thought and took the issue no farther. Time to handle the Ellerslies.

"How old are you?" Joey asked the new guy as soon as the doctor exited the basement. The horror of learning about and then becoming an undead creature seemed bearable since laying eyes on Androni.

"Just shy of two hundred and fifty," the man said, his gaze intense— much more focused than the doctor's or Pastor Tony's. Androni looked at Joey like he was *there,* as if Joey's presence enhanced the magician's life. It felt good. Scotty liked him, Abby maybe a little more, but even they didn't have a fraction of the intensity in their eyes this man had.

"You look at me as if I'm… I don't know," Joey said, not embarrassed to speak his mind. "Like I'm interesting." The vampire's face softened and he nodded with a grin.

"Oh, you are," he cooed and lifted his fingers to touch Joey's cheek. "And only eighteen years old… so young… Maybe too young."

"Why? Too young for what?"

Androni grinned and gave Joey another long look. "I have never met another vampire until I met the doctor. I am no authority on this."

"I'm happy you're here," Joey said and turned for the pool table. His mind on the events of the night, now and in a few minutes. He grabbed the cue ball and rolled it to the far corner. Still in thought, he walked to that pocket and reached inside. The ball he retrieved was red and made of foam. He held it up for Androni to see.

"My ball! Ah! That doctor, he's a sneaky one!"

With his mouth open and his cheeks bunched in a wondrous grin, he tried to figure out how that happened. How did Doctor Corescu get that ball in the pocket in that short period of time without them seeing? Still marveling, he rolled his gaze to his compelling new friend.

Androni stepped close, very close, and looked down his nose on Joey a few inches shorter. When he had Joey's eye, he licked his lips in slow motion and removed the ball from Joey's fingers.

"Mark is a tricky one," he said in a whisper inches from Joey's face. "He seems proper, but he has a rascally streak."

"Yeah," Joey replied, not disturbed by the proximity and he wondered why. Somewhere in his mind he heard, *because you're a vampire, too, dummy.* But was that enough reason? So what, the guy was a million times more interesting than anyone he'd ever met. Joey moved his gaze around Androni's face, so close, and then grinned. "Tell me some stories from your life. I know you have the best stories around."

"Funny," the vampire said then and backed away, moving toward the couches against the wall. Joey felt a sadness when he did so but followed, listening. "I want to hear about you. Your friends, your family, your plans."

"Oh gosh. My plans…" Joey replied and when Androni dropped into a sofa, he took the adjacent one. "You go first."

"I will tell you about Androni the Magnificent, but it will be a trade. One for one?"

Joey smiled and said okay. "But I warn you, I'm boring."

Androni shook his head in slow motion. "No, you are mesmerizing. You go first. Tell me about this incredible physique. Do you swim?"

Joey blushed and started the tale. One part of his mind listened for his parents, but tonight, looking into a vampire's eyes—a vampire who found him more interesting than anyone ever had before—Joey hoped they had a flat tire coming over.

27

So then, my beloved brethren, let every man be swift to hear,
slow to speak, slow to wrath; for the wrath of man does not produce
the righteousness of God.
James 1:19-20

JOANN ELLERSLIE GAWKED AT THE HOUSE AS THE SECURITY gate opened before them. She hardly knew the evangelist, and what little she did know never indicated he was wealthy. "How in the world does this man afford this kind of set up?" she asked her husband behind the wheel. "Isn't he unaffiliated? Just who is this guy?"

"Don't know," Bob replied. "Maybe he inherited it. Maybe he's on the take. God doesn't pay folks this sort of money for preaching *right,* I guarantee."

Bob Ellerslie steered the Town Car down the long drive and pulled to a stop at the front door. There were marked parking spaces for five cars, and he pulled in next to a dark blue SUV. "Agricola drove to our house in a little green pick-up. I don't see it. Joseph's here, right?"

"That's what he said." JoAnn narrowed her eyes, fingers to the door handle. Bob motioned for her to wait.

"Let's have a plan. We want Joseph to come home with us. No ifs, ands, or buts." Robert hit the unlock on the doors and waited for his wife to nod. "You remember how the guy was at church. He's persuasive, but we are united. There's no room for discussion. Agree?"

JoAnn gave a slow nod and offered a compromise. "But we let him join their team. I mean, Bob…" she looked at the ornate front facia. "They're famous."

Her husband shook his head. "Agricola is spooky. Something's off with him and I can't figure out what it is. Plus, didn't you think that was fishy when he ran off with our boy? We get Joseph home and go from there."

JoAnn sighed her agreement and followed him to the double front doors. Barely had the bell ceased its ring when the right-side pulled inward to reveal a stranger, a tall sophisticate in slacks and a white tailored dress shirt open three buttons, no tie.

The man smiled with a small bow. "Good evening," he said with the tiniest accent. "I am Dr. Mark Corescu, a friend of the Agricolas."

Bob Ellerslie stepped past the man pulling JoAnn behind him. "Good evening. We're here to pick up our son Joseph. Please tell him we're here."

"Right this way." Their host turned and JoAnn and her husband followed, her gawking at the sky-high ceilings and the decorative scrolling on the trim. When they reached the room he suggested—a library by the look—it was empty. He gestured they should go in.

"Wait a darn minute," Bob said without stepping inside. "Where's Agricola? I didn't see his truck out front."

JoAnn turned her face to their host. The man appeared bored, looking at her husband's upturned face without replying. In two full seconds, Corescu only parted his lips and JoAnn turned her face to the ceiling. "Joseph Ellerslie!" she called in her mom voice, "Come here right now! Your father wants to talk to you!"

The doctor closed one eye in response to her shout and gestured again for the library seating. "Please have a seat. Mrs. Agricola and Joseph will be with you any moment."

"Well, I just…"

Bob didn't finish his complaint and since he went into the room, JoAnn followed. He was right; something was off, and she didn't have to be able to name it to act upon her instincts. Her baby was coming home. She sat after her husband, both of them on a flowery short sofa. Corescu did not sit but stood at the threshold as if awaiting the others.

"Dr. Corescu," JoAnn said sounding out his name. "Are you a physician?" She wanted to mentally compartmentalize the man and learning if his PhD was medical or scholastic would help.

"Yes," the man said and added, "but I am retired."

Her husband scoffed looking to the side. "Must be nice." She bumped his elbow and he added, "He's younger than I am."

JoAnn gave the doctor a strained smile and licked her lips. Where was her son? Before she called him again, Bob cleared his throat.

"Dr. Corescu, I don't know what sort of boy you think we raised, but he's not going to just call his mom and tell her he's moved out. We're a tight knit family and that's too disrespectful. Present him now, or I'll assume something nefarious is going on." Bob rose to his feet and JoAnn followed suit, placing her hand to his arm.

"Doctor, does Joseph know we're here?"

Their host turned his face to the dark hallway and then stepped back as if someone was about to enter. JoAnn dropped her husband's elbow to greet Joey, but it was Agricola's wife, Reverend Tracey.

"Hi! Oh, gosh! I'm so sorry you had to wait on me!" the woman said with sincerity and zoomed in to grab JoAnn in a hug. When Bob put out his hand, she moved around it and hugged him, too. She turned her face to the doctor still in the hall. "Will you go get him? I guess he didn't realize they're here."

JoAnn was ready to shout again, but Corescu left her vision and the reverend faced her with a smile. "What can I get you? Coffee? Tea? Whatcha need?"

"We need our boy, Ma'am," Bob said, a little too rudely for JoAnn's taste. She tossed him a glare and sat down when Sarah did.

"No, we're fine. Sorry about Bob," she said and flapped her fingers at him until he lighted beside her. "Joseph hasn't said anything to us about that night he spent away from home. Then, your husband showed up and took him away and we still didn't get to see him. We're just worried, that's all. We're spooked. We gotta see if he's okay. You understand, right?" JoAnn didn't know if the woman was a mother, but she was a Christian. That alone should help her understand.

"I do and he'll be right down. I'm not even sure what happened after that charity auction. He confided in my husband and the doctor, but from what I understand, he ran into some trouble and he didn't want to burden you two with it. When he joins us, he'll explain everything."

JoAnn nodded. "Thank you for that, Sarah. We appreciate Pastor Tony for trying to help." JoAnn ignored her husband's warning look. "I'm glad he wants to join your ministry team. He always wanted to be a preacher. Ever since he was a little boy."

Sarah clapped her hands, her face shining. "He's anointed, that one."

"Don't get ahead of yourself, Hon. Joseph has a lot to answer for before he makes his next move."

JoAnn did not comment on her husband's statement, but engaged Sarah in small talk about the house and grounds. The doctor seemed weird, Agricola was rude, but Sarah Tracey Agricola? She was an angel and JoAnn allowed her friendly smile to lighten her mood as they waited. For Bob's sake, she hoped the boy hurried up and didn't give him any lip.

❖

Standing beside Androni both leaning on the pool table, Joey listened to those upstairs. He sighed when the reverend asked the doctor to fetch him. "I can't face them," he said and looked at his toes. Androni bumped him by moving sideways one time.

"Why not? You heard Mark. Make up your mind what you want and let no one waver you. I do it all the time."

Joey tilted his chin enough to look to his new friend's handsome face. The magician grinned and double-raised his eyebrows. Joey smiled back, his mind divided. Right here, this moment, flanked by such a powerful example of what he had become, Joey could imagine simply telling his parents what he planned to do. But once little Joey got upstairs and faced his mommy and daddy, he was certain they'd convince him to leave. The sound of the doctor's footsteps approached and Joey's lips tightened. As comfortable as he was with Androni, he was tense and fearful around the doctor and Pastor Tony.

"Will you go, too?" he asked low just as the doctor appeared at the top of the basement stairs. He cleared his throat and Joey wondered if it was possible for him to escape the house.

"Go to the library now," Doctor Corescu instructed. "Your time has come and gone."

Joey chose his words with care. "They're going to win. I can't face them. I'm not ready."

Mark inhaled to reply but beside him, Androni held up one hand with a respectful grin to the doctor. "I will go with you. I am certain I can be of service." The magician looked to the doctor for approval.

Mark backed and swished his hand to the stairs. "Please, go to it."

He sounded weary of the entire exercise and with Androni right behind him, Joey jogged up the stairs. When he reached the library door, he bounded in pasting on a grin. His mother and father hopped up and grabbed him into a three-way hug. He patted their backs. With his eyes in Androni's, he began the placations.

"Mom, Dad, I'm sorry about all this. The guy who bought me at the auction never showed up. It must have been a prank, but he had that car drive me all the way across town. I waited where instructed and no one ever came. I fell asleep waiting and when I woke up, it was after ten the next day." Joey kissed his mother's cheek and both parents released him to begin saying their piece.

"Son, that's horrible, but you should have told us. You don't have to go to strangers when something like this happens," his father said and blew his nose in a handkerchief. Joey apologized but his mother started to say the same thing in her own words. When Joey apologized enough that both parents ceased the topic, they withdrew and stood a distance away, much more like the way they stood with him at home. Before he could open the discussion about remaining with the Agricolas, his mother's gaze moved to Androni in the corner.

"Who is this?" she asked and his father also turned his head.

From the hall, the doctor stepped in, but it was Reverend Tracey that answered. She crossed the room and grabbed the magician in a hug and kissed his cheek.

"Androni the Magnificent!" she said with aplomb and turned to the Ellerslies with one hand to Androni's shoulder. "This is one of our friends from Europe visiting for a time. Back home, he's a magician."

The reverend's voice sang and Joey peeked at his parents' faces. They were buying it, mostly moved by Sarah's voucher.

Joey watched his mother, ready to change the topic to Androni, not near as upset as his dad. But as she walked toward the corner, Joey's father called her back.

"JoAnn, really! Let's keep our focus." He turned to Joey, thankfully standing ten yards away and out of physical reach. "Joseph, go to the car. We'll settle everything tomorrow."

Joey didn't move but glanced right to meet Androni's eyes for courage or advice.

"Joseph Robert!" his father barked, now pointing for the front doors. "Now! This is not a negotiation!"

Androni circumvented Joey's mother and stepped to his father with purpose. When he passed Joey's position, he sent him a wink and Joey thought he heard him say, *"deal with your mother"* telepathically. Before now, they hadn't experienced any sort of link in that way, but he turned to his mom and distracted her with questions about Luke. Behind him, Androni stopped close enough to her father to drop one hand to his shoulder. Joey listened and watched peripherally as his mom's responses continued on his other side.

"Mr. Ellerslie, is it?" Androni's smooth voice.

"Reverend Ellerslie. What do you want from my boy? And why are you wearing this ridiculous get-up?"

"These are my clothes. Have you never seen a real live magician?"

"Please, I never... Joseph—"

152

"Step with me outside, Reverend Ellerslie," Androni said and Joey did all he could to avoid looking fully over to watch. "I will tell you…" The magician's voice fell to a whisper and Joey realized only he and Dr. Corescu would overhear. "I will tell you what the boy is too embarrassed to say. Come. You will understand. I promise."

"Well, make it quick. I don't like being jerked around, especially by my own kid!"

Joey's mother looked at them as they left the house and he expertly drew her attention back. Out of the corner of his eye, Dr. Corescu moved quietly along the wall until he, too, stepped into the night. What they were saying to his dad he would have to ask later. For the moment, he distracted his mom and Sarah Tracey helped.

In another three minutes, Androni and the doctor re-entered the house. "Reverend Ellerslie asked if you would join him outside. He has a little headache and said he will call Joseph tomorrow."

Joey hid his grin and his mother began making goodbyes with Sarah. When she kissed his cheek and told him to be good, his mother left and he exhaled with drama.

"I don't think I want to know why Bob Ellerslie suddenly had to go," Sarah said and hugged Joey's neck. "I'm turning in. Ya'll be good, okay?" She met the eyes of each man and turned for the stairs. When her foot hit the first one, she swiveled to say to the doctor, "Will you tell Tony I love him?" Her request was spoken with strength, but Joey read the sadness too. The doctor offered a genteel nod combined with a bow and she grinned and trotted up.

Joey sighed and rubbed his face. "Thank you," he said then to Androni. He raised his gaze to the doctor. "Thank you."

"You're welcome." Dr Corescu checked his watch. "It is nearing 9. Joseph, show Androni to a spare bedroom. Tomorrow, take him into town and help him choose some appropriate clothing. Will you do this?"

Joey nodded once and turned his face to Androni. He grinned, simply looking into the guy's eyes brought him a feeling of happiness he'd been missing a long while. Androni sent him a wink and fluffed the silly collar of his tasseled smock ties.

"Androni," the doctor said then and moved closer to them both, "remember the risk I took bringing you here. Do not make me regret my kindness."

"That will never happen, master," Androni said in the old way and Joey liked the medieval sound of his words.

"Make sure that it doesn't. I have to leave for a short time. Stay here, wait for my return."

He and Androni both nodded once and Joey wanted to ask him where he was going. When the doctor said nothing more about it, he decided not to ask. In another minute, Androni invited Joey back to the cellar before they set up his room for a round of pool. With a new goodnight to the doc, they headed down.

Androni raced him to the door and then popped his head when he passed him for the cellar stairs. Joey laughed and felt his heart fill with joy. He should be worried or upset, after all, he was already wishing he had another hit off that black horse. But he wasn't. He was happy. And Androni the Magnificent was erasing his sorrow millimeter by millimeter.

28

Day and night they never stop saying:
"Holy, holy, holy is the Lord God Almighty,
Who was, and is, and is to come."
Revelation 4:8

"DOCTOR?"

Mark turned his face upward, Tony's wife looking down on him from the upper landing. He lifted his brow and awaited her needs.

"You can use my car as much as you need," she said and dropped a set of keys which he caught. "I'll lease a car tomorrow for Joey."

"That is very generous of you," Mark said and waited for more. He had ordered a car tonight online and arranged for it to be delivered by 8 AM.

"Outside with the reverend," she began and stopped. Mark did not want to guess what worried her the most. She'd been violently assaulted by Paul when he lived and only 3 days ago, Haman Troye took advantage of her kindness in a way that still haunted the edges of her gaze. Mark tried to toss her some comfort.

"Hypnotic suggestion," he said softly. "Androni used it in his performance overseas and it worked very well on a certain Baptist preacher we know."

Sarah smiled with a blush. "He has some crazy-compelling eyes."

Mark chuckled in a nod. "Anything else?"

"Tony," she said and swallowed. "How did he look? I mean, he had a forty-day fast not too long ago and… well… I don't want to worry since God has it in hand, but I am worried for him just the same."

"He will be fine. It is my feeling that this forty days will be cleansing for him…" Mark stopped short as the end of his thought cascaded past his consciousness. He did not want to face it, but somewhere deep down, he figured this was his last month in the flesh.

"This punishment seems harsh," she said, maybe interpreting his abrupt speech as worry. "I can't hear God on it. I wonder if I'm not also in need of chastisement."

Mark sighed. He was not a seer or a prophet, but she had hit on something he intuited from the angel. He decided he'd try to explain.

"When we come across something evil and detestable, we are not to take hostages, or loot the enemies camp. Tony did both. The Spirit warned him and he barged ahead, following the lust that we immortals encounter when under those circumstances. The blood your husband ingested would have killed him. More correctly, it would have driven him insane, driven him to kill each of you one by one, and then himself. Almighty God stepped in again and saved his skin."

"Jesus is always jumping in to save my Tony isn't he?" Sarah laughed softly.

"And you discern that Tony is taking your chastisement onto himself?" The woman nodded. "I am not privy to your sin, but this is what he did. He asked the Father to allow him to carry it for you."

"He is wonderful."

Mark nodded and waited for anything else.

"You said he can't use a phone, but you can hear him, right? Mentally?"

Mark looked aside and peeked to the place he'd find the preacher. Tony was praying, noticed Mark's presence and sent a sentiment of doing well. Mark met Sarah's eyes.

"He is safe. He is praying."

"Thank you," she said and a tear slid down her cheek. "Joey and Androni, is this a good idea? The boy seems overly infatuated with him."

Mark nodded. "I will keep an eye on them. I am guarding all of you. I will be vigilant."

She blushed again and had a new thought. "Tony does not sleep much. He sleeps about nine hours every five days. Is that the same with Joey? Androni? Will they simply be awake all the time? Here, in the house?"

Mark didn't know. He offered what he could. "It is different for each of us. I will watch Joey and determine his needs. Androni confided that he also sleeps only one night a month. They will spend their home time in the basement. I advised them to study the Bible."

"Androni does not know our Father," she said with a sad expression.

Mark gave a tip of the chin. "But he's also not hard against the idea. We will show him the way."

"Yeah," she said sounding like a teenager. He held her eyes another long moment and she turned bright pink. She faced away and said as she walked to her room, "Save those eyes for Elizabeth. You know she can't wait to see you again."

Mark chuckled and picture the young woman's face. He needed to go to Germany and find Hope, and then he needed to check in on Tony. When would he find the time to see his new favorite person?

Mark chuckled when he realized he sounded whiny—just as Tony accused him some days ago.

Androni called the boy with his will, using talents honed over a century of longing for company in a lonely country. It must be a vampire skill but he taught himself since he had no master, no teacher, nothing. And he didn't call his name or send telepathic messages—which he didn't sense a tangible mental connection with the guy anyway—rather, he simply "wanted" Joey Ellerslie to come. Thirty minutes ago, he'd been summoned upstairs for a "God chat" with the homeowner. Androni had listened in, but could make no sense of it. These vampires who refused to drink blood confounded him. As much as he wanted to bask in Mark's presence, he wouldn't... *couldn't*... give up the blood.

And it was time for the boy to return.

I want what I want.

Right now, leaning against a pool table in Agricola's furnished basement, Androni wanted Joey fiercely.

The door at the top of the stairs opened. Androni smiled at the pale face that peeked at him around the post when he reached the floor.

"Sorry that took so long. Were you calling me?" he asked, his blue eyes so light they seemed translucent. Was he an albino? No, but almost. Since Androni hadn't responded, he continued to enter the space and crossed to the pool table. "You okay?"

"I was lonely," Androni said and watched his eyes. Decades of communing with mortals had left him woefully unable to relate to vampires, even brand-new ones like the kid. By the time Joey's mouth formed a shy smile, Androni recognized what he was doing—he was seducing the boy as if he was one of his blood donors back in Country.

"It is sort of lonely," he agreed and with an exhale swiveled to lean against the table mimicking Androni's position. "I've been this way only a few days and I don't have anyone to go to." He shook his head with a *tsk*. "Before I met that Haman Troye, I was never alone. Now?" He huffed.

"I've been this way for two hundred and fifty years," Androni said in a soft voice, mostly watching the boy's face and studying its shape and what appeared to be very smooth cheeks. Did he yet shave?

Joey grinned at the scrutiny and blushed, a very light pink rushing to his face. "You are a zillion times more interesting than Tony or Dr. Corescu," he said with a new grin. "Why are you looking at me so hard? I look weird, don't I?"

Androni lifted his brow, enjoying the question and the opportunity to banter. Corescu despised chatting, but he had always loved the sound of his own voice. "Oh, my boy, no," he told him and stood to turn and face him head-on. "I was born in Hungary and have lived mostly among Gypsy caravans. I am quite fascinated by your coloring." Androni lifted one hand; would the boy allow him to feel his face?

"I'm really pale," he said and leaned close, causing his cheek to meet Androni's palm. "Even before this happened, I was called Casper behind my back."

Joey chuckled his nickname but Androni saw it didn't disturb him. He cupped the cool cheek and then lifted his other hand to even the grasp. Joey met his eyes.

"What are you thinking about?"

"You," Androni answered in a whisper, unintentionally continuing his seduction mode. How would it work on baby vampires? And what was the goal? To taste his blood?

"I just had a lecture from Ms. Sarah. She thinks I've been idolizing you," Joey whispered, a careful sentence spoken after double and triple consideration.

Androni allowed a half-grin. "I don't think he wants us too close." Androni held on, now allowing his thumbs to stroke the youth's chin, free of stubble, covered with the fine down of a prepubescent.

"Is that it?" the boy asked, still barely above a whisper.

"Maybe, maybe," Androni replied in the same decibel. "Joey, may I call you Ghost? I think I'd enjoy sharing code names with you."

"Hah, yeah," he laughed, still close, nose to nose. "And I'll call you Gypsy. You look like a Gypsy prince from long ago…"

Androni grinned and dropped the contact with his face. He spun on his heel and headed for the low couch along the wall and invited the boy to sit. The basement lighting was limited to the lamp hanging over the pool table and he very much enjoyed the dim coziness of the room. When Joey sat down, he sat only inches away, with an exaggerated exhale and sticking his legs out long.

"Comfortable, Ghost?" Androni said with a twinge of humor to see how it would play. The boy nodded with a spreading grin.

"Very, Gypsy, my friend." He looked right to catch Androni's eye and chuckled. "You make me glad. I don't know what or why or how, but before you got here, I was pretty sure my life was over. I mean, Reverend Sarah swears up and down that God did all this for my good, but…" The young man looked front again and swished his head once. "I had zero hope before I saw you."

"Tell me," Androni said when he stopped speaking. There was more and he wanted to hear it.

Joey smiled and looked at his hands. "Before he left me for the airport, the doctor said, 'I'm bringing back a vampire from Europe,'" he said in an imitation of Mark's voice. "'Be on your best behavior when I return.'" Joey stole a quick glance and looked down again. "That's all I knew about you. I had no idea you would be so… Well, so…" He stopped sharing and shrugged.

"Tell me," Androni said again in earnest and put two fingers to Joey's near thigh. The boy turned.

"When I saw your face, I just got … happy. Hopeful. It's stupid." He again dropped his eyes to his lap.

"Why is it stupid? Can't vampires have instant attraction?" Androni offered. The household members resisted their true nature. Could he prevent the baby among them from adopting the same traits?

Joey shrugged one shoulder. "Maybe."

"No maybe. It has happened. It is a fact." Androni popped his leg. "I want you to smile. Why don't you look happy? Androni is right here!"

Joey grinned and re-met his eye. "You know they made us rooms up there. One for me and one for you. Pretty soon, the doctor is going to tell me I should go there. Why?" the boy asked and it did not seem rhetorical. "I don't want to go in there by myself. I won't be sleeping. I want to be here with you." His grin fell and he huffed. "I wonder if I swapped parents."

"Only if you allow it," Androni said in a secretive tone. "You are on a precipice of your new life. You can choose the next step. The direction of your future. Are you a man or a child?"

"A man," Joey said with a nod.

Androni clucked his cheek. "You are the funniest boy."

"I'm the funniest *man*," Joey said with a new grin.

Androni transitioned from two fingers to his entire palm across the boy's leg and Joey's face turned to the contact. "It was the same for me. When you came down the stairs, when you played my game. I am smitten."

"Smitten," Joey laughed and shook his head. "I love your accent. Reminds me of movie vampires. Very cool."

"What accent?" he teased. "Tell me about yourself. Do you have a girlfriend?"

Joey placed his palm atop Androni's hand. "Naw," he huffed. "I had a girlfriend in high school, we went to the movies some."

"Did you kiss her?" Androni sat up from the back cushion to turn and see the boy's face.

"Naw," Joey replied and watched Androni's movement, still without revealing anything in his face of how he perceived the magician's movements.

"Have you ever kissed a girl?" he asked, lowering his voice. Joey shook his head, an adorable pink tinting his cheeks. Androni waited for the boy to meet his eye and he shot him a grin to add, "Have you ever kissed a guy?"

"No!" he said with force, but laughed, as he grew embarrassed. "What about you? You probably have kissed tons of ladies."

Androni nodded. "Thousands upon thousands."

"I'd like to hear some of your stories," Joey said and meant it, but Androni couldn't leave the current topic.

"I would like to kiss you," he said, and Joey's eyes widened.

"Why?" he asked back to the whisper and holding Androni's gaze.

"I think it might feel nice." Androni waited a second and then another, the boy thinking it over, imagining it, and wondering if he would think it felt nice, too.

"Um," Joey said with an obvious swallow. "Is it important? I mean, it's not something I'd normally... well, it's weird."

"Ah..." Androni relaxed back, hand still on the boy's leg. "What used to be normal is gone. You said looking at me gives you hope for a future. It might be because I can show you everything I know about being a vampire. I taught myself how to move objects with my mind. I can teach you. I taught myself how to swoon people for their blood, take it carefully, and leave them alive and oblivious. I can teach you..."

"And magic and blood and kissing guys is normal for European vampires?" he asked with a half-grin. His blush remained, but his tone had returned to his calm cadence. Androni nodded once and Joey's smile

160

opened. "Okay, but I can't promise you magic," he said with a laugh. He froze with drama to see if Androni would laugh at his joke. He rewarded the boy with a chuckle before rising to his feet and tugging Joey's arm.

"Lesson number one," Androni whispered and positioned the boy facing him, toe to toe. "Taking blood from mortals to leave them alive starts with the swoon. This move right here," he said and cupped the young man's cheeks as he had earlier, "gets their attention."

"It's working on me, too," Joey said as a joke, but his voice had wavered.

"You like my face?" Androni asked, now wanting more of those compliments. *I want what I want,* and his mantra never grew tired.

"Yes. You're very good-looking, Gypsy," Joey said, using the code name to lighten the moment. "And…" The boy swallowed and licked his lips, his eyes dropping to Androni's mouth. "And your lips are big. I think the ladies like that, right? Mine are so thin. I don't think…"

"Shhh," Androni said and put a finger to his mouth. "Now, study how I do this. Are you paying attention?" Androni's eyes were on the young man's lips, which were not as thin as he purported. More than ever, he wanted to know if kissing the boy would be pleasurable. And would he reciprocate? He had to. Who didn't love Androni the Magnificent?"

"Yes," Joey whispered, mostly as an exhale.

"Good." Androni moved close enough to allow their mouths to touch, the skin barely in contact. Joey had stopped breathing and his muscles tensed. Androni moved a tiny bit in, his lips compressing the boy's a fraction, and Joey tensed further. It was time to do the deed, perform the test, and Androni released the air from his lungs and moved in, conforming his open mouth to Joey's gently parted lips. The young man didn't move back, and he did allow it, his jaw was not rigid, but there was a sense the boy was waiting for it to end. Androni noted all this and moved onto part two. With his right hand cupping the back of Joey's head and his left hand gentle at his throat, Androni pushed his tongue past the barrier of the boy's lips.

"Hah," Joey laughed around the obstruction, not resisting, but also not assigning any pleasure to the move.

Androni grinned and pulled away, still holding him, but now met his eye. "Nothing, eh?" he asked with a friendly wink.

Joey chuckled soft with an apologetic shake of the head. "You wanna try again? I'll try again. It's just weird…"

Androni huffed with a wide smile. He dropped his hands and Joey reached forward in a blur and grasped his left wrist.

"I like your touch," he said and put the hand back to his cheek. "This feels nice." He held Androni's gaze, so serious, and still sorry the kiss did nothing for him.

With a nod-blink, Androni conceded, "Two-hundred and fifty years and no one has ever rejected Androni's kiss."

"Maybe it's because I'm a vampire," the boy said lowering his voice. "Maybe it's because since Haman Troye did this, there's nothing twitching down there... know what I mean?"

Androni grinned. "You're a virgin." The boy didn't have to answer. He'd had one girlfriend and never kissed her.

"Hey, are you mad? Did I screw it up? Can I still call you Gypsy?" The boy was joking but also concerned his rejection affected their connection. Androni gave him a new smile.

"Yes, and you and I have a big future ahead of us. I will teach you how to enjoy a kiss. And so much more. Vampires *aren't dead*. I will show you this." He dropped his hand from the boy's cheek only to search for and find his hands, holding them both between them. "Can you get a car? Can we go to town? The doctor has departed and I do not intend to drink blood from a horse tonight."

Joey allowed a cautious grin and he looked to the basement door and back. "Sure, we can get an Uber if my dad hasn't cancelled my credit card."

"Do it," Androni said and watched Joey operate his phone. He had seen commercials about Uber, but in Europe, hadn't been involved enough to have a cell phone, credit cards, or a vehicle of his own. He needed Mark and his people to find a foothold in America, and when he looked into Joey's face, he felt he'd found the perfect person with whom to discover her secrets.

Joey was finished with his chore and he dropped his phone in his pocket. "Let's go. They'll be at the security gate in ten minutes."

"Impressive, Ghost," he answered and Joey's eyes flashed with humor.

"Let's be Ghost and Gypsy tonight. Show me how you get blood without killing and I'll show you how to use Uber."

"This is a good plan," Androni lobbed back. He rolled in his bottom lip, holding the boy's eye. This was going to be a great night.

29

Deliver such a one to Satan for the destruction of the flesh,
that his spirit may be saved in the day of the Lord Jesus.
1 Corinthians 5:5

LEAVING THE BOY ALONE WITH ANDRONI DID NOT SEEM like a good idea on the surface. Was Mark supposed to *babysit* the youth? The more he thought about it the more he truly questioned his responsibility regarding the newest vampire. How much coddling did the boy require? How much support did God expect Mark to provide? Perhaps Tony could give him some advice in this arena.

Mark chose to drive to the cabin and use the quiet time in the car to consider his options. Happily, at 8:00 o'clock that morning, as promised, his new Lexus arrived. He had ordered one similar to his favorite coupe when Paul lived. The memory brought a sad half-grin and Mark gazed out the windshield.

Paul. Life had been better then, happy, peaceful. True, Mark lived in denial, but at the time, he didn't know it and every day brought the knowledge that he ruled his world and Paul worshipped him with his whole heart. But God wanted Mark back into the fold and used Hope Brannen to knock him out of his comfort zone. Mark grinned. The spunky blonde had surely turned his head. He'd never paid women any attention and so his attraction to her must have been supernatural. God, again, having His way.

But I lived those days seeking the woman God had promised...

Decades ago, before Whitford City, before Paul, before he came to America, he had been given a vision that one day a woman would come into his life and ease his burden. Mark interpreted it to mean this special woman would take on his yoke and aid him in his calling. Thus, he watched for her. When he locked eyes with Hope Brannen that day in his office, he had been certain she had arrived. Mark chuckled. He had thought she would join him as a vampire. It was laughable now, since he knew the truth, but maybe God was telling him all along that he'd meet a young woman

163

like Elizabeth. One who would ease his burden another way. One who would be a balm on his tortured memories.

Enjoying the idea, Mark's mind traveled back farther, to 1640, when The Other attacked him, eventually leaving him alone to figure it out on his own. But before then, Mark pondered, before that night, wasn't I happy?

He pictured Father Marcus Corescu, accepted as the village clergy at twenty-five. He enjoyed his calling, his flock, his purpose.

And then farther. Mark pictured himself as a boy, a new twelve, running along a forest path with his best pals. They raced to the caverns, a forbidden destination for children, but they could get away with it. Play in the caves and be home before their fathers returned from the fields.

Mark watched his younger self chasing the other two boys his age, Petroff and Yoki. They reached the entrance and used the opening to prepare their torch. Yoki removed a pre-oiled muslin wrap from his pouch and Petroff trimmed a goodly branch he'd found along the way. Marcus had brought the flint and char, well known among the youths as the best fire-starter among them.

Spisak, his home village a hundred kilometers east of Budapest, sat nestled in a valley surrounded by forest and mountainside. Natural tunnels criss-crossed the underground, and at different points in time the menfolk used the caverns for different purposes. Men had found caches of precious jewels there over the years and more than one claimed to have found gold. In recent years, interest in the tunnels waned and the children, although forbidden to play there, did whenever they could sneak away.

The torch came to life and oh! What a magical place the cavern became. Black walls running trickles of water, the obsidian sand turning the floor a sparkling onyx that bounced back the light of the flame as if littered with diamonds. Marcus and his friends began inward, they'd been here many times, but today they would turn right instead of left and explore. Yoki counted the turns and in a half-hour, the game became who could make up the most fantastic story of those who used the space for magic in the past.

At some point in the game, a tussle broke out. Shouting led to pushing which led to Petroff falling to the wet floor. The torch extinguished and the boys clung together, working to determine the way out. After multiple false starts and violent disagreement of which way to go, Yoki began walking, the other two boys holding his coat.

But we were separated…

Mark recalled the terror of losing contact with his friend's jacket tail. It only took moments in the heavy blackness to be utterly separated, no one able to see well enough to even find one another. When his friends' calling voices were no longer audible, Marcus became hysterical, screaming and walking fast, bumping into the walls and tripping over nothing in the pitch. Finally, young Marcus sunk to the wet floor and sat on his rump to cry. He would die here. The dark fell on him like a blanket, suffocating him and clogging his ears, even his mind, preventing him from thinking straight. Time had no meaning and between fits of terror and shouting for help, Marcus dozed. When he awoke, there was no way to tell if he'd been out minutes or days. What kind of danger was he in? Would he starve? He could thirst to death since he was too frightened to search out the source of water he heard far off. Were there wild animals down there? Criminals? *Monsters?*

Afraid he might never be rescued, Marcus then remembered God.

Marcus's father put a lot of stock in the traveling preacher who came to the Spisak annually, sharing the Gospel. Although the majority of Hungary was Catholic at the time, Spisak had been founded by folk opposed to the Catholic church. The Gospel of Jesus Christ, however, was as welcome as ever, and when the preacher came, all the menfolk welcomed him.

Marcus bowed his head and prayed to be delivered. "If You would save me," he had whispered in the black cave, "...I will become a preacher. I will spread the Gospel all the days of my life. Amen."

God indeed rescued me, Mark mused as the memories rolled past his mind in black and white like an old movie. And though it seemed days had passed in the miserable abyss, it had only been three hours. Little Marcus's father, joined by a few of the menfolk, found him, directed by his friends.

Mark smiled again. This is why he entered the clergy. When he became a man, he traveled to the town and studied under the traveling preacher. When ready, he had returned to Spisak where the town fathers welcomed him as their clergyman.

Mark looked at the dark road, he would be at the cabin in twenty minutes and he was no closer to knowing what to do about Joseph.

Why don't I ask God directly? The answer flashed across his mind as it always did—*because I am a monster.*

But no, that was an excuse. An excuse to avoid doing what God wanted him to do. If he believed he was too evil to speak to God, then he wasn't responsible for whatever he was supposed to do for Him.

He will hear me if I speak to Him...

Mark *tsked*, not quite ready to open that box. *I will use Tony's help.*

Mark said goodbye to the resurrected memories of more than four centuries past. He'd been thirty-three and unmarried when The Other brought him into the dark world of vampires.

Unmarried. Mark thought of Elizabeth Hawken.

When he compared the two women in is life, and he had often since meeting the police detective's daughter, Mark acknowledged the disparity of how he viewed them both. His emotion regarding Hope Brannen had been levered to the novelty of having the perky blonde attach herself to him seemingly out of the blue. Hindsight told him that God had set that up, caused him to look at her when women in general had not interested him in centuries. Then came along Elizabeth, wise, mature, and beautiful. God had allowed Mark to fall for her much like a mortal man. Why? Why would God give him such thoughts of commitment, soul mates, marriage—human relational abstracts as a vampire he could not entertain. Mark didn't know and he didn't truly want to ask God for fear He would answer.

Mark turned on to Lady Bird Lane, the dirt road that led to the cabin. A sad memory arose of he and Paul heading to the cabin to collect their thoughts. Paul had murdered Mark's other servant in cold blood. Reuben. A tragic event that only signaled that Mark had lost control of his life. And now a different vampire sits in the cabin, Tony Agricola, seeking God and seeking peace for defying God's instruction.

Mark pulled to the only roughed-out slot at the cabin's front door and switched of the engine.

This is why I'm here, Mark thought. *Tony hears from God. He will help me decide the next course of action with Joseph.* Mark exhaled with a nod, adding, *If God has allowed me—nay, caused me—to fall for a woman, maybe He is going to leave me alive when this is done. Maybe, her prayers will be enough to move the heart of the Creator.*

Mark didn't believe it, but as Tony's face appeared in the open door, he met the man's eyes and allowed himself a measure of hope.

It had only been seventy-two hours, but looking at Doctor Corescu gave Tony a sense it had been longer. "I'm glad to see you," Tony said welcoming him inside.

Corescu entered and crossed the room. "You look well. I see this plan is working."

Tony nodded and gestured they should sit. He settled on the near couch and Mark in the stiff chair across.

"It is, I have all the company I need with the Holy Spirit and absolutely no bloodlust." Tony watched his eyes and had to speak his mind. "I might be delivered when this forty-days is up." He didn't wait for Mark to comment. "I know that sounds familiar, but it's different this time. I don't feel like a vampire. My night vision was weaker last night. I think I'm transforming."

It occurred to him that Mark may be able to discern his status with his own vampire skills, but he wouldn't ask. Instead, he directed the conversation to the doctor's countenance. As handsome and dashing as any movie star, tonight the vampire seemed softer, his shoulders slightly rounding and a humble crease in his brow. Tony asked Mark about it.

"Humble, eh?" Mark huffed in reply. "I suppose that's as well as any way to describe the new Mark Corescu. God has removed the control box on every aspect of my life. He is working our situation from multiple directions and I'm afraid I need your help to decide my next move."

"Shoot," Tony said with a nod. "When we parted, Joseph had joined the household. Were you able to convince his parents to leave him there for the time being?"

Mark nodded. "I had some help from Androni, but yes, the Ellerslies allowed him to stay."

Tony grinned at the way the name Androni lit up Mark's face. "You like him."

Mark nodded. "I do. If you meet him, you'll see, but he is extremely likable. Even when Hope became entangled with him which brought me to his circus caravan, I liked him on sight. He has no guile, no agenda, and had no one to explain how to be a dark master." Mark grinned at his own words and Tony chuckled. "And he is appealing to the eyes."

Tony raised his brow with a comical noise. "He looks the part."

Mark chuckled and averted his gaze. "He is funny and interesting. Living among circus folk the past century has made him even more affable than his original personality allowed. Joseph is in love with him." Mark stopped sharing and re-met Tony's eye.

"Oh? He likes him a little too much, then?"

Mark offered a slow nod. "I am unhappy about it. Why? I request your advice, ask God, am I worried for them or is it something else?"

"Tell me what's on your mind. I'm listening," Tony said and Mark exhaled with what sounded like relief.

"When you were removed, Joseph received the truth of it, that I had taken charge of the household. He allowed me to show him my stallion, teach him to draw from animals until such a time that he wouldn't need blood, but he fears me. He doesn't like me. He'd only been with us a few hours when Androni flew to the States. I chose to drive the distance with Ms. Hawken. On the way back, I felt comfortable enough to share our lives with the magician. When I introduced Androni to Joseph, the boy's eyes…"

Mark made a *shew* and Tony nodded in thought.

"What worries you about this," he said trying to guess at what Mark was reluctant to say.

Mark sighed, resigned. "I sense that because of Joseph's sheltered existence coupled with his virginal state before his change, his attraction to Androni is of the romantic nature." Tony huffed with interest and Mark continued. "Not sexual, obviously, but everything the youth romanticized about vampires is found in this flashy magician. More than anything, Joseph wants to emulate Androni. He wants to know Androni inside and out."

"Well," Tony said with muted humor and Mark gave a half-shrug.

"Who's to say? If he wasn't a vampire…" The doctor wiped his face with one hand. "Androni has perfected the art of drawing blood and leaving his victim alive and unaware. He has become an expert in providing sexual stimulation to his victims in exchange for a non-fatal blood meal."

Tony nodded in thought, recalling his consummation with Sarah, where with his vampire limitations and her physical conformation, they were still able to find pleasure in the marriage bed.

"When I overheard Androni seducing the youth before I left the house, I did not interrupt. I do not want the two of them so close because Androni does not know God. But what if God is putting them together for His purposes? I can't hear God's will on this, so that is why I am here with you in person.

Tony had a sense of the two and decided to share it with Mark. "I see them leaving us, together, arm in arm."

Mark sighed and shook his head. "I see that, too. But this wild one and the youngest vampire? Out in the world?"

Tony raised one hand. "No need to list the ways they could find trouble," he said in a gentle laugh. "It's not up to us to hold them in place.

You're right about that. You and I, and Sarah and Elizabeth, should pray for God's will to be done with the both of them. It's okay to be concerned, but not to worry. If they leave, they are in God's hands." Mark had no argument so he moved onto the next worrisome topic—Hope Brannen.

"She is with friends, our connection is up and strong," Mark offered. "When I leave here, I will go there, check in, see if I cannot convince her to return with me. She is leaving the path and it is dangerous."

Tony nodded. "Ask her to come home and then accept her answer. We will pray that she is kept safe and that she does not die while outside of her Father's house."

With a grave nod, Mark agreed and added, "Add a prayer for Ms. Hawken. She wants to know me as a man, as a life-mate…"

Tony squeezed his fingers. "I know. Don't say it. Let's pray for God's will to be done."

Mark had no complaint and he bowed his head and Tony lifted them all to the throne.

30

ANDRONI SAID HE'D NEVER TAKEN AN UBER AND AS THE driver piloted them toward downtown, the magician launched into explaining the origins of the word. Joey listened, laughing at his put-on German accent and amazed at the vast bank of knowledge the vampire had accumulated over the decades. Sure, he'd been localized, it would seem, within a four-hundred-mile radius in the Carpathian Mountains, but he devoured life. No complaining, no fear, no worries. And although he avoided direct sunlight because of headaches, he wasn't destroyed or afraid of garlic and crosses. Such silly vampire deterrents Joey would never discuss with Tony or the doctor, but Androni enjoyed their discussions. In fact, *Gypsy* enjoyed everything about Ghost, and he read this in the man's eyes. Never did his new friend seem bored or tired of his presence. This was new and welcome and as the hired car reached the busier streets of downtown, Joey began asking what he wanted to do.

"Does Montgomery have dance clubs?" he asked.

Joey smiled when the driver glanced at them in the rearview mirror. It was a middle-aged woman. She had eye-balled them both when they got in, but hadn't made small-talk.

"We do," he said and asked the driver to pull over. Once free of the stranger, he and Androni faced the strip of opportunities. Three busy clubs to choose from and Joey asked him for a preference.

"What's the difference," he asked his eyes scanning the patrons on their every side.

Joey wondered the same thing and gave him a grin. "I guess there's not any." They chose the closest door and in they went.

Joey wondered what they must look like to the club patrons. With Gypsy looking very much like a Vampire King and Ghost looking his

170

namesake—pale, young, but attractive enough. Joey grinned at his thoughts and, noticing the action, Androni sent him a wink. They had chosen two stools at the bar, facing the dancefloor, watching, listening, and absorbing the life of the place. Being underage, Joey did not attempt to order afraid of being carded, but Androni ordered a martini for himself and a cola for Joey so they'd look the part.

"For the record, you're my big brother," he told Androni leaning in to be heard. "It's my 21st birthday and you're taking me out on the town."

Androni grinned. "We need a story, eh? Is that how you do it in America?"

His intonation held something else and Joey raised his eyebrows. "What are we here for?" he asked with friendly suspicion.

"Blood," Androni said in his normal voice, not whispering and not hiding his meaning.

In his peripheral vision, Joey noted no one looked over at the word. Maybe he was paranoid. Maybe pretending he knew how to "go clubbing" had been a bad idea. He'd wanted to impress Androni, but he'd never been to a dance club or legitimate bar. He must have blushed because his friend leaned in close as if to speak in his ear. Instead, he kissed his cheek. Joey blushed deeper, certain other patrons would have taken notice. But with a tiny peek, no one had.

"You worry too much," Androni said still close and leaned out just enough to look him in the face. "Life isn't hard. It isn't complicated. IF," he stressed and leaned out a little more. "IF you know who you are. Will you let Androni the Magnificent show you? Your friend Gypsy will show you how to live. Yes?"

Joey nodded like a child, his eyes in Androni's, their faces so close, he expected another kiss. But his friend resumed his spot on the stool, one leg to the brace and one to the floor, watching the dancers. Joey wanted to ask him more and then wished they could speak telepathically. He'd had miniscule snippets from the man, but the doctor and Tony could hold entire conversations. How was that possible? Neither was sharing the secret, but Androni would. Joey built up his courage, remembered how much the guy liked him, and touched his sleeve to have him look over. Joey leaned close to him this time and said in his ear, "Why can't we speak telepathically like Tony and Dr. Corescu?"

When he withdrew to hear the answer, his friend's face had brightened.

"Mark explained it as common blood," he answered in a low voice.

Joey nodded; he and Androni had no common blood that he knew of. He was wondering how to remedy the situation when Androni slid off the stool and took his bicep. With a half-grin, Joey allowed the tug and followed across the space to a far corner marked restrooms, and then trailed Androni inside. The space was clean and dimly-lit with smooth brown walls and brass-trimmed sink hardware. It was smallish, with two stalls and one free-standing urinal. No one was inside and with a quizzical smile in place, Joey watched Androni choose the next move. He scoped the two stalls and pulled Joey inside one with him and latched the door.

"What?" Joey asked in a whisper, intrigued and wondering what the guy had cooked up. Androni's expression was open and gleeful which made Joey grin wider. "What's up?"

"We will swap blood. This is the magic required to allow us to speak to each other's minds." Androni faced him square on, looking down and only two feet apart.

"Oh, wow," Joey whispered, enjoying the idea suddenly of drinking Androni's blood. Then he remembered the doctor's edict and frowned. Androni held up one hand.

"It is a risk," he said with a sad nod. "We must weigh the pros and cons, eh? I live my life a certain way and I will not change—it works for me too well. But you have to live your way. You decide if this risk is worth it to you."

"The risk that the doctor will kick me out," Joey said still whispering and Androni offered a single nod.

"I don't know what to do." And he didn't. His entire life, Joey turned to his parents and authority figures to know what to do, to make the next move. Now he needed to make a decision on his own. What should he do?

Androni gave him a new smile, maybe intuiting his inner struggle. "You're only eighteen. It's understandable to wrestle with these deep decisions. If I may mentor you a little," he said, his chin lowered and his eyes up.

Joey gave him a small nod. "What would you do?"

"Instead of asking that, ask yourself if you can stomach any negative consequences. Then you will make an informed decision."

It made sense, and before Joey put his mind to the task, Androni added, "Remember; whatever you choose, own it. Take full responsibility and have no regrets."

Joey ran it down. If he broke the doctor's rules, he might get kicked out. If he got kicked out, where would he go? Would he stay with Androni? He'd be kicked out, too. How would they make a living? Androni admitted he came to the country with only the clothes on his back.

And I can't go home as a vampire...

With that in mind, how was he going to explain this to his parents after a week goes by? A Month? Longer? The issue of swapping blood with Androni and possibly being evicted was one small problem among dozens of larger issues. Suddenly, Joey wished they were not in a noisy bar restroom. He wanted to talk, to listen, and to get Androni's advice on the future. With a wince at his inner weakness, he asked if they could leave.

Androni unlatched the door without pause and stepped free of the stall. "Where shall we go?"

Joey sought his mind for quiet places they could relax and share information without being interrupted. Tony's house was out. His own house, of course, a non-issue.

"Let's get a hotel room," he suggested, and then, afraid his idea would send the wrong message, he followed up with, "so we can talk in private."

"Fantastic," his friend said and turned for the exit.

Joey followed, wondering about what the next hour would entail. Yes, they would find a room. Yes, they would sit down and relax in private.

And no one will be there to stop us if we swap blood.

Joey's stomach fluttered at the thought and he rolled in his lips. Androni noticed and draped an arm across his shoulders.

"I will teach you to stop this worrying," he said and pulled Joey toward the car.

Twenty minutes later, Joey slipped the keycard into the lock and pushed open the room door, Androni right behind him. Inside, he thanked God his dad hadn't shut off his card. He had a bank account, but his father was on it. If he had a notion to cut Joey off, it wouldn't be difficult. For now, however, he was able to get a room. The downside being, of course, that if his dad decided to snoop onto the app, he'd see exactly where his boy was holed up. Joey kept this information to himself, *part of not worrying so much,* he said inside.

"Very nice!" Androni said and flopped onto the large king bed with drama, landing on his back, arms and legs wide. "Such luxury!"

Joey grinned at his abandon. It would be very nice to be so lighthearted. Even before Haman changed his DNA, he had lived a careful and stressful existence. Trying to please his parents, his teachers, everyone.

What if he learned to relax? Would God allow it?

"Over here, Ghost!" Androni said, scooching to one side and then patting the comforter. "Imitate me!"

A smile reached Joey's lips and he crawled onto the mattress, first on his hands and knees looking down on the vampire's gleeful face. He held his eye a little too long because his cheeks pinked. Something about Androni's intense gaze brought a blush every time, and this was accompanied with a deep-down hunger that didn't yet have a name. Joey maneuvered to lay beside his friend, both of them facing the ceiling tile.

"Ghost, you beautiful, beautiful boy, you did that all wrong." Androni turned to his side, brought his knees to his chest to put the soles of his boots to Joey's hip. With gentle but steady pressure, he used his feet to push Joey off the bed.

"What? What do you mean?" he asked laugh-talking and now standing over his friend and awaiting an explanation.

"Think about it. Did Gypsy carefully get onto the bed and come to rest on his back?"

Joey laughed, shaking his head. No, Androni had flopped down with abandon. Joey measured the distance, the height of the mattress, and then the amount of space between his friend and the side. Then with a shout of "hi-yah!" tamping his new vampire leg strength, Joey leapt into the air to land on the bed, his back to the thick duvet, arms and legs out. His hand dropped across Androni's chest and as he relaxed into the pillowtop mattress, his friend lifted that hand to his mouth.

"Much better," he said, his lips against Joey's skin. The magician breathed against it a few seconds then released his hand.

Joey sighed, his smile as wide as when he first met the gregarious vampire. Now what? Should he begin the conversation? He got his friend in private, so he needed to proceed, right? Joey turned his face and caught Androni watching his profile as he pondered his next move.

"I want to see in your head," Androni whispered, his voice so silky and welcome to Joey's ears. "If we swap blood, it will likely come easier for us. Have you decided? Will you defy the doctor and possibly lose his affection, but no longer remain deaf to Androni the Magnificent's amazing telepathic sentiments?"

Joey smiled despite the seriousness of the situation. "You have a way with words," he said then, holding his friend's eye. "I want to swap blood and accept the consequences."

"Yes," Androni replied and reached again for his hand. "Me, first."

Joey rolled onto his side facing his friend and watched him bring the wrist to his lips. "You're going to bite my arm?" Joey asked in a whisper, wondering what to expect, how it would feel, and if he'd be afraid when it started. When Haman attacked, Joey had all but blacked out from terror. He'd been bitten in the neck, but he couldn't recall any details of the event. Only that he'd been afraid for his life. Now he was going to experience it all in slow motion—and this time, he was in no danger, and he knew it. He decided to ask the question and was happy he could without fear of being teased. "Why don't you bite my neck?"

"You would like that better?" Androni asked with a grin. "Because I am your mentor, right?" Joey replied with a single nod. "Then learn this. I will bite you here and you will bite me in the same place to practice for when you bite *them,* the mortals. I will show you how to take their blood and leave them alive. In the throat, you can easily hit the carotid. You and me? We will heal. A mortal can bleed out and die."

"Oh," Joey said thoughtfully and watched as Androni put his lips to the offered arm. He drew his tongue across the spot and held Joey's eye, which made him smile and blush anew.

"I love those pink cheeks," his friend said and opened his mouth wider.

Joey witnessed the man's fangs then, elongating as he watched, and they slid past the barrier of Joey's skin as if made of surgical steel. Joey inhaled but felt no pain, only the pressure of the act and then the suction Androni created at the wound site. One, two, three. Five, seven, nine... Joey counted the seconds. Then, his friend's tongue pressed against the wound and Androni closed his eyes tight. He groaned softly and from deep within and did not move another several seconds.

"You okay?" Joey asked and Androni nodded, remaining as he was. When another minute passed without the man moving, Joey grinned and prodded his shoulder. Androni laughed one chortle and collapsed onto his back. He didn't move, his eyes closed, and Joey propped upon his elbow. "What? Good or bad? I can't tell."

"*Uh... May... Zing,*" Androni sounded out in slow motion and he finally turned his head to Joey, lazily opening his eyes. "Here. See if it's the same for you." He flopped onto his side, lifting his wrist.

Joey trained his gaze to the blue veins beneath the vampire's skin. What would it feel like, biting down... breaking through? Would it be like biting an apple? Or a peach? Should he be disgusted?

Joey cleared his mind recalling Androni's top teaching—stop

175

worrying. With that final consideration, he allowed his teeth to touch the surface. For the first moment, nothing happened, but barely had he pictured the blood in his mind that his fangs slid free. Joey bit down.

Oh.

It's…

It's nothing like…

Joey stopped his brain and allowed his eyes to roll back as the thick fluid poured into his mouth and sloshed his palate. He swallowed only when forced to, enjoying the flavor more than he ever imagined.

"The blood of a brother is better than any other…"

Oh, God, he was right…

"I dreamed about you. Are you okay?"

Mark considered the illuminated text screen, his old mind first thinking it wasn't so long ago that cell phones didn't fit in your pocket. Three seconds later, a second note came in.

"It's absurd, but you know… With all that's weird, why not dreams, too?"

Mark grinned at her grammatic exactness. He hadn't been texting long, but he had already started truncating words and he would never use commas. He'd been reclining on the veranda of his German home after leaving Tony at the cabin. Joey and Androni were "on the town," Hope was safe but not answering his calls, and here was a nice surprise. Elizabeth Hawken thinking about him at what would be 1 AM in her part of the world. He pushed the call icon and she picked right up.

"Hey! Sorry about the hour," she said, the sound of her voice giving him a new smile.

"I do not sleep, so please, no need to apologize."

Elizabeth huffed an embarrassed laugh. "I forgot about that."

"I regret causing you distress," he told her wondering as she must have been – was it a dream or a nudge from God?

"No, never. I just wish you were here to talk to," she said in a softer voice. "I feel time running out and when we said goodbye tonight, I couldn't rest my mind."

Mark sensed she had an entire litany of things she would discuss if he were there, but propriety prevented her from asking him to come. He had no such restrictions, so he posed a suggestion. "Invite me over and I will come. Right now."

"Really?" she said her voice happy again. "Yes, come on. Do you have my address?"

"Just a moment," Mark said with a tiny new grin she might hear in his voice. He rose to his feet and in his mind, pictured her cottage. He had been there many times without her knowledge, reconnaissance being important before when she was just a girl imbued with Rakha's blood. With no effort he blinked, and then he stood in her yard, on the fence line, under an oak where he had been weeks ago after The Other was killed. "Your wish is my command. Front door or back?" he asked so she would hear his humor.

"Really?!" she exclaimed and disconnected. A moment later the porch light came on and she opened the door. "Hey!" she shout-whispered and waved him close when she met his eye. "I'm so happy to see you!"

Her expression pulled him with its power. Mark crossed the trimmed lawn and her face lit up the night. She put her hands out as if to pull him inside and he instead brought them to his lips.

"You look lovely," he told her when he released her fingers.

"Aw! Thanks! This is the real me."

She wore no makeup and was freshly showered—Mark inhaled her soapy aroma and it made him happy. She wore pajamas, the blouse being loose-fitting but so thin, she had no secrets. The instant he noticed, she did too, and comically folded one forearm across her breasts.

"Come in!" she said with a giggle and ushered him across the threshold. She scooted away to the back of the small home, calling for him to make himself comfortable.

Mark chuckled to himself and dropped onto her short sofa. The room was close, cozy, and decorated with earthy artwork and silk flora. Elizabeth returned in a t-shirt and sweats, jogging in on her toes, looking all of ten years old, her long brown curls tied loosely in back. She sat beside him, turning sideways, and stared into his face.

"You popped over here, eh? That's amazing." Her eyes were huge as always and she blushed as if embarrassed at her comment. "I understand all this is old-hat to you, but, just… wow."

"You think I'm amazing," Mark said with levity and she gave a happy nod. "Good, because I am." She laughed and his joke helped her relax to her normal posture. She reached for his hand which rested on his leg and she covered it with her own.

"When we said good night, I knew you had things to do. Important things, but I wanted to be there with you. I wanted to stay with you. If you were a normal man and your problems were normal," she said with quotation marks, "I'd just assume I was in puppy-love. But there are big things at stake here, and I'm involved up to my ears."

Mark followed with a nod awaiting more.

"When I got home…" She hopped up to grab her phone. She pressed a button and turned the screen to Mark. "Listen to the message Dad left me."

Mark dropped his eyes to the phone. It read, "Dad" and was 15 seconds long. Elizabeth hit play.

"Honey, Reverend Tracey called. She said you know about them. So listen—I told Agricola to protect you from that voodoo crap. I don't know why they decided to tell you. It's bad. Really bad. I want you to be careful. The reverend said you're safe, and I trust her completely. But I don't trust that doctor, or even Agricola anymore. Just be careful. I'm not telling Jenn. Please, God, don't tell her anything about this. Okay, honey, call me back. I love you. Be careful."

Mark raised his eyes to hers when the message ended.

"I called him back. I told him you are a good man, that you and Tony want to be normal again. I think he got it. I think he understands and when we said bye, he said he would pray for you guys to be successful in getting un-cursed."

"Un-cursed," Mark repeated with a slow nod. "I am sorry to be the cause of this trouble."

"No, no, no," she said and set down her phone to scoot closer. "Don't be sorry about that! I wanted to play it so you'd know where it stands with Dad. He said that Jenn doesn't remember meeting you at the hospital. How about that? He said she dropped her P.I. hobby and last month, got into mini-goats and mini-horses."

Mark huffed a laugh.

"Did you hypnotize her to forget you? That's what Dad thinks."

Mark nodded. "I thought it was best."

"I think so, too. Whatever God was doing using her and Dad to get us to that point is done. If God lets her forget, I'm all for it. But it got me thinking."

"Yes?" Mark asked and didn't try to guess ahead what she would say.

"I'm asking God to deliver you and keep you alive. If I get my wish, I'm going to try my best to keep you forever. Then you and I will eventually see Jenn." Elizabeth grinned and blushed as she embarrassed herself revealing her plan. "Imagine if you're delivered and we go see them. Will she recognize you? Remember you and start it all up again?"

Mark raised his eyebrows. Her question had no answer, only speculation, which wasn't his forte. She rushed ahead in his silence.

"I know it's out there. I need to stay in the now. I know."

Mark sighed and reached for her near hand. "Every hour that passes feels like my last. Is this what your dream entailed?" he asked, seeing something in her eyes. She nodded very slowly and lowered her gaze. "Let's live in this moment. Right now."

"Yes, I want to. I will," she said and re-met his eye. "Tell me how it went with Androni and Joey. Did they make friends?"

Mark laughed once and enjoyed her corresponding grin.

"What? They did, right? He's nice. Did he like Joey?"

"Yes, they are best friends," Mark said choosing his words. "The reason I find myself alone tonight sitting on a roof across the globe is because Androni took Joey on a date." Mark smiled with a new chuckle and Elizabeth interpreted correctly.

"Oh, so he really liked him a lot, eh? Too much?" she asked.

He gave a small shrug.

"Well, look—try not to worry. I have a good feeling about that guy. He's like a little baby being introduced to a gigantic new world. If he and Joey can be pals, maybe that's what will bring Androni to know God. What do you think?"

Mark smiled, "Tony said the same thing."

Her eyes dimmed with concern at the tone of his voice. "Mark, what's bothering you tonight? Let me tell you my dream. I think it was from God."

Mark nodded; dreams had always been a big part of his life, even before meeting Tony and learning the truth regarding the Judging.

"Before we decided to get to know each other, I dreamed about you watching the world go by, not living, not participating. Remember that?"

Mark again gave a nod. He had floated between the worlds since learning the truth and the death of The Other left him untethered to either realm. Now that he had a friendship with Tony and more recently, Elizabeth, he felt more alive than he had in a long while.

"Tonight when I dozed off, I saw you standing in a field at night, the moon over your shoulder and it was enormous." She brought both arms up to make an "O". You whistled and an entire herd of black horses came from all sides, creating a gigantic dust cloud that obliterated my view. I could hear the hooves and the sounds of squealing, but could only see dust. When they grew quiet and the haze filtered away, all of the horses were pure white. They turned and walked calmly back the way they had come."

Mark rolled in his lips picturing what she described. She did not continue for a long moment and he sought her eye. "And me?"

"You were gone."

"Ah," he said with a single nod.

"I think it means even though in your past, you killed a lot of people, many of them repented. You were able to do some good despite the curse. I thought you might find that encouraging." She shrugged one shoulder. "So, I texted you."

"I'm glad you did," he said and leaned close to kiss her forehead. They were both quiet for a time, staring into each other's eyes until finally, Mark stood to his feet, bringing Elizabeth along with him. "Get your sleep. I will come get you around lunch and we'll have some adventures. Would you like that?" Her face brightened. "What will we do next?"

"Ummm," she hummed looking up, her sweet face breaking his heart. "Have you ever played putt-putt?"

Mark chuckled. "In 1972, I was invited to golf with the chief surgeon of the hospital where I worked at the time. Paul bought me all of the appropriate materials and I learned the rules of play, but when he showed me the outfit…" Mark leaned out to meet her eye, a half-smile in place. "…I suddenly came down with a case of flu."

"The pants?" she asked and he nodded. "Oh! I wish I'd seen you wearing plaid golfing slacks!" Elizabeth laughed hard and grabbed him about the middle. He hugged her back and kissed the top of her head.

"Never happen," he laughed and then stiffened his spine. When he swallowed, he tasted blood in the back of his throat. And, oh God, it was ambrosia. He had already learned when Tony imbibed, he could taste it— also, when Tony starved, Mark felt the same pain. But right now, wherever they were, the boy was taking blood from the magician.

Elizabeth pulled out of the proximity to see his face. "What's wrong?"

"Joseph and Androni are swapping blood," he said, not hiding the ugly truth.

"Oh, no," she whispered. "They're not supposed to do that, right? I heard you telling Androni not to do that."

Mark rolled in his lips with a nod. What should he do? Anything? Was God even watching?

"Is Joseph going to be okay?" she asked in full concern.

Mark sighed and folded her back into place, snugged against his chest. She fit into him like a glove, as if they could melt together if they tried hard

180

enough. "Joseph's attitude in short is, God did this, God is responsible, and God will forgive me if I mess up."

"Okay…" Elizabeth said to prompt him to continue.

"All of those are true, but when we sin on purpose, we make our lives more difficult. God can forgive him for choosing blood over holiness, but following the sin instead of the Truth will cause him heartache. I know because I have been there."

"Then tell him. Warn him. Tell him you've been there, done that, and the consequences. He'll probably choose the blood for now, but he'll remember what you said when God makes things tough for him. I'm speaking from experience too."

"I think you are exactly right." Mark swallowed again and the telepathic blood meal massaged his sleeping hunger. He reined in his thoughts with incredible skill, but it thrilled his stomach to fantasize such food might slide down his throat, too.

I could do it. God would forgive me. Just sink my teeth into the boy's throat, take a portion of the blood of a brother. But I won't. I won't. I definitely won't…

And inside, he attributed such willpower now to his affection for Elizabeth.

Isn't God clever, he thought and left it alone.

31

But the Lord is faithful,
Who will establish you
And guard you from the evil one.
II Thessalonians 3:3

THE BLOOD OF A BROTHER IS BETTER THAN ANY OTHER...
The phrase looped itself, mantra-like, as the ecstasy Androni's blood brought his system tickled Joey's mind. And he barely cared that he first heard it from the demon, Haman Troye. Right now, this moment, he understood what it meant.

Still gripping Androni's wrist, Joey dropped his weight backward to the mattress. It must have been three minutes before he realized he still held the vampire's arm.

"What do you think, beautiful Ghost?" Androni's voice had come from within Joey's head, not from without and he whipped his face to the side.

"It worked!" he rasped and his friend touched his temple. Joey grinned and sent with concentration, *"it worked!"*

"Try a harder one," his friend sent back.

"The blood of a brother is better than any other," Joey sent, watching Androni's eyes. His friend smiled, first a little, and then a lot, before wiggling his captive hand for Joey to drop.

"So true, this is so very true," Androni said this time speaking. He remained lying on his side, his head in the soft pillow and facing Joey. "The doctor will know when he sees you, smells you—I smell my blood in your body."

Joey furrowed his brow and worked to see if he discerned any such thing about Androni. Maybe he did, but didn't have enough experience to know. He assumed it was so and still had no good response.

"So we shall proceed with living, eh?" Androni asked in the same soft tone. "Drawing blood from mortals... You'll want to do it sooner than later. I've not taken animal blood, but it cannot be near as satisfying."

"Aren't they afraid of vampires? I sure would be."

Androni smiled with a secret sideways grin. "They're not afraid of Androni. This is why I am your master, eh? I will show you how to do this right."

"My master?" Joey said with a grin. "My vampire master, I like it."

"I never knew my master, as you know," he replied and lifted his now healed arm to touch Joey's cheek one stroke. "It does not have to be so difficult for you, Ghost, as it was for Androni. I will teach you everything I know and you will find abundant life."

Joey's expression slipped as he recalled a Bible teaching about abundance. Such was for the Lord to give man, and it was for the purpose of fulfilling God's will on earth. Androni moved on to his next topic, but Joey's mind rolled through more Scripture pertaining to vampirism, the drinking of blood, the divided mind, the lust of the eyes…

"These phrases… they are religious teachings?" Androni asked, obviously seeing much of Joey's thoughts.

"Yeah," he replied in a sigh and rolled onto his back. "There's no way around it—the Bible is against vampires." Joey turned his head to say the last word with an apologetic frown. "This is why the doctor and Tony don't want me to drink from people. They want God to deliver them. They want to be normal again."

"And what do you want?" his friend asked in a near-whisper.

Joey knew the answer and it frightened him as well as brought up excitement. "I want to stay with you."

"You want to be a vampire?" Androni asked in his mind.

Joey's answer to that one took longer. He hemmed and settled with saying, "…for now."

The expression in his friend's eyes grew softer and he propped up to again press his lips to Joey's face, this time to his forehead. Then with a terrible jangle, Joey's cell rang from his back jeans pocket. One glance and he read the landline from Tony Agricola's home.

"Joey, honey," Reverend Tracey said as sweet as ever, "something happened to your brother. He's in the hospital and asking for you."

Joey got to his feet, his eyes on the door. "Which hospital? Where? What happened?"

"Hush, now, honey, it's going to be okay. Dr. Corescu is there. He assured me your brother will recover. He was hit by a car. Go to Baptist South, ICU, okay? I'm going to text the doctor that you're coming."

"Yes, thank you, I am," Joey disconnected and barely glanced at his friend as he crossed to the door. "I… I…" He didn't know what to say to

Androni so he left the room, allowed the door to close, and jogged to the elevator.

The room was rented for the next 24 hours so he'd be fine. Joey wanted to worry about leaving him like that, but then, in the most peaceful voice he'd ever heard, Androni sent, *"Take care of your brother. I will be here when you are finished."*

Joey sent a heartfelt thank you and zoomed to the hospital. Poor Luke. He would run into his parents. He would run into Dr. Corescu. The Doctor would discover when he'd done with Androni.

But Luke needs me.

Joey drove faster and did his best not to worry about every detail. Such as, did God orchestrate this to make him return to this family?

Nope. Nope. Nope.

Joey cleared the thought and prayed for his brother.

32

No one among you shall eat blood,
nor shall any stranger who dwells among you eat blood.
Leviticus 17:12

JOEY LAY HIS HEAD IN HIS HANDS AND STARED AT THE ceiling. Luke remained in the hospital two days and nights. Joey's parents grabbed onto him when he arrived, questioned him within an inch of his life, and in the end, seemed to hate him for choosing the Agricola's home over theirs. But Joey stood firm, the image of Androni's teeth in his arm keeping him anchored.

And mine in his...

Joey's stomach rumbled with the thought. He hadn't taken blood since then. The black stallion had a mate, a mare the doctor added that was kept in a stall, easier to catch and more convenient for blood. Joey didn't want horse blood. He craved Androni's.

For the moment, the house was empty. Sarah had gone into town on errands, but being the saint she was, she'd handed Joey the keys to a leased late-model luxury sedan. He never would have chosen a Jaguar, but it was fancy. He had thanked her, and she scooted away, as if still uncomfortable in his company.

Oh, well... Not my fault, he thought and then wondered where the doctor had gone. He never told Joey where he was going, rather simply expected him to wait around.

This is NOT fair!

Androni had been indeed excommunicated without fanfare and Joey had not seen him since the hotel room. That was four nights ago. Joey pondered his situation. He missed him and he was angry.

NONE of this is fair.

Besides missing the magician's company, Joey missed his blood.

The blood is the life.

Joey said the scripture aloud in the room.

Didn't Count Dracula say that in the movies?

185

But the original One who spoke those words was God. This phrase was a fragment of a larger, more meaningful sentence from the Holy Bible. *Thou shall not eat the blood of any animal. For in the blood is the life.*

Carrying his thought even further, Joey looked to the end table on his left and lifted the leather-bound Bible Corescu was bugging him to study. Flipping through, he mumbled aloud again, "The blood is the life…" Inside, his internal questions continued.

What was God trying to get the Israelites to stop doing? Were they drinking blood? Had this become a problem in the camp? Or did it have to do with pagan rituals that involved blood? Devil worship? Idolatry? And… does this law apply to me?

Joey opened the Bible at random and it fell on 1 Timothy. He glanced at the words on the page, not really seeking anything, his mind still pondering the imponderable things of before, when his eye stopped on the word 'immortal'.

"God, the blessed and only Ruler, the King of kings, Lord of lords, who alone is immortal and lives in unapproachable light…" Joey read it again, and then once more aloud. "Who alone is immortal…"

Then that means that I am not immortal. This means that the doctor, Androni, and Tony…we're still mortal.

"I ran across that quandary many times as I searched my spirit on these matters."

Joey startled and sat up as the doctor came fully into the room. He allowed a nod, but did not reply.

"If only God is immortal, why have I lived so long?" Doctor Corescu sank into a leather chair and looked into Joey's face. Running his hand through his black hair, he sighed. "Have you an answer?"

Joey didn't and he looked back to the book in his hand.

"What are you thinking about?" the doctor asked, sounded truly curious.

Joey shrugged one shoulder. "Why do you think the Lord let this happen? I've been good. Do you think God found something offensive in me? Something He needed to purge?"

"You haven't learned yet that none of this is about you. It's also not about me or Tony or your friend, Androni. Our breath is for the Lord. He allows us to use it any way we choose, but it was created for His purposes. You being here is part of His divine plan and we cannot understand the details while in this flesh."

Joey marveled at his logic. Still such truth brought with it no comfort. "I guess He's accustomed to us being mad at Him then," Joey whispered looking aside. "I don't like being separated from the one person in the world who truly wants me around." Joey sought Mark's eye. "Why do I had to take blood from an animal when Androni can feed me without hurting anyone? Your rule against this makes no sense."

"Turn your ire to the heavens, young man," the doctor said, his patronizing tone in place. "It is your God who wants you to remain pure in this way. You think I don't long to take Androni's blood? Or yours?"

Joey narrowed his eyes, not considering this.

"I think about it all the time. Before I listened to God's will, I took human blood every night. And when I wanted to, I drank from my servant Paul. If God did not hold my hands, I'd sink my fangs in you right now."

Joey was surprised and he lined up his questions. Corescu shook his head.

"You want me to do it—you want me to suck blood from your neck. Androni touches you and his contact brings you comfort. My touch would not do the same."

Joey didn't believe him, thinking the doctor just didn't like him enough to touch him in the first—

"Look."

Joey startled as Corescu reached his side at the speed of thought and stood against him, their chests touching. The vampire's right hand cupped Joey's neck and the left arm held him in place.

"Is this comforting?" he asked in a rasp and Joey heard the hunger in his voice. *"Feeling calm?"* he teased, sending his question with an eerie quiver. Haman's attack returned to mind and dread pierced Joey to the core. His every muscle tensed, and he prepared to fight or run, whichever he could do first. Corescu gripped him more tightly and pressed his face beneath Joey's jaw, speaking now against his taut skin, "Nothing about this is wholesome. Nothing about this is pure or godly. Nothing…" the doctor hissed and drew his tongue across one swipe before finishing silently with, *"absolutely nothing about this has anything to do with the holiness of God."*

"I know, I know—please!" Joey yelped pushing against the doctor's broad chest. *He's going to do it! He's gonna… he's!*

But he didn't. The doctor was gone, out of the basement, and likely, out of the house. Joey collapsed to the sofa and buried his face in his hands. His mind reached out for Androni, but for the first time since they swapped blood, he made no connection. Instead, he heard the doctor's telepathic voice.

"You will not be able to reach him this way. I have blocked such communication.

187

Grow into God's image, boy. Not Androni's."

Joey frowned and looked at the floor, his eyes narrowing with anger. *None of this is fair!* he shouted inside. For his own edification, he tried to reach Androni a few more times with more and more concentration, but nothing. And his friend did not carry a cell phone.

Joey's stomach rumbled.

The stupid mare was in the barn.

Angry at the doctor and maybe also at God for allowing such a state to land upon him, Joey headed up the stairs.

In less than five minutes he stood in the center of the barn aisle. It was was wired for electricity, but Joey kept it dark, allowing light to spill in from outside the fourteen-foot-high sliding door. He was hungrier than ever now that disgruntlement had set in. Earlier tonight, he had prayed in private to God and asked for His will to be done. Now, ten minutes ago, he begged God to let him see Androni again, to taste his blood, to enjoy his fellowship.

Am I splitting into two people? *Joey of God* who sought the Lord's will, and *Joey of the Dark* who ached in his flesh for blood.

Joey grimaced as his stomach grumbled. Drinking blood was abominable, so why did God allow him to be cursed? And what about Pastor Tony and the Doctor? These men loved God; why did they have to suffer under this terrible curse?

Joey rubbed his eyes and ran his fingers through his hair. The truth was that he needed to eat. Would God want him to starve? The doctor wanted Joey to be stronger than the temptation. He was supposed to be able to *ignore* the gnawing pain.

But I can't do it.

With his hand to her halter, Joey pulled the horse out of its stall. The mare lumbered forward, big and dumb and ready for whatever its master demanded.

Master... My vampire master...

Joey looked off at nothing, recalling Androni's face, smiling. Smiling at his Ghost. This man, his friend, Gypsy, liked him without reservation.

And I can't see him? How is that fair?!

Angry again, Joey jerked the mare's lead line and she flinched. He barely gave her any notice and continued to complain in his heart. When he tied the horse to the ring in the wall, he stared again into the dark corners of the barn.

"Androni?" he called out with his heart and mind. *"Gypsy? Are you*

188

there?"

Nothing. How had the doctor ruined their connection? What sort of power did he have and why was he allowed to use it?

"Androni would feed me…" Joey spoke to the quiet barn, to the crickets, to an owl somewhere in the rafters. He listened to the slow beating of the horse's enormous heart. "Androni is the only one in this whole mess who loves me, who wants me to be happy…"

Having grown now more melancholy than hungry, Joey abandoned the horse and walked to a vacant stall. The thick pine shavings wafted fragrant dust as he stepped through. In the darkest corner of the fourteen-by-fourteen space, he dropped to his knees. Inside, advice arrived: *Leave the barn, pray, stop focusing on yourself, do the right thing…*

Joey huffed and after turning his arm, he considered the underside of his wrist. Here is where his closest friend, Androni the Magnificent, took his blood. Joey's middle rumbled. Why did everything have to be so complicated? Didn't Androni tell him to worry less?

I'll drink my own stupid blood. It's gotta be better than from that stinky horse.

Joey flexed his tendons. Greenish-blue veins did their important work beneath the translucent skin. Barely had the thought crossed his mind when he felt the change in his gums, the tingling reminiscent of days gone by when as a child, he wiggled loose a tooth. Joey ran his tongue against his newly sharpened fangs.

No one will know. I can't hurt myself, can I? Why not?

Joey paused to listen to the empty barn, still squatting in the clean shavings, a cocoon of wood plank and dust on all four sides. With a new pain from his gut, Joey brought his arm to his mouth and pressed his teeth into his flesh. Hot blood immediately came forth and filled the cavity of his palate. His first swallow assured him he'd made the correct choice, the fluid bringing him the exact same pleasure Androni's did. In another three gulps, he noticed a sharpening of his mind and his muscles surged with adrenaline. He could probably jump over the barn with this power! Joey studied the delicious ache that searched his nerve endings and didn't notice when his body slumped against the stall wall. His mind grew fuzz and he pulled more and with increased volume. When no more blood would come, he opened his eyes.

He was on the floor, eyes to the open stall door. Sawdust stuck to the tears on his face and he opened his mouth only to find he could make no sound.

What's going on? Did I drink all of my own blood?

189

It didn't seem possible but when he attempted to lift an arm, he could not move at all. Joey was paralyzed.

This can't be happening...

Then, he began to retch. Violently and with no muscle control, Joey's upper body contorted to force the liquid from his stomach. Wave after wave, pulse after pulse, he shook with the effort of his stomach emptying of its own accord. Joey's abused system vomited volumes of dark, red fluid onto the shavings, staining his clothing and whatever of his body pressed against the floor. Finally, Joey remembered he had a Savior and he begged God for help.

"Jesus, help me! I can't move!" Joey prayed gagging still until he lost his voice, the convulsions continuing even after he'd ejected the last drop.

I'm going to die...

Squeezing his eyes closed, Joey wished someone would help him and he wished it would be Androni. And then, everything went black.

The stable had been closed when she left earlier that day so when Sarah noted the half-open door, she crossed the yard to close it not considering someone might be inside. Once she reached the barn, she paused, recalling why they had started using it in the first place—for the vampires to drink blood.

Sarah gulped and prayed for strength as she poked in her head.

"Hello?" she called and listened for a reply. "Doctor Corescu? Joey?"

The horse nickered and Sarah noticed it tied to the wall. She had not dealt with equines much, but it probably wouldn't do to leave it fastened to the wall all night. With a quick scan of the aisle, Sarah entered and approached the horse in a big circle, recalling some childhood teaching of not sneaking up on horses from behind.

"Hey, horsie, horsie," she said in a soft tone and reaching for the huge head. She had no trouble freeing the lead and she turned for the closest stall. Then she heard it. A noise in the back of the barn.

"Help..."

The tiny plea sounded like Joey and when she scuttled the horse in its stall and closed the door, she rushed to the back of the barn. Out of the corner of her eye, dark wispy creatures flitted away, up through the roof and into the night sky. Demons. Sarah had been seeing them since her youth and she ramped up her internal prayers.

"Joey? What's wrong? Are you hurt?"

Then she saw him, slumped like a ragdoll on the shavings, blackish fluid underneath and staining his clothing. The boy gagged once, a dry heave, and opened his eyes.

"Help…" he rasped, not truly focusing in her gaze. Sarah steeled her nerve and stepped closer.

"Who did this?" Sarah asked and stooped to her knees, near, but not in the expelled blood. The boy appeared to be the victim of a violent attack. "Can you stand?" she asked and touched his shoulder. "Let's get into the house. Doctor Corescu will know what to do…"

Joey shook his head once, his cheek making a liquid noise in the disgusting effluence. Sarah pushed against his upper arm, speaking with urgency

"You have to get up. You can do it. Get up!"

She didn't know precisely what to expect, but when he worked to focus his eyes, he sought her gaze and she did not recognize him. His face was right, but the pale blue eyes she knew had turned red. Sarah thought to stand and back away, but Joey's inert hand came to life and grasped her forearm, jerking her to the sawdust with violence. Sarah yelped with surprise, but even as she formulated a prayer of protection, the boy pulled her captive arm to his mouth and sank impossibly evil fangs into her flesh.

"Stop! Stop in the name of Jesus!" she screamed, falling to her rear to kick the boy with both heels. Three strong kicks and another shouted command and she broke free, Joey's body flinging against the wall with much more force than Sarah alone was capable of. Terror and unbelief crossed his features and Sarah told him to stay put.

"I'll get help!" she shouted, kicking through the shavings to scramble to her feet. Sarah covered the bite wound, but it had healed by the time she reached the outdoors. God must have sent an angel. How else had she thrown the vampire off with such strength?

God will deal with Joey and Corescu better pick up the phone! she thought as she ran for the house, dialing the doctor's cell. Corescu said he'd control the vampires. *He better get here and do it!*

Once in the house, she waited for the doctor to pick up the line, calming her panic with sheer will. Joey hadn't meant any harm. He'd been starving—she saw that plainly. And Sarah didn't blame God; on the contrary. Jesus had again sent an angel to save her from a vampire. He had done it before. A year ago, before she met Tony, a vampire named Paul Black (a.k.a. Saul White) had stalked and then attacked her in a shopping mall. It was because of that assault she found herself tainted by the man's blood. When God's angel helped Sarah fend him off, some of the creature's blood landed on Sarah's lips. Only later did Tony track her down and tell her what all that meant.

And I fell in love...

Thank you for Tony, but please make Mark hurry!

The doctor picked up the phone and she lit into the story. He was heading back and Sarah closed her eyes and thanked God.

Again.

The Angel's face held no expression, it's fiery gaze piercing Joey's soul. He gaped at its size, its head appearing to brush the high rafters. It put out a hand that emanated light and Joey held his breath. Had he crossed the line? Was this an angel of death?

"Give me your hand." The angel's deep voice vibrated like a cello bow released.

No longer paralyzed but still weak, Joey touched the angel's fingers. In an instant, his strength was renewed, and he sprung to his feet.

"Thank you," Joey said but the being was gone. Joey turned a circle, his eyes round with amazement.

I just saw an angel! I got to tell Abby! Oh, she'd never believe it!

A horse snorted out of sight and Joey's exuberance evaporated.

Tell Abby an angel rescued a vampire from killing himself?

With more questions than answers, Joey stepped into the barn aisle and stared at the half-open door. Sarah said wait. He'd wait. But tomorrow, he'd start hunting for Androni. God wanted him to live, not starve to death sucking blood off a horse.

God wants me to live.

Androni wants me around.

Plan set, Joey watched for the doctor's arrival.

33

THE NEXT EVENING, JOEY WAITED FOR DOCTOR CORESCU to leave. Although he did not expound to Joey where he went, it wasn't hard to guess, since he constantly returned with Ms. Hawken's aroma on his clothing. Plus, Joey had a notion he also went to check on Pastor Tony, which was nice since God wouldn't allow anyone else to do so. Tonight, again, he found himself on his own recognizance. Joey left the basement and stood on the landing to call up the stairs for Reverend Tracey. She popped out, her sweet smile in place.

"I wanted to apologize," he stammered, looking up at her from the first floor. She did not start down, but gave him a warm smile.

"Forgiven," she said with a nod.

"Did you see the angel? He touched my hand and made me better."

"Praise the Lord," she replied. "But I didn't see him, no."

"Okay." Joey looked at the door and then back up to his hostess. "I'm going out a while, okay?"

"Okay. Be careful," she said and fell quiet.

Joey didn't know what else to say, mortified that he'd attacked the woman. He remembered it, every second, but the way she looked to him through the starvation haze had been frightening. Sarah Tracey had turned into a framework of blood vessels, as if a special effects department photoshopped her in. Even recalling it now caused an involuntary shiver and Joey turned for the door.

In the parking lot, he reached his borrowed car and pondered what Tony had told him about the doctor and Paul Black. He had been very close to Corescu. Close enough to be called a brother and a trusted friend. He had also served the vampire for a hundred years. Joey huffed at the thought.

It's not right for Doctor Corescu to keep me away from Gypsy. He knows better. He knows we need each other...

The doctor had kicked Androni out, but not Joey. The reverend tried to explain it, saying that because Androni was not a believer, the forgiveness did not extend to him. The reason Joey was still part of the household was because of his faith.

It still isn't fair.

All the way into town, Joey thought of places to search for his friend. Androni would stay in Montgomery, Joey was certain. And he liked to hunt the clubs. Joey decided his first stop would be where they first went together. Sadly, that bar and three others turned up no Androni and Joey walked North on Union wondering where to try next.

I know he wouldn't leave town. No way. He knows I would look for him. He wanted me to make sure Luke was okay, but then he's gotta know I would come find him...

"'Scuse," a man said and bustled past, knocking Joey's elbow. The movement jostled him to the present and he looked at the building the man presumably exited. It was a college bar, evident by the football and fraternity logos plastered on the outer walls.

What the heck, Joey sighed and entered. He wouldn't give up. Not yet. Didn't Androni enjoy the energy of young people? By the rowdy noise at the entrance, this place was packed. Joey pulled open the nondescript black door and stepped across the threshold. He hadn't been carded at any of his stops so far, and here, no one stood at the door checking IDs.

Joey moved toward a small round-top table with a single seat, assuming the others had been bogarted by nearby patrons. Settling into the tall-backed chair, he watched the dance floor, every inch filled with dancing men and women. To his left and right, every pedestal table lining the walls was also occupied, the clientele ranged from early twenties to late forties. He scanned the heads, the faces, the forms, and did not see his friend. He inhaled the aroma of the place, seeking Gypsy's scent, but he either did not have the needed expertise to weed him out, or he wasn't there.

"What can I get you to drink?"

Joey swiveled his face to meet the bright gaze of a perky server carrying a tray.

"How about a water?" he replied by reflex.

"Water for the movie star at Table 7. You got it," she said with a wink and spun away.

Was she flirting?

194

Maybe it was because the whole town knew him to be the preacher's son, but women did not usually notice him. As he pondered, another woman eyed him from across the room. She was medium height, late-twenties, with shoulder-length brown hair. She was not familiar and approached now with bold intent.

Does she recognize me? Why would she come over here?

The woman reached him and leaned upon the tall table. She gave him a smile and batted her long eyelashes.

"You look like you might be in the wrong place."

"What?" Joey replied, working to figure out if he knew her.

"My name's Katie. You're Pastor Ellerslie's son, right?" She looked him over, lascivious and as if he was just her type. Hollywood movies flashed across his memory again, Dracula always so appealing to his victims. Was this what these people saw when they looked at him now? Had he drawn them to him because of his condition?

"Oh, you're just so cute! And grown up, too!"

"Um, hi," he replied scoping for her companions.

She giggled. "Um, hi." She touched his near sleeve. "My girlfriend deserted me. Can I get a lift? The pastor's son is safe, right?"

Joey wanted to be polite, but his plans for the night were set. They also did not include rescuing a stranger at a bar. Then when he didn't say yes right away, she wiggled her upper body, wavering her shoulders at him and he did not look at the shadow in her cleavage that her movements created.

"Come on, don't say no. I need a ride and I'll make it worth your while. I promise."

Joey couldn't think up an excuse fast enough so he got to his feet and she allowed him to stabilize her at the elbow as he noticed now that she had been drinking.

"I'll call you a cab," he said and steered her to the exit. Once they'd stepped into the damp night, she stopped moving and he turned to see her face.

"Pastor Ellerslie's boy, what's your deal? Are you gay?"

Joey's eyes widened and he shook his head, his mind going to Androni for no good reason. "No, ma'am. I-I'm waiting for someone." He stuttered and wondered if it was a lie.

"Come home with me. I'll help you grow into your height. Put some hair on those baby cheeks."

Joey offered a nervous chuckle and waved a cab close. He opened the

195

door for the woman and she slipped in, still inviting him to join her for the ride. He made a few more polite refusals and then the car drove away.

That was awful, Joey reflected and turned to gaze at the club entrance. Music leaked past the front doors and patrons were coming and going. *He's not in there. What do I do now? Keep searching?* Part of him wanted to ask God for help, like he would have done before he met all the vampires, but now? How kosher was it to ask Jesus to help him find his monster friend? With a sad chortle, Joey turned away from the club and looked over the parking lot.

I don't want to go back to Tony's yet... That doctor, sheesh...

I can't go home. I can't call Abby... not yet. I need to figure this out first...

"Joseph Ellerslie?..."

Joey turned. A stranger walked right into his space and put out his hand. Joey shook it. "Yes, sir. I'm Joey."

"Harold Bax," the man said and shook too long. When he released, Joey wiped the man's sweaty transfer onto his jeans. "Geez, you've grown," he said in a chortle, his wide middle bouncing with the move. "I worked the sound board at the community center when you played that recital. Remember? You were about fifteen, so, you're what? Twenty, now?"

"Eighteen," Joey replied, not recalling the man, but he remembered the performance. The stranger was mid-forties with messy brown hair and a ruddy complexion. Faded blue jeans and a plaid work shirt finished his look. Joey offered an apologetic shrug and thought he would move along. When instead the man took a step closer, setting off Joey's alarms. Not of fear, not like before Haman attacked. Tonight's alarms reminded him to watch out for bloodlust. He felt nothing right now, but when a pumping heart came too close, it could awaken.

"I live nearby. Can you give me a lift?" Harry tilted his face to one side and held his eye.

"You need a lift?" Joey said, his voice soft and his stomach waking up and yawning.

"Nearby, yep."

Joey's middle grumbled and an aroma hit his nostrils that tickled his hunger. In his mind, he took the man home and somehow figured out how to take his blood. The mere thought caused Joey to want to panic, but he calmed himself, remembering Androni's lessons of calm and confidence in all things. The guy needed a ride and Joey had a car.

Joey nodded and started away, turning his back on the guy. "I'm parked over here."

At the Jaguar, Harry climbed into the passenger side and whistled. "Nice wheels. Preaching pays your daddy good, eh?"

"Well, it's not mine. Some friends loaned it to me, that's all."

"Nice friends," Harry remarked and Joey got them underway.

They were on Madison in only a minute and Joey watched for the cross street.

"You have a friend named Gypsy, right?" the man said and Joey inhaled, swiveling his face as much as was safe in the late night traffic.

"Yes!" Joey said with exuberance and turned left as directed. "Why? Have you seen him?"

"Yep," Harry said with mystery and pointed to a white work van half a block ahead.

"Where? Where did you see him?"

"In my living room," Harry said his face out the windshield.

Joy spread across Joey's frame and he barely got the car in park before leaping to the curb.

"Is he there now?" he asked and looked at the two possible houses the man would belong to. Harry took his time, enjoying the suspense and then headed for a seafoam green Victorian with a crumbling porch. Joey tossed his trepidation out the window as he shadowed the stranger to the door. Bax unlocked the deadbolt and put his hand to the knob. Before turning it, he looked at Joey over his shoulder.

"He's going to reward me for finding you. You ready?"

Joey didn't comprehend the man's beady-eyed sentiments, but nodded. The musty space came to lackluster life when Bax flipped on a lamp and Joey sought the corners for his friend. "Androni?" he whispered.

"Androni!" Harry announced. "So that's his name! He wouldn't tell me. Such a tease he is!"

Joey ignored the man and focused down, listening for his friend's heart. Finally he heard him in the next room and Joey moved past Bax in a semi-shove and headed down the dark hall.

"Gypsy? Answer me," he whispered, his heart hammering and tears threatening his eyes.

"In here," his friend said and Joey shoved open the door.

Joey surged inside without thinking or wondering why he'd not come out. He was well into the room when he realized they were not alone. The magician was shirtless and sitting on one leg upon a mattress. Asleep longways on the same bed a woman lay on her front, maybe nude, but mostly covered with a white sheet. Androni met Joey's eye and put a long finger to his lips.

"I've missed you so much," Joey mouthed and Androni smiled wider, he opened his arms, inviting Joey to come near. He did and when close enough, the magician pulled him into a hug. For five long seconds, Joey bent at the waist and clasped onto the vampire, the man's long wavy hair tickling his nose, his aroma bringing to mind leather, canvas, and sawdust—as if still at the circus.

With a sudden giggle, Androni tugged him down and then harder, flipping Joey onto the bed, causing his upper body to fall across that of the sleeping woman. Joey complained he might hurt her, but Androni shushed him, pulling Joey to a lying down position facing him. Joey's ribcage was impeded by the sleeping woman's torso and he braced to avoid crushing her.

"No need to be so careful," he said with a laugh in his voice, still speaking low. "She will not awaken for hours yet. I whisper to hide our conversation from little Harry."

His friend whispered the man's name with a comical wrinkling of his nose. Then he shoved the woman away with a lifted knee until Joey's body made full contact with the bedcovers.

"Better?" he asked.

"What are you doing here? Is this where you're staying? Is that man…" Joey didn't know what to ask about Bax but Androni wasn't listening. He was looking into Joey's face like he always did—as if Joey was the most wonderful person in the world.

"Did you say you missed your Gypsy?" he asked, his voice low and silky.

Joey's grin widened as he took in his friend's face, slow and as if he hadn't seen him in decades. Emotion zoomed across his spirit and he nodded, afraid if he spoke he might break down.

"Kiss me," Androni said, his eyes pools of affection.

Joey leaned in without hesitation, but paused millimeters away. He held his eye and whispered with a grin, "Okay, but I still can't promise any magic."

"This is as it should be. I'm the magician, not you," he said and closed the distance.

Joey was still grinning and laughed a little when their mouths made contact. In the first second, he tasted blood on his friend's lips and then his tongue. This time when Androni took the kiss deeper, Joey tried to follow his lead, to do what he did. It didn't feel good but it also didn't feel bad. The magician's hand came up to cup his throat and Androni took to sucking on his tongue. Joey got tickled and laughed around his efforts.

"Here," Androni said when he ended the kiss. He shot his jaw to the side bearing his throat. He used his hand on Joey's neck to guide him and he allowed it, pressing his face into his friend's nape. Joey opened his mouth and his teeth slid out, so smoothly, so mechanically. His heart and mind were thanking him for his kindness, but his fangs slid home, bringing thick and life-giving blood into his body. This is what he needed—not some stupid animal's blood. Androni was hurting no one, and certainly not Joey. The blood tasted sweeter than he remembered and when he'd had enough, he slipped onto his back with a wide grin.

"I'm never leaving your side," Joey whispered his eyes closed, enjoying the afterglow of his meal. "I don't care who demands it. Pastor Tony, Reverend Sarah... the doctor..." Joey tapered off and didn't list the biggest name of all. But he was thinking it. Even God Himself couldn't convince Joey that being with Androni was wrong.

"Do you have a passport?" his friend asked and Joey swiveled his face to Androni's. "Come back to Europe with me. This country is wonderful and amazing, but it is also in such a hurry. We can slow down time, you and I. We can live every minute the full sixty seconds over there."

The vampire's tone had turned poetic and his bright eyes spoke promises. Joey believed every one. He owned a passport, although it had only a single stamp in it for Canada. His mind went to his parents and his little brother. Then to Abby and even Scott. All of these people would be angry if he left the country. He said this to his friend and sighed, disgusted with himself and his lack of decision-making prowess.

"It's not complicated. You want to be with your Gypsy, right?" Androni asked as a secret, his outside hand coming to stroke Joey's cheek. "Your parents and your brother and your friends will forgive you. They will also die natural deaths while you live hundreds of years."

Joey's eyes grew wide. Somehow, he'd never walked it that far ahead. Androni nodded.

"Add this to your pros and cons. I have watched generations come and go, friends, lovers, enemies. They all die and I go on. But you and I would be together. I would show you everything you need to know and I will make sure you are happy."

Joey believed him, but wasn't he supposed to seek after God? Seek holiness? Doctor Corescu pretended to attack him to remind him of the unholiness of their curse.

But I didn't do this! It's not my fault!

Joey set his jaw and covered Androni's hand still at his cheek. "Let's do it. Let's run away together. I can clean out my bank account. Let's go now before Dad has a thought to screw it up."

Androni nodded with a quiet grin and rolled to his feet. He dug into his slacks pockets and displayed a stack of bound hundreds. "Harry gave me everything he has in savings. This is nine thousand dollars. We will start new in Europe and the wealthy will take us in. Their daughters will invite us right into their vaults. Do you believe me?"

Joey tried to picture it, but Hollywood movies kept replacing the images in his head. Women in period costumes and horses pulling carriages. Still, he grinned and got off the bed. He circumnavigated the crumpled mattress to meet him face to face. He wore the same colorful breeches he'd arrived in and Joey grinned anew.

"I'm glad we never got those stupid American clothes for you," he said in a giggle. "Where's your fancy pirate shirt?"

Androni was still bare-chested from seducing the woman. With a matching grin, he searched behind him for his discarded garments. Found, he shrugged it on, leaving the smock strings untied to hang open.

"That's you. Don't ever change," Joey said and grabbed his friend into a hug. Androni embraced him, too, both long arms wrapped about his upper body. Then as Joey expected because of his friend's growing romantic behavior, Androni pressed a kiss into Joey's neck. It felt nice to be wanted and wasn't as weird this time. Joey thought ahead, over the next few hours and how they would arrange their flight and where they would go. His friend now kissed his jaw, tender and with care. Joey allowed it. He'd found a true friend, a soulmate, and just because he happened to be a vampire and a man, that wasn't Joey's fault.

None of it was. Not a single bit.

34

For God so loved the world that He gave His only begotten Son,
that whoever believes in Him should not perish but have everlasting life.
John 3:16

ALTHOUGH HE USED TO BE ABLE TO FIND ANYONE ON THE planet with a bit of concentration, Mark was unable to lock onto the boy's current location. This loss of power was unnerving, but shouldn't he expect it? He'd been steadily turning more "human" since Rakha passed. *Or maybe that is when I gave myself over to the idea of being delivered...*

Elizabeth Hawken had a lot to do with it. Mark wanted to be mortal for her sake, because she was so pure and his curse, so evil. After all, the only reason he'd been so good at searching out "sinners" was because of the unclean spirits that traveled the globe and reported back information. Mark no longer listened to those muses, although now and then, they reminded him how much he loved blood and the power he had wielded for centuries. Their chats revealed Elizabeth understood all this, yet, Mark had no confidence the Lord would allow him to live once he was delivered. Still, he sought to make the woman proud. And as he feared, the Ellerslie boy was barreling headlong into trouble, wrestling with Mark as well as with God.

Elizabeth had said what if God lined this up to save Androni's soul? It made sense and Mark had long ago learned not to shake his fist at the heavens.

I need to find the boy. It is my duty to all those who care about his well-being...

His senses had led Mark downtown, following his nose and supernatural awareness, he found an old Victorian nestled in an established neighborhood off Union. Something in his middle called him to the porch, and he had no doubt he had reached the place Joey Ellerslie sought refuge. And recently, for his body scent hung in the air. With another moment's thought, Mark recognized the magician's scent as well. It was a little past midnight and the street was quiet. He climbed the crumbling front stairs and paused before ringing the bell. Reaching up to the bulb in the porch light, he unscrewed it two turns until the light went out, cloaking the stoop with darkness. Whoever gave sanctuary to Rakha and now Androni would be one who enjoys the mystery. Mark rapped the front door with his knuckles.

Inside, the shadowy form of a short stocky man appeared through the glass. When the homeowner hesitated before opening the door, Mark smiled.

"Hang on…" a man's voice chirped and rushed about within view; Mark could only guess at his thoughts. Several months ago, this man allowed Rakha into his home on a regular basis to drink his blood. On one occasion while under the ancient demon's influence, Tony also came here, although he bravely refused the offered meal. Now, somehow, the same man became aware of Androni and Joey. How? Was it spiritual leading? Mark had a guess and would ask the man for details if given the opportunity.

Then the door pulled inward and Harry Bax stood inside the storm door looking at Mark with suspicion. But after a millisecond, his hard gaze softened—he recognized the vampire in his visitor. *How is this possible?*

"Um, hey?" the man stammered. "Can I help you?"

"Open the door," Mark said with authority and the man did so without pause.

He stepped aside and Mark entered the home; Harry Bax toddled behind him with his hands clutched at his chest. At the center of the room, Mark turned to face him. Bax right behind, backed two steps to face off. He raised his eyebrows but hadn't spoken since the initial greeting. Mark listened to the house. The magician and the boy left their scent behind, but they were gone.

"Do you know where they went?" Mark asked, skewering the man with his gaze, pushing his will like the old days and vaguely wondering if he had such power still.

"You – you – who are you?" Bax stammered. "You're their master?"

Mark sighed and narrowed his eyes. He had expected a better response to his hypnotic force. Then Bax's eyes widened.

"Mr. Smith was your master!" he said with new awe.

Mark did not need clarification of whom he spoke. And, he was out of patience. In a surge of movement, he had Bax about the throat, his palms encircling the man's slimy skin. "Where. Have. They. gone?" He spoke directly into the man's face this time with an evil edge he had no trouble resurrecting.

"I – I – I don't know," he rasped, his horrible breath difficult to ignore. "Please, I gave him my money. The boy used my computer." Bax's eyes looked left, but the rest of him could not move. "It'll be in the browser memory. I'll look. I'll look!"

Mark allowed one more hard gaze accompanied with a snarl and dropped the contact with drama. "Do it. Now."

Mark watched him back away, clearly afraid, and scramble to a cluttered surface, the centerpiece a laptop computer. He hadn't played "mean" in many months and marveled at how easily it returned.

If I chose, I could fall right back into my old life. I would live on...

But he remembered Elizabeth and his promise to God. He had made his decision.

I choose God.

He stood over the trembling man's shoulder and watched him pull up the history. Bax scrolled a few pages and pointed with a fat finger.

"There, look, British Airways." Bax typed a few keys and hit print. "His itinerary. Is that good? Are you happy with me? Is this what you needed?"

Mark received the offered sheet of paper and scanned the information. Androni was taking Joey home, to the circus by the looks of it. Mark's jaw tightened with frustration. What should he do now? Chase after them? Mark stared at nothing and ignored Bax's continued requests for a pat on the head.

Tony would ask God... maybe it's time I did, too...

Mark turned away and walked toward the door. He did not exit, but facing away from the homeowner, he closed his eyes, chin tilted up.

"Father-God, what would you have me do?"

Mark waited. God had sent an angel to dispose of Haman. Maybe He would help this time, too. Behind him, Bax mumbled a prayer of his own and Mark turned to watch him, still holding an ear open for God.

"Who is it? Is he for me? I serve you, it's my turn. You owe me..." the man whispered and did not seem to realize Mark's keen ears picked up every syllable. When Bax noticed his interest, he hushed. "What can I do for you now? Do you need blood?" the man asked and removed his graying undershirt. He turned three-quarters to reveal multiple healed lacerations and puncture wounds, some more than a year old by Mark's medically trained eye. His offer was open, but his pock-marked and rashy skin repulsed Mark more than he expected. He hadn't had human blood in ages, and he had no desire to touch this man again.

"Get dressed," Mark commanded and eyed him hard until he covered himself once more. "How did you find Androni?"

Bax's eyes widened. "What is your name?" he asked, but Mark's question did not mean the initiation of a conversation. He repeated his first question with a threatening step in.

"Tell me how you wound up with Androni."

"Okay, okay!" he said and backed until his rear met the messy desk. "Jasmine, she's my spirit guide, she showed me where to go. She showed me Mr. Smith, too. She led me to the boy." Harry spoke in a rush. "She never showed me you before. You are the one I needed all along!"

"Silence," Mark said, not loud, but with the edge to frighten the man back. "Close the blinds and dim the lights."

Bax jumped to attention, circumvented Mark by a wide margin and reached the front windows. He pulled the thick curtains together and clicked off the overhead light, leaving the room lit by two small lamps on either side of the sagging sofa.

"Okay. Okay. What now?" he asked, his eyes begging. Mark refused his blood and wondered now what would be required.

"Sit down," Mark commanded and the man plopped his weight to the couch atop newspapers and discarded fast food sacks.

Mark pondered the man's explanation—a spirit guide. A few responses filtered to his mind and Mark realized they were his help; God had sent him a chore. He was supposed to lead the seeker before him back to the path.

"Listen," he said and had the man's rapt attention. "This spirit you call Jasmine is working for the devil. You know this, correct?"

Bax allowed a small shake of the head. "No, she's helping me..."

"God gives His prophets and disciples visions that edify and encourage man. Satan gives psychics and mediums distorted views of what has passed, or lies of what will come. You have given your loyalty to a demon. You are being played."

"Oh, no I'm not. I am a powerful sorcerer. She is making me great..." His words carried no conviction but he did not cower.

"She told me if I gave my blood to her children, I would grow in power, and I have. Every time I give my blood, I have visions of the future and material wealth falls in my lap..."

Mark huffed. "What does she say about me? If I took your blood?"

A small grin reached the man's mouth. "She said you are very powerful. She said if you would accept my sacrifice, I would have more power than ever!"

Mark laughed and Bax's smile vanished. "She lied." Mark stepped into him. He needed the man to fear him and the adoration and subservience was not helping God's cause. "When I drink a man's blood, I take it all…" Mark grasped the man by both upper arms and jerked him to his feet. Speaking too close for the man to focus, Mark walked him backwards until his back met the wall. "Two hundred thousand men and women have died in my grip…"

"No, wait," Harry pleaded, his voice shattered now with new fear.

"…Thousands of putrid, shriveled corpses in graves across the globe…" Mark had employed his spookiest voice and it was working. Bax lost his bladder and the room filled with the acrid aroma of urine. "Mr. Bax. …Harry." Mark squeezed the man's fleshy biceps, holding his eye. "Your spirit guides are demons. You are doing their bidding. They have deceived you, pulling you into hell, hoping you will die in their care. Do you know what happens then?"

His eyes enormous, Harry shook his head.

"If you die in their care, you will go to hell. For all eternity. Harry… do you want to go to hell?"

"I don't…believe…in that," he mumbled without force.

"Hell believes in you, Harry. Here… let me help you understand. Just relax…. shh."

With a new idea, he looked deeper into the man's eyes. When Mark judged sinners in his old life, he would telepathically read the victim's dark deeds. Now he sought Harry's thoughts, seeking an interaction with Jesus in the man's past. Any positive interaction with God would do. He had to look quite a few years back, but he found a bright spot during a youth retreat when Harry was in middle school.

"Harry, remember Camp Chandler. Remember Sammy Hatcher on the lake that morning. Tell me what happened. Tell me what happened on the lake."

Bax inhaled and covered his mouth. "Sammy told me about Jesus," He answered slowly, as if in a dream. As Mark watched, Bax recalled more details. "I had a problem."

"What did Sammy do about your problem, Harry?"

"I was deaf here," he said his hand to one ear. "I had an ear infection as a baby. It ached a lot, too. It made my life miserable. Sammy told me that if I believed, Jesus would heal my ear."

Mark saw a hazy vision of what Bax recalled. Two boys in a small boat

205

floating on a quiet lake, the sun up only an hour or so. An errant wind whipped the boy called Sammy's hair and then quieted. The air smelled of fish and pine trees, and not another soul was in sight.

"Sammy told me that Jesus was still alive. That He was in heaven right now praying for me. Hoping to save me from hell. I was a bad kid, bad to the bone…" Harry's eyes glazed over, no longer looking at his dark visitor. "Daddy sent me to that Christian Camp, I was bad. It was my last chance before juvvie…"

Mark remained quiet and the man continued.

"Sammy told me that he would pray for my ear to hear again. Sammy said that Jesus would make my ear right again to show me that He was alive and that He loved me…"

"And what happened, Harry? What happened when Sammy prayed for your ear?" Mark offered gently. He was immensely pleased with how the session was going. *Oh, I wish I had learned three hundred years ago that I could help these people without killing them.* But that was old history. Mark did not kill anymore. He returned his focus to Bax.

"He put his hand on my ear and asked Jesus to make it hear again." Harry put his own hands to his ears and closed his eyes, as if reliving the prayer. "Sammy prayed a really short prayer, like maybe two sentences, and then pulled his hands off my ear. At first, nothing. But Sammy started singing one of his church songs, and my ear started to pop." Harry's eyes refocused in Mark's. "When his song was done, I could hear just fine." Harry licked his lips, his respirations up. "Jesus healed my ear. He was alive with us in the boat, just like Sammy said!"

Mark nodded and disentangled from the man's thoughts. He backed two steps holding Harry's gaze. "Jesus is alive right now. Ask him to help you right now. Ask Him to show you who Jasmine really is."

Mark wanted out. He needed to go. He wanted to get Joey back. God had not answered that part of his question. He watched Bax thinking through his next move. With a thought, he was at the cabin. He would ask Tony. It was the next best thing to being able to hear from God.

35

"MAYBE YOU'RE JUST A HEDONIST," JOEY SAID WITH A LAUGH and his friend rolled his head to the side.

"This is a big word, Ghost. Do you know what it means?" Androni's eyes flashed with humor.

"I certainly do." With a dramatic exhale, Joey faced the dark ceiling, both of them lying on top of the hotel comforter. They were hours away from escaping the country, leaving the dreary sad-sacks (as Androni called Tony and the doctor) behind forever. For the moment, they were sleeping a few hours during a layover, a handy Bed and Breakfast offering a cozy place to while away the next seven hours.

Androni chuckled deep in his throat when Joey didn't complete his thought. Then he also rolled his face front to stare upwards. "I like to feel good and I like things that make me feel good." The vampire was silent a few ticks and added, "You make me feel good. I'm keeping you around, Ghost. You are mine. I'm claiming you."

"Claiming me," Joey said as a statement. "Do I get to claim you back or is this some sort of vampire master thing?"

"I'm making it up as we go," Androni said, still with a smile in his voice. "I have two centuries of figuring out what I like and don't like, of this I am an expert. Beyond that, I will wing it."

"Then I'm claiming you, too. You're mine."

Androni rolled onto his side and propped his head into his hand. "I'm yours for what? Blood? Mentoring? Companionship?"

Joey also rolled onto his side to look into Androni's face. Then, there it was again, a breathless amazement filled his mind and he couldn't speak for several moments. As if from far away, Joey lifted his outside hand and moved a curl of black hair from his friend's forehead. The vampire's eyes flashed in the low lighting and he smiled, moistening his lips as if knowing Joey would look there.

"Are you doing this?" Joey asked as it occurred to him that maybe he was. "Are you hypnotizing me every time I look at your face?"

"No," Androni replied. "You love me all by yourself."

Joey grinned and rolled back into position looking upwards. "Yeah, I guess that's it. When I look at you, I'm so hopeful. I see a lot of good things ahead."

"I see the same thing," his friend offered in a quiet voice.

Joey had an idea. "Doctor Corescu had a servant named Paul. I think he loved him. I mean, like a brother. Have you had someone before me? Someone you wanted to claim?" Androni was still on his side watching Joey's profile and he felt the man's attention, so intense and thoughtful. Why?

"No," he said in the same low volume as before. "The humans are food to me. You? I see you as a friend."

Joey smiled and rolled his face to meet Androni's eye. "The humans are food to me," he repeated in Androni's accent and chuckled. Since running off together, Androni had feasted on a few people and left them confused but alive. So far, Joey had only taken blood from Androni. Would he really bite someone? Or could he skirt the sin by sticking to vampire blood?

"We must figure out how Mark ruined our telepathy. I am unhappy about that. Very unhappy. Seeing your thoughts gave me great joy."

"Me, too," Joey replied, still looking into his face, Androni propped on one hand and Joey on his back. "You said we're going first to your circus company. What then?"

"There, I play a Satanist with amazing mystical Dark powers. It is pretend. But there is a sorceress who practices in earnest. I believe she can restore us. She has power. I have witnessed this."

Joey's scalp prickled at the thought of using witchcraft for gain. His friend noticed the change and rolled into a sitting position, cross-legged facing Joey lying down.

"You are afraid," he said, scrutinizing Joey's face.

"It's holy fear," Joey said not expecting his friend to understand. And he didn't. He held his same expression and waited for more. "God abhors witchcraft. 'Do not seek out spiritists or mediums, you will be defiled by them'." Joey shrugged one shoulder and put his near palm to Androni's closest knee. "That's a Bible quote."

"Ah." His friend nodded, incorporating his entire upper body and covered Joey's fingers with his hand. "You want to maintain your religion?"

"Yeah." Joey couldn't lie; he wanted Jesus. He couldn't leave God no matter what. Would this ruin Androni's affection for him? Joey ran it down in his mind and felt his entire body rush with emotion.

"Curses," Androni growled. "I want to hear your thoughts!" In a reflection of concern, he fell onto his side, but this time against Joey, their bodies in contact all the way down. "This expression," he said in a kind whisper. He tucked one arm behind Joey's shoulders and the outside hand he put to his cheek. "I hate it. It is a look of fear, uncertainty, and distrust." Androni held him in an embrace now and Joey felt as if he hoped such a hug would erase all those negative things.

"I'm sorry," Joey said and lifted his outside hand to Androni's cheek. "I don't want to make you upset."

"I wouldn't be upset if we had our telepathy returned. I wouldn't be upset if you would cease doubting my affection and commitment to our union. I would be happy if you would allow me to be your god and dump this restrictive religion."

Joey's blood ran cold. He shook his head. If he wasn't white as a ghost anyway, he would be now. In that instant, he expected Androni to push away from him, leap from the bed, and disappear out the door forever. He even peeked at the door as the thought touched his mind. But the magician instead pulled their bodies together so now his cheek pressed against Androni's chest muscle.

He held him there, rocking him, and then he whispered into Joey's hair, "You will not have to choose, beloved Ghost. I would never make you choose." Androni kissed the top of his head. "I have claimed you from all flesh, humans and vampires. But as for God, I do not know Him. He owns your spirit. I will share that part of my Ghost."

Joey exhaled staring at nothing, his mind thanking God even though he hadn't felt a reciprocating movement in days. Androni kissed his hair again and moved to kiss his forehead. Then his nose tip and when he met Joey's eyes only a moment, he rolled lower to press his mouth to Joey's. Joey was learning how to mimic his efforts and maybe he was going to finally give the guy some pleasure. It was weird, but it made his new friend super happy.

With a giggle of relief, Joey grabbed Androni with both arms and flipped them both to the center of the giant bed. Now Joey lay half across his friend and the laughter in Androni's eyes was worth all the anxiety of the past ten minutes.

"Okay, let me try," he said with a triumphant grin. Joey pressed his lips to Androni's and did his best to measure up.

36

Be hospitable to one another without grumbling.
As each one has received a gift,
minister it to one another, as good stewards
of the manifold grace of God.
1 Peter 4: 9-10

TONY'S QUARANTINE WOULD END IN FOURTEEN DAYS. Would God deliver him? If so, what would that look like? Sarah sighed; she rarely received direct answers regarding her own life. *Tony is my life now,* she said inside and looked at her hands. *I miss him so much!*

A sharp noise caught her attention and Sarah looked to her closed bedroom door. Was the doctor building something? Did he trip? A wry grin hit her mouth and when the sound didn't recur, she returned to her prayers.

The door is closed.

Sarah raised her eyes. That thought had come from her spirit and she sought a deeper interpretation.

Am I closing out something, Father?

She narrowed her eyes and waited for a nudge. Had she been shirking her duty to the young man? To the doctor? Sarah asked the Lord directly in her heart and the same sentence passed over her soul: *The door is closed.*

Sarah stood and walked over, praying for guidance as a word from God bubbled deep down. She had become familiar with the sensation; the Father wanted her to speak to someone on His account. As Sarah turned the knob, she saw in her mind who it was for. As a new shiver hit her flesh, she stepped into the hallway and steeled her nerve. God had a word for the four-hundred-year-old vampire downstairs. Sarah would need to find him.

Since Tony left for the cabin, Sarah had spent every waking minute distracting herself. She visited with Elizabeth, most often away from the house, although the young woman and the doctor visited sometimes on the grounds. Sarah went to church, taught Bible classes at different

211

facilities, and she took long walks at the city park. But she hadn't spoken with Doctor Corescu in any valuable way since he arrived. She had closed herself off from him and the boy. Now that Joey had fled the country, she worried for him, took calls from JoAnn Ellerslie to pray for him together, and had no idea when the Lord would bring him home.

But I closed the door to the doctor.

That thought returned and Sarah was pinged with guilty regret. She reached the first-floor landing and called the doctor's name. In a moment, he came up from the basement.

"Yes?" he asked, spearing her with those eyes that caused fluttering where it ought not.

"Can we talk a minute?" she asked aware that besides tiny snippets of conversation, they had never sat down alone. Something about him… A new guilt stabbed her heart; she feared him because of her previous experience with vampires. Paul's attack had been terrifying. Haman's less so, but still filled with the violation that left a woman feeling vulnerable and helpless. *But God is my strength,* she said inside with meaning and hoped her expression was more calm than her spirit.

"I apologize for what you have suffered. If I could change any of it, I would," the doctor said reminding her that he saw some of her thoughts. He accepted when she gestured that he sit with her. The first room off the foyer had been set up as a music room with a grand piano on one side and two wide soft armchairs on the other. They sat and he waited for her to begin.

Sarah trusted God to give her the correct words and she cleared her throat. "Doctor Corescu, for three weeks I have shut you out. I was afraid. It wasn't God's will that I hole away up there in my room." She swallowed with a shrug. "I want you to know that. I want to apologize."

"That is not necessary," he began and she gave him a tight grin and continued.

"He has a word for you. The Lord tells me that you're worrying about Elizabeth, about how she will handle your departure…" This time, Mark rolled in his lips and Sarah recognized her error. "No, honestly, I have not heard from God on what the result of your deliverance will be. I sense you will be delivered in His timing, but I have no knowledge on…"

Corescu offered a single prominent nod and she let that part drop.

"You wonder about how God sees you. How He regards your efforts to cleanse your soul of—" Sarah inhaled sharply as images from the doctor's past arrived in morbid detail. With a hiss, she slowed them down, but her dedication to delivering God's prophecies required her to see. Corpses. Thousands. Tens of thousands of dead bodies. Screaming, begging for their lives, a cacophony of expelled terror exploded in her mind, and every soul that left the flesh at the doctor's hands screeched at once and Sarah literally yelped when they were done. Sarah prayed for the images to disappear, the ocean of despair in his past threatening to devour her strength.

Oh, my sweet Jesus, You are good. Your mercy is endless. Your grace is without measure. You have forgiven that monster out of Your bottomless love. Oh, sweet Lord, please take his memories out of my head. Please...

As she waited for her prayer to be answered, her thoughts turned to Tony. Was he capable of committing even a *fraction* of what the doctor did? Sarah was shocked by what she had seen. She had seen evil in Paul White, but never so much *death*. Corescu had brought about the demise of thousands of people and God let him do it. Why? It was such a perfect example of divine forgiveness that she marveled.

Jesus forgives the penitent, but this man has killed far more than any one mortal could accomplish in his short life. Just... Father! Help him repent and leave it forever!

She refocused on the doctor who had leaned forward, pensive, his hands on his knees and concern in his handsome face. Sarah met his eye and shook her head once, *just wait. Just wait. Just a moment...* she needed time for the images to filter away and then the word would come. *Just wait...*

And then it arrived.

Like water on a parched tongue, the Father touched Sarah's pain and put His word in her mouth.

"My son, you are my strong warrior. You go into battle and bring home what the enemy has stolen. You carry a banner for the Lord your God as bright as the morning sun; every foul spirit can see it and they fear you for it. The more time you spend with Me, the more powerful you will become *for* Me. Your humility serves you well and I long to bless you with your heart's desire. I have watched over you as a babe in my arms, nursing you, nurturing you, and chastising you when you went astray. I love you more than you will ever comprehend. And My son..."

Sarah paused with drama, her next words giving her a chill before she spoke them. The doctor hung on, obviously breathless and she finished in a soft voice.

"My son, it is time to release your past. Release your past as I have."

Sarah brought her hands to her face. Without looking up, she whispered the interpretation, hating the words because of how she despised their curse.

"You have to stop drinking blood, Doctor. To walk in God's ways is to reject vampirism. Entirely."

She couldn't look at him. Sarah remained covering her face with both hands, wishing she was done. That the doctor would say thank you and walk away. But that wasn't how it worked and she knew it. Sarah listened as he gathered his response, a shuffle of movement as if crossing his legs or leaning back in his chair. Then he sighed and said in that smooth voice, "Did *God* say I should stop or do *you* say it?"

"It's what *I* say, but it's what *God* meant," she replied and raised her face. "That's all I have."

She watched him think it over and he had leaned back, stretching out long legs, his ankles crossed. She considered asking the Father hints regarding the man's deliverance. Would he live on? Would he turn to dirt?

"I have not touched human blood in over a year," he said in a low voice and she nodded once. "He wants me to give up the animal blood, too." The doctor spoke in a statement and again, Sarah nodded. With a heavy sigh, he gave a weary nod. "Thank you for your obedience to our Father, Ms. Sarah."

"He wants us to prosper. To succeed in His purposes," she offered with a nod. "Have you heard anything about Joey? Androni?" The duo had been gone three weeks and she hoped the doctor would have supernatural insight to save her unneeded worry. He sighed in response and lifted his shoulders in a shrug.

"I cannot locate them, and this reveals a loss of power." He stopped there and she waited. Then he huffed once to himself. "I feel he is alive," Corescu said touching his sternum with one palm. "But that is because of our common blood. I do not sense Androni at all."

Sarah licked her lips and nodded to reassure him that she felt they were safe and that God would keep them that way.

"I believe that, as well," he said and rose to his feet.

Sarah did, too, and asked a happier question. "Are you seeing Elizabeth today?"

He dropped his gaze to the side, a smile hitting his mouth. "At five, she will escort me to a jazz concert," he said inside a chuckle and a small head shake. He returned his gaze to Sarah's. "No matter what the Lord decides to do with this vessel, I am thankful to know you. And thank you for helping Ms. Hawken see the good in an old monster."

Sarah enjoyed his humor and sincerity and she nodded. "Go have fun," she told him, and after a genteel bow, the vampire left the room.

"God, help him fulfill your purpose. And help Elizabeth, too. Amen."

With that internal prayer, Sarah returned to her bedroom, but she did not close the door.

Androni was amazing, end of story.

Alone for the moment, Joey stood hidden in the caravan's toilet stall as his partner wooed a woman for her blood in the main room. The past three weeks had passed like minutes as every moment with his new friend seemed packed with new things to learn and experience. Most of it had to do with adjusting to his vampire senses, but he hadn't taken anyone's blood. Only Androni's. Was that okay? Joey wasn't ready to ask God about it, knowing he would have to eventually. But tonight…

When they arrived in Europe, they toured England and France ten days before coming to Germany. In the larger cities, and besides the foreign language spoken, London, Paris, Berlin, were very much like those in the States. Joey was able to read some of the signage using context, but Androni was teaching him to read and speak German. So far, learning and concentrating was much easier since his transformation and his mentor was happy with his progress.

My mentor…

Joey grinned at the word; his friend had become so much more.

A moan from the other room. Joey remained quiet. Androni did not go a single day without a blood meal and so far, Joey remained out of sight. He hadn't said so specifically, but he wasn't ready to watch his friend feed. Even at the thought, an unnamed terror tickled Joey's inner mind and he pushed it back.

"Ghost," he heard then through the wall and Joey opened the door.

As most other instances, the "victim" appeared asleep, lying in the bed as peaceful as can be. What was different this time, Androni waved him close lifting the woman's wrist. Joey closed the distance wondering what he was thinking and wishing they still had their telepathy. Before he gave his polite refusal, Androni grunted he be still and bit the same wound. He pulled a moment, wrapped a cloth to the woman's arm and stood to face Joey.

Joey gave him a quizzical look and he grinned, lips closed. Then with

215

a hand to the side of Joey's neck, he tugged, pulling their mouths together. Then he realized what his friend was doing. Once in contact, Androni pushed the woman's blood from his mouth to Joey's.

"Mmmm!" Joey objected but swallowed, held fast by Androni's hand. The fluid hit his stomach and a tingling calm spread instantly to every extremity. He hadn't had feeling in his nerve endings since Haman's attack and his eyes grew wide as the forgotten sensations filtered away. It had been fleeting, but definitely real.

Androni dropped the contact and stood away holding his eye. "This is your lesson tonight, my beautiful Ghost," he whispered even though the woman on the bed was unconscious. "Drinking from me gives you pleasure here and here." Androni touched his head and mouth. "Human blood will awaken your body from head to toe. It endures only a moment, but it reminds us we are alive. Do you understand? I told you this before; vampires are *not dead.*"

Joey held his gaze and slow-nodded. His friend had put great emphasis on the last phrase and after another moment, Joey asked, "Did you used to think you were dead?"

With an exaggerated sigh, Androni pushed past and gestured Joey should follow. He led him out of the caravan into the dark night. The inky sky was littered with stars and the moon was full. Joey marveled anew at his amazing vision, halos of lights emanating from every surface, including his friend. Joey looked longer at Androni's aura and grinned.

"What color is it?" his friend asked reading from Joey's movements what he was studying.

"Lavender," Joey replied with the same goofy smile. "What color is mine?" When Joey looked at his own arm or torso, he saw only white light.

"It is a delightful hue of blue," Androni said with a wink. "Walk with me, Ghost."

He dropped his arm across Joey's shoulders and led him toward the path. The caravan sat on the outer edge of the circus campus and backed up to the woods. They had already explored the forest and easily saw where to place their feet along the rustic trail. They were a hundred yards from the caravan when his friend began the conversation.

"When I left that cave two hundred years ago, I did not know I was a vampire. After internalizing that I could no longer eat food or drink wine, I had a notion to try blood. Where that came from, I never gave much thought, but after meeting the doctor, I am guessing it was one of those spirits."

216

Joey nodded his head in agreement and waited for more.

"Once I realized I was only able to consume blood, I supposed I was dead. That I had become a vampire. Over time, I drank live human blood daily to remind myself that I was indeed alive. Not an undead creature. Not a monster."

"Yeah, I understand," Joey said with meaning. "I felt it. It was... too short." He grinned and Androni laughed and hugged him one-armed. Then he relaxed, draping the arm again along his shoulders as they walked.

"You wonder why I kiss you so much," his friend said and Joey huffed a laugh. "It is because only a vampire's mouth, palate, and stomach enjoy such sensation. Because of this, I put my mouth on my favorite things."

"That makes sense," Joey said in a nod. Besides those areas, his body was numb. Since Haman Troye left him in this state, Joey experienced pressure, but no sensations of pain or pleasure, as if his body had *gone to sleep*. But his nerve endings of his lips and tongue were as alive as ever. "I should have thought of that." Then he added in a low voice, "I thought maybe you were gay and thought I was, too..."

This time Androni laughed. "Before my change, I had a wife, planned a family. Men were friends, comrades, fellow soldiers. But now? Combine my affection for you with how wonderful it feels to put my lips to yours, I look forward to every kiss. I think I am using our embraces to affirm my life, even more so than the blood."

Joey liked the sound of that, loving how no matter what Androni said about him, it was always more positive than anyone had ever thought of him before. Then he chuckled and Androni stopped walking to turn and face him, one hand now to his shoulder.

"Yeah, I was just thinking how horrible a kisser I am," Joey said with a laugh. "I'll get better. I promise."

Androni swooped in and covered Joey's mouth with his own, no tongue, just pressed tight. In another five seconds, he pulled back, the familiar twinkle in his eye. "Nothing about you is horrible. You must know this by now. You have become everything to me. I am not ashamed to admit it."

Joey shook his head in wonder. "I feel exactly the same way," he whispered.

"Good. Now I will share with you," he said and lowered his throat to Joey's level. "Try to enjoy the sensation, use your imagination of the old Joey Ellerslie, allow your mind to bring back feeling to your body. When I drink blood, I do this. I have an amazing imagination and I am betting you do as well."

Joey licked his lips and opened his mouth against his friend's skin. The woman he fed from left her aroma behind and Joey enjoyed it. When his fangs slid home, Joey's eyes rolled back in pleasure. He assigned a mental reminder to his flesh as Androni instructed, but mostly he felt his own tongue pushing against the punctures, controlling the flow, savoring every drop. Then he closed his mouth, remaining close, clutching his friend about the torso. Androni stroked his hair with one hand and supported his back with the other.

"Thank you for running away with me, Ghost," he whispered over Joey's head.

"Thank you for having me," he replied and held tight.

They stood together in the cool night air, trees and forest greenery pressing in on all sides, the canopy revealing half of the sky. Joey had never been happier. He sighed and did not let go for a very long time.

37

And on My menservants and on My maidservants
I will pour out My Spirit in those days;
And they shall prophesy.
Acts 2:18

SARAH AWOKE CRYING, HER HEART LONELY FOR TONY AND her spirit worrying over his last day of quarantine. The Father comforted her every minute, but her flesh still worried that like the last time he fasted forty days, God wouldn't do what Tony expected. What if, again, God leaves him as a vampire? How would her husband react?

Asking herself as well as God, Sarah put her feet to the floor. Her carpet was gone, replaced by earth. Sarah froze in place, her heels hovering over lush green grass that as she considered it, began to wave in a cool breeze. She raised her gaze and her bed sat in a pasture, a wide expanse of countryside with only a tree line far away along the horizon. The azure-blue sky was peppered with white cumulous clouds and the sun shone as if it were high noon.

"Father?" she said using her voice and sound waves left her mouth, rippling from her body outward until disappearing in the distance. "What can I do? What is this? I am here for You." Every word had the same effect, moving like visible waves into the air.

The sound of hoofbeats filtered in, slowly building to combine with the gentle coo of birds and the whistle of crickets. Sarah scanned the field until a wisp of pale mane fluttering in the wind caught her eye and she watched a beautiful white horse gallop toward her position. It stopped fifty feet away and reared, pawing the sky and neighing with joy at its power and glory. When its celebration ended, it stood square, still and quiet, its body parallel to Sarah and its face looking east. Then it turned its head and she discerned a mark in its forehead... *Jesus' mark!* Once she noted it, the grand stallion maneuvered carefully into a lying down position until it lay flat to the earth. Sarah felt an urge to walk closer so she did, the cool grass tickling her feet in the lucid vision.

"This is Corescu?" she asked aloud and in her heart and she had the answer. The horse did not make any sign that it knew she was there. It breathed small puffs of air through its nostrils, its cheek flat to the earth, wildflowers framing its entire body. Sarah didn't breathe as the air around her grew still, every bird, every insect, even the wind fell to complete silence until all she could hear was the beating of the steed's giant heart.

Lub-dub.

The flowers touched the animal's shimmering fur and then strained away, leaning as if repelled, as far as their stems would allow.

Lub-dub.

Royal purple, deep crimson, sunshine yellow, all of the flowers shone with the glory of God's design and all of them wriggled to avoid contact with the beast, its breathing slowing.

Lub.

Dub.

It was dying, she knew it, but why did the flowers pull away with such drama?

Lub.

Sarah dropped to her knees, still not close enough to touch the horse, but she might reach a flower. Stretching as far as she could without coming near the dying animal, she plucked the only flower she could reach, a bright sprig of lavender. It came up from the root and she stumbled backward as simultaneously, the horse slumped into a death rattle that shook the ground.

Grasping the sprig to her bosom, Sarah turned and ran back to her bed, still sitting comically in the field, and she hopped upon the covers.

"I see, Father. I see. I understand!" she called aloud, marveling at the soundwaves leaving her mouth as before.

Fifty feet away, the animal grew still and melted into the ground. Every flower touching its flesh turned black and died. Sarah hugged herself, the single sprig in her hand.

"I'll tell her, Father. I'll tell her. Thank You! You are full of mercy!"

When Sarah blinked, her bedroom had returned to normal. The morning sun streamed in through her picture window and she thanked God again. After she'd rushed through her morning ritual, she laid down new prayers for Tony before jogging to the landline in the study. She dialed Elizabeth's number and prayed for God's guidance.

"Hey! How are you this morning?" the young woman asked when she picked up. "I'm seeing Mark at one. This is it, isn't it? Day forty."

Sarah smiled and agreed. Then it was time to share her vision. "Honey, I had a vision from God. I'm telling you first and then I'll call Doctor Corescu."

"Oh, God," Elizabeth whispered and Sarah had a sense she was taking a moment to sit down. "Okay…"

"The Father loves you and Mark so much, so much! You know that, right? He sustained Mark all this time and used Tony's obedience to bring him from the dark back into the light of his youth. Do you follow?"

"Yes, ma'am, I am thankful for that," she said low, with meaning but growing sad, too.

"My vision this morning confirms what we have all been feeling." On Elizabeth's end, Sarah heard sniffles now and cloaked crying. "I know, honey, I know. But God wants me to tell you how important it is for you to not be anywhere near him when he goes. I feel God will move the doctor far away from us to a safe place where no one else will be near. The vision showed me that anyone with him when he departs will perish."

"Okay," she said no longer hiding her sobbing. "Praise the Lord," she added with a choke in her voice.

"Yes, so I will tell the doctor. Your job is to love him and have a beautiful time today, right?" Sarah asked, aware of how horrible it was to hear.

"I will. I promise," Elizabeth replied and blew her nose. "Thank you for that. Thank you for your obedience. I'm sad but I understand. I know God sees the end from the beginning. Thank you, Sarah."

Sarah prayed with Elizabeth several long minutes and let her go. She needed to call the doctor and she prayed for the right words and hit his number. He had spent the past thirty days with Elizabeth doing everything they could think of, but he knew in his heart he was on his final run. She waited for him to answer and trusted God to put words in her mouth. He always did. He was dependable 100%.

The sun filtered through the thick pine canopy surrounding Mark's woodland cabin. Tony considered the enormity of the date and swallowed. Day forty was upon him and his body, mind, and spirit were alive with excitement. In his hand he held his journal, a red leather bound booklet that matched his Bible. Sarah had given it to him soon after they wed knowing he used to keep such a handwritten daily account before being introduced to the world of vampires. He stepped into the cool morning and inhaled, taking in the mountain air, feeling wholly restored. He crossed to the stump of a shorn-off tree and sat, facing the woods and listening to the myriad of forest noises. After thanking God aloud, he flipped the journal to the first entry.

Day One: I'm not hungry. Jesus said, "If anyone thirsts, let him come to Me and drink."[7] I'm going to read through the Bible. I read it start to finish when I was twelve. Time to do it again. I love You, Jesus.

Tony grinned. Forty days had passed quickly. So much more easily than the last time, further reminding him how God does things in his own timing, not that of man. He flipped a few pages and stopped at a headline he had bolded by writing over it several times.

Day Fifteen: I AM NOT A MONSTER AND I DO NOT NEED BLOOD.

Tony snickered wistfully recalling that night. He whiled the hours doing one of four things: reading Scripture, walking through the woods, writing in his journal, and dozing. Sleep came only every nine days or so, but he truly had no complaints. In the first fifteen days, he finished reading the Bible all the way through. When he reached the Book of Revelation, a hunger for blood hit him that he hadn't experienced since arriving at the cabin. From a dead sleep he had been awakened by the growling in his stomach, an aching and acidic pain that wrenched him into a ball. Then it passed. He thanked God, feeling that He must have sent angels to dispatch the devil. And that hunger pain did not recur.

Tony flipped again and landed on last week.

Day thirty: Mark came by again. He's in love with Elizabeth. I prayed for him and he left. He must have been a wonderful pastor before that monster got a hold of him. I can see amazing depth in him now and he confided in me that he hasn't craved blood in weeks, really not since meeting Elizabeth. He's concerned for Joseph Ellerslie, but I convinced him God has the boy in hand. Jesus—make my words true. Amen.

---

[7] John 7:37

Tony nodded to himself and sighed. He hadn't heard anything new on the boy or the magician in a week, so maybe Mark had no news. It was worrisome, but they both agreed they had to turn the boy over to the Lord if he was to be saved. And the boy's parents? According to Mark, they were livid. They had hired a private investigator to track their son down and Mark and Sarah had been questioned. One bright spot had been Elizabeth's father used his pull to call the dogs off Tony's people after the first interview.

Thank God for that.

Tony flipped the book to Day forty and pondered the headline. He had no doubt he would save this journal to remind him in the years to come of the mercy of God.

"I will be there at 6 PM."

Tony's eyes widened at the doctor's voice in his head. Then he chuckled. *"I forgot I was able to do this,"* he sent back and after a gentle laugh, the doctor was gone.

"Well, Abba, I guess I'm still a vampire. At least to some extent. Tonight, when Mark gets here, please work Your will with us. We want to do things Your way. Amen."

Tony strolled back into the cabin to write. He'd try not to think of what might happen to his friend, Mark. And what of himself? Was he guaranteed to live once he was delivered? Sure, he was young, but his body had technically died when Paul poisoned him.

"No!" Tony said aloud. "This is in God's hands. I will do what You want. The end! I'm taking the day off."

Tony would put up his feet and doze. And he would praise the Lord.

38

The Lord bless you and keep you;
The Lord make His face shine upon you,
And be gracious to you;
The Lord lift up His countenance upon you,
And give you peace.
Numbers 6:24–26

THE AIR WAS WEIRD BETWEEN THEM, BUT ELIZABETH WAS happy to see her dad. He and Jenn had come into town for other business and he asked if they could stop in. She had plans with Mark in an hour and wasn't sure how or if to say anything about how deeply they'd taken their relationship. Fifteen minutes into the visit, Jenn took a phone call and stepped outside and her father leaned forward catching her eye with his new secretive posture.

"Thank you for not saying anything about you-know-what in front of Jenn." He peeked the way she left. "Are you okay? Is it okay? You know, with…"

He couldn't finish and Elizabeth offered a tight-lipped nod. She wished with her whole heart that she could ask him for advice, but if he can't even say Mark or Tony's name, how could he help?

"So you're still seeing him? The doctor?" he asked still as a whisper with a side-eye watching for Jenn. Elizabeth nodded and her breath hitched. Her dad noticed. "What's wrong? You can talk to me. What is it?"

"Dad, I don't hold it against you that you don't want to know. I know it's weird and unbelievable what God is doing here. I'm okay. You don't have to worry about me. It's okay."

Her dad shook his head and sat up a little. "Nu-huh, I shouldn't hide from it if you need help. I pretend it's not real, all of it, but what? Let me help? I'll try. I'm sorry. I guess I'm still a bit shell-shocked. I know the doctor's not a bad guy. Go ahead. What's bugging you?"

Elizabeth was encouraged and she took a deep breath. "I'm in love with him, Dad. Big-time. Head over heels forever love."

Her father nodded, unsure or unable to respond.

"But there's a death sentence over his head," she said, not happy with the words, but they were words her father could understand. "Very soon, maybe tonight or tomorrow, he'll be gone, and I'm about to die from heartache." She was crying now, holding back the sobs, but her eyes and nose had filled with fluid.

"Gone? He's moving or…" Her father read her body language. "He's going to die?" He sounded incredulous and curious, too. Very gently, he asked, "How, honey? Why? Are you in danger?"

Sarah's dream came to mind and she wiped her eyes and then grabbed the box of tissue. "Daddy," she said low, the childhood moniker escaping on its own, "God is taking him home. All this time, we became such good friends and we knew there was a chance he might die when God delivers him—"

"—from… *vampirism?*" her dad interrupted with a mouth-only whisper.

Elizabeth nodded. "He and Tony both expect to be delivered and Sarah had a dream that Mark is going to Jesus." She blew her nose and wiped her eyes several times before continuing. In the meantime, her father leaned closer and gave her back a gentle pat.

"Oh, honey, what can I do? I'm sorry I've been avoiding you and him and all this. I'm ashamed but…"

"No, it's not your fault. We needed our space. I just wanted to testify of my love for him I guess. I can't tell anyone outside, you know…" She shook her head. "And you and I only just reconnected. If this separated us, that wouldn't be right, either."

"I agree, you're right, honey," he said low and left his palm to her back with comforting weight. "Okay, here's my dad advice and it is about love and Jesus and friends, not about… *vampires.*" Again, he whispered the last word barely audible. Elizabeth gave him a nod, her eyes begging for comfort. "We can fall in love with someone who's dying of cancer. We can fall in love with someone with a expiration over their heads. How long we have together with them is not the issue. What's important is how your time together has enriched your life. When you're together, you're happy?"

"Oh, yes, Daddy. So happy. My heart bursts for him," she said growing more comfortable sharing her feelings.

"Then this is what you'll treasure. If he indeed dies, ask Jesus to help you remember all those wonderful times together. God will take care of him and you will keep his memory alive with your love." Her dad waited for her to react and she gave a tiny smile. "And don't forget; Elijah and

Moses visited Jesus long after they were dead.[8] You'll see him again in the Kingdom. I know it."

"That sounds right," she said low. "I will. I will keep his memory alive. He let me take his picture." Elizabeth pulled free her phone and opened the photo app. Mark allowed two photos, both selfies, both with the phone in his hand because of his height and longer arm. Photo one, they both looked into the lens, smiling, and no one would ever know the man was a vampire by the light in his eyes. Photo two, he had dipped low and smooched her face with drama—also, precisely as a normal man in love would do. The shutter click caught that sweet moment with his face in her cheek and her eyes and mouth open in laughter.

"Oh, he's cute! Who's that? What did I miss?"

Elizabeth and her father both sat up and Jenn completed her entry, reaching for Elizabeth's cell phone.

"I'll show you later, I promise," Elizabeth said thinking fast. Mark had hypnotized Jenn to forget him, but there was no need to test that it held. *Wait until he's gone,* a little voice said inside, and it hurt Elizabeth to think of it that way. But her father's advice helped. Just being able to announce her love and then have a caring and supportive ear made all the difference.

"Oh, you two have been keeping secrets!" she said joking and found her spot beside her husband. "That's okay. I'm an awesome detective. I'll detect Jonah when he least expects it." She tickled his side but he wasn't ticklish. His deadpan expression gave Elizabeth the giggles and it was a long time before she stopped laughing. When they headed out, her father sent Jenn to the truck for a final word.

"Honey, call me tomorrow. I'm here for you." He kissed her forehead and when she assured him she would, he turned away.

Elizabeth took a deep breath and exhaled with care. In fifteen minutes, Mark would be by to pick her up for what they both expected to be their last date.

"Father, let me keep him. That's the last time I'll say it, honest…"

She paused in her prayer to look at the noon-time sky. It was November 5 and winter wanted to barge into the edge of Autumn, sending a cool, wet wind through the greying sky.

That's a death sky, Elizabeth thought. *The way the sky looks when you go to a funeral…* She returned to her prayer with a sigh.

"Your will be done, not mine. Amen."

---

[8] Jonah is referring to "the transfiguration of Jesus," Matthew 17:1-13)

At the top of her road, Mark's Lexus turned in and she put on her smile. It was as real as the melancholy of losing her best friend.

"It has been decided. Tonight at 6 m I will go to the cabin. From there, it is up to God." Mark touched Elizabeth's cheek. She had been crying before he arrived and she already informed him of her father's helpful advice. Since he arrived and came into her home, though, she had been all smiles. Her heart was ready and he hoped his was, too.

"Okay," she said deep in his gaze. "Good. It's good. You are in very good hands."

Mark grinned at her repetition, as if convincing herself along with him. "What would you like to do until then?"

"I have it all planned out. You ready?" she asked and he enjoyed her enthusiasm. It was real and obvious that she had prepared herself as well as she could. "We've done and seen just about everything we can in the tri-state area except one thing. It's sort of dreary outside, but we're driving to Calloway Gardens. It's two hours away. We'll have a long drive, long chat, and then we'll walk the gardens and look at the fall foliage and the new butterfly sanctuary. Have you ever had a dozen butterflies land on your bare skin?" He shook his head smiling at her joy. "Oh, boy. You'll really enjoy this then. How does that sound?"

"Let's go." Mark put out his arm and she took it.

On the way to the door she tugged his arm. "Give me one of those special Mark Corescu kisses."

With a new smile, he took her into his arms and did as she asked. He'd kiss her forever if the Lord allowed it, but he also sought God's will. They consumed more time than expected, but then got on the road to the gardens.

Butterflies on my skin.

Mark was looking forward to how such a thing would make his beloved's face shine with joy. It was what he lived for. And now, something he needed for his final few hours.

Mark gave her one more photo.

At the butterfly sanctuary, he had removed his jacket and rolled up his sleeves to see if the insects would land on him. Elizabeth loved his muscled forearms, and she made a big show of kissing them once she'd latched on. When she let him go, several humungous fluffy green and white butterflies fluttered close and landed on him, two on his shoulder, one on his back, and two on his uncovered arms. Together they watched them, the wings robotic in their open-and-close motion, the coiled tongues tap-tap-tapping his skin and clothing. Mark and she both held their breath when a golden butterfly landed on his nose. With a stealthy movement she lifted her phone, opened the camera app, and clicked before the creature fluttered away. With a laugh, she checked the result.

The angle was low, from her hip, but she got it, a comical spreading of its wings causing a mask of yellow across her lover's handsome face. When she showed him, he shook his head, the joy in his face shining like the face of God.

"Come here, my beauty," he said with a half grin and pulled her into his arms. Standing in the center of the path splitting the sanctuary greenhouse into two halves, they embraced, butterflies and moths fluttering about their business all around them.

"Mark, I love you so much. You know that, right? I mean, no matter if you go home to Jesus tonight or come home to me, I am going to love you for the rest of my life."

"I know, and I am blessed by it," he responded and touched their lips together. "I have kissed you more than I have kissed anyone in four centuries," he added with a laugh.

"That makes me special!" she retorted and hugged him tight. The clock was closing in on six and they both felt it. "Hey, you're wonderful. When you and Tony talk to Jesus, tell Him you want to stay." She waved away his response before he offered it. "I know it's up to Him. Just say it. For me. Will you?"

Mark grinned. "The Creator of the universe requested an audience with a lump of clay," he said serious, but with a smile. "I'll not push it." He chuckled to lighten her mood and it worked.

Elizabeth hugged him again. His body tensed after a moment and she knew the time had arrived. He would sense it in his bones, and she somehow knew that, too.

"Okay, go ahead. I love you. I'll see you tomorrow." She looked into his face and he gave her a nod.

"Okay, my beauty, go to the car. I want to see you safe in the car."

She backed a few feet down the path and turned for a two-step exit that helped keep the insects inside. Mark remained on the path and would watch her through the glass. Once in the night air, she waved through the opaque walls and he still watched. When she unlocked the Lexus and sat behind the wheel, he blew her a kiss. Elizabeth's heart swelled just then and she cried out for him to wait. But he was gone. In a blink, he'd gone to the cabin.

Elizabeth slumped behind the wheel and looked at her hands. It was dark and the park was closing, but she would pray. For five minutes, until the Park Ranger knocked on her hood and asked her to move along, Elizabeth begged God to let Mark stay.

She could ask some more. God would forgive her.

He knows I'm only human.

And she promised she would accept His decision.

But hoped just the same.

39

Trust in the LORD with all your heart,
And lean not on your own understanding;
In all your ways acknowledge Him,
And He shall direct your paths.
Proverbs 3:5-6

THE DOCTOR ARRIVED AS THE CLOCK STRUCK THE HOUR, appearing in the center of the small cabin main room. Tony had been at the desk, reading, praying, and to some extent, dreading what was to come. When he met Mark's eye, he asked the first thing on his mind.

"How is Sarah?"

Mark gave him a sad grin. "She sends her love. The Lord sent her a vision that no one should be present for this process. You and I must proceed alone."

Tony offered a single nod, having intuited some of this already. "And how is Elizabeth?"

Mark this time gave a sigh. "She is prepared. Her heart is broken but she is in good hands."

Again, Tony nodded and stood up. "How is Joseph? Is he with Androni?"

With a regal head tip, Mark replied, "They are also in God's hands. And before you ask," he said with a mischievous wink, "Miss Brannen is safe at present but refuses my contact. I gave her current address to your wife. Perhaps…"

Mark shrugged once and Tony also did not know what to add. Hope's personality had changed so much since meeting the doctor that Tony wondered if either of them really knew her at all. Her identical twin had murdered two husbands and more than one child. Did Hope suffer the same mental instability? It was too much to ponder at the moment and Tony took a cleansing breath. Mark did too and put his hands together.

"Let us begin," Mark said, his voice carrying throughout the small space with substance.

Tony grinned when he noticed and Mark did, too. "That was very vampir-y, Doc," he said as a joke and Mark grinned. "It's good we can keep our humor, eh?"

"Indeed."

Tony crossed to meet him where he stood and put out his fingers. "I reckon we proceed by praying." Mark joined hands and they looked into each other's eyes. "First, allow me to say how much I appreciate you. I don't know when it happened, but I've been seeing your potential all this time. Even when we met and I was frankly, terrified of you."

Mark huffed a sad sound and remained silent.

"I somehow knew that you were a true man of God. Heck, I needed you. I can see how all this crap we've been through has saved me as much as scared me. I had lost touch with God and didn't even know it. He used you to help me." Tony's words choked and he forced down emotions threatening his composure. "So, thank you."

Mark made a nod with his upper body and re-met Tony's eye. "That is a gracious position, thank you."

That was all there was to say. His friend could count on him to watch after those left behind, including Elizabeth and Joey, Hope and Androni. All that was left to do was ask God to show them the next step.

"You ready?" he asked for no good reason and Mark nodded, maybe choking up himself a bit now that the hour had arrived. "Okay, I'll go first." Tony took a deep breath and closed his eyes. "Father, please deliver me from this curse. In the name of Jesus Christ, I am ready. I am ready to perform Your will. If it is within Your will that I could leave this cabin delivered, please let it be done." Tony paused, looked in his heart and could think of nothing else to say. "And please work Your will with Mark. Amen."

He squeezed the doctor's fingers without opening his eyes, sort of afraid to know if he would see in the dark corners like a vampire. Then his friend's deep voice filled the room with its masculine timbre.

"Istenem, apám, hallgasd meg imámat. Az akaratomat keresem."[9] Mark said aloud in his first language and focused on the memory of Elizabeth's face one last time. He was about to do it, he would leave the world of the flesh,

---

[9] "Father-God, hear my prayer. I seek Your will." (Hungarian)

he had no doubt, and when he kissed her mental image, he allowed her to go. "I have destroyed Your children, disobeyed You, and sinned against You for too long. I ask You to forgive me. Wash me clean with the blood of Jesus Christ, *Jézus Krisztus,* because He went to the Cross for me and sacrificed His life for me. Thank You for allowing me these friendships," he said and Tony squeezed his fingers in camaraderie.

Mark parted his lips to continue and Sarah's prophecy returned to his mind. He asked inside, *"Do You mean Tony, too?"* As he awaited an answer, his friend dropped the contact. Mark opened his eyes and he was alone. With a careful exhale, he turned a circle, ending with his eyes on the door.

I am going home, so I will go from my own earth.

Mark owned many properties in Europe and he pictured his castle overlooking his home village, now long incorporated into neighboring cities and renamed. But his estate remained, aged, a bit brittle from disrepair, but still private and locked tight, kept that way by hired realtors. Like he'd been doing centuries, Mark pushed his physical body there and opened his eyes in his abandoned dining hall, dark and in the middle of the night, six hours ahead of Alabama time, thus technically the next day. Mark hugged his body and turned his heart back to his God.

I'm about to do it. I'm going Home…

In his memory, his mother calling him to supper. His father, patting his head when he performed his computations on the slate tablet. His first kiss, age ten, Jesia Lowyn, her brown eyes and fire-red hair vivid to recall. A vicious fistfight with local youths at age fourteen, protecting the reputation of that same girl, but then just a friend.

Mark's mind moved to adulthood, the clergy, and being attacked by The Other. Mark zoomed ahead to avoid the thought of blood-letting and pictured Paul. … *"Oh, I'm sorry, Father. I repent, I repent,"* he said inside, recalling how he changed the bright young man into a servant, kept him close, and brainwashed him for a century. And then Hope came to mind and Tony, and finally Elizabeth bringing him to the present moment. Mark hugged himself tighter and looked to the ground.

"If You will have me, Father, I repent of all my sin from my birth to now, I beg Your forgiveness. I ask You to deliver me from this curse and bring me home. I love You. I need You, and I will not go a single second without You." Mark licked his lips, a light-headed sensation approaching with cat's feet.

It's about to happen…

"Amen and amen," he said to the room, eyes to the dusty stone floor.

"You are My son and I love you, too," he heard in his heart.

Then, with a soft wind that seemed to lift him off his feet, Mark's vision exploded with light. Marveling at the splendor of the moment, his mind filled with beautiful music and Marcus Sebastien Corescu, formerly of Spisak, Hungary, went Home to the Creator.

And it was good.

40

My sheep hear My voice, and I know them, and they follow Me.
And I give them eternal life, and they shall never perish;
neither shall anyone snatch them out of My hand.
John 10:27-28

"IT IS DONE."

Joey sat up from a light sleep, gasping for air. He stared at the dark space, his heart hammering and his ears popping. When he wiggled a thumb to the source of discomfort, a cool palm rubbed his back.

"We're not rising until dark. What are you doing?"

Joey slowed his breathing with effort. He swallowed hard and his tongue felt too large in his mouth. *Is the doctor dead?*

Androni sat up and grabbed his shoulder. "Did you just think *Mark is dead?*"

Joey whipped his eyes to Androni's. *"I think the doctor is dead,"* he sent as a thought.

Androni's face exploded into a grin, and he leapt from the messy mattress to pound the caravan's metal ceiling. Then he stopped himself as if realizing what he had just heard. "Why do you think he's dead?"

Joey shook his head. "I don't know exactly. I had a chill and I heard in my head, *it is done.*" He narrowed his eyes looking in thought. "It sounded like the angel that helped me in the barn." He turned his gaze to his friend. "If it was, then I think God wants me to know that Doctor Corescu went Home."

"He went home, eh? That is a romantic way of saying someone died, right?" Androni asked in a laugh, but Joey wasn't offended. "Are you okay?" he asked.

Joey gave it some thought and looked out the tiny window into the late afternoon light. They had not contacted anyone from home in more than four weeks. Joey decided to let his parents think he ran away and maybe down the road he would send them a card. He didn't want them to worry but he could not bear to see them. Plus, how could he explain himself? He also had not contacted his friends. But as for the doctor and Tony? He did feel bad that the man was gone.

"Well?" Androni pressed.

Joey and Androni's relationship had only improved over the last month. As much as Joey felt he needed the magician, Androni admitted he needed Joey even more. Although their symbiotic relationship extended beyond the blood, Joey still had not taken sustenance from any other source. *And I hope it stays that way…* The thought of biting a person turned Joey's stomach.

Just then Androni developed a wide grin.

"Oh, I have missed you!" he announced and zoomed into Joey's space to grab him around the shoulders. He covered Joey's face with kisses hugging him tighter than before. Joey couldn't help but laugh but it would be a new adjustment; he had fallen out of practice of guarding his thoughts.

Now he's going to know I don't want to bite anybody else…

"Oh, beautiful boy!" Androni said and kissed both cheeks European style. "You will never have to do anything you do not wish to do. You are here to live! Remember what I told you, we will live! And that means you will be happy. I promise."

Joey received the affection and when his pal backed away, he thought again about the doctor. He couldn't know exactly what happened, but it was most likely that the doctor and Tony received the deliverance they desired. If that was true, it followed that Joey could, too. If he wanted to leave his new life, God would allow it.

Androni's face fell, and Joey surged close to take his shoulders. "I'm not going anywhere. I want to be with you. Let's do it, let's live."

Androni's smile returned, and he collapsed onto the bed. "This is going to be great!" Then he sent Joey a thought. *"Tonight, I will show you how to do magic. We will wow the crowds with two magicians, the Ghost and the Gypsy. The ringmaster will change our sign this month. Oh, the adventures we will have."*

Joey recalled the ball flying through the air and he grinned. What would God do if he stayed a while? Enjoyed his friend? Didn't Pastor Hawken preach that God wanted His children to be happy and wealthy? Joey nodded to himself.

God will help me figure this out, he thought. *I love Jesus and I love Androni.*

His friend double-raised his eyebrows. "Ghost, my love, we will live!"

Joey clapped his hands, believing they really would.

pilogue

The next day John saw Jesus coming toward him, and said,
"Behold! The Lamb of God who takes away the sin of the world!
John 1:29

TONY AWOKE TO THE SOUND OF SARAH'S SINGING AND HE creaked open his eyes one at a time. The last thing he recalled was holding hands with Mark and asking to be delivered.

"God of wonders, you are holy! Holy-y-y-y-y…" his wife sang and he focused his gaze her way. The soft halo of light he'd been seeing since Paul forced the vampire's curse into his flesh …

It was missing.

Tony sat up and his urgent movement attracted Sarah's attention. She rushed to his side of the bed and grabbed him around the neck, showering him with soft kisses. Tony allowed it, but still needed to check a few things.

With a gentle movement, he slipped out of Sarah's grip and got to his feet. Testing a tiny jump and then a larger one, he grinned. He was heavy, his super strength had evaporated. He turned to Sarah and the smile on his face could not have been wider.

"It's gone! Praise the Lord! Thank You, Jesus!" he shouted looking into his wife's beautiful face. Sarah sang those words to the Lord and clambered back into his embrace. He joined her in a new song and they held hands, singing God's praises out loud, the music heading right through the ceiling.

Finally, they relaxed to a quiet reflection and sitting side by side on the edge of the bed, they leaned against each other. Tony pondered the doctor, certain in his spirit that the man had gone Home as they figured he would. But knowing he was in paradise did not assuage the pain in his heart at losing a friend.

"He was a wonderful man, really, I see that now," Sarah said softly intuiting what he'd been thinking. "And he loved you so much. His face lit up when you came in. I saw all that. And when you were away, he spoke

236

with me of what a great man you are. He never stopped singing your praises."

Tony huffed a sad laugh and nodded, draping his arm around her back. He kissed her shoulder and sighed. "I wish I'd known him longer."

Sarah nodded once and squeezed his near thigh. "I'll call and check on Elizabeth," she said low and turned her face to Tony's.

He met her eye with a cautious half-grin. "Do you think she'd be okay for a little bit? Like maybe, thirty minutes or so?"

A slow grin also hit Sarah's mouth and she smacked her lips. "Tony Agricola, are you hitting on me?"

Tony moved in and she met his effort, touching their lips in a barely-there kiss. Remaining close, he said, "I am if your name is Sarah Agricola."

Sarah smiled with a joyful laugh and rotated her torso for a new embrace. When they tumbled back to the mattress, she met his gaze shaking her head.

"What?" he asked low, his face surely shining with joy.

"I love you, I love you so much," she said and came in for a new kiss.

Tony returned the move and the sentiment, inside wishing the memory of Mark goodbye. When Sarah giggled at his hands on her waist, he shut out the world, thanked God for her all over again, and focused on his bride.

E*N*D *Anathema*

The story will conclude with...

NOVUS, Book Five of the Corescu Chronicles.

Androni wants to show Joey the wide world, sharing the glory of a vampire magician's life. How will that fit with the boy's love of God? Joey needs to share the Truth with his new best friend; will that push him away? Back home, the Ellerslies do not understand or forgive their son's disappearance. The private investigator they hire to bring him home is familiar with supernatural creatures and bringing the boy back alive might not be his first inclination.

Read now and enjoy the final installment of *The Corescu Chronicles.*

More Vampire-Themed Novels by Ellen C Maze:

THE RABBIT SAGA

#1 Top-Rated Bestseller *Rabbit: Chasing Beth Rider*
A bestselling novelist writes of vampires, unknowingly infuriating an ancient real-life race of blood-drinkers who vow to destroy her because her books endanger their way of life.
Join the chase today!

The Judging and Rabbit: Chasing Beth Rider Connection

In Ellen C. Maze's *Rabbit: Chasing Beth Rider*, a bestselling novelist finds herself on the run from a bloodthirsty race of beings whose leaders despise the affect her novel, *The Judging*, has on their people. Here is what readers are saying about *Rabbit's* fascinating and unique look at the vampire mythos:

Praise for *Rabbit: Chasing Beth Rider*

"Maze's storytelling is fast and fun, overflowing with ideas and spiritual insight."

~ Eric Wilson, author of *Fireproof*, and *Valley of Bones*
(The Jerusalem Undead Trilogy)

"What a great book! It kept me on the edge of my seat, waiting for what was going to happen next. With all the strange powers at work in this world, this book reveals the greatest Power of all."

~ Rabbi John Giddens, *www.ChavurahShalom.org*

"I absolutely love it when an author can take a myth or legend and weave them neatly and efficiently into a brilliant and original tale. This book is definitely not simplistic in nature. Ms. Maze gives us a fast-paced plot with many twists and turns, not just in the action, but also for the mind. *Rabbit: Chasing Beth Rider* will grab your attention from the first page and will not let go until the end, and maybe not even then. Enjoy the chase!"

~ Stephanie Nordkap, *Bestsellersworld.com*

Maze takes us on a vampire journey with a one-of-a-kind twist! Rabbit is a fast-paced, action-packed, exciting vampire thriller. As an avid reader of vampire fiction, this gem unexpectedly has become one of my very favorites.

~ Marcia Freespirit, CEO, *JimSam Inc. Publishing*

"Riveting and eye-opening...a powerful testament to the often overlooked spiritual strength within us all."

~ *Apex reviews*

Please sign up for Ellen's newsletter to be alerted of all new releases and freebies. Link: https://dl.bookfunnel.com/z0c7dpe1am
Or at the CONTACT link at www.ellencmaze.com
Or by clicking "Follow" on Amazon.

www.ingramcontent.com/pod-product-compliance
Lightning Source LLC
Chambersburg PA
CBHW061617170626
46811CB00001B/451